Regulus: Clara

Lorena Bisset

Bisset House Press

REGULUS: CLARA

ISBNs

979-8-9911069-4-8 (eBook)

979-8-9911069-8-6 (Paperback)

Chapter Headers by Sinéad MacAskill

Chapter Header Digitization by Devin Arnold

First Edition 2026

For Sinéad, the one who stitched everything back together.

From your guardian, Leon.

Content Warnings for Sensitive Readers

Although this is a love story, there are a few things we'd like you to know about before you dive in.

As follows:
Explicit Sexual Content
Major and Minor Character Death
Attempted Sexual Assault
Emotional Abuse
Physical Abuse
Mentions of real-world events such as the Titanic sinking, 1918 Pandemic, and WWI

November 7th, 2010

On the phone, he'd sounded relatively normal. Not happy, given the circumstances, but able to form coherent sentences and get his request across. I'd expected it would be much the same when I saw him. But that day, in my makeshift office in the corner of the archives, Leon Regulus looked like he belonged with the artifacts all around him. His face was gaunt, blue eyes hollow. Even his normally sunny-blond hair was somehow paler. He was staring into the corner of my office, fingers touching the spot on his right ring finger that was a little less tan than the rest of his hand. A stack of three books rested on one of his legs. If the topmost cover was to be believed, they were five-year, Line-A-Day diaries. And they were old. Everything about this poor man looked as if his internal sun had gone out.

But I suppose it had. Sinéad MacAskill was dead.

Even those who didn't know the pair well could see how much Leon and Sinéad meant to each other. It was obvious in the most blatant of ways. They were always seen together at every public appearance of the Bruadarach and her bodyguard, the Heir Apparent tagging along as we all expected. But now both the Bruadarach and Heir Apparent were gone, one struck down in a targeted assassination and the other taken out by...well, we hadn't been told yet.

I stayed quiet for a moment longer, watching Leon stare into the middle distance. His forehead was resting on his hand, elbow on the arm of the chair he'd slumped in. He looked more like a pile of laundry than the man who was meant to be head of security. Finally, I cleared my throat to get his attention.

His head jerked up, eyes blinking rapidly as he came back to reality from wherever he'd been. "Sorry, Miss Bisset. Sorry." He lifted both hands to cover his face, rubbing his eyes and dragging his fingers down his cheeks. "I can't...think well these days."

"I understand." The entire island was in turmoil, many citizens wailing in grief as the others stared off in despair. Even Bruadarach Mariana's right-hand man, Milo, hadn't been able to keep perfect hold of everything. It all felt like it was teetering on the edge of the cliffs near Dubhan. I sighed very slowly, through my nose, allowing myself to close my eyes just briefly. If I thought about it too much, I'd probably have another panic attack. *Best to get right to it then,* I thought, and opened the new notebook I'd purchased for his request. "You said you wanted help recording some history?"

Leon nodded. "Yeah." He straightened in the chair, one arm laying along the armrest, the other hand resting protectively on the three Line-A-Day diaries that were in his lap. "It's a story from when I was a lot younger, but if I don't record it somewhere, I'm afraid it's going to be lost forever."

"Alright. I'm happy to help however I can." Leon couldn't be more than thirty years old, so I was absolutely expecting a story from when he was a teenager or younger. I quickly titled the first page of the notebook and smoothed it out, pen at the ready. "Start wherever you like."

He paused, fingers tapping along the armrest and gripping the books. "Can you keep a secret, Miss Bisset?" It wasn't playful, or even ominous. Usually in movies and TV shows when someone asks that, it's a bit cheeky, said with a smirk or a wink. But Leo asked it with such grave seriousness and sincerity, I felt cold for a second.

"O-of course, yes, I'll keep whatever you share with me private, Mr. Regulus."

He nodded, his eyes falling closed. If it weren't for the hard swallow bobbing his throat, he would have looked like he was asleep. I waited.

"I need your help recording a story about a girl. She meant the universe to me, and I can't bear to see her story lost to time. Our...our story." His voice got small, choked. "My story." His hand gripped the armrest, and I was about to get up and tell him to come back when he felt stronger and more ready to share, but he sucked in a shaking breath, rubbed his face again, and looked at me. His eyes were the clearest they'd been since setting foot in my office. I nodded.

"Whatever you tell me, I'll record and preserve."

"Thank you." After another moment of what I assume was preparation, he spoke clearly, his voice warming with the memory. "I met a girl who turned my life inside out. I was just a young man working in New York, trying to help my mother get through life and fend for myself. But then I met her. I met Clara. And suddenly...very few other things mattered."

His pause was long enough I felt it was alright to ask a question or two. "Where did you meet her? How old were you?"

"I was twelve, or, I was about to be. She lived in New York too, but not in the same neighborhood." Leon shifted, resting his elbows on his knees and lifting his hands, fingers circling his right ring finger as if to twist a ring that wasn't there. When his touch didn't find it, his hands dropped back to his lap. "She grew up to be the most beautiful woman I've ever seen, even now. I'm starting to forget some things about her, but her voice is as clear as day in my head." His eyes grew distant again, but this time they didn't look hollow.

"I assume something happened to her?" I was writing notes as quickly as I could, making short bullet points to expand upon later.

"She's gone. I lost her to a fire."

"Oh, I'm so sorry. I didn't mean to bring it up so soon." I made a note of it, then glanced up. Leon was looking at me, and I furrowed my brow. Was I interrupting too much? I didn't get a chance to ask or apologize, as he spoke again.

"This is..." He sighed, squeezing his eyes shut then looking at me more seriously. "This is where the secret comes in. Unless I say so, please don't share this story with anyone else."

I nodded intently, probably a little too eagerly. "Of course. You can even take the original copy home with you." This was some secret; I could feel Cabinet-level red tape wrapping around my new notebook.

"Alright." Leo relaxed into his chair, looking at the shelf of old ledgers stored near my desk. Maybe less eye contact would help him get the story out more easily. "I met Clara a few days after the Titanic sank."

Despite his serious tone, I laughed, a small two-note trill of disbelief. "On one of the anniversaries?"

"April 17th, 1912. I met Clara the day before the Carpathia docked in New York."

I wanted to believe he was pranking me, wasting my time, but there was absolutely no denying the solemn set of his jaw, the sadness in his eyes. I put my pen down. "Mr. Regulus, are you expecting me to believe you're over a hundred years old?" I hadn't done all the math in my head yet, but I knew the Titanic's 100th Anniversary was a couple years off, and if he'd said he was twelve when it happened—

"I'm not expecting you to believe it, but I'm hoping you will at least try for long enough to help me with this. Then you can pretend I'm however old you think I am." Even though I expected his response to be flippant or joking, all I got was resignation. I sighed, shaking my head.

"Alright. I'm going to believe you for now, to get this story on paper for you. Then I might...I might ask for an explanation, or I might just ignore you for the rest of time. I don't know what to think right now." I could feel the edge of a panic attack sinking into my chest, and I gripped my pen to try and ward it off.

"I'll explain it; I'm happy to. I might get in some trouble for it, but I'll do it." He sounded cowed, like he'd been scolded or harassed for this before, and my heart softened.

"I'm sorry. You startled me, and I am still not sure how to react to this, but I understand this is important to you. Please, continue with your story."

"You're fine." He laughed, the sound a sad-but-amused chuckle, and pushed his hand through his hair. "I've had worse reactions." The smile he gave me was still tinged with grief, but I could feel the hastily-built wall I'd put up crumble because of it. It was becoming impossible to think of him as a human, but he was still a grieving man who'd asked for my help. So help I would give.

Leon spent five hours in my office that day, and six the next. He told me every single thing he could remember about his time with Clara, mostly out of order and mixed up, but in the end, we got everything in chronological order. I had to do some side research on New York City and the surrounding areas, just to make sure everything was accurate, but I shouldn't have been surprised when it was. Leon had lived there for many years, after all.

This was the first citizen story I was ever asked to record. I never thought I'd share it with anyone other than the man who asked for it, but he's given me his blessing and encouragement to share it with the world.

It's been a hundred years since this tale ended, so let's go back and start at the beginning.

April 17th, 1912

"Get your copy! All Titanic saved on the Carpathia! 1,535 dead!" The newsboy was shouting at the top of his lungs when I got to the corner, and I had to squint against the mid-morning sun just to see him. I couldn't see past the surge of people surrounding him, waving coins to try and grab this morning's edition of the paper.

Everyone was learning about the great wreck of a maiden voyage that had also been the Titanic's last. The numbers were still in contest, with some papers even reporting that there had been no loss of life at all. It wasn't until news of the Carpathia reached our ears and newsstands that relatives and friends of the passengers started camping out at the docks, hoping and praying that their loved ones hadn't been among those who were now lost at sea.

I was only eleven at the time, unofficially an unpaid apprentice to the local fire brigade in my corner of Brooklyn. It was supposed to be paid, the ad in the paper had said it was paid, but they'd decided I was too young and needed to learn some life skills first. According to the chief, life skills were picking up after everyone else, washing the trucks, and picking up the kitchen after meals, all around my normal school days. I didn't have much choice in the matter, so I did as I was told, happy to at least have steady meals since Mom couldn't afford to buy for two. As soon as I learned enough to start getting paid, *I'd* be buying *her* food. Maybe once I turned twelve over the summer it'd be different.

It had been raining off and on the entire day, and during a break in the weather I'd been sent out with a meticulously counted amount of money and a shopping list, and was halfway through it when I'd reached the newsboy. I stepped closer, peering around the crowd to try and read at least the headlines, but the gaggle of people was too thick. So I listened instead.

"I heard they turned off the wireless in the Marconi room and ignored everyone."

"I heard the White Star Line and the banks were cohorts in an insurance fraud scheme."

"That can't be true, weren't there a lot of bankers as passengers?"

"Rival bankers."

"How horrible, it's just horrible."

"Stanley was supposed to be on that ship. I'm so glad he got delayed. Of course he's out the ticket money now but, I'd rather he be alive and broke than dead and rich."

So much was going on, and the crowd was pressing closer and closer. I was suddenly reminded of the eggs in one of my parcels and the threatening glare of the chief if I returned without them. I slipped away, perching myself in an alcove under a shop window where I could still hear without my groceries getting crushed.

Most of the words got jumbled in the din of the crowd, and I lost track of the rumors and possible facts pretty quickly. Giving up, I gathered my parcels back together and set off, looking down at the list instead of where I was going.

Of course, I ran right into someone. She was an older woman, old enough to be my mother probably. She glared down at me with deep blue eyes under the brim of a small hat which partially hid dark blonde hair beneath it, and brushed her skirt off very pointedly, as if I carried a special type of dirt and had just soiled her dress with it. I immediately shifted my groceries to swipe my hat off my head, bowing it just slightly.

"Beggin' your pardon, ma'am, that was my fault. I shouldn't read and walk."

She narrowed her eyes almost imperceptibly and nodded. "You should not, young man." And with that she set off, and I settled my cap back on top of my hair. As I watched her go, I realized two things: one, we were headed into the same shop, and two, there was a girl about my age with her, hands held behind her back and a bored expression on her face. I cringed at the idea of having to go in the same building as the woman I'd just run into, but it was my last stop and I was on a timetable, so I sucked it up.

I ended up behind her in line, but thankfully she didn't notice. The girl with her did, though, and glanced back at me curiously. I met her gaze a single time then looked away, back at my list, trying to act nonchalant and unbothered. Unfortunately for me, it didn't work at all. Because she was very, very pretty, and kept looking back at me.

After a few moments of near-arguing with the grocer, the woman stepped away to peruse the stocked goods and the grocer went to fill her order. That left me and the girl on our own, me still pretending to read my shopping list for the tenth time and her pretending she wasn't sneaking looks at me. The silence was unbearable; I was about to just head back outside before she spoke.

"Unfortunate about the Titanic, don't you think?" Her voice was high and soft, and held none of the Brooklyn accent mine did. She must not have grown up in this neighborhood.

"Oh, yes, I-I suppose so," I stammered. She wasn't hiding that she was looking now.

"Suppose so?" Her tone was probing, and her hands shifted behind her back. I noted a rolled-up magazine under her arm, the *All-Story*.

"Well, all I've heard is rumors, so I don't know what to believe yet. I keep hearing people say it was an insurance scam or a planned attack on rival bankers or other godawful things." I shrugged, shifting the packages I was carrying to my other hand. The twine on the parcels was starting to cut off my circulation, and I regretted not bringing the little cart the firehouse owned. I gave up and sat them on the floor between my feet as the girl studied me silently. "What?"

"I hadn't heard any of those things, just that it had sunk and a lot of people probably died." She shrugged, looking a little embarrassed now.

"I heard that nobody died, but I also heard that everybody died." I shrugged in solidarity. Neither of us really knew what was going on.

"I wonder when we'll know the truth," she mused, almost mumbling to herself. She looked down towards her shoes, and I took the chance to really look at her, nutmeg-colored hair and storm-gray eyes hidden behind her lashes. Her skin was cleaner than mine had ever been, and it looked soft; for some reason it made me think of the peach cream pastries I had seen in the display of a bakery once. Cream and spice and storm. What a combination. All wrapped up together to form the prettiest girl I'd ever seen in my life.

"Clara?" the older woman called from the opposite side of the shop, coming back over as the grocer returned with a crate packed full of her order. "Fetch Luis. We'll need him to carry this." The woman made a shooing motion at the girl, and Clara shot me a quick look before slipping out of the store. I tried not to stare as she left.

Luis turned out to be a burly Hispanic man, and the woman directed him to pick up the order and carry it to the cart, then they were off and it was my turn.

"Kid, hey kid," the grocer called me, and I snapped away from the window that gave me a view of Clara and her party heading down the sidewalk to look back at him.

"Sir?"

"You orderin somethin or what? I don't got all day."

"Sorry! Sorry sir, yes, I have an order from Chief Duncan."

"Well stop ogling Manhattan girls that are out of your league and give it to me." The grocer held his hand out impatiently, and I immediately laid the list in his palm. The firehouse did regular business here so I was grateful no questions needed answering. I was way too distracted by the fact that Clara had spoken to me to even think of any answers.

The grocer was right though, she was out of my league by a mile. I was reminded of that as I got back to the station, arms full of parcels, carefully cradling the one holding the eggs in my hands where I could guard it.

"What in all the heavens took you so long, Leo?" one of the firemen—Gregory, second in command—called as I stepped inside, carefully wiggling my way through the door without putting any of the packages down. He came over and took a few from me, including the eggs, and I sighed in relief.

"All the news about that ship that sunk is forcing everyone outta their houses to go buy papers." I followed his orange-red hair to the kitchen, dumping the groceries on the giant table as quickly as I could. "All the streets are packed and everyone's just stopping and talking about it in the middle of the sidewalk."

"Of course, big tragedy like that. Everyone wants to know what's happening." Gregory set about putting the groceries where they belonged, and I did the best I could to help while staying out of his way. No more words were exchanged between us, and after we were done, I gathered all the paper and twine to take it to the back.

It was early afternoon then, and I stopped in the alleyway to sit and finally rest from my travel across what felt like the entire borough. An old crate served as my chair, and the brick wall of the fire station cradled my head as I tilted my face toward the sky, welcoming what little sun slipped between the buildings.

The city was always loud, even back then. Full of people talking, yelling, singing, arguing. Horses clip-clopping down the street amidst the huffing and puffing of early car engines. There was always some sort of buzz going on, always some sort of noise.

The grocer's words floated back to my mind and I smirked, eyes still shut. There I was sitting in a dirty alleyway in Brooklyn, just as dirty as it was, thinking about some scrubbed-clean heiress with new clothes, and hands that had probably never carried anything heavier than a little dog or a kitten. I heaved a sigh. *It's a good thing I'll probably never see her again,* I thought, slumping down against the bricks. *I might start liking her too much for my own good.*

April 25th, 1912

Little did I know how wrong I was about half of that thought. A week later, I was back out shopping and picking up groceries yet again, performing my normal duties. And there she just so happened to be, standing by the stairs of a milliner's shop, looking bored out of her mind.

"You're out here all alone?" I asked, not thinking then of how my question could have sounded. She was startled at the sound of my voice and shrunk back against the railing of the stair, shaking her head.

"No, my governess is inside the shop. I'm waiting." Clara was eyeing me warily, and I took a half step back. This seemed to appease her, and the grip she had on the railing relaxed enough that her knuckles weren't white.

"Oh. I'm sorry for just...barging in like that," I mumbled, kicking at a crack in the sidewalk.

"You should know what sentences would frighten a girl. I was ready to scream if you tried anything." She was glaring at me still but also suppressing a grin, and I cracked one of my own.

"I wouldn't have."

"I know that now!" Her smile finally broke. "Why are you back in this area?"

"I'd like to ask you the same, miss. You don't exactly fit in here," I teased, tugging on the collar of my worn out, hand-me-down shirt. She looked me over.

"We're out shopping. Miss Horne says this is the best hat shop in all of New York, so this is where she wanted to go. She likes this neighborhood." Clara shrugged, clasping her hands in front of her, leaning back against the railing. "Now, you answer me."

"I live three blocks away." I said it with a snicker that grew louder as I watched her cheeks flush. "I'm always in this area." My grin widened.

"I should have guessed."

"Probably."

She stood in silence with her embarrassment for a moment, then looked up as the door opened. The lady I'd barreled into was talking over her shoulder to someone in the shop, and Clara stood straight, perfect posture. Then she dared a look back at me. "What's your name?"

"Leon Ardin. Most everyone calls me Leo, though. I heard your governess call you Clara, is that right?"

She nodded, smiling softly. "Well, since you live right here on this street, perhaps I'll see you around again." This last part was a little hurried, almost whispered, and she slipped away as soon as her governess, whose name I assumed was Miss Horne, stepped off the stairs and onto the sidewalk.

I was left holding my list and parcels again, staring at her as they walked away. I didn't know how much of a rebel she was being back then, twelve and already trying to give her governess the slip. All I knew was that I really liked her curls and the way the corners of her eyes crinkled when she smiled, especially when she smiled at me.

After that, I took to spending whatever free time I had on the street where the two shops I'd seen Clara were. I perched on a lot of stoops to do my schoolwork while waiting. More days than not she wasn't there, even though I'd been going to the area at about the same time each day. But she didn't live in Brooklyn like I did, so I probably shouldn't have been surprised. Two weeks went by after our second meeting and I only saw her twice, just a glimpse while she climbed into a train car to head back to wherever her home was.

I was distracted, and it was obvious. The chief noticed, and Mom even noticed when I was home, and I got the life teased out of me for it at all angles.

"Aw, little man, who has you staring out the window like that?" Mom's voice was laced with her grin, filtering over from where she was stirring up dinner in our old cookpot. "I haven't ever seen you that dreamy-eyed."

I weighed my options, thinking if this was a good tidbit to share or not, and decided to give it up. "I met a girl."

Mom's soft, fake, dramatic gasp and chuckle caused me to turn a soft glare on her, but I quickly dropped it as she grinned. "Who is she?" she asked.

"Her name is Clara. She was out shopping with her governess. I've only managed to talk to her twice but..." I sighed in spite of myself. "I can't stop thinking about her."

"She must be some fancy little lady if she has a governess that takes her out and about." Mom started sounding a little indignant, and I set my chin in my hand, wondering if I was about to hear a rant about "damned rich folk" again.

"I guess so. The grocer said she was some sort of heiress, but I don't know if he knows what he's talking about."

Mom hummed in thought, finishing whatever precise number of stirs was required for our the dish she was making. She placed the pot on the table, filled our bowls, and we dug into our stew. Mom didn't bring up Clara again and neither did I, even though she was the only thing I wanted to talk about.

May 2nd, 1912

A few days later, I was strolling around looking for her when I heard someone talking with clear ill intent.

"Hey little girl, where's your daddy? Did he send you out here alone?" The man's voice held an awful, sour note of lechery that made me lift my head from the newspapers I was stacking. I'd knocked into a paper boy's stack as I rounded the corner and was helping him gather them back up. A man about Duncan's age—at least in his thirties, if not older—was leaning over someone much smaller than him, his arm up against a wall that I assumed the girl he'd mentioned was trapped against. "Why would he send you out with no escort? What a terrible daddy he must be to you."

"He's not!" The voice was one I knew, and I immediately abandoned the papers in favor of walking across the street to the alleyway. "I'm with my governess. She's in the shop, I swear!"

"Sure, sure. You're just trying to scare us off."

The man I finally recognized as a drunkard who rarely left the bar down the street reached up to stroke the cheek of the girl he was looming over, and once I got close enough, I confirmed it was in fact Clara he had trapped.

"Get away from her!" I called, forgetting the man was easily double my size and strength, not to mention he had his two cronies as backup. They all looked over at my call, and Clara visibly relaxed, but not enough to give the man any chance to grab her. "She's here waiting for me. Leave her alone." I somehow kept my voice from shaking, and the drunkard leaned back, dropping his arm but gaining an evil grin.

"Well now, if it ain't the little station boy. She's meeting up with you, eh?" He looked back over to Clara, the grin not dropping. "I have my doubts."

"I am. I'm meeting Leo here, now. We made the plan last week." Clara eagerly hopped onto my lie, trying to sidestep along the wall toward me. The drunkard planted a hand against the bricks, blocking her path. "Please, he's telling the truth."

"I don't know what kind of governess or rich fella daddy would let a nice girl like you hang around the likes of him."

"The kind that wants me to have friends of all types!" Clara pleaded, looking over to me with wide eyes, begging for help. I was running through options in my head when an older female voice cut through all of the tension.

"The kind that will call for the police right now if you don't step away from her ward." Miss Horne was standing at the corner of the building, arms crossed, her tall frame drawn up to its full height. The drunkard dropped his arm and stepped back, his cronies doing the same, and Clara took her chance to dart away and hide behind the skirts of her governess. "Now get out of here before I call them anyway." Miss Horne, despite being a thin slip of a woman the men could have picked up with one hand and ran off with, had a countenance about her that sent them scrambling. Then she turned her cold gaze on me. "And you, were you just standing there hoping nothing would happen?"

"N-no ma'am, never. I just—I couldn't—" I stammered, flushing, suffering trying to think of a reason I hadn't been able to protect Clara.

"He wasn't here until after they trapped me. It's not his fault. Please don't scold him," Clara pleaded at Miss Horne's side, giving her governess a beseeching look. Miss Horne softened, resting an arm around Clara's shoulders with a sigh.

"Fine. Come here, boy." She beckoned to me and I obliged, sweeping my cap off my head and clasping it in my hands behind my back.

"Ma'am?"

"Whenever we're in this area, I'd appreciate it if you could help me keep an eye on this troublemaker." She jostled Clara lovingly, a small smirk on her face. "Is there a way I can let you know when we're going to be here?"

I mulled it over before answering. "If you want to tell Chief Duncan at the firehouse nearby that you've hired me as a bodyguard, he wouldn't mind you calling the station phone to get ahold of me." Then I flushed, ducking my head and gaze from her face. "I don't mean to act like this is a paying job, ma'am. I'm truly not expecting to be paid."

Miss Horne chuckled softly, then sighed, and the noise was almost fond. "That's a good thing, because while I get paid well and Clara's father could just buy you outright, this sort of arrangement would end with me getting the boot for being irresponsible. So, let's just keep it between us for now, and if there's ever a time when you do deserve compensation, we'll discuss it. Please tell your Chief that Juliana Horne will be calling."

I nodded eagerly, just glad for the chance to be around Clara without sneaking about like I had the past few times.

"Really? You'd just ask some boy off the street to look after me?" Clara was asking when I came back to my senses. My heart sank a bit. Wasn't she just as glad as I was? Miss Horne chuckled.

"I saw him at the store weeks ago, and I heard you call him by name. And if you think you've managed to duck around corners before I see you, Leo, well you're sorely mistaken." Her grin was sharp and I found myself returning it.

And so it went, Miss Horne would call the station asking for her "cousin" Duncan and plan a visit. Then I would wait an hour, meet them next to the milliner's place, and spend the rest of the time they were in the area at Clara's side, keeping anyone and everyone at bay. Chief Duncan was glad to have me out of his hair, Gregory was happy to add an errand or three to my normal weekly shopping duties, and luckily Clara didn't seem to mind tagging along on them. She even helped carry parcels back to the station, but only after we argued about it.

"I can carry them, Leo, I'm not fragile. It's just a package of flour."

"It weighs ten pounds and we have to walk five blocks."

"It's nothing; just let me help."

I sighed, hard, but relented. I was carrying the heavier packages anyway. "Are you sure you're not going to get in trouble with Miss Horne for this?"

"I'm sure she won't mind. It wouldn't hurt me to be a little stronger." Clara was keeping pace with me, and I purposely picked up a little bit of speed just to try and prove to her that she wasn't able to help. Little did I know she was about to show me up. We alternated picking up speed, until we were flat out running the last block to the station. I was panting with my heavier load, Clara only lightly huffing, by the time the trucks were in sight. She grinned.

"Told you." She dropped the package of flour at my feet, then crossed her arms. I glared up at her from where I was bent over with my hands on my knees.

"You were carrying one thing, and you're the one who started running. You set me up."

"Oh, spoken like the boy who set me up from the very beginning." She kicked at my shin lightly, and I swatted at her arm.

"Yes, and?"

"And that means I was right." She stuck her tongue out at me and I returned it, both of us acting like we were much younger than twelve. Or at least, that's what Chief Duncan said when he found us bickering outside.

"I didn't know you were still eight years old, Leo." He was frowning, and I ducked my head into my shoulders. Duncan always looked stern, even when pleased about something. His full dark beard, hooked nose, and small, deep-set eyes always gave him an intense look. He held himself to a high standard, every strand of hair on his head and face perfectly arranged to be neat and tidy, and he held the rest of the firehouse to the same standards.

"Sorry sir."

"Why did you bring your charge all the way here? You're a bit far from that governess that's hired you." Duncan relieved my arms of the other parcels, and scooped up the flour sack as well, lifting it all with ease. I shrugged.

"Gregory sent me on an errand while I was out, and she insisted on helping me bring it all back."

Clara nodded, standing straight with her hands clasped behind her back. "I hope I didn't cause any trouble, sir." Her tone had shifted from the haughty, teasing one she'd used with me into a perfectly polite, light little voice that I narrowed my eyes at. "I did want to help." Duncan did something I'd only heard him do twice before. He laughed.

"Not a problem, miss, as long as it was your idea. Don't let this rascal talk you into anything." He nodded toward me then disappeared into the station, and Clara turned to meet my glare with a grin.

"What? I did want to help. You tried telling me I couldn't."

I glared harder, then rolled my eyes. "If you were my sister, I'd have wrestled you to the ground already." I grumbled, straightening my cap. She plucked it out of my grasp and set it on her own head, grinning wide.

"And if you were my brother, I'd have pinned you and made you cry for Mother," Clara teased, dancing away with my cap still on her head. I gave chase.

We ran all the way back to the shops, Clara laughing and dancing out of my grasp every time I reached for her, until she finally stopped and let me catch her outside the milliner's.

"Alright, you can have it back." She was panting between her giggles and swept my hat off her own head to place it back on mine. "I wanted to see if you could beat me without your burden."

I tugged the cap firmly onto my head, as if pulling it down farther would prevent her from stealing it again, and made a face at her. "You only wanted to beat me again."

"Well, I wasn't sure if I could, but now I know. And I did beat you." Clara's words were sprinkled with laughter, and it only made my glare deeper.

"You are supposed to be this fine lady and yet here you are, running around Brooklyn with some dirty station boy. Your father must be so pleased."

She stuck out her tongue. "He never has to find out!"

May 22, 1912

A few weeks into this arrangement, someone else joined Clara on her trip to Brooklyn. She and another girl showed up with their arms linked, holding each other close like sisters.

"Leo, this is Marie. She's my best friend." Clara held out her free hand toward the other girl, who bowed her head shyly, keeping her gaze away from my face.

"Nice to meet you, miss."

"Enchanted, Leon." Marie's voice was so quiet; she was the exact opposite of Clara. They looked like they could have been sisters, though. Their hair was nearly the same shade, though Marie's was lighter, and they almost had the same color eyes. Where Clara's were storm gray, Marie's were more like silver. I didn't see Marie's often at first, but when she did look at me, it was like being pinned with metal darts.

The times Marie joined us, Clara never held my hand unless we needed to stay near each other in a crowd. She was always slightly reserved, a little withheld, as if she was on her best behavior in front of her friend. Despite all this, I had a feeling that if our secret arrangement got out, it wouldn't be because of Marie. She was trustworthy, I could feel it.

She proved her trustworthiness over and over throughout the years we all knew each other, and I was always terribly thankful to her, even if I never quite figured out how to show it.

Weeks of us meeting up turned into months, with me following Clara around on various errands and her doing the same with me. Sometimes I'd do my homework while she read her magazines or she and Marie chatted, and a few times Clara and Marie even helped me with it. We would bicker over who would carry what and how far we could run, so much so that some of the regulars at the deli and bar would bet on us. Somehow, Clara kept winning even though I never let her. We were kids, running around the sidewalks and in the shops, stealing our time together around school and work and whatever else we had on our plates. We were happy.

July 14, 1912

Following Clara to the newsstand every other week was starting to become a chore. She would always buy the same magazine I'd seen her with on our first meeting, tuck it in her bag, and then I would never see it again. I couldn't understand why she did it.

"What is this thing you need to get so desperately?" I asked, hands in my pockets as I trudged behind her. It had been drizzling lightly all day and we were darting in and out of shops as it started and stopped.

"The next part of my story is out." That was all she said as we finished our walk, she spent her fifteen cents, and we made our way to an empty, dry staircase. Clara sat herself upon the second stair and flipped through the pages before settling on the first page of some story about Mars.

"You're going to read it right now?" I knew there was a pout on my face and I didn't bother to hide it. She didn't usually do this, and it would cut into our time together.

"Unless you actually had plans today, yes." She rolled her eyes at me and flipped the magazine like I'd seen Duncan flip out a newspaper, returning to Mars.

I settled beside her and put my chin in my hands, watching people on the street until I grew bored of it. She turned a page, and I shifted to peer over her shoulder. Someone named John Carter was finishing some sort of glorious battle, and I tried to piece together what had started it as I read. But I couldn't, obviously. I opened my mouth to ask her what was going on, but she spoke before I even made a sound.

"I'm not going to explain it. This is the very last part. If you want to find out what happens, I'll bring you the others." Clara had continued reading while speaking, and I remember being amazed by that. "You have to give them back though!"

She glanced at me while turning the next page, and I grinned. "You'd bring them all the way here just for me?" Her cheeks turned a soft pink and her glance turned into a glare.

"Only if you give them back!"

I chuckled. "I will, I will."

"Good." She flipped the magazine again, and I set my chin back in my hand to watch her.

"I look forward to reading it."

Little did I know that this singular instance was one of the beginning moments of a lifelong adoration of the world of Barsoom, and Clara would buy every single *All-Story* magazine from then on. It was her absolute favorite series.

May 20th, 1913

"Sorry to bother, ma'am, but could you get Leo for me?" I heard Gregory's voice from the front door and came out of my room before Mom had a chance to call for me. She was standing with her hand still on the doorknob, brow furrowed as she looked between Gregory and me.

"Is something wrong?" I asked, coming to stand beside mom. It was my day off, I thought. Had I gotten my days mixed up?

"Well, I'm not quite sure." Gregory lifted a hand to rub the back of his neck. My brow furrowed to match Mom's. "That gal you hang around with and her friend are at the station without their governess."

My eyes widened. Clara and Marie had shown up without Miss Horne?

"They were asking for you, and we told them it was your day off and to head back home, but Clara refused. I think she'd been crying." Gregory continued, and Mom's hand went to her mouth.

"Was she hurt?" She asked, that same hand landing on my shoulder. She'd been about to leave our apartment for work, her bag in her hand and all.

"No, ma'am, thank goodness." Gregory shook his head, and Mom nodded.

"I need to go, but Leo, you best go tend to them. See what's wrong, and get ahold of that governess."

"We called her already. She said she'd be on the next train," Gregory said. Duncan had probably placed the call.

"Good, very good. Alright. Leo, if you need to bring them home, go ahead. They'll be safe here. We don't want them out on the streets alone again." Mom leaned over to kiss the top of my head, but she didn't have to lean far, as I was catching up to her in height.

"Thank you, ma'am." Gregory stepped out of her way, settling his hat on his head. He motioned for me to follow him, and I did after grabbing my own hat and locking the door.

He told me a little more on the way to the station, how Clara had knocked on the kitchen door until someone had opened it and demanded that I come and see her and Marie immediately. Since I wasn't there, the others had tucked the girls into the kitchen, made them some tea, and asked them to wait. Duncan had stayed in the kitchen with them while Gregory came to get me.

As soon as I set foot in the station kitchen, Clara jumped out of her seat and ran over, flinging her arms around my neck. She nearly toppled us both, but I found my balance just in time and hugged her back.

"What's wrong? Why did you come without Miss Horne?" I asked, pushing her back gently so I could see her face. She had definitely been crying. Her eyes were red and a little swollen underneath, and there was still a small tremble to her lip.

"Marie and I are leaving. We're running away." Clara lifted a hand to wipe under her eye, and I dug in my pocket for a handkerchief. She dried her eyes while I looked over her shoulder at Marie and Duncan. Marie looked sad and concerned but was letting Clara do the talking. Duncan just looked glad the girls weren't on the streets alone.

"Why do you want to run away?" I asked, leading Clara back to her seat and coaxing her to sit. She did, sniffling into my handkerchief.

"My father hates me. He'd probably be happier if I wasn't around, if he didn't have to argue with me all the time."

"He doesn't hate you, Clara." Marie spoke softly, her hand lifting from her mug to rest on Clara's shoulder. "He was cross with you, but I truly don't believe he hates you."

"You saw only the last bit of his anger." Clara wiped at her eyes again, and I took the seat across from her, next to Duncan. He was staying quiet, but I could tell he didn't feel like he could leave just yet. I would have bet real money that he was trying to determine if Clara had been abused.

"Tell me what happened." I laid my hands on top of the table, reaching out to Clara with both. She took one, keeping the handkerchief to her face with the other. After a moment's pause, she spoke.

"I wanted to help in the garden. The gardener was happy about it; he seemed thrilled that I wanted to learn about flowers and caring for them. I asked him how to take care of our rose bush, and the lilacs."

Clara continued recounting the morning. She and the gardener had gone around the entire garden and he told her the names of all the plants in it. He showed her all the tools he used and was in the middle of teaching her how to use them when Clara's father had come outside, red-faced and shouting, and demanded Clara come inside at once.

"He had barely shut the door to the patio when he'd started yelling, telling me that it was inappropriate for a young lady of my status to be kneeling in the dirt and befriending the *help.*" She said the word "help" with a slightly displeased face. "I hate how badly he treats everyone who works for us. They are all so lovely to me, and to Marie too. And father just acts as if they're automatons there to do his bidding. So of course, I argued back. I told him that the gardener was a wonderful man and he'd been polite and educational, and didn't father want me to be well educated? But that was apparently the wrong thing to say, and he started yelling more about disobedience and impudence and everything else he could think to call a girl who'd just wanted to learn to garden."

Clara's voice shook as she spoke, and broke as she finished, the handkerchief covering her mouth. She breathed through it, her eyes shut, and I squeezed her hand. Marie scooted a little closer to rub Clara's back.

"I came into the room right as he was finishing his tirade. I'd just gotten to the house, and as soon as her father left, Clara took me by the arm and we came straight here." Marie was speaking softly, and Clara leaned into her. "She told me everything on the train."

Duncan sighed into his mug then set it down, rubbing his eyes with one hand. I'd nearly forgotten he was there. "Young miss, I understand being upset, but that was a rather reckless thing you did. Coming all the way here on your own, I mean."

Clara looked up at Duncan and her hand tightened on mine. I pressed my thumb into her fingers, shaking my head. "He's not going to yell at you like your father did." I looked to Duncan, who nodded to confirm my words.

"I won't. You've been yelled at enough, and you aren't my daughter. But I do know you now, and I consider you under my care every time you're here." Duncan stood up and rounded the table to stand next to Clara, kneeling on one knee to be closer to eye level with her. "Is your father hurting you at home? Are you in danger?"

Clara shook her head, releasing my hand to wrap both of hers around the handkerchief. "He yells at me a lot, and is cross often, but the worst is just the shouting."

"I'm glad to hear it." Duncan patted Clara on the arm, then stood, turning to the doorway right as Miss Horne burst through it.

"Clara! Marie! Girls! What on earth were you thinking?!" she called to them, moving to stand in the spot where Duncan had just been, wrapping her arms around Clara and reaching to hold Marie's shoulder. "Why did you just leave? I would have come with you. Oh, girls." She bowed her head to the top of Clara's, and I could see all the tension melt out of her body.

"I'm sorry," Clara whispered into Miss Horne's shoulder, who huffed a sigh.

"I would hope so, young lady." She stood, planting her hands on her hips. "We are certainly not telling your father the full truth, so you and Marie had best figure out a cover story that we can all agree on." It seemed so odd for a governess, a lady of authority, to suggest lying to her employers, but Miss Horne's job would be on the line if Clara's parents knew she was traipsing around Brooklyn with me as often as she was. Marie too I would assume. I didn't even know if Marie's parents knew anything.

"We will," Marie said, standing up now that Miss Horne was there. She folded her hands primly in front of her, looking at Duncan. "Thank you sir, for taking care of us. And for the tea."

"Of course, miss. You are both welcome here, but please don't try and run away again." Duncan smiled at Marie, then turned to Clara. He held her gaze for a moment then spoke. "Miss Clara, if your father reprimands you any more harshly than he has already, please come and tell me."

"Yes, sir. I will. Thank you." Clara stood and bowed her head to Duncan, who just nodded in response.

"Leo, stay here with the girls for a moment." Duncan held out his arm to Miss Horne, and they turned to leave the room. I assumed they were going to Duncan's office to discuss what had happened.

I turned to the girls, who were both fidgeting nervously. "Is Miss Horne very strict?"

They both shook their heads. "No, she really isn't. She's kind and lovely, and she's taught us both so much," Marie said, and Clara nodded. "My governess is only with us part of the time, so Juliana has been mine nearly as much as she's been Clara's." It sounded a bit odd to hear Marie call Miss Horne by her first name, but it made sense if they were that close.

"She's like our older sister more so than our governess." Clara sniffed, and dabbed at her eyes with my handkerchief again.

We were quiet until Duncan and Miss Horne returned, then Clara and Marie both hugged me tight before they left. Miss Horne had taken both girls by the hand and was leading them down the sidewalk as if they were three instead of thirteen.

"Come now, girls. Clara, would you like to pick up the *All-Story* on the way home?" Miss Horne was already settling back into her patient, watchful governess role as they walked out. Clara nodded and seemed to brighten a bit at the suggestion.

"It should be the last part of the second Barsoom story today," I called after her, and she looked over her shoulder with a smile and nod. Then they were swallowed by the crowd on the sidewalk. Duncan sighed and rubbed his eyes with one hand, the other clapping onto my shoulder.

"You've brought such drama into our firehouse, Leon." I believe he was teasing, but at the time I was unable to see it.

"I didn't bring it myself!" I shouted, pulling away from his hand. The single comment had turned me into a cat with its hackles raised. "I never told them to come here at all. I wasn't even supposed to see them today!" I was scowling, and Duncan just looked down at me tiredly.

"Leon, you have no reason to be up in arms right now."

"You just told me this was my fault!"

He crossed his arms, shaking his head. "I did not. You're twisting my words."

My twelve, almost thirteen-year-old brain was struggling to understand what he meant. He'd literally said I'd brought drama into the firehouse. "You just said—"

"I know what I said. Come here." Duncan took hold of my shoulder again and I only struggled against him for a moment before he tightened his grip and led me back inside. He sat me down at the kitchen table and then sat across from me. "Listen, boy. I didn't say what happened was your fault." I was about to respond but he snapped his fingers. "I said listen. Not talk back." After I nodded, he continued. "All I meant was that your friends now see this as a safe place, and in all my years of being here, I've never had this happen before. Women have brought us their newborns because they can't take care of them, but two girls running away from Manhattan and ending up here is brand new."

"Then why did you say it was me?" I didn't shout this time, but it was a struggle to keep the bite out of my tone.

"Because if it weren't for you, this wouldn't be a safe place for them. Does that make sense? Because you"—he pointed at my chest—"are a safe person for them, anywhere you are is safe. You have become their guardian, and they trust you enough to run to you when upset."

My anger dissipated so quickly it felt like it had never been there in the first place. Clara and Marie had run to *me*, not the station. Not just away from Clara's yelling father, but to me. I lowered my gaze, suddenly at a loss for words. Duncan chuckled softly, but tiredly.

"Now you have it." He pushed himself up, patting my shoulder as he left the room. "Don't let it go to your head. You're a fireman, not a knight in shining armor."

He was right, you wouldn't find me in chainmail on the back of a magnificent steed, but boy I sure felt like one just then.

November 7th, 2010

"What about the war?" I asked as our conversation turned to that period of time. Leon shrugged.

"We were only fourteen when it began, so for a long time it didn't really affect us. The States didn't even join right away, as I'm sure you know." He glanced at me and I nodded. I did know.

"Your parents didn't talk about it? People at the station?"

"Well, sure, all the adults around us were always talking about it. But we were so removed from it. I remember Marie and Clara going to charity dinners with their families and such, but to them it was just another party, another public appearance to be made. 1914 was just another year for us." Leon's gaze had drifted to the shelves again, and I made note of what he said. "We played in Brooklyn, chased each other around the park, were menaces in all the stores. I think once we even got kicked out of a store." The corner of his mouth lifted into an amused smirk.

"Sounds as if you were all troublemakers." I chuckled softly, noting that as well. Leon laughed, breathlessly, just a few notes.

"I wouldn't say that. It was mostly Clara. She liked to tease, play little harmless pranks. I caught her 'stealing' Marie's purse and books multiple times, and she routinely took my hat." He air-quoted stealing, the fond smirk still on his face. "We just always got caught up in her acts. We were kids having fun however we could."

August 8th & 9th, 1915

Went to Brooklyn again with L. Spent $4 on his gift. __Very__ well received!

The summer I turned fifteen, Clara already had been for months and had been gladly holding that fact over my head. So, the morning of my birthday, I sat and waited for the call I figured would come, so I could shove the fact we were the same age again in her face.

But it never did.

I waited around all morning, into the afternoon, and finally about an hour before dinner, I gave up. If it had been any other day I would have stayed until after dark, but Mom had made me a birthday meal and demanded I be home for it. And I wasn't about to pass up a special home-cooked meal, even for a chance to see Clara. I ran through the light rain that'd been falling all the way home.

"You were nearly late." Mom had her hands on her hips as I came in, giving me a look of displeasure. I bowed my head sheepishly.

"Sorry."

"What kept you? Were you with that girl?"

"No, actually. I didn't see her at all today." I was about to sit down at the table, had my chair pulled out and everything, when Mom pointed at the sink and I hurriedly went to wash my hands.

"You know she's from an entirely different world than us, Leo." Mom's voice had a tinge of sadness to it, and I sighed. We'd had this conversation countless times over the past few years.

"I know, Mom."

"You shouldn't get so attached to her."

"I know, Mom."

Mom sighed through her nose and turned to the cupboard to retrieve a little round dish. Inside it were two little pastries from the nicer bakery at the end of the neighborhood, the one we didn't normally go to because it was way more than we could afford.

"Oh, you didn't have to..."

"I wanted to. They're both the kind with peach cream, like you like." She was grinning now, and I returned it, reaching forward to wrap my arms around her. Even though we disagreed on how I spent my time, she just wanted what was best for me.

"Thank you. This is such a great surprise, I really mean it. Thank you." I held her shoulders and leaned forward to kiss her gently on the forehead. At fifteen, I was starting to grow taller than her already. She laughed and patted my chest.

"Sit down and eat them then, you can have your dessert before dinner tonight."

I didn't, simply because it was too ingrained in me to have sweet after savory and not the other way around. But I went to bed that night with a full stomach, which was more than I could say for my heart.

I lucked out the next day though when Duncan told me that Miss Horne had called nearly at the crack of dawn and asked him to tell me to be prepared to stay with her and Clara all day. My surprise must have shown clearly on my face since Duncan took a little bit of pity on me and explained as best he could.

"All I know is that something has happened and Miss Clara doesn't want to be in her house for as long as possible. Miss Horne didn't explain further. I'm sure they'll tell you once you meet up. Now scat." He shooed me away, waving his hand toward the door, and I obliged, heading out into the drizzling rain.

I scampered down the wet sidewalk, dodging people as best I could and doing my best to avoid running into anyone. It didn't take me long to reach our normal meetup spot by the milliner's shop.

"Leo!" Clara called out, and I lifted my head to see her making her way toward me with an umbrella held over her head, trying not to run. I met her in the middle and she threw her arms around my neck, hiding her face against my shoulder. Heat crept up my back and settled on my cheeks. It took a second, but I settled my arms around her waist, hugging her close. She smelled like lilacs.

"I'm so happy to see you." Her voice was muffled against my collar, and she squeezed me tight.

"I am too. What's wrong? Duncan said something happened but he didn't know what." I leaned back and tried to look her in the eye, but she was avoiding my gaze. A quick glance told me Miss Horne had left us to our own devices. "Clara?"

Her mumble was inaudible.

"I can't hear you at all."

She pulled back, sighing, keeping her hands linked behind my neck. I hoped it didn't feel as hot to her as it did to me.

"I got caught out in the garden again. You know father doesn't want me helping the gardeners, but I really like working with the flowers." She was pouting a little, and my shoulders sank in relief that it wasn't something worse. "I just don't want to be near him for as long as possible. I don't understand what's so wrong about a young lady learning how to keep flowers." Her pout grew stronger.

"So is that why you didn't come yesterday?" I was trying not to remind her it had been my birthday; it felt selfish.

"Yes. I was told to stay in my room until dinner and then go right back after. As if I'm some sort of child." She rolled her eyes, which was not helping her case. I tried not to laugh.

She released me and took my hand instead, and we made our way to the street where the shops were. At least, we started to, then Clara gasped and turned to me, squeezing my hand. "Leo! It was your birthday! I missed it! I'm so sorry!!"

I was relieved that she'd remembered, but to tease her I pretended to be upset instead. I rubbed the back of my neck and looked down, mumbling my words. "It's alright, it's not important." She saw right through me, swatting the hand she held. I snickered.

"It is too! Now you stop it. I'm shopping for you." I had no choice but to agree.

"As you wish, Miss Clara." I chuckled and earned another light smack on the arm as the friendly, pleasant atmosphere that normally surrounded us returned.

Despite a few more protests, I was dragged into the grocer's and gifted a bag of candy, all the pieces chosen and paid for by my companion. I tried not to cringe as the grocer told her the price. It was more than I'd ever had in my pocket, even as a paperboy, but Clara just handed over the coins as if they were nothing. It was a struggle to be grateful instead of jealous.

"Anywhere else you want to go? A different shop? Something to eat?" Clara slid her arm through mine as we walked away from the grocer, stealing one of the candies from the bag and popping it in her mouth. The rain had let up and her umbrella was hooked on her other arm. We didn't usually walk like this. We'd held hands a few times just so I didn't lose her in the crowds, but now she didn't seem to care who saw her on my arm. I was in no position to protest since I was serving as her distraction and celebrant, so I let her keep her arm where it was.

"I don't know. You're the one glad to drop money on me today so it should probably be your purse's choice." The statement earned me a light pinch on the arm and I laughed. "What?"

"It's for your birthday, you're supposed to be choosing!"

"Alright, alright." I grinned, squishing her arm to my side lightly. If I'd have been looking I would have seen her blush, but I only found out that she had later. I looked up and down the street, turning this corner of the world over in my mind until I remembered somewhere I'd never been. A little music shop tucked away, almost in an alleyway, that was pretty much always empty every time I passed it.

I led her there, and we were announced with a little ding of the bell hanging over the door. The shopkeeper poked his head around the doorframe that led to a back room, and grinned.

"Why hello! A pair of young lovers in to peruse my wares, how dandy." He came out of the room dusting himself off and we were suddenly reminded Clara's arm was through mine. I was about to pull away but she held me tighter. I didn't fight her.

"It's his birthday! Or well, it was. We're celebrating today since we couldn't yesterday." Clara was smiling, patting my arm just below where she held it, and the shopkeeper returned her cheerful expression.

"Well how lovely, what are you looking for? An instrument? Some sheet music perhaps?" He was gesturing to different parts of the store as he spoke, and my eyes followed the movement, then paused.

Hanging on the wall was a brand-new guitar, shiny and beckoning and practically begging to be touched. I did drop Clara's arm then, and she let me. I moved toward the wall, magnetically pulled to the string instrument.

"Ah that's a fine choice, my boy, a fine choice indeed. We just got that one in last week. Only two people have played it: the man who made it, and me when I was buying it for the store. It's a

Buegeleisen and Jacobson 430." The shopkeeper chuckled, beating me to the wall and using a little stepladder to pull the guitar off the hook. "Here you are, put the strap over your head like this." He showed me how it sat and adjusted the strap to my body. "Hold the neck like this, it puts less strain on your hand."

After a quick instruction on how to hold a single chord—not that I knew what a chord was back then—he handed me a pick and showed me how to strum properly. The music I made was shaky, a little out of tune, and only had one note. But the electricity up my arms to my heart was blatant. I was absolutely meant to play guitar.

"Well now, listen to that. Have you played before?"

I shook my head. "I haven't ever touched a guitar before now, sir." I couldn't meet his gaze because I was still transfixed by the instrument in my hands, pressed lightly against my ribs. "I swear I haven't."

The shopkeeper laughed softly again, patting my shoulder. "I believe you, boy, you don't have to sell your story." He moved to the counter, then to the back room. "We have a case for it if you want to take it home."

Suddenly the guitar felt like glass in my hands, and I moved to pull the strap over my head, setting the instrument on the counter. "Oh, sir, I'm sure I can't afford this." My voice cracked a bit on my words, and the heartache forming in my chest was quieted by Clara's hand on my shoulder.

"I can." It was only two words, but they inspired a whirlwind of emotions. Gratitude, that she'd even be willing to do this for me. Jealousy, that she could without a second thought. Suspicion, that she had an ulterior motive of using me to get back at her father by spending his money on something this frivolous.

"Clara, no, don't," I whispered, out of habit more so than me believing the words. She shrugged.

"How much would this one be, sir?" she called, and the shopkeeper reappeared with the case. He grinned and settled the guitar inside of it before answering.

"Well normally it would be seven dollars and twenty-five cents, but we do have payment plans available if you need one." He said the price as if it wasn't one of the biggest sums of money I had ever heard in my life. I paled, and Clara saw, her hand remaining on my shoulder.

"What's the payment plan look like?"

"Two dollars today, twenty-five cents monthly until it's paid off. Then it's yours." The shopkeeper snapped the case shut and turned to his cash register, pulling a little ledger out from beside it. "If you're wanting it, the strap comes with it, but not the case."

"And how much is the case?" Clara's voice was so calm. How could she be this calm about such a staggering amount of money?

"The case is only a dollar sixty-three."

"That's much less than I was thinking." She laughed and squeezed my shoulder before nudging me gently out of the way. "Can we put the balance in my name?"

"Clara..." I sighed, shaking my head. "You shouldn't do this."

"Leo, I heard how you sounded with it. It's meant to be, and I'm making it happen." She glared over her shoulder and I cowed, returning to silently warring between gratitude and jealousy.

The transaction happened without my noticing, and I only came to when I felt a blunt stab on my cheek. It was Clara, poking me with the guitar pick that I'd set down on the counter. I blinked and looked at her, batting her hand away as she grinned.

"Leo, my dear friend, you are now the owner of a brand-new guitar." The case was in her other hand and she lifted her arm to hold it out. I stared, absolutely in shock that she'd done what I said she didn't need to. "I can't hold it like this for long, take it from me."

I quickly did as she bid, my fingers wrapping around the case handle so, so carefully. Clara tucked the pick in my shirt pocket, patting it with a smile. I settled the case by my side and lifted my head to look for the shopkeeper, finding him behind the counter with a pleased look on his face.

"You enjoy that now, boy, and if you want to learn properly, you come back and see me anytime." His grin was so bright it sparked one of my own, and I nodded.

"Yes, yes sir, I will. Thank you." I turned to Clara, taking hold of her hand. "Thank you so much."

She giggled, squeezing my hand, then waved to the shopkeeper as she led me out of the store. "Thank you, Mr. Weis!" Apparently she'd learned his name while I was fighting with myself.

"Have a nice day you two!" He called, and the bell rang above our heads once again as we left.

One of Brooklyn's largest parks was nearby, and Clara led me to it before I could suggest somewhere else. She settled under a tree and patted the grass next to her, and I obeyed. Thanks to the tree, that patch was dry.

"Well take it out, let's see what you can do with no lessons." She chuckled, and I nudged her foot with mine as I sat. But I was grinning.

"I can't believe you just did that. Isn't your father going to be furious?"

"He's not going to know. It's my allowance money; it's been burning a hole in this purse for as long as I can remember." She shrugged, leaning back against the tree. Her dress was probably going to get ruined, but she definitely didn't care. "I can't think of anyone better to spend it on than you, or maybe Marie."

"I'm sure you've never spent that much on Marie."

"You weren't paying attention, Leo." She sighed, faking annoyance. "I asked for the payment plan. I spent less than four dollars on you today." Despite the lower price, the amount still stabbed me. She'd bought the case outright, then.

"Clara, that's so much money! You can't—" She leaned forward to press a finger to my lips.

"I already did, and it's not a problem. Really. You can pay me back by learning to play properly."

As she lowered her finger, I quickly did the math in my head. "Clara it's going to take you two years to pay this off." I sighed. I was trying not to be ungrateful for the gift. She just shrugged at me.

"Oh Leo, what a terrible future, to have to visit you at least once a month for the next two years." Her tone was false tragedy, and she lifted a hand to press the back of it to her forehead. All of the drama was erased with a brilliant grin. My heart eased, just a little.

"Are you really sure? I can make payments too once I start getting paid by the station."

"I'm really, really sure." Clara chuckled. "But if it'll make you feel better, sure, make all the payments you like. I'll make them when I'm here, and you make them when you can."

Her agreement to my offer to help pay released the rest of the tension from my chest, and I banished it with a long sigh, my eyes closed. "Thank you, I mean it. This is amazing."

"You deserve something amazing." Her voice was quiet, and I lifted my gaze to find her looking back at me, smiling far more gently than she ever had. Now that it wasn't straining to beat, my heart flipped. I swallowed and quickly looked back down, settling my fingers onto the strings like Mr. Weis had shown me. I didn't know what chord it was then, but later on down the road he'd tell me it was G.

And so, with a single chord and aching fingers scored by the strings, I played Clara a makeshift song that had no lyrics but carried every bit of my gratitude across the foot of space between our hearts.

August 15, 1915

Took M. to see L. Played guitar for us. Was so lovely.

A week after Clara purchased the guitar for me, I got to see Marie and Clara both. We forsook the normal shopping spree to sit in the park Clara and I had gone to the day after my birthday, and the girls demanded I play for them.

"I'm really no better than I was last week, Clara." I shook my head at them, pulling the instrument onto my lap and tuning one of the strings. That was the first thing I'd asked Mr. Weis to show me how to do, take care of the thing. It was an investment after all.

"I don't care. You could be the worst player in the world, and I'd still sit here and listen." Clara's words caused my heart to stutter a bit, and I covered it by clearing my throat. Marie chuckled lightly. She'd gotten more and more comfortable around me the longer we'd known each other.

"I very much would like to hear, Leo, if you don't mind. Clara was raving about it all week, about the little song you made up."

I flushed. I didn't fully remember the off-the-cuff "song" I'd made up just to thank Clara for the gift, but it helped that I still only knew the single chord. "Alright, well, I'll try. But it might be different."

The girls settled happily against the tree, leaving me to sit in front of them hunched over the instrument the same as I had been for the past week. I pressed my fingers to the strings, a little more used to them now that they were nowhere near as hurtful as they'd been at first, and found a familiar rhythm of seemingly random strumming. The little tune started to filter back into my memory, and I adjusted to it as I remembered.

Clara closed her eyes and leaned her head back to listen while Marie's eyes fixed on my strumming, as if trying to puzzle out how it all worked just from looking. They both remained like that until I slowed my hand, plucking the single string at the top to signal the end of the tune. Marie grinned, lifting her hands to clap. I laughed and bowed as best I could over my guitar.

"See, isn't it wonderful? Leo's definitely a natural." Clara was smiling when I looked at her, but it wasn't really joy, it felt like pride, like warmth. I felt the back of my neck heat up.

"Oh, absolutely, I agree! You need to learn all of the ah...chords, was it?" Marie looked at me curiously.

"That's right. I'm going to go back to ask Mr. Weis to teach me more tomorrow. So by the time I see you both again, I'll be able to play a little better."

Clara shook her head fiercely. "Don't you dare change that. Make up a new one. But your first one has to be the same!"

"Oh, well, yes ma'am. As you wish." I chuckled, and Clara nodded, satisfied.

"That would be nice, actually, to make up a new song every time you finish learning another one." Marie adjusted her position, tucking her legs up underneath her. I grinned at her.

"I would have so many songs."

"As if that's bad!" The girls spoke in unison, and we all fell into laughter.

"We want all your songs, Leo!"

"Yes! We do!!" Marie agreed eagerly.

"Hahaha, alright, I'll do my best to make something up for everything I learn." I idly strummed the strings, enjoying the little ripple of untamed music. I knew very little about guitars, but I did know that there were a lot of chords. So I'd be making things up for years, most likely. I didn't mind the idea, and I don't think the girls did either.

Things stayed much the same over the next four years: we met up, strolled around the shopping areas of Brooklyn, lounged in the park, and sometimes went to the music store together for my guitar lessons. I picked it up quickly, but it seemed there was always something new to learn with this instrument. A new song, a new way to tune, a little thing called a capo that clamped across the strings to change the key—the lessons were endless. Every time Clara and Marie accompanied me, they perched in the corner on a couple of stools, flipping through sheet music or just listening. Quite a few times, I'd look over and find them both leaning back against the wall, quietly dozing against each other's shoulders. It was only once when I strummed loudly and fast to startle them awake, but that once was worth it for their reactions.

"Leo! Why?!" Clara whined, rubbing her fingers against her ears as she shot me a look that was half-scolding and half-pleading. Marie was just staring at me sadly, but I could see the glimmer of mirth in her eyes. I grinned, wide and pleased.

"Oh, Miss Clara, just a wakeup call." I chuckled, leaning my elbow gently on top of my guitar and settling my chin in my hand. Both girls narrowed their eyes at me, which only made my grin grow wider.

"Well, I would like to file a complaint with the wakeup service," Marie pouted, scoffing in my direction. Clara nodded in solidarity.

"I would too!"

Mr. Weis laughed from his counter; he'd had to help a customer in the middle of our lesson. "I was waiting for that to happen." He was grinning too, and it was fond. He'd definitely gotten used to our little trio hanging around.

"You shouldn't have let him." Clara scowled at him too, much less fiercely than she had at me, and he only chuckled before returning to counting his day's earnings.

"He just shouldn't have done it." Marie leaned back against the wall, shaking her head.

"Aww, alright, I'm sorry. I'll play a song for you, will that make it better?"

"Yes," Clara stated, and Marie nodded in agreement.

So they received a rendition of a parlor song Mr. Weis had taught me the previous week, a lilting little thing full of joy and sounding like bluebirds. Both girls were pleased by the time I finished. I was definitely forgiven.

July 7th and 8th, 1916

L. bought lunch today! First real paycheck. Was so charming about it all.

It was a little before I turned sixteen that I was finally allowed to undergo training as a firefighter, instead of being just a station boy. I'd suffered as the errand lad for four years, and finally Duncan had deemed it enough. Lucky for me, I was already pretty strong and fit, so the training wasn't nearly as tough as it could have been. I lifted the heavy buckets with ease, managed to learn to control the hose, and could get a hydrant open nearly as quickly as Duncan could. It turned out that wasn't the hardest part of using a hydrant, water pressure and I weren't getting along very well at first.

"You'll get there, Leo, just keep trying." Gregory was holding his hand out after the hose had gotten away from me and I'd toppled over. I accepted his help and pulled myself up, swallowing a frustrated sigh. "That beast is just slippery as hell."

"And wet too." I grinned at my own joke, and Gregory snickered briefly.

"It fights all of us, we just learn how to fight back."

My first paycheck was pretty miniscule, even by 1916 standards, but it was still a cause for celebration. I was only allowed to work when I wasn't in school, after all. But I took the money home to Mom as quickly as I could, keeping just a dollar for myself and giving her everything else.

"Oh honey no, you keep more of it for yourself. I have my own income, remember?" she protested, trying to push the bills back toward me. I shook my head, dancing out of the way while laughing.

"Absolutely not. I said I would bring home money and I have. I've kept what I want and the rest is all yours. Get more groceries, buy yourself something pretty—I don't care what you do with it, but it's yours."

Mom finally relented and tucked it away in an old coffee can, then pushed the can underneath her dresser. As she stood I wrapped her in my arms, squeezing her tightly. She chuckled gently and hugged me back, resting her head on my shoulder.

"I am going to help take care of you and this apartment as best I can now. I promise."

"I believe you, my son." She squeezed me again before leaning back, her hands staying on my sides as she looked me over. "Now if only you could stop shooting up like a beansprout. You're much too tall. You're going to dwarf all your dance partners."

She'd said the word "dance," so I immediately adjusted our stance and spun her about the room until she was cackling and grinning just as much as I was.

"Alright! Let me go!" She was breathing hard, mostly from laughter but also because I'd led her around the entire apartment. "Let your mother rest, boy."

"Yes, mother dear." I leaned forward to kiss her forehead softly, and she sighed happily.

"You're a good boy. Don't let anyone ever tell you different." She patted my chest.

"I was raised right." My grin was infectious and sparked another on her face.

"That you were, son, that you were."

The very next day, I took my saved dollar and waited for Clara to show. I'd gotten the call from Miss Horne myself, since I just so happened to be near the station phone when it rang. As a proper fireman, I was allowed to answer calls now. It took them a little longer to get into the area, and I whiled away the minutes watching a group of little kids play kickball in an alleyway. A cigarette dangled idly from my fingers. I'd picked up the habit a few months prior, but Clara and Marie had told me quite blatantly that they hated the smell, so I'd resolved to only smoke when they were nowhere nearby.

Finally, as I was staring off into space, I felt a tap on my shoulder.

"I found you, fireman."

I turned to see Clara grinning wildly, and I immediately returned the expression. She narrowed her eyes at my cigarette and I immediately dropped it, crushing it beneath my boot.

"Afternoon, heiress." It wasn't what I'd wanted to call her, but 'dearest' was probably off the table for a boy of my status to call a girl of her status. She made a face of displeasure at the title, batting me softly on the shoulder.

"Never call me that again," she commanded, and I chuckled and nodded.

"What should I call you then?"

Clara's gaze shifted to the middle distance as she thought. I stood upright from where I'd been leaning against the wall, hands sliding into my pockets. One of them curled around the dollar bill, and I allowed myself a little smile, remembering my plans for the day.

"You could just call me Clara."

I couldn't help it: I burst out laughing.

"What?"

"All that time in thought just to tell me to call you by your name?"

She crossed her arms. "I couldn't think of anything else."

"Alright, Clara." Every bit of warmth and affection I'd wanted to put into the word 'dearest' went into her name, and I was rewarded with her eyes widening and a soft blush crossing her cheekbones. "Clara." This time it was softer, and I turned to step closer to her. I watched as she swallowed and took in a steadying breath.

"Y-yes?"

"Would you like to have lunch with me today?"

She reached out to swat me on the arm, and I grinned. "You get all...all...lovely on me just to ask me to lunch?" Her stammering was the ultimate reward; it took so much to get her to lose her composure.

"Yes?"

"Ugh."

I suppressed my grin, turning it into a smile. Clara glared.

"I'm sorry, Clara." I said her name the same way I had before, the grin breaking through when she blushed again.

"Stop it or I'm not going with you. I'll go find Juliana."

"Hahaha, alright, I'll stop." I offered her my arm, though, and she took it. I led her to what was probably the cheapest dining counter in the area, but it's what I could afford with the money I'd purposely set aside for this.

We took over two stools at the end of the counter. Clara's knee pressed against mine in a long-practiced act that kept everyone else away from her, but as used to it as I was, it sent my heart racing that day. Any touch I could steal, I would. So I pressed my knee back softly against hers, savoring this bit of thievery.

I ordered for us, stretching my dollar thin and having a moment of panic when our order ended up being a few cents more than I had. Clara retrieved the remainder from her purse, handing it to the waitress with ease, while I sat embarrassed and ashamed, feeling my plan was ruined. Clara's hand slid onto my knee, under the counter, and patted it softly.

"Don't worry about it, you still paid the lion's share. I'm definitely going to count this as your treat." Her gentle smile eased my shame, and I returned it as our food was set before us. "Why are you so adamant about paying today, anyway?"

"You've spent more than enough money on me. It's high time I treated you once in a while."

Her shoulders shook gently with mirth. "Leo, you've never had money before now, and I never minded. You're my favorite person to spend money on."

Her words set off another war in my heart, between gratefulness, pleasure, and jealousy. It was a battle fought valiantly ever since we'd met, and jealousy had only managed to win at night when I was lying awake ruminating about all the things she'd bought for me.

"Well, I have it now, so you can't use that excuse anymore." I jostled her knee with mine, and she laughed. The sound was a balm to my soul.

"Alright, alright, but you're still my favorite person." She surely meant the full sentence, the one she'd said earlier, but that didn't stop the little flip of joy my heart did.

"And you're mine," I replied softly, and she looked over.

"What?"

I cleared my throat, a mimic of her earlier blush now gracing my cheekbones. "You're mine." I was met with silence for longer than I was comfortable with, and looked up, hoping not to see disgust or anything similar on her face. To my delight, she was smiling, her eyes just a little bit watery.

"You're mine," she whispered, and I grinned. My heart felt like it was swelling, growing with happiness every time she said it.

After a brief moment of basking in our contentment, we turned to our usual topics of conversation. I told her about the new song that Mr. Weis was teaching me, she described the latest family dinner gossip and nonsense. It was all so blissfully, wonderfully normal.

We walked to the park afterward, her arm returning to mine, and we strolled in silence, just enjoying each other's company.

There used to be a small pond in that park, and that day there were a few ducks in it, so we sat to watch them. I laid my jacket out on the ground so Clara could keep her dress clean, and then I laid myself out on the grass next to her. The weather was calm, peaceful. Warm but not hot, with a soft breeze that was just enough to lift a few strands of hair from Clara's hairpins, waving them gently in the air currents. I looked up at her from where I lay, studying the shape of her nose and jawline, memorizing each curve of her profile. She caught me staring.

"What are you doing?"

"Just looking at you."

She laughed. "Why?"

I took a breath before answering, knowing I was about to cross another line I shouldn't. "You're really lovely." My eyes lifted to the sky, away from her gaze. "I've always thought so, even when we were younger, but you're growing up into a beautiful woman, Clara."

She was silent again, like at the diner, and my heart froze in my chest before I dared to glance over. There was a smile on her face, water in her eyes again, but it wasn't the same pleasure as before. I sat up immediately, reaching to lay a hand on her upper arm. She started, looking up to meet my gaze.

"You shouldn't try and court me before my debut, you know," she whispered, dropping her gaze to her lap. Mine followed. She was trying to make it sound like a joke, but something else lingered underneath it.

I found out years and years later that the thought of being with me had always been on her mind, and that was the first time she'd ever allowed it past her lips. I'd had similar thoughts, but had always fought them. I was so far below her station it wasn't even funny. I was just about on the bottom of New York City's social ladder while she floated near the top. We weren't even meant to know each other, really. All of this settled heavy in my heart as we sat there with it between us. We'd had such a beautiful day, and the remembrance that we didn't actually live in the safe little bubble we'd created for ourselves had ruined it.

My hand dropped from her arm, and I sighed as I flopped back down on the grass. I lifted an arm to cover my eyes, tucking my face in the inner crook of my elbow. "I'm sorry, Clara," I whispered, just loud enough she'd hear me over the city noise.

"I know." Her response was just as soft, but her voice gained a little bit of its typical fervor back as she spoke again. "Once I'm out, you can try."

The sentence made my heart do a little flip again, and I swallowed down a wave of emotional nausea. I knew she meant it, but the reminder of all the trouble she'd get in if her parents knew about me weighed on my heart. I shouldn't have done what I did. I should have kept my distance, remained just a hired kid looking out for her. I shouldn't have fallen for her. I shouldn't have let her fall for me, if I was reading her right.

We continued sitting silently, inches apart, me hiding from the world. Her hand shifted in the grass and I felt her fingers slide between mine. Involuntarily, I squeezed. She squeezed back.

"I'm not going to stop visiting even if you tell me to."

"I would never tell you to."

"Good, I'd have to chase you down." She laughed, softly and not quite happily, but I smirked gently at it.

"You'd catch me. I can't beat you anyhow. At least, last time I tried." I lifted my arm just a little, enough to see her beneath it. She was smiling properly, her eyes tinged with the ghost of upset.

"We haven't tried in a while, not since before you started your training." I could hear that she was taunting me into racing her again, so I sat up, leaning closer.

"Is this a challenge, Clara?" I purposely didn't say her name with affection, and if she caught that, she didn't let on.

"Why, mister fireman, I think it is." She stood, lifting my jacket and tossing it on me. By the time I had it off my face, she was off, down the footpath already and laughing wildly.

I gave chase, and managed to catch her around the waist at the other side of the pond. She was breathless in my arms and patted my chest in surrender.

"You win, you win, I give up!" I released her so we could collapse onto a nearby bench. I couldn't stop grinning, despite the small pang of hurt still lodged in my heart. This was normal, this was how we were with each other. It felt right, even though being found out would mean the end of it all.

"That's the first time you've said that to me. What's my prize?" I teased, shifting to rest my arm on the back of the bench, my head in my hand. She moved to copy me.

"Your prize is hearing 'I give up' from me."

I ducked my head as I laughed. "You know, I'll take it. I'll probably never hear you say that again anyway."

"No, no you will not." She giggled, dropping her arm to use it as a pillow for her head. She was even more beautiful then, her cheeks lightly flushed, her hair just a little more wild than it had been, her eyes brighter. But I kept it to myself. I'd hurt us both enough for one day.

July 30th, 1916

VERY loud explosion in the harbor. Maria's windows shattered!

It felt like the world itself was shivering. I was up and out of bed, at the window immediately. Something had happened, and now all the men in the station were crowding at the windows to try and see. Of course, all we could see was blackness and the buildings closest to us.

"Was that an earthquake?" someone asked, and I moved out of the way so people behind me could take over peering into the dark.

"I dunno. Nothing's fallen over."

"Maybe something blew up?"

"What would blow up at two a.m. and wake everyone up?"

Everyone was talking, and I took the chance to pull my boots on and go up to the roof. Something was burning on the horizon, out in the harbor, a little bit north. The Statue of Liberty was silhouetted by it. Some of the other firemen followed me up, and were making noises of awe and confusion.

"What's out there? That's Jersey innit?" I asked, and Gregory appeared at my side, nodding.

"Black Tom Island I think." He didn't sound sure, but the newspapers the next morning proved him true.

A bunch of munitions warehouses and barges and other things that were meant for the war had blown up, and the sheer force of it had shaken up the surrounding area. We all listened for reports about the damage from people who'd been nearby as fellow firefighters from other stations called Gregory up to tell him all about it. Even though it was our job to help, there wasn't anything we could do, so we just read the papers and talked to people, trying to piece everything together.

August 2nd, 1916

Saw L. Reassured nothing happened to him.

The explosion had been on Sunday, and the following Wednesday, Clara ran into my arms when she saw me. I nearly fell over from the force of it, but I wrapped my arms around her and held us both up.

"What's wrong? Did something happen?" I asked, and she pulled back to look at me, bewildered.

"Did you not see the newspapers all week? That big explosion? It woke me out of a dead sleep and shattered Marie's windows!" She had gripped the front of my shirt and almost seemed as if she were going to shake me.

"Oh, I knew about that, but you came running over here like something had happened to y—"

"I was worried about you! Marie was close enough to it that her house is damaged and she has these little scratches all over. Everyone says she'll be fine and they won't even scar but I just kept thinking, what if it had been worse, what if a big chunk of glass had hit her? And then I thought about you and how your part of Brooklyn isn't very far from where it happened either and I just, I just..." She drew in a shuddering breath, and I wrapped my arms around her again. Miss Horne was standing not too far away and came over when I looked at her.

"Hello, Leo." Her hand rested on Clara's back, and she gave me a small but sincere smile. "Glad to see you unharmed. Clara here was hardly able to sleep all week. We came out as soon as we could to come and find you."

"Well, here I am." I grinned, and Clara's fist hit against my chest weakly. I laughed, softly. "I'm really all right. Everyone at the station is. I don't think we were close enough to get anything but shaken up. Nothing even fell over."

"I heard there's even damage to the Statue of Liberty." Clara's voice was muffled against my chest, and I squeezed her. Miss Horne smothered a chuckle, coughing into her hand.

"I have some errands to run, You two enjoy your afternoon. Clara, meet me back here at four." She waited until Clara turned her head and agreed, then waved as she headed off. I gently pushed Clara away from my chest just so I could look at her.

"Are you better now that you've seen me?" I asked, and she nodded, wiping her eye with the back of her hand. "Good. Let's go get your magazine, huh?" She nodded again and slid her arm through mine as we turned in the direction of the newsstand. Her Barsoom series was over for the moment, so she wouldn't be taking any trips with John, but there were others she'd been following.

With the *All-Story* safely in one hand and her other arm looped through mine, we went to the music shop. It was one of the few places where the owner didn't care if we were there for a few hours, and we didn't quite feel like going to the park.

"Ah, there's my favorite pair." Mr. Weis waved at us from a shelf he was stocking as we walked in, and we called our greetings back. He left us to our own devices and we ended up perched on a couple of stools that were shuffled around the store as needed, leaning against one of the only empty patches of wall in the whole shop. Clara had calmed down considerably, and I was glad. As she read, I thumbed through a few sheet music booklets, but my mind was elsewhere.

Fires were terrifying, I knew firsthand. I was still on edge every time I set foot near one, even with the full crew behind me and in proper gear. I'd only been on three big calls, but luckily, with each one I was getting more used to it, and my training made me more confident in my abilities.

As if she was reading my mind, just then Clara asked, "How do you do this on a regular basis?" Her voice was soft, and she hadn't looked up from her story. I realized she hadn't turned the page in a while.

"Do what?"

"Just...face something like that. Fires, explosions—it's terrifying. I never thought about how scary your job is before." Her hands tightened around her magazine, crumpling the pages just a bit. I reached over to tap her chin and get her to look up.

"It's the job. It's scary, and it never gets less scary. But my job is to know what to do in the scary moments. Gregory trained me very well, and so did the others." She had looked down again so I tilted my head and leaned closer, catching her gaze. "Whenever we go in, we're always really careful and wearing lots of gear to keep us safe. You don't have to worry."

She caught her lip between her teeth, and she swallowed with difficulty. "I'm going to, though."

"That's fine." I smiled, tapping her chin again. "If I have you worrying about me, it'll just mean I have to be even more careful."

She laughed a little at that, and her hands relaxed around the pages. "For me *and* your mother, of course."

"Well that's a given." I chuckled, and her shoulders dropped, tension sinking away from her body.

We spent the next little while in the shop, until Clara finished her story, then wandered until it was time to meet Miss Horne. As they headed off, Clara called over her shoulder.

"Be careful! Remember who's thinking about you!"

As if I could ever forget.

January 11, 1917

Another explosion. Can't get out of the house. Mother frightened.

Not even a year later, the world shivered again. But this time from the other side. In Jersey, a giant munitions factory had caught fire and blown up, and we could see it from the rooftop of the fire station yet again. This one happened during the day, and we found out later that no one had been hurt thanks to the switchboard operator telling everyone to leave. She ended up getting a medal.

Everyone who was at the station that day was on the roof, hands shading our eyes from the sun as we looked into the distance at New Jersey.

"Glad we're not in that area," someone commented, and subsequently got elbowed in the ribs. He got called a coward, and a brawl nearly broke out until Gregory shouted at them to knock it off. We were all thinking the same thing, though.

Fires themselves were bad enough; I couldn't imagine an explosion as well. I tried not to let my mind run away with the idea.

It wasn't long after that Miss Horne called, and I was the one to answer the phone. "Hello?"

"Hello Leon." I wasn't sure how she knew it was me from one word. "It's Juliana. I have to tell you we aren't going to be able to come today. We were planning on it but we've had to cancel."

"Because of the explosion?" I couldn't see it from the window in the room where the phone was, but I looked outside anyway.

"Yes. Clara's mother doesn't want us to leave the house until we've been reassured it's safe."

"No one's called here yet to talk to Gregory, so it's probably under control at least." I sat down on the edge of his desk. Of course I wanted Clara to come to Brooklyn, I hadn't seen her all week, but I wasn't about to argue with Miss Horne.

"That's good to know, thank you. I'll give you a call again when we're headed there next. Thank you, Leon."

"Of course ma'am." She hung up, so I did the same and made my way out of the office.

"Off to your second job?" Gregory asked, ruffling my hair as he passed me in the hallway. I shook my head, unsuccessfully righting the style he'd ruined.

"Explosion's got Clara's mom scared, so they're staying in Manhattan."

Gregory nodded. "Understandable."

I knew he was right, but my sixteen-year-old brain that just wanted to see the girl I liked best completely disagreed. It was a war for the rest of the day between my head and my heart, but in the end I forced my head to win out. What kind of fireman would I be if I didn't take something like this seriously?

After all the newspapers came out, I gathered them all and studied what had happened, trying to understand how they put out the blaze, how it started, trying so hard to learn. It was the first time I genuinely started taking the job seriously, and all because I felt guilty for being upset that the whole ordeal had kept Clara from me.

December, 1917

Wonderful Christmas present from L.
He also loved his!

"Now where are you headed off to?" Gregory called behind me as I shouldered open the kitchen door. I grinned, waving a few dollars at him.

"Off to get my ma and my gal a Christmas gift." Clara wasn't my gal, exactly, but that's what all the other firemen called her. "Leo's gal," or "Leo's girl," or "that wee girlie." She had a lot of nicknames at the station, but I was fine with it so long as none of them were crude.

I was greeted by a rush of cold air digging under my scarf and trying to take my hat. I took a minute to re-wrap my scarf, tying my hat on my head with it, my ears bundled under both. With my hands tucked in my pockets, I was plenty warm as I made my way to the only bookstore within walking distance.

The bell on the door chimed merrily as I pushed it open, and the shopkeeper called a greeting. I couldn't see them beyond the shelves but knocked the snow off my boots and headed toward their voice.

"Hello there! How can I help you?" I came face to face with a man not much older than me, red hair mussed, glasses askew, and a pencil behind his ear. "I'm James." He shifted some books to one hand and held out the free one, grinning widely. I couldn't help but return it.

"Leo," I said, shaking his hand. "I'm looking for a book. It's a gift."

"Oh, which?" James put the books he was holding down and came around the counter.

"The new Burroughs. Came out this year."

I followed him back to the window and watched as he plucked a novel from the shelf. It was wrapped in a dust jacket with an illustration of a man fighting to protect a princess, and I smiled at it. The bookseller handed it over, and I flipped it open to look at the book under the dust jacket. The green cover had red lettering, and a little red circle to represent the book's setting.

"That's the one, thank you," I said, following him back to the cash register. A dollar later, I was leaving the shop with *A Princess of Mars* in my coat pocket.

The next stop was for Mom, and I managed to find her a much nicer hand cream than the cheap brand she normally used. Her hands were always dry and cracking, even in summer, thanks to her work doing laundry. Plus, the cream smelled like roses, her favorite. It was more than Clara's book had cost, but it was worth it for Mom's hands to not hurt anymore.

It wasn't until the week before Christmas that I was able to give Clara her gift. She told me as we strolled down the sidewalk that day that she wouldn't be able to come visit again until after New Year's, since her family was going to go visit her grandparents. I had her book in my pocket, waiting for her to be done telling me all the things she and Marie had done that week. It sounded like they'd gotten into a little trouble, switching some Christmas decor around Marie's house, but they'd gotten off lightly because, "'It is just too close to Christmas to be angry at such a small thing,'" Clara mimicked Marie's governess, whom I'd never met, then started giggling. "She convinced Marie's father that, since nothing had been broken and we'd put things back right when caught, there was no harm done. And he listened!"

"Aren't you lucky he's not a Scrooge." I nudged my elbow into her ribs, making her laugh again.

"Bah, humbug! These girls are having fun and I don't like it!" She did her best Scrooge voice and covered her mouth as she laughed through the last few words. I laughed with her, and we made our way to the diner.

Once we'd sat and ordered, I reached into my pocket but didn't bring the book out. "I have something for you."

"Oh, what a coincidence, I have something for you as well. Goodness, one would think it's Christmas or something." Clara giggled, turning to face me better while also digging in her little purse. I resisted the urge to be childish and stick my tongue out at her.

"Close your eyes for a moment. I didn't wrap it," I told her, tapping the book in my pocket. She grinned, paused her search, and did as I bid. I pulled the book out and set it on the counter at her elbow. "All right."

She opened her eyes and looked down, picking up the book and running a finger alongside the edge of the front cover. "Oh, Leo."

I smiled, resting my head in my hand, elbow on the counter. "You probably bought it when it first came out, didn't you?" Her smile turned shy as she nodded.

"I did! I'm so sorry, I did. I like this so much better though because it's from you." Clara looked up at me, a sincere grin painted across her face and pulled the book to her chest. "You have to mark it for me somehow, hold on." She turned her attention back to her purse, digging up a little pencil, then pushing it and the book to me. "Don't sign your name but do something."

I knew why she didn't want my name in the book, so I didn't ask or argue it. She returned to her purse as I flipped the book open to a page in the middle, turning it so the inner margin was horizontal. I scratched out "Forever on Barsoom" with the pencil, drawing a star at the end of the phrase. I pushed it back to Clara, who looked up.

"That's perfect!" She set a little box on the counter and pulled the book up, examining my words closer as a waiter set down our food. "Oh, thank you Leo, this is wonderful." The book was closed and pressed to her chest again, and I could feel a blush creeping up the back of my neck.

"I'm so glad you like it." I rubbed the back of my neck, willing the blush to go away, then nodded to the box. "Is that mine?"

"Yes!" Clara pushed it toward me, between our plates, and picked up her fork as I untied the ribbon. Lifting the lid, I found there was another box set inside, but this one was velvet and dark blue.

"Clara what on earth..." The box looked expensive; just the color alone seemed to scream its price.

"Just open it," she urged, waving a hand at me impatiently. I tipped the smaller box out of the larger one entirely, then flipped the lid up.

Inside, on a matching velvet cushion, was a band of gold engraved with a repeating star design all around. It had no stones, just the engraving, and I stared at it.

"Clara...what is this? My goodness." Words were starting to fail me. I knew it wasn't a wedding band, and it didn't look like a signet ring either.

"It's fashionable! Wear it on your right hand so no one mistakes you for a husband." She giggled and took the box from me, plucking the ring from its cushion and motioning for my hand. I gave it to her, and the ring slid onto my right middle finger, fitting perfectly. I laughed.

"How did you know my size?"

"I measured against the size of my fingers and then guessed." Clara grinned, patting my hand as she turned back to her food. "It just suits you. I saw it in a shop and couldn't stop thinking about it and then realized why as I was trying to sleep."

She said it so nonchalantly, as if it were a normal thing to buy a friend a gold ring. As if they weren't normally an indicator of commitment, of marriage, partnership. I stared at it on my hand for a few long moments before turning to my own food, mulling over the gift as I chewed.

"Do you not like it?" Clara asked, after we'd both been silently eating for a while. She looked nervous, and I shook my head immediately.

"That's not it, no. I love it! I do." I tried my damndest to inject every bit of sincerity I felt into my voice. "I'm only...a little surprised?" I looked back at the ring, curling my hand into a fist. "A gift like this usually means something really important, and you just bought it for me because you thought it would look good on me?"

"No!" Clara's nervousness dissipated as she giggled softly. "It is important. You're very dear to me, and I like spoiling you. I like giving you nice things because you're always so good to me. You've been such a wonderful friend to me all these years and I thought it could be something of a thank you for all of that." Her cheeks were growing pink, and I let myself smile. It was still a much too expensive gift, and had my mother been with us, surely she'd tell me to return it, but only because of the cost. I'd deal with her reaction later.

"Thank you," I breathed, and I meant it. The initial shock had faded, and although I still wasn't sure if I deserved something like this, I was sure that the ring wasn't ever leaving my hand again.

On Christmas, I was with my mother but only for a little while in the afternoon, since I'd agreed to work the night shift at the station that no one else wanted. We didn't waste a single bit of our few hours together, making what was a feast for us, taking a stroll around the block to hear all the carolers, and returning home to exchange gifts. Mom was overjoyed with her hand cream, gushing about the smell and delighting in how lovely it felt on her hands. She had a bit too much of the cream on her palms when she took my face between her hands, and I smelled of roses for the rest of the night.

"I made you something this year, dear boy," she said with a mischievous smile on her face that made me grin.

"What is it?" She shooed me into a chair at the table and went to her bedroom, ordering me to close my eyes as she came back out. Soon after, something soft but fairly dense was dropped in my lap. I opened my eyes to find a new quilt resting on my legs, various colors and patterns all sewn together to create a repeating block design. My name was stitched into the corner, with hers below it and a heart underneath. I stood, lifting the quilt high to let it unfold fully. It was big enough for my bed and then some and was thick enough for the winter.

"This is wonderful! Thank you so much!" I folded the quilt over the back of my chair to hug my mom close, squeezing her tenderly. "Thank you, thank you. How did you make it without me seeing?"

She laughed heartily. "Well, when you're at the station more often than not, it's easy!" I laughed with her, and took her hand, spinning her around the kitchen in a gliding dance. She gripped my hand, then paused, turning it to look. "Now what's this? This is new, and fancy."

I lowered my hand between us, flexing my fingers as she studied the ring. "Did your girl give this to you?" she asked, and I could hear the layer of disapproval under the curious tone.

"She did." I held Mom's hand softly, letting her look, but not letting her take it off. She ran her finger along it, then looked up at me.

"Don't lose it." Her tone was solid, serious, and I nodded without a word. Then she patted my chest, grinning again. "Come on then, let's have dessert before you have to work."

I smiled gratefully, glad she hadn't made a fuss about the ring. "I'm sure you'll stuff me so full I won't be able to move if there's a call."

Her laughter rang through the apartment.

March, 1918

Juliana dismissed. Heartbroken. Have to figure out how to see L.

A little over a month before Clara turned eighteen, I was informed by a very sad Miss Horne that she had been dismissed, since Clara was no longer a child and she'd already stayed on as governess and tutor for far longer than was standard. She had a job lined up already with another girl, so she wouldn't be out of work, but it meant that Miss Horne and Clara's trips to Brooklyn weren't going to be possible anymore. My heart ached, not just for Miss Horne, whom I knew had genuinely enjoyed her position and Clara and Marie's company—and even mine, the few times she'd joined us on our excursions—but for myself as well, because it meant seeing Clara regularly was going to be next to impossible now, unless Clara herself figured out some scheme.

By that point, I had been working as a firefighter properly for some time. I'd managed to get my diploma as well, and Mom hung it on the wall of the apartment. Gregory had taken Duncan's place when he retired, and even seemed to be looking to groom me into taking over when he decided he'd had enough. This meant I had been able to answer the phone without proxy when Miss Horne placed her last call to me. I didn't know it would be the last time I'd ever speak to her.

That night at the fire station, as I lay on one of the beds in the bunk room, surrounded by my snoring squadmates, I did my best to try and fall asleep. Even past midnight in 1918, New York City was loud as anything, but nowhere near compared to now. It still made it hard to sleep if you were already struggling, though. And oh, how I was struggling. Miss Horne was our confidante, our go-between. We relied on her to bring us together and I just couldn't see how it was going to work without her.

This resulted in about four hours of extremely broken, light sleep that did basically nothing for me the next day. Gregory, bless him for it, took pity on me and told everyone else I'd come down with something and would be staying with my mother for a few days, even though I was meant to be on call. Then he ordered me to go home for a while.

"Oh, my son, I feel bad for you." Mom was holding my head to her chest as I sat at our table after I'd told her what had happened, my eyes growing watery but refusing to spill over. I sighed, letting myself rest against her. Even if she was only saying it to placate me and was secretly happy to not have to worry anymore, I'd take it. I'd take whatever comfort was offered.

"Thanks, Mama." My voice was quiet, and I turned to wrap my arms around her waist.

"I know how much you cared about her. I may not have liked the arrangement, but I know it made you happy, that *she* made you happy."

"She really did."

There must have been something in my tone that made Mom upset, because she held me tighter, dipping her head to press a gentle kiss to the top of my head. "Oh, my darling."

The tears spilled over. I couldn't restrain them. Mom held me close, letting me dampen the front of her apron.

"Oh, my son. My dear sweet son."

The following three weeks were some of the bleakest of my life. I went back to the station after a couple days, shorter than Gregory had sent me away for, but I wanted the distraction of work more than anything else. I did what was expected of me, and thankfully there were no truly serious blazes for me to get distracted during and make worse. I followed my chief, played out his orders, and went to hide and fall asleep when it was all over. And when I couldn't sleep, I lifted my hand to watch the gold band catch the light from the window.

Then one day, Gregory had finally had enough of my moping. He kicked the side of my bed, arms crossed when I looked up at him. I stared, questioningly, silently, and he sighed in exasperation.

"Get up, kid. Enough of this. You're acting like your life is over just because you haven't seen a girl in three weeks."

"I might not ever see her again, and we didn't even get to say goodbye."

"I don't give a damn, kid, you can't live your life in this bed."

"I get up every time there's a call."

"You know what I mean, damnit. Now get up. You're doing the grocery run this week."

I hadn't done that in years, and we had a new station boy that had taken my place. My stare got more quizzical, and I sat up on my elbows.

"Shouldn't Timothy be doing that?"

"He's going with you." Gregory turned to leave the bunk room, calling over his shoulder, "He's waiting, get a move on."

Begrudgingly, I got a move on. After fixing my hat onto my head and shrugging my jacket on, I headed down the stairs to the back kitchen door where I found my replacement hopping from foot to foot impatiently. I didn't know Timothy well, but from the expression on his face, he had a very precise view of me. He didn't even talk to me as we set off together, my hands in my pockets and about a half-step behind him. To everyone else, we probably could have been mistaken for brothers out doing errands. He looked enough like me, in facial structure and physical build at least. He had deep, dark-brown hair that curled under his cap and golden-brown eyes. Sometimes he reminded me of a black cat in the sun.

"I'm going to the grocer's!" Timothy called, darting off before I could respond. Clearly he wasn't happy about the arrangement. He probably thought Gregory thought he needed help. I'd let him prove himself. I knew Gregory's only goal was to get me out of the station for more than a call. So I let them both have their wins, strolling around the shops, waving at Mr. Weis as I passed his window, and automatically making my way to the milliner's where Clara and I had always met. I felt the pressure on my heart increase, and my gaze dropped to where I could just barely see what was in front of me. I lit a cigarette to distract myself from it. The rush from the nicotine didn't hurt, either.

I'd just passed the shop when I heard familiar chattering. But not a familiar response. I lifted my head at the sound, and my heart soared as I saw Clara and an older woman who just had to be her mother having a polite disagreement near the stairs of a different shop. I couldn't stop my grin or my feet as they picked up pace and I made my way closer, ducking into an alcove in the shop neighboring the one Clara's mother was headed into. I quickly dropped the cigarette and crushed it, hoping the smell would fade by the time Clara reached me.

I waited until she made it to the sidewalk, then reached out to snatch her upper arm and tug her to me. Her shout of surprise and indignation was cut off immediately as she realized who had pulled her away, and her scowl shifted into a brilliant smile.

"Leo," she breathed, hands lifting to press against my chest. I chuckled, my arms settling around her waist.

"Clara."

The moment stretched as we held each other, thankful our last visit hadn't actually been our last. Then bravery overtook logic and I leaned forward to kiss her.

Her little gasp of surprise was silenced as our lips met, and her hand lifted to slide along my jaw, into my hair. My fingers pressed into the small of her back, pulling her just that little bit closer. A soft, gentle little hum of pleasure passed from her lips to mine, and after a moment more, we parted. We were both flushed, grinning in happiness and embarrassment, and Clara held a hand over her mouth. Our gazes didn't part.

"Sorry," I whispered over the din of the crowd. She snickered.

"No, please, don't be."

I leaned my forehead to hers, closing my eyes and sighing in relief, pleasure, happiness, and a little guilt. Clara's hands dropped to find my chest once again, and I felt her shoulders relax.

"I've wanted you to do that for a really long time." She chuckled, then pulled away, moving to take my hands from her waist and hold them. Her grin could have lit the whole city.

I matched it with my own. "I've wanted to do it for a really long time."

"As much as I want to do it again, my mother could come out at any second." She was laughing but leaned around me to peer down the sidewalk. "I need to tell you about my plan."

The fact she'd thought of a plan made my heart soar for the second time that day. I had been too lost in my own misery to come up with anything and was just barely recovering from it.

"Yes, please, I need to know." Our hands parted and I took a half-step back, returning to the polite distance required of us.

"Miss Horne phoned the station, and I'm thankful, but it left me without a way of reaching you."

Clara grinned, and I was confused. How could that be something to grin at? "That was part of the plan. So she could accurately claim ignorance about the rest of it. Because I didn't tell her. She asked me to do something but not involve her, so my parents wouldn't bring retribution down on her head." Clara had started giggling softly between her words, and I swear she looked as if she was about to start dancing. "Marie and I have joined a painting studio, you see." Her hand lifted to her mouth again, keeping her laughter private.

"How does that help us?"

She rolled her eyes, shaking her head at me. "It's our cover story. I haven't actually joined the studio but Marie has, and we have a friend who is already in it who will be sending us information about the classes and doing a few extra sketches for us to copy. That way, it looks as if we are slowly working on learning anatomy, perspective, all those things artists use, in a beginner's course."

My eyebrows lifted in surprise. She'd put a lot of thought and work into this, just to make sure we could continue seeing each other. Her sly, pleased grin was mirrored on my lips.

"Clara, dearest, I could kiss you right now." I laughed, shaking my head in wonder. "You are so clever. Just so, so clever."

She laughed, clasping her hands behind her back. "I know." Her voice was sing-song, pleased. "Also you can kiss me again, but be quick about it." She peeked down the sidewalk again, then looked up at me expectantly.

I leaned forward once more, lifting a hand to cup her cheek. She kept her hands behind her back as our lips met softly again, just quickly, but no less sweetly. Her cheeks were pink when I pulled back to look at her.

"The painting class is every Thursday, at three p.m. If you're not out on a call, I'll meet you here at that time." It was more often than we'd ever been able to meet before.

"Of course, yes! Yes, I'll be here as often as I'm able." I knew my excitement was audible, and normally I would have been embarrassed but at that moment I genuinely did not care. Clara and I were able to see each other, *and* she'd let me kiss her twice! I'd have danced in the middle of the street if she'd asked me to.

"It's a deal then." She leaned around me once more, and sighed. "I have to go, Mother is finished with her shopping. I'll see you on Thursday!" Clara stood on her toes to kiss me again, shorter than the second time but still just as wonderful. Her smile as she waved and darted away kept my heart pounding for the rest of our time apart.

That first Thursday took ten years to arrive. I was awake with the sun the morning it finally came, cleaned up, dressed, fed, and ready to go. Clara had said three, and it was only eight. I had nothing to do besides wait on her and pray there weren't any calls that needed the entire squad of firefighters today.

I was sitting alone in the kitchen, working my way through a mug of coffee I really didn't need when Timothy came down. He was sleep-rumpled, yawning, and I watched this thirteen-year-old kid pour himself a cup of coffee.

"Should you be drinking that?" I mused, and he startled.

"Why are you up so early?" He scowled, and I chuckled.

"I'm meeting someone later and I can't sit still about it."

"Oh, the girl, right." He said it so dismissively, returning to his mug preparations, and I stared at him curiously.

"What do you know about her?"

"Just that you've been in love with her longer than I've been here, she's out of your league, and you'd run away with her given the chance."

The laughter that escaped me was both amused and slightly nervous. Who was feeding this kid his info? "Where did you hear all of that?"

"Gregory."

Ah, now it all made sense. The current chief was the source of my gossip, so of course he'd be the source of everyone else's. I hummed in acknowledgement, wrapping both hands around my mug and staring down into it.

"Does she love you back?" Timothy's normally dismissive tone had dropped to reveal pure curiosity.

"I..." I grinned, remembering how she'd been the one to kiss me before she left last week. "I think she does, I really think she does."

"Well, good, maybe you will be able to run away with her sometime." His regular tone was back, but I was glad to know he had a different one. He disappeared with his mug off to station parts unknown, hiding in wait until someone called him like he normally did. I drained my own mug, then stood at the sink to wash it and a few other dishes that were lying around just to kill a few more minutes.

I bided the rest of my time much the same, tidying the kitchen and scrubbing the table before the other men started coming in and I got nudged out of the way. After getting kicked out of the kitchen, I moved back to the bunk room and tidied my own bed and the trunk I kept at the station. By the time I was done, it was barely ten.

"Damn." I sighed, flopping back down on my bed and ruining all the work I'd just done to make it perfect. I was running out of things to clean.

Eventually, I had bothered everyone else in the station enough with my random chores that Gregory shooed me out and told me to go wait near the shops.

"What if we get a call?"

"Oh no, we'll be down a single man," he said dryly as he sighed at me. "Just go, we can handle it."

"Are you sure?"

"Yes, please just go. You're making everyone jumpy." Gregory was speaking out of frustration, but I could hear the underlying fondness.

I gave in, listening to my chief's orders and leaving the station three hours early. Noon in New York City, even then, was hectic and bustling. Lunchtime brought everyone out of their offices and houses in search of sustenance. The few businessmen not in Manhattan lined the dining counters, seamstresses gathered on the front steps outside the shops they worked in, kids released from inside screamed and laughed their way down the streets. It was a pleasant, noisy bustle, and I took advantage of it to keep me distracted from the slow passage of time.

Somehow, it worked. I spoke to the shopkeepers I knew, caught a little kid as he was about to topple over and made his mother's day by telling her she was lovely. Her light blush and laugh would have made mine were it not for the fact Clara was on her way to meet me. We made small talk, nice enough, before the mom herded her kid back toward home.

Clara's hand found my shoulder before I even knew she was nearby. The gentle smile that had been on my face for most of the day widened into a grin, and I held my arms out to her as I turned. She stepped into them, wrapping her own around my waist.

"Hello! Put that out," she ordered, nodding at my cigarette, and I immediately obliged.

"Hello, Clara." Two years prior, I had said her name with such affection that her cheeks and the tips of her ears had turned pink. I did it again that day, and she sighed happily.

"Oh, Leo." Her head fell against my chest, her arms squeezed me just a little tighter, and I matched her pressure. We remained like that for a few glorious moments before she leaned back, hands sliding from my back to my sides. "My parents don't suspect a single thing. I told you this was a good plan."

"Where's Marie?" I glanced around, having fully expected her to be here as well.

"She decided she'd rather go to the painting class, remember?" Clara giggled, her hand lifting to her mouth as it always did.

"It's just us then?" My grin was turning mischievous, and Clara caught it, returning it with one of her own.

"Why yes, sir, it is."

"Oh my, however shall we spend our time together then?"

"Actually, I'm positively famished, so if you want to come with me, I need something to eat." Clara's laughter broke the romantic mood that had been there, hovering just above us.

"Anything you want, dearest," I replied, laughing along with her. I released her and turned only to lift my arm and slide hers through it, patting her hand gently. "I'm just happy to be with you."

We ended up at the same dining counter we usually frequented. Ever since that day two years ago, we'd nearly become regulars, and now, with our schedule figured out, we could actually be regulars. Our late lunch was quiet, joyous. I couldn't tell you what we talked about, only that Clara laughed enough I felt sure it added forty years onto my life.

Regular, weekly visits from Clara had brightened me significantly. I'd always loved just seeing her on whatever day Miss Horne brought her to Brooklyn, but now I knew exactly when to expect her. By that point, she'd kissed me more times than I'd kissed her, and I was very, very alright with that. I spent more time learning my guitar, becoming intimately familiar with it and trying to copy songs I'd heard others play. I'd asked Mr. Weis to teach me to read music, but that was even more slow going than learning to play the guitar. Nonc of it made sense, until suddenly it did. I mentioned that once, and he just laughed and said that's how it worked.

My visits with Mom had become a little less frequent, as I spent almost every night at the station instead of with her at the apartment. But I tried to make it a point to visit her once a week, at the very least. I was still giving her the majority of my paychecks as well, and she finally felt comfortable enough with my help to cut down on her own hours as a laundress. She was brightening as well, her eyes less tired, her hands nowhere near as roughed up. They'd always have the calluses, but they weren't as red and cracked dry anymore.

I was sitting at the dining table with one of her hands in both of mine, massaging it gently, when she sighed so deeply I had to look up to be sure she hadn't suddenly fallen asleep.

"What is it?"

"I'm just...very relieved. It's been so hard since your father passed. But things have been steadily getting better the last four years. I'm very grateful." Her words were soft, her expression tired. But not tired from a long day's work, tired from finally being able to relax. I grinned up at her, squeezing her hand gently before reaching for the other one to tend to it as well.

"It'll just keep getting better too, Ma. I'll make sure of it."

She chuckled softly, closing her eyes and relaxing into her chair. "I believe you, my son."

November 8th, 2010

Leon had returned to my office, two more notebooks in his hands. He was looking a little better now, some light had returned to his eyes and the gauntness of his face was starting to disappear. If I had to guess, someone was probably tending to him, making sure he ate a few full meals and got a proper amount of sleep. It was good to see. I didn't know him very well, but it seemed like he had gotten more of himself back.

Finding his voice as well, he lifted the notebooks. "I found these while sorting through her room, I thought they might be useful."

Her room. Surely he meant Sinéad. And now here he was presenting her belongings to me. "Are...are you sure you want to use them?" I was already lifting my hands to take them from him, despite the idea of holding a recently deceased woman's belongings sending a shiver down my spine. My fingers wrapped around them gently, eyes roaming over the doodles and scribbles on the top cover. Leon stepped back and sat in the chair he'd been occupying, slumping comfortably into it.

"Yeah. Add her words to mine. There are stories in there that I wouldn't be able to tell." He closed his eyes, leaning his head back against the top of the chair like he'd done while telling me his and Clara's story. I looked back down at the notebooks, setting them on my desk.

I paused a moment before I spoke again. "Are you sure you want to leave them here?"

"I..." He sighed, rubbing his eyes with one hand. "I don't." His voice was cracking. "I really don't. I want to hoard everything of hers and never let it go." His fingers moved to try and spin the non-existent ring again, just like they had yesterday.

I trailed my fingers down the spine of one. It would be easier to copy all the pages quickly if I took the notebook apart first. "Well, they're spiral bound. Here's what I can do: I can take the spirals out temporarily, make copies of all the pages, put it back together, and give it back to you. Would that be alright?"

"Yes." The single word was so earnest, so full of gratitude, I felt pinpricks of tears behind my eyes. He didn't have to lose another part of the woman he was mourning; he didn't have to watch another bit of his history slip away. "Yes, that would be perfect. Thank you so much."

"I'll turn Clara's diaries back over to you as soon as I'm finished with them too. I can't take them apart to make copies as easily as I can these or el—"

"It's okay, Lorena." Leon chuckled softly, his head still tilted back and eyes still closed. "I know those are a lot more delicate. I don't even know how to keep them from falling apart."

"I can ask the archival team to work their magic." In truth, I already had. The diaries were in great shape, but I'd already been handling them for hours and was worried about ripping a page or breaking the spines.

Leon visibly relaxed, sinking further into the chair. He was smiling, still a little weak but sincere. "You make me wish I had relied on you all along."

I laughed bashfully. "I'm happy to record all of your stories, Leon."

"Thank you, Lorena."

As he settled back into the chair in the corner of my office, I stepped out to hand the notebooks to Raphael and ask him to handle them. He agreed, and said he'd leave them in the basket near my door when he was done. I thanked him and returned to Leon, who was staring at the ceiling.

"Where were we?" I asked, settling in my chair and flipping open my notebook. "1918?"

Leon's mouth curled into a little smirk, but a humorless one. "That was quite a year."

"I know the war ended and the Spanish Flu pandemic started that year. What else?" I made a note about the pandemic, reminding myself to do some research about it later.

"The pandemic, yeah, tragedy. Absolute...tragedy." He sighed, closing his eyes again. "Almost everything was shut down for a while, the businesses were all supposed to open at different times to keep the subways from getting crowded. The mayor made everyone wear these gauze masks so we couldn't sneeze or cough on each other. A lot of that happened the year after, though. 1919." Leon lifted a hand to rub his eyes and pinch the bridge of his nose. "But in 1918, Clara didn't visit nearly as much, and of course there was Newport, and the ball."

"The ball?"

He nodded. "She debuted that year." His eyes opened and fixed back on the ceiling as he fell into his story. But he wasn't actually at the ball, so he only knew what happened afterward.

April 2nd, 1918

Mother told me about Newport.
Not looking forward to it.

My debutante ball happened in what seemed to be three distinct parts. First, Mother informing me it was happening and that Marie's parents were thrilled that she was to be included. We were being introduced to society together, despite both of us already having our (supervised) run of the city.

Second, the planning and preparation for it. My parents bought each of us a new gown, new shoes, new everything. They were all in white with delicate lace trim, sashes of the same fabric but not the same color, and we went to so many fittings for them I lost count. In the end they fit us like gloves, every stitch placed perfectly, every ruffle tousled just so.

Our ballroom was scrubbed from top to bottom, the paint touched up, the woodwork all freshly oiled, and the chandelier lowered so each crystal could be made sparkling once more. The entire room was gleaming, shining, and one afternoon as I stood in the center of it, I imagined it to be made of dreams.

"Do you approve, my dearest?" Mother was grinning as she stood in one of the doorways that led into the room, and I spun, holding my arms above my head.

"It looks divine in here! How gorgeous!" I spun once more, laughing to myself, and Mother came to join me, our hands locked together as we twirled around the ballroom. Father found us there a minute or two later, smirked fondly to himself, then wandered off to smoke his pipe. Mother and I slowed our spin, giggling, then she linked her arm with mine and led me from the room.

"I have wonderful news that you may have already guessed." She was struggling to keep laughter from her voice, and even pressed a hand to her lips to try and smother it. I giggled at her side, pressing a hand to my mouth in mimicry.

After she'd taken a moment to calm herself, she brushed a stray hair behind her ear and spoke. "Since you'll be out properly after your ball, you'll be joining your aunts, grandmother, and me for the seasons in Newport." She was grinning, and I returned it falsely.

I had known this news was coming. I'd seen older cousins and friends go through their own debutante balls enough times over the years now to understand the ins and outs of it. The girl gets brought out properly, then shown off in every public setting she'd previously been excluded from. I was looking forward to the ball itself, but not what came afterward.

Because going to Newport for the season meant missing Leo's birthday every single year.

I bemoaned this fact to Marie the next day as we lay on the grass in her family's garden, on top of the rug her mother insisted we use so as not to ruin our dresses. We spoke so quietly that we had to rest our heads together to hear each other. Marie's curls were tangled with mine, our shoulders pressed together and hands intertwined.

"At least we'll be together; neither of us will be alone all the way in Newport." She was right, and it heartened me.

"But Leo," I whispered, squeezing her hand. She squeezed mine back, and sighed.

"If only we could hire him as a kitchen boy or something for the summer and take him with us." Marie had said it solemnly, then started to giggle. "Although, I think we'd see him even less than we do now if we did that."

That set me giggling too. She was right. If Leo were working in one of our houses, the extent of our interactions would be glancing at each other in hallways and probably leaving notes for each other in some secret place we could both access.

Marie and I daydreamed that up for a while, lying there as the clouds shifted across the sky. She imagined herself up a beau as well, and we giggled imagining clandestine meetings in the middle of the night, like the romance novels we'd read together.

A few days later, it was time to tell Leo.

April 4th, 1918

Told L. about Newport. Very displeased. Me too.

"Wait, did I hear you right?" My hands went to my hair, pushing it back and definitely ruining whatever was left of my comb work. "You aren't going to be here for the entire season?"

Clara nodded, arms wrapping tighter around herself. I was struggling not to let my intense displeasure show, struggling not to show how deeply my heart was breaking at the thought of not seeing her for three entire months out of every year. Why she'd chosen to tell me right as we'd found each other on the street was beyond me. She'd led with the bad news, and there wasn't even any good news to soften the blow.

"And it's going to be every season. From now on, every single one of your summers will be in

Newport." I pushed my hands through my hair again, not caring that it would be sticking up at all angles soon.

Clara nodded again. "Believe me, I hate it just as much as you do. Perhaps more, even." Her arms finally released their hold and she planted her hands on the bench we were sitting on. "You don't have to go up there and be paraded around like a trophy and introduced to every young bachelor there is just so your parents can hope for a marriage propos—"

"This is about you getting married?" The breath had been ripped from my lungs and I pressed my hand against my chest, hard, making sure my heart was still beating. The gold ring pressed to one of my ribs. Clara wasn't mine, we weren't involved in that way, and I'd probably never be able to marry her, but the thought of her being put on display like a piece of meat was destroying me.

"I thought it was obvious." Her voice was so soft, I almost didn't catch it. "I always forget how different things are in society's little bubble." The words had a note of bitterness, and I looked up to see a deep frown crossing her face. "I'm basically going to be sold off to the highest bidder. Whoever will bring the family more prestige and money." The final word was spat, and Clara slumped against the bench. I felt myself crumple more as her words matched my thoughts. "I'll just run away.

You and Marie can come with me. Then none of us will have to do what's expected of us."

That pulled a chuckle from me. "Not much is expected of me." I closed my eyes and breathed out a long sigh, tilting my head back against the top of the bench. "I'd hate to leave my mother though."

"Bring her, too."

We sat in silence on the bench, I'm not sure how long, until Clara looked at the little watch she had on a chain and let out a heavy sigh.

"I can only stay for another hour or so." Her question went unasked, but I knew what it was. Were we going to sit here and pout or go somewhere? At that moment, I didn't want to go anywhere at all with her, but also I wanted to go anywhere but New York with her.

"Let's just walk." It would give us something to do besides brood, and moving around would rid me of the anxious buildup of energy in my legs.

So we stood, Clara slid her arm through mine, and I led us out of the park and back toward the street we always met on. Even though I was trying so hard not to let my displeasure show, I was clenching my jaw and couldn't seem to relax it. The idea of losing my summers with Clara to a parade of young, wealthy, probably good-looking men was playing on repeat, looping my thoughts.

"You're going to crack your teeth." Clara's voice was just as gentle as her touch on my arm, and I started, forcefully unclenching my jaw.

"Sorry." It came out harsher than intended, my bitterness leaking out. Clara felt it and her brow furrowed. Her hand started to pull from my arm until I caught it and put it back.

"Let go." Two words to deepen the crack in my heart.

"Why?" Again, harsher than intended. Her hand pulled fiercely from my arm. I regretted it instantly, swallowed, and tried again with more gentleness. "Why, Clara?"

She'd turned her head from me, but with a gentle touch to her chin, she looked back. Her eyes were shining and watery, her lower lip pulled between her teeth to keep it from quivering. I tugged her into an alcove, out of the way of the foot traffic, and held her face softly between my hands.

"Please, tell me what's wrong."

It took her a moment to find her breath. "None of this is my idea, and I don't like it any more than you do. Do you think I want to be paraded around and shown off? I never have. I've always hated the idea of it, always dreaded this." Her words were catching in her throat and she coughed through her last sentence. "I never wanted any of this. I've tried so hard to not have this."

I pulled her into my arms, letting her muffle sobs against my chest. My cheekbone rested on the top of her head, and I felt her gripping the front of my shirt. I hated myself a little just then. I'd been so upset over not seeing her during the summers, over the possibility of the woman I loved being practically sold to someone else, that I'd lost myself to my own emotions.

I'd hurt her. The one thing I had sworn I'd never do.

"I'm sorry," I whispered, leaning my head down to her ear so she'd hear it. "I'm so sorry. I let my own anger overtake me. I'm so sorry."

Her hands gripped tighter, and she sucked in a long, shuddering breath. "Please don't snap at me like that." She was whispering too, and I basically had to hold my own breath to hear her.

"I won't. Never again," I promised.

After a moment or two more, she had stopped crying, and with our two handkerchiefs we cleaned her face up. She smoothed my shirt out and apologized for the wrinkles. We went to the diner, shared a plate, and not long after, she headed back home. It had been one of our worst visits the entire time we'd known each other, and it was mostly my fault.

April 9th, 1918

Have no words. Extraordinarily happy.

Next I saw her, I broke my promise.

We were in a secluded part of the park, tucked as far away from everyone else as we could be, but our argument was threatening to break out of our little bubble.

She'd just been complaining about the situation again, and for the most part, it was proving easier to bear this time around. I'd griped along with her and we'd joked about running away, but then she began thinking aloud about how to keep meeting with me once she was married. I'd nearly collapsed.

"What do you *mean*, 'once you're married'? I thought you didn't want to marry whoever they picked? I thought you hated the idea of being sold off!"

"Leo, I already told you I have no control over this! What am I to do, abandon my entire family?! Abandon Marie?! If they find someone they want me to marry I'm going to be pressured and pushed into it and I'd have to cut all ties to get out of it!" Clara hadn't yet cried this time, but I felt like I was about to.

"I never once thought you'd go through with their wishes. You stand up to everything else they say, you talk back to them all the time!" My head was in my hands, fingers twisted into my hair.

"This is different, Leo." Even though her tone was trying so hard to stay icy, I could hear the tremble of heartbreak underneath it.

"You *kissed* me, Clara. Kissed me."

"I did." Her voice cracked.

"You kissed me so many times. What is this, have you just been leading me on? Toying with me until your family decides it's time? Am I just an escape from your gilded cage?" I could feel my anger building as I wrote this narrative in my head, and I couldn't stop my words. "Your fun little poor boy to run around the city with and pretend you don't have your life all planned out for you?"

Clara had been trying to answer my questions as I'd stabbed them at her, and by the time I'd finished speaking and looked up, she was trembling with rage. As I stared at her, tears streaking down her cheeks and fists balled at her sides, my anger faltered. I'd hurt her again.

"Damnit, Clara, I'm sorry. I'm so sorry. I didn't mean a word of it." I dropped my head back into my hands, sinking to the ground in a squat. "I didn't mean it." She had no response for a few moments, surely gathering herself.

"Can I talk now, or are you going to just...just keep blabbering to yourself?" she asked, shakily, clearly trying to wrangle her confidence. The rain that had stopped earlier in the day was starting back up.

"Please, talk," I begged, keeping my voice as gentle as possible.

She sighed, sharp and heavy, then crossed her arms. "You are an escape for me, that much is true. You can call it a gilded cage all you like but it is absolutely suffocating. I hate it. I hate all of it, and I don't want to be a part of it, like I've told you *many* times before." I looked up to find her staring at the ground, chewing on her lip. Our anger was starting to ebb away, but neither of us was ready to take the few steps toward the other yet. I felt a raindrop slide down the back of my neck.

"Then why would you go through with it? Why not just tell them that *you* want to pick who you spend the rest of your life with?" *Why won't you dream of marrying me instead? Why did you buy me a ring if it wasn't a promise?* These were the answers I needed most of all, the ones that could break my heart but make it all understandable.

"I'm afraid of being cut off. From my mother, the rest of my family, from Marie. It would be like getting excommunicated from the church. It's not about money or the house or anything like that. I don't want to lose anyone." Her lip started to quiver again and I finally stood up, taking hold of her arms gently. Her shoulders were growing damp in the drizzle.

"But you're fine with losing me?"

"No! Heavens, Leo! No! I am not!" She shook her head fiercely, a few curls falling into her face. "I don't know what to do here! I don't want to lose my family, I don't want to lose you, but I'm probably just some dalliance for you anyhow, just some rich girl that spends money on you and kisses you and you'll probably end up with a wife who is better suited to you anyway so losing you when you're not even serious about me is hurtful but eas—"

"I'm in love with you, Clara. I have been for years. Why are you making up this story about me? To fool yourself into thinking abandoning me is alright? To give yourself some closure for something that hasn't even happened yet?" I barely knew what I'd said, my anger was at the back of my throat and I was doing my damndest to swallow it down. "Why would you tell yourself I'm not serious about you when all I have wanted for years is to run away with you?"

I waited for her answer for longer than I thought necessary, staring at her awestruck face and wondering why she was awestruck. Her curls were being weighed down by the rain, a couple clinging to her temples. I could feel my own hair sticking to my forehead. What a sight we must have been.

"What? What now?" I asked with forced gentleness. I was trembling with the effort of not snapping at her. I'd said I wouldn't, and I had already broken that promise once.

Clara reached up slowly, holding my face between her hands. "Repeat what you said."

"What?" I shook my head, trying to pull away, but that only made her press more firmly.

"Leo, repeat what you said." A smile was beginning to form on her lips, fighting her serious tone. It clicked.

"I'm in love with you." The words, finally said aloud, dissolved any lingering anger I felt once and for all. Clara started laughing, wrapping her arms around my shoulders, and I slid mine around her waist to pull her close. "I am absolutely, head over heels, stupidly in love with you, Clara. I have been for so long." I felt each word lifting a weight off my soul, and I pressed my face to her hair. She squeezed her arms around me tight. Our clothes clung to each other.

"I'm in love with you, Leo."

Her confession was enough to finally let loose the tears that had been gathering in my eyes, and a sob from my throat. The weight had slammed back into me as I remembered everything else. "Clara, I can't even find the words to explain how much the idea of you marrying someone else hurts me." I genuinely hadn't intended to say it aloud, but I had. Clara's laughter died down quickly and her hands gripped the back of my shirt, then she pulled my right arm from around her waist to twine our hands together, to press my ring into the sides of her fingers.

"I'm sorry. I wish I knew what to do besides act aloof and distant to every possible suitor so they lose interest in me." She chuckled half-heartedly at that, and I smirked against her hair.

"That's a great idea, actually. If no one ever goes to your parents with a proposal, you won't be forced into anything."

"I'll do it then. And we can figure out what to do about us." The way she said "us"—like it was a tangible, real thing, something you could see—made my heart beat faster, my arms hold her tighter.

"Us," I repeated dreamily.

We managed to get ourselves together not long after, cleaned up our faces just like we'd had to the previous week, and made a promise not to fight over this again. As much as the idea still pained me, I had no right to take that pain out on Clara, who was hurting just as much. After we'd finally stopped dancing around the issue and let our feelings be known, it should have gotten so much easier. Instead, Clara was forced to face a reality we never saw coming.

April 19th, 1918

Father being ominous. Dislike it.

The ball was a week away. Everything had been planned down to the minute. Friends and family and important members of society had been invited. Mother was happily flitting around the ballroom, instructing our staff how to decorate to her liking. Father hadn't spoken a word about anything, just left us women to our own devices.

My devices consisted mainly of staying out of the way, complaining to Marie, and trying not to think about Leo. I failed, often and regularly. I thought of him so much I nearly slipped and told Mother about him. She did notice my moping, and I had to assure her it had nothing to do with the ball, and everything to do with the books I was reading instead. She suggested I get happier books. I agreed, and she pulled some from her own collection to leave on my vanity. This touching, unasked-for gesture from my mother moved me more than any plan she'd made for the ball. From then on, I made greater efforts to appear pleasant and excited.

One night that same week, we were lounging in the parlor after dinner. I was reading *A Princess of Mars* again, an ever-constant companion by my side. As a novel it was much easier to carry than a stack of Argosy magazines. The volume was barely a year old, my most treasured gift already showing how much I'd handled and adored it. Then my father spoke and pulled me back to Earth from Barsoom.

"Clara, we're going to have guests tomorrow for dinner. I want you to wear your best, and be the gentlelady we all expect you to be."

I tilted my book down to look at him over the top of it. Guests were normal, but he usually only made such a request when someone very important was joining us. I laughed and righted my book. "Who is it, a duke or count or someone?"

I realized quickly my levity wasn't appreciated, my father's *harumph* and the creak of his seat as he stood signaled his displeasure.

"Young lady, you will do as I say. You remember that you have no voice here, not under my roof." He had come to the edge of the sofa I was on, looming over me and shaking the end of his pipe in my direction. He wasn't truly angry, not yet, but I could see it brimming in his eyes. I nodded.

"Yes, Father, I understand."

Mother remained silent throughout the interaction, her needle paused over her embroidery as she listened. She only had half a voice under this roof after all, and the majority of it was reserved for household decisions. We looked at each other as Father made his way back to his chair and fell into it, his pipe set back between his teeth and the newspaper rustling and flicking as he found his spot.

The rest of the evening passed in uncompanionable silence.

April 20th, 1918

Ominous was correct. Met R. Unhappy.

All of the next day, I strived to keep a wide berth between myself and my father. Mother had already approved the menu, the table settings, and everything else, so all that was left was her choosing which dress I ought to wear and getting me primped and polished and shining like the proper young lady I was meant to be.

Rather than following her around or planting myself in the kitchen or garden to speak with the staff, I stayed in my room, pacing around it while reading a bit of this book, a page of that one, and trying to untangle the knot of uncertainty and anxiety trying to take over my heart. My home had never felt more like a prison, despite my sequestering being my own decision.

In the early evening, Mother sent her maid to help me get dressed in the gown she'd picked out and pull my hair up into a smooth and fashionable style, with what must have been hundreds of pins to keep my curls from slipping out. Something inside me mourned as I realized I was on the edge of never being able to let my hair down in public ever again. Another piece of freedom stripped away, infinitesimal as it was. At least I'd been allowed to wear one of my favorite blue gowns.

Coming downstairs for dinner, Mother met me in the hall outside the parlor and took my arm. I noted that she was wearing some of her most expensive jewelry, the set she saved for special occasions. I'd last seen it on her for a Christmas party. My suspicions about this dinner rose, reaching record heights. She leaned close to speak softly. "Be nice to the young man here. He's a bit brash and full of himself, but please don't call him out on it."

From that description alone, I hated him already and hated even more the idea that I wasn't going to be allowed to give voice to that fact. But I nodded my understanding, and Mother escorted me into the parlor. A young man and a couple whom I presumed to be his parents were occupying my normal sofa, and they all stood to greet us as we came in. The man I assumed was the father grinned widely and held out his hand to Mother and me in turn, and as he spoke his greetings I realized I recognized him. It was Cornelius Warburton, a man who had worked with Father for years on end, as far back as I could remember. His family was stationed in Connecticut, but came to New York frequently for some business or another. The others were definitely his wife and son. Father and son shared the same black hair, but the son had his mother's dark eyes. They'd attended various parties of ours in the past, and I'd seen Mr. Warburton exiting father's office on a few occasions after meeting to speak about whatever joint venture they'd been working on.

"Ladies! How lovely to see you both! It's been much too long." His suit was impeccably well-tailored and looked nearly brand new. I figured that since he and Father were in business together, we'd be of similar financial statuses. Mr. Warburton's attire, along with his son's obviously new suit and his wife's fashionable gown and expensive jewels, confirmed this.

"Since the Christmas party, at least." Mother chuckled politely, nodding her head to the man and then turning to his wife. "Hello, Sybil dear! How are you?" Sybil had her copper-colored hair pulled up high in an updo that elongated her already long neck, making her resemble a swan. The effect was quite lovely and would have been lovelier if not for the barely-hidden look of distain on her face. I hoped I'd learn what it was directed toward later.

The pair of ladies chatted quietly off to the side, leaving me to be introduced to the son who was standing near the fireplace, looking for all the world as if he'd rather be somewhere else. At least we'd have that in common.

Mr. Warburton gently took me by the arm and turned me toward the fireplace, eager to make the introduction himself.

"Miss Clara, please allow me to properly introduce you to my son, Reginald. Despite being at your home so many times, we've never had the chance. But I suppose that's the way when you send your boy off to school." The man chuckled, holding out his hand to his son. "And Reggie, this is Clara."

Reginald bowed his head, his jet-black hair shining as it caught the light, and I held out my hand, each of us conducting ourselves as expected. He took my fingers and squeezed them in his own, but it was not gently. "Charmed, Miss Clara." The combination of his curious tone and the touch set my heart racing unpleasantly, and I forced myself to remain in the room, to smile and give a proper demure little nod back.

"Much the same, Reggie." I kept my voice steady, aiming for a casual friendliness even as his dark eyes bored into mine like a predator's would as they stared at their prey. I didn't want to feel like prey.

"*Reginald,* if you please." His tone had snapped to something much crueler than before, and I felt the urge to lean away from him. *Should I be afraid of him?* I didn't have much time to ponder this, as the butler came in to announce dinner.

We'd been seated next to each other, of course, since we were of similar ages, and that's simply how things were done at a properly balanced dinner party. The two sets of parents spoke among themselves for a bit while Reggie—I had decided to call him that in my mind as a form of rebellion—and me focused on enjoying our meal. At least, he enjoyed his. I was still quite unnerved. There had only been one other man who had ever looked at me in that same manner, and it had been a very old man, another business friend of my father's. At least then, my father had very cooly and quickly gotten him out of the house and even let me sit on his knee, apologizing for the discomfort. But I'd been six at the time, and things were very different now.

Reggie and I didn't speak during dinner, besides a few small platitudes from him to which I gave short answers. He didn't seem bothered, in fact he seemed pleased and amused. Then I found out why. Father and Mr. Warburton were all but chuckling to themselves, looking nearly secretive in some mischief or another. They discussed who shall share the news, which one of us? Before deciding Mr. Warburton should have the honor, he's the guest after all, it's only polite. So he pushed his chair back and stood, grinning and holding his hands out to us.

"Now that we're all introduced and in the same room, finally, we can share our plan that is years in the making. This old man here and I have been business partners for quite some time now, as you all know, but we'd like our families to be tied even tighter." Mr. Warburton looked at my father with a mischievous smile at his little joke.

My stomach dropped. Surely he wasn't going to say what I thought he was about to say. Surely not.

"We've made the decision that as soon as Reginald is finished with his schooling, and we get him installed at the office properly, he and Clara shall be wed. A bond like this can only prove how much our companies trust each other, and that can only serve to demonstrate to the rest of the world that we are the most trustworthy in the industry!"

Oh, the way he spoke about it! As if it were just a publicity stunt, just some marketing scheme, as if Reginald and I were just two little chess pieces to move about a board. I imagined myself throwing down my fork and napkin, shoving out of my chair, and running all the way to Brooklyn. Of course this is what the dinner was about. This is probably what the debutante ball was all about. And of course they'd kept it from me all these years! They knew that if they waited until I had no choice, until they'd gotten all the other pieces into play, that it would make it nearly impossible for me to find a way out. I hated them all in that moment, despite mother's books, despite the planning for the ball being suited exactly to my tastes, despite every kind word they'd ever given me. It was taking great effort to not flee the room.

As the others—even Reggie—clapped and celebrated the news, I kept my eyes on my mother, finally catching her gaze and letting her see through my expression that she'd betrayed me. Her smile faltered and her gaze fell to her lap. I had a brief shot of petty pleasure at the sight of it.

My father chuckled and held out his hands so everyone else would quiet. "Allow me to tell the other part. Of course, this means at your ball, Reginald will be your escort and we'll announce the betrothal then. We can't have anyone else messing with our plans, now can we?" He was all but winking at Reginald and me, and I tightened my grip on my fork, thinking of hurling it at him.

So that's how it was to be then. Just as Leo had said, my life plan had been laid out in front of me. I didn't get to choose my own escort, I didn't get to choose my own *husband*. I was feeling more and more like a bird in a little gold cage with every word from my father and the Warburtons.

Reginald turned to me, his grin sharp and pleased. It wasn't pretty. "Even though you're half mute, you're quite pretty, so I'm pleased. You'll make a fine trophy. I'll be glad of a wife who doesn't talk back."

I stopped myself from stabbing him with my fork, still clenched in my fist. I had no response, and this seemed to please him. I barely knew him, and yet I hated him.

I tried in vain to speak to Mother later that night, after they'd left and Father had happily retired to his study for a cigar and brandy, utterly pleased with himself. I cornered Mother at her vanity, but she refused to hear a word against the plan.

"It's all set already, Clara. I don't think you understand what kind of damage it would do to untangle all this now." The fact that she said this as she untangled her hair felt like some sort of hideous joke.

"I'm not allowed to even have a proper season? Not allowed to speak with all the eligible bachelors?" My protest was weak and I knew it.

"Clara, this makes it easier on you. Now you don't have to deal with the falsehoods and fakery they would all use to woo you. Do you not understand that most of them would just be after your money, not you?" She looked at me directly in her mirror, and I saw tears in my own eyes.

"I'm not allowed to find out for myself?" My voice was cracking through the entire sentence, my knees threatening to sink to Mother's plush carpet. She sighed and set down her brush.

"Darling, this is all around easier. I hope, in time, you'll come to understand that. We're saving you a lot of heartache." She laughed, lightly, not fitting for the conversation at all. "It isn't as if you've some childhood crush to fall back on anyhow."

I do, but I can't tell you about him. My thoughts weighed heavy on my tongue, and I excused myself back to my room. I wished so desperately that I could fall back on Leo. After all, he had just confessed his feelings to me and I to him. We knew where we stood with each other. And now, after promising to find a path forward for us, all doors had seemingly been closed.

And the worst trouble was, I wouldn't be able to see Leo again until days after the ball.

April 26, 1918

The Ball.

The third part of the debutante ball was the thing itself. The day of the ball arrived with as much dread as there was excitement. I hadn't been forced into Reggie's company since our introductory dinner, but his family had arrived at our home that morning, carting their party finery with them into a few of the guest rooms. Luckily, no one expected to see me until that night when I made my grand entrance with Marie, so I took the chance to remain in my room and wait for Marie to come to me.

If there ever was a soothing balm to my weary soul, it was Marie. My best friend, my confidant, my secret-keeper. The girl who'd held my hand through everything and I hers. We'd met at some party or another as small things, our parents having known each other since before either of us existed. Much by chance, we had both escaped into the garden, and ended up hiding behind the same rose bush. I could hear Juliana calling for me from the doorway, but I didn't heed.

Marie and I had exchanged a look, knowing immediately not to give each other up as Marie's governess called from the door as well. Our unspoken pact led us to staying behind the rose bush for hours, until a larger portion of the party had been conscripted into finding us. Juliana had been so cross, holding me by my upper arm and clearly trying not to shake me in front of the partygoers.

"I will always find you wherever you end up, Clara. You cannot hide from me." The way she said it sounded more like a promise than a threat, and somehow, I felt more comforted than afraid. Juliana had promised, under the guise of scolding me, that she would always be on my side, that she would always do her best to save and protect me.

Juliana was invited to the ball as well, as a guest instead of a governess. I hadn't seen her for several very long and sad weeks. I missed our daily interactions quite desperately, and when she stopped by my room while I was still staring out the window and waiting for Marie, I sprang from my window seat to wrap my arms around her.

"Oh, Juliana! I'm so happy to see you!"

Her soft chuckle and the light touch to my hair relaxed my shoulders, and Juliana squeezed me tightly back. "Hello my dear girl." As always, her voice was soft and firm, a gentle command of whatever room she found herself in. The familiarity and surety of it soothed my spirit, just as Marie would when she arrived. "Are you well?"

The expression that crossed my face was surely one of discontent, even a touch of anger, and Juliana pulled back to hold my shoulders and look directly into my eyes. The grip steadied me, and I felt more of my frayed nerves float away.

"I can see you're not, dearest." She sighed, gathering me back into her arms, and it took every single shred of self-control and all of my etiquette training not to just start crying in her embrace. Juliana bowed her head to mine to kiss my hair, just a feathery touch, and her hand smoothed down the back of my dress.

I felt like a child again, wrapped in my governess's arms after skinning a knee or having some mean boy call me a rude name at a party. Except what has happening now was so much worse. I didn't even know if I could tell her the entire story, at least not without tears. And if I showed up to my ball with red eyes, I knew there'd be talk about town and hell to pay at home. What good was a crying daughter on the day of her debut? What good would it do if all the newspapers wrote about New York's newest debutante sobbing at her own ball instead of how delicious the food was, how bright the music, how sparkling the ballroom?

What terrible publicity I would bring my family, and the announcement of my loathsome engagement that I'd never agreed to would be buried under everything else. The precise opposite of what they'd wanted, what they'd planned for years.

Juliana asked nothing by way of an explanation, just continued holding me firmly but softly until there was a quiet knock on the door. "Clara?" Marie was on the other side, and we two women turned to open it. I flung myself at Marie as soon as the door was shut once more, and she returned the embrace, a little surprised. I hadn't been able to speak with her since the dinner, not in private anyway. She knew something was bothering me, but I couldn't confide in her among mixed company. Juliana, keeper of secrets, guardian of girlhood, was not mixed company. We trusted her more than we trusted our own mothers.

"Can you speak of what's bothering you now?" Marie asked, tugging me back to the window seat and settling in beside me. Juliana sat herself in a chair not far away, close enough to hear us, but also close enough to the door to be the one to open it should someone knock. She wasn't even employed by my family anymore, but she still took it upon herself to protect us.

I nodded, releasing a long, slow breath, willing the last bit of nervousness to leave my body with it. "Yes, I'll tell you both. You cannot say anything until after tonight, though. After tonight, everyone will know."

"Oh, dear." Juliana sounded like she knew what I was about to say. She shifted her skirts just so and folded her hands in her lap. I noticed Marie copying her out of the corner of my eye. My own hands found the end of my sash and started twisting it, giving the fretting things something to do rather than flutter about.

"My parents betrothed me to one of Father's business partner's sons. I just found out a few days ago. They mean to announce it tonight, during the ball." I continued my story, describing Reggie's predatory gaze and the terrible chill he seemed to give off, the endless trepidation I felt the entire time I'd been forced near him. Marie's face held only horror and worry, while Juliana looked on, seemingly deep in thought. Marie reached for my hands as soon as I stopped speaking, pulling me close to her and squeezing my fingers.

"Clara, we must go to your mother! Surely she could see how unhappy you were! She can try to put a stop to it!" As much as I adored her for it, Marie's plan wouldn't work.

"I already tried. I told her I didn't like him. She said to just give it time." I pulled one of my hands free from Marie's grasp to brush away a curl that had fallen to my face. Marie kept the other surrounded in both of her own. It kept me tethered, for the first time in days I no longer felt like I was free-falling through my own life, no rope or sail or counterbalance, anything I could use to correct or chart my own course. Leo's comment of having my life planned out for me was in my head, blazing like a headline across my mind's eye. I shuddered at the thought of telling him all that had happened, was yet to happen, during our next meeting. Juliana seemed to be reading my mind, as she spoke for the first time since I'd begun my story.

"What will you tell Leo?" She whispered it; we were in my parents' home after all. I briefly thought of my parents listening at my door and finally discovering my secret. There would be no leaving the house ever again were that to happen. Not without an escort or three, and not until my dreaded wedding day. How many years would I remain in this estate? Never going past the garden wall, my only reprieve being visits from Marie? I didn't want to think about it, but my mind couldn't stop.

"I don't know," I finally whispered back, pulling my other hand from Marie to bury my face in my palms. "I just don't know."

And finally, risking the unsavory headlines that my father would surely have *things* to say about, I let myself cry in the safety of my room, held by two of the people I trusted most of all.

Five hours later, my eyes had cleared thanks to Juliana fetching a cool cloth to put on my face and both she and Marie forcing me to rest for the majority of the afternoon. Juliana had gone to speak with my mother, told her I'd had a case of nerves but she was handling it. That was all it took to make my mother leave us alone. Somewhere deep in the back of my mind I felt a petty voice saying, *See how little she cares for you? She will gladly hand you over to someone else the moment your emotions become too much to bear.* I didn't let that voice win, but oh, how valiantly it tried. It resurged when she didn't come to my room until just a few minutes before I was due to make my entrance, simply so she could remind me to smile and not just glare at Reginald the entire time.

"It will be a great struggle," I mumbled, but she was already back in the hallway, closing my door behind her.

So it was with Juliana's and Marie's mother's help that we dressed, our hair was tied up elegantly, and just the lightest bit of rouge was dusted onto my cheeks. Face paint was still quite unwelcome in our circle, but Marie's mother convinced me that this little bit was better than my ghastly pale complexion. She used much nicer words, but the meaning was the same.

Trussed up, laced up, everything tied down and made to remain in place for the remainder of the night, Marie and I went downstairs arm in arm. If we'd just been allowed to enter like that, I think we'd both have been overjoyed. But of course, there are traditions to follow. Marie was handed off to some boy her family had picked to be her escort. Neither of us had ever met him until the week before. Thankfully for her, there was no nursery room betrothal. She dutifully stepped through the door, head held high, grinning widely as we'd both been taught to do.

Reggie was waiting for me next to the door. I kept my chin up, my gaze level, and settled my hand on his arm with the least amount of contact possible. If I thought it would be easy to disguise, I would have floated my hand half an inch above his arm to provide the illusion he was leading me without having to actually touch him. Mother had reminded me to smile and not glare, so I reminded myself I was here with Marie and some of our other friends, and I wouldn't be forced to be at Reggie's side all night long. I had the brief thought of imagining I was on Leo's arm, but I knew it would bring more trouble than the comfort was worth if I allowed myself to act the same way with Reggie as I did with Leo. I'd already resigned myself to being civil, polite, and nothing more with him. It simply would ruin that decision if I started laughing and being more comfortable with him. Not to mention, of course, the fear of letting the wrong name slip through my lips.

We entered silently, both of us plastering smiles on our faces as the crowd came into view. With that one simple action, I'd been formally introduced to New York City society. All of this fuss just for me to walk through a door. Internally I was seething, trying not to let it show through my eyes. *Keep up appearances, Clara, darling. Don't let anyone know your thoughts just by looking at you*. I was mocking my mother and father both in my head, all their reminders of how to act and what to say and with whom I should speak to make a good impression.

And it must have worked because, despite my internal mockery, an hour later, long after my required dances with at least three suitable young men (Reggie first, of course) had ended, Father had pulled me aside. I thought I was about to be quietly scolded, but to my surprise, he offered up a glowing review of tonight's behavior and how charming my conversation had been with all his business friends. The man was actually grinning, and it's genuinely difficult to convey how rare that was.

"Were you not already engaged, I'm sure we'd have a line of proposals out the door by morning." He was chuckling to himself, tapping his pipe against the balcony rail. I gave him a polite smile, but he couldn't see it didn't hit my eyes in the dim light, not that he would have paid attention to such a thing, anyhow.

"Well, you haven't made the announcement yet. Perhaps you could bide your time and see if a better offer comes along?" I giggled, trying to make sure it sounded like a joke, and to my relief, Father laughed along instead of flying into fury. He truly was in good spirits.

"Tempting, tempting. But this union has been years in the making, my girl. Now I just know you're up to the task. Your mother's made a proper young lady of you, she has."

With those words, he left me to the balcony on my own, and I slumped forward against the rail. The air was a little chilly, winter still trying to reach the earth in the deepest parts of the night, steadily failing as the warmth of spring took back over. It was bracing, comforting almost, and I lifted my head to the dim stars, blotted out by the city's light. Even if I could see them, I wouldn't have been able to find any of the constellations; such knowledge was not my own. Still, wistfully, I searched for them.

I'd thought I had seen Orion or perhaps Gemini, I had no idea, when Marie came out and took my shoulder.

"Dearest?" There were a million questions in that single word, but the most evident of them was, *Are you alright?* I shook my head, lifting a hand to rest it on hers.

"Father actually praised me tonight." The words came from me shakily, and Marie held my shoulder tighter. Our matching skirts tangled together as we leaned into one another, hands held tightly in front of us. More than ever, I wished we could be genuine sisters. Growing up in her household would have meant so many different things. As if she could hear my thoughts—and I thought perhaps she could—Marie rested her head on my shoulder and lifted her hand to point out a grouping of stars.

"Look here, you see this stretched out rectangle here, with the hook on top?" I followed her words and finger, nodding and resting my head against her hair. "Here, at this point," she said, pointing to the brightest star on the little rectangle. "That star is called Regulus. Guess what its other name is?"

I shrugged, lightly so as to not dislodge her. "I'm not sure." I didn't see her smile, but I felt it. She squeezed my hand.

"It's the heart of the lion, the Leo constellation." Her hand tightened on mine a little more. "The very heart of Leo. Visible right from your window."

I felt the tears gathering in my eyes, but I didn't let them fall. I closed my eyes instead, closed them against the ball, against my father's schemes, against everything besides Marie and Leo.

"Thank you, my darling friend. Thank you so much."

"Anything you need, dearest one."

May 2nd, 1918

Finally got to see L. Feel more secure now.

I hadn't seen Clara for over a week and was starting to get antsy. She'd told me why, of course, but being away from her for that long right after we'd confessed our love felt like some cruel trick of the universe on us both.

I was literally pacing along the street while I waited, spinning my ring around my finger. I wanted so badly to have a cigarette, but I was trying my best to keep the scent of smoke off me for the day. I kept glancing up and around every time I made it to the edge of my pacing, and finally spotted Marie. As much as I wanted to be with Clara alone, Marie was a welcome sight.

"Marie!" I called, lifting a hand to wave to her. She looked up and waved back, reaching to grab someone's—presumably Clara's—arm, and pull them in my direction. Sure enough, Clara appeared a moment later, and both girls were standing in front of me.

"Hello, ladies." My grin was stretched wide at them both, and it took me a moment to look past my own mirth to see the dismal air about them. "Oh no. What's wrong?"

Clara hadn't even met my gaze, Marie was trying to find a smile, and I rested a hand on each of their shoulders, stepping closer. "Come on, let's find somewhere to sit, then you can tell me what's happened." They both nodded and slid an arm through each of mine, and I led them to the park where we'd spent many long afternoons.

We found a bench, settled in, and I spoke again. "Was the deb ball a disaster? Did someone fall into the buffet?" I was teasing, but they both winced at the mention of the ball. "Wait, was it really? After all that planning and fuss?"

Clara's hands covered her face as Marie sighed, looking up to the sky. I knew neither girl was pleased with what came after the ball, but I'd expected lighthearted recreations of the night's antics, them making fun of every eligible bachelor of New York. This was the opposite. I had been perched on the top of the bench between them, and lowered myself to sit properly, taking their hands.

"Please, tell me what's wrong. I want to help."

Clara finally looked at me, with tears in her eyes. "It's worse than we ever could have imagined, Leo. Far worse."

I felt my heart drop. It took me a second to respond. "What...what do you mean?" My mind was already trying to answer the question, running through all sorts of situations, trying to figure out what could be worse than Clara leaving me behind every summer. I gently released Marie's hand and took Clara's in both of my own. Marie settled her hand on my back, as if she could reach Clara through me.

"You have to tell him." Marie's voice was so tender, so careful, all it did was make me worry more. I squeezed Clara's hand, urging her on. Marie spoke again. "Do you want me to do it?"

Clara shook her head fiercely while still supporting it with her free hand. "No, no, I'll damn myself."

I laughed, nervously. "Now I'm really frightened." A glance to Marie showed her offering me a small, half-hearted smile, and Clara offered nothing more than moving her hand from her head to her heart.

"They've chosen for me, Leo. They picked someone. They picked someone years ago and just told me two weeks ago. They waited until now to drop all of this on me and suddenly I'm left with absolutely no choice at all, when I might have been able to have one before. They chose *for me.*" Her words dissolved into tears with her last sentence, she bent over her lap and sobbed, her hand gripping mine tight.

I didn't know what to do. I sat there, my mouth slightly open, squeezing her hand as tightly as she squeezed mine. Marie stood and came around to Clara's other side, sitting on her heels in front of the bench to wipe Clara's face with her handkerchief.

"Dearest, please breathe. You too, Leo." Marie had taken over as caretaker so effortlessly that I immediately obeyed and sucked in a huge, shaky breath, letting it out as I lifted a hand to my hair.

Everything was off kilter. I leaned back against the bench just so I didn't feel like I was going to fall over. They'd picked someone for Clara to marry already? All this time, they could have told her, we could have known, I wouldn't have let myself—

No. I would have fallen in love with her all the same.

Clara was breathing, gripping Marie's handkerchief to her chest, eyes shut tight. I let out a slow breath, standing and gently pulling my hand from hers. The shock and despair on her face stabbed me in the heart, but I comforted us both by taking Marie's spot and kneeling in front of Clara, reaching forward to wipe a tear from her cheek with my thumb.

"Did they pick a date, also?" I asked, cupping her cheek in my palm. Her tears stuck between us. She shook her head, then paused and reconsidered.

"They said he has to finish his schooling. I assume university, so another four years?" Clara looked to Marie for confirmation, and Marie nodded, then spoke.

"I heard he's going to Princeton. Definitely four years, starting fall semester this year."

I tried to do some mental mapping of how far away Princeton was from New York, then gave up when I realized I didn't really know. Another sigh escaped me as I stood up, catching Clara's hand as I did. "So we have four years to figure out how to get out of this. Four years to hatch a plan and make it work."

Marie had taken my seat in the middle of the bench, rubbing her hand along Clara's back. She smiled at my words. "Four years is a long time, don't you think? And now that we're both out in society, our parents will be much less strict about how often we go out and to where. We could drop the painting class lie." Marie giggled softly to herself, tugging gently on Clara's sleeve. "Although I may still go for my own amusement."

Clara had been ever so slowly brightening as we spoke, and she gave us a little half-smile at Marie's joke. "It is a long time." She looked a little better than before, and wiped her eyes again. "I still am so upset that they kept it from me for so long."

"As you should be, that's an enormous betrayal!" Marie, who had obviously come prepared, switched out the soaked handkerchief with a fresh one. "I think anyone would be just as upset. I would be."

"I would be too," I confirmed, and Clara looked up at me with a bit more of a sure smile. I returned it, and reached out to grab both their hands again. "Let's not speak of it any more today. You've told me what's going on, now let's go act like everything is normal for one more day. We'll start planning after we've all rested and had time to think." *Gregory would be so proud of me right now,* I laughed to myself. *Taking charge and keeping everyone calm just like he trained me to do.*

The girls nodded, Marie hopping up to take Clara's other hand, and together we pulled her from the bench. She was still a little sniffly and wrapped her arm around mine a bit tighter than was proper, but it made her feel better. She held Marie's hand with her free one, and we made our way back to the street in our linked chain, heading toward the music shop. Clara had already paid off my guitar, but we shopped for music together and chatted with Mr. Weis like it were any other day. I kept a light tone to my voice and a smile on my face and watched Clara's shoulders slowly loosen and her jaw unclench. My heartbeat was pounding a terrible, aching beat against my ribs, but I ignored it for her sake.

They didn't tell me what else had happened at the ball, and I didn't ask. We spent our hours together pretending it hadn't happened, acting as if nothing were hanging over us, as if a new, looming threat weren't casting a cloud. The girls headed off hours later, their newfound freedom letting them be a little looser with their timing. They were tittering and singing as they headed back to the train station, and I was glad for it.

But the moment they were out of sight, I turned and headed to the fire station immediately, my smile dropping to the pavement with my heart. Gregory would still be around; maybe I could talk to him. My mother was a comfort, but I knew what she'd say, some version of it being doomed from the start. I didn't want to go to her just yet.

Clara was getting married. Married! To someone she'd just met, to someone I would never meet. She hadn't even told me his name, and that was probably a good thing. It was a good thing I didn't know exactly where Princeton was, either. I'd probably march there come fall and just slug the guy.

Gregory was indeed still at the station, and I slammed into his office and fell into the chair in front of his desk. He stared at me over his coffee mug, an eyebrow raised.

"Can I help you with something?" he asked, lowering the mug. I leaned forward to put my head in my hands.

"Clara's engaged." It was all I could manage to say before the tears started falling. I heard Gregory's sigh and his chair as he pushed it back, his footsteps as he rounded his desk. His heavy hand fell on my shoulder, patting it.

"I'm sorry, son." He'd called me that before, but in that moment it meant more. I collapsed into sobs. Gregory sat on the edge of his desk and reminded me to breathe, and waited out my crying fit. As my sobs faded to sniffles, he handed me his handkerchief and set his hand on my shoulder again. "Tell me what happened."

I told him everything I knew, the ball, the betrayal from her parents, the betrothal. It wasn't much information but his eyebrows rose in shock all the same. He rubbed the back of his neck, laughing painfully.

"You'd expect them rich folk to act a bit more civilized about these kinds of things, but I guess not." He sighed, hand still on his neck, and looked off to a corner of the office. "I'm sorry, son," he said again, shaking his head. I lowered mine back into my hands. My chest still ached, but it no longer felt heavy after letting Gregory help carry the load.

"I don't know what to do."

"I don't either. This is one hell of a situation you've found yourself in, kid. Makes me wish I would've echoed your mother and warned you from the start. She's just such a sweet girl, it was always nice seeing her around. Kept spirits up, you know?"

"Don't talk about her like she's some station darling." I hadn't meant to snap, and Gregory leveled me with a look. I cowed.

"You know that's not what I meant, Leo." He shook his head again. "She's just a real nice girl and we all like her. We all like you two together. You make each other happy." He shrugged, crossing his arms.

"She truly does make me happy, Gregory." Tears were gathering in my eyes again, and I pressed his handkerchief over them. Both his hands landed on my shoulders.

"We'll figure something out, boy. But for now, let it all out. Don't carry this in your heart. It'll only hurt you."

Gregory had hugged me twice the entire time I'd known him, and that was the first. He squeezed me tight, like he was trying to push all the broken pieces of me back together, and it actually worked somewhat. It was only thanks to his sheltering hug and the strong whiskey he'd poured me afterward that I was able to sleep that night. The rest of the summer, until Clara returned, was an entirely different story.

July 29th, 1918

Laid on beach with M.

Mostly pleasant.

Everything about Newport was beautiful. The houses, the landscaping, the beaches, the water itself. Going to the ocean from New York City wasn't exactly a pastime, not for society girls like Marie and me. Our parents considered public beaches *indecent.* I rolled my eyes at the thought, looking out toward the private beach that bordered the house we were renting. There really wasn't that much of a difference. Sand, sea, gulls.

It had been parties and dinners and luncheons all summer, and admittedly a good number of them had been enjoyable. But we were expected to be even more available here than at home, and it was tiring. Marie was staying with us at that moment but had been flitting between here and other friends' houses—both rented and owned—as society asked of her. I wished desperately she had been under the same roof as me all summer, but I wasn't going to cage her.

I folded my arms on the windowsill and laid my chin on top of them, wondering if I could make it to the edge of the water and back before anyone noticed I was gone. It was calm today, the waves small, but I'd been expressly forbidden to go anywhere near the water on my own. I could understand the rule for safety reasons, but just standing on the beach shouldn't have been a problem. Somehow, though, it was. And I didn't want to have my access to Marie taken away. It was the only redeeming thing in this seaside prison. I knew if I crossed them, my parents would make Marie stay elsewhere until it was time to go home, punishing her just as much as me, even if she'd done nothing.

So I stayed indoors, pushing the window open to at least smell the ocean. I fell asleep on the windowsill to the sound of the waves.

"Clara! What on earth are you doing? You're going to let all of the insects in." Mother jolted me from my nap, and I lifted myself up, wincing against a tight muscle in my shoulder. She reached past me and tugged the window shut, and suddenly the waves were as distant as New York.

"I just dozed off, I'm sorry." I forced myself completely upright, my hands folding in my lap instinctively, ever the perfect lady. Mother scowled down at me, shaking her head once in disappointment before leaving the room.

I heaved a sigh. I wouldn't see Marie until afternoon. She'd agreed to go on some outing with some of our other friends who had come up from the city, but I'd declined. I was regretting it now.

"Whose idea was it to stay home, Clara?" I sighed to myself, pushing up from the window seat and clasping my hands behind my back. I had fallen asleep in the small library of this house, and I do very much mean small. Only two bookcases, and most of the books seemed to be old ledgers and an encyclopedia set. A small smattering of fiction was also housed on the shelves, but nothing that was catching my interest as I idly perused. I should have brought some of my own.

I should have just stayed in New York. I surprised myself with the thought, but realized I believed it. Newport had sounded exciting before, like an adventure, but now I knew that it was just the same people, the same parties and discussions, the same rules, just in a different town. The ocean was the only novelty here, and I was more or less barred from enjoying it.

I couldn't stand it any longer. My proposed gamble from earlier suddenly felt like nothing. I made my way to the door that led out to the large, enclosed porch, plucking a parasol Mother had left behind from the little rack near the door. It was still so calm, hardly a breeze. Opening it, I settled the parasol on my shoulder like a good debutante trying to protect her complexion, but spun it round and round like a child. What good was a private beach if you couldn't do as you pleased on it?

The sand was softer than I thought it would be, and I sank in a bit with every step. *Good. It will take me longer to get back even if I'm told to hurry.* Some part of me cursed the rebellious notion, but I silenced it. I wasn't doing anything out of the ordinary for a beach vacation.

I wandered a little way from the house, keeping it in sight, twirling my parasol. It had been a while since I'd been genuinely alone. If I weren't at Leo's side, I was at Marie's, and if not Marie, my parents. If not them, servants. The list could keep going. I sighed again, and knew I was being dramatic. Marie had been my constant companion since we were so small, but right then, even though she was in the same town, she felt worlds away.

I really should have just gone with her; I've done this to myself. I spun the parasol harshly and winced as it caught a stray lock of hair. *I've done that to myself, as well.* Untangling my hair, I spun on my heel and walked back the way I came. I could pace the beach until Marie came back.

I could pace the beach until Leo walked here. That thought stopped me in my tracks, and I looked out at the water. I'd known I would miss him while we were up here, but these months away from him, with nothing to look forward to on Thursdays for the entire summer, had worn me as surely as the waves wear the coastline.

I'd wandered too close to the surf. Water was toying with the heels of my shoes. With another sigh, I stepped back, looking out over the water but not seeing it. I was thinking of Leo's eyes, bluer than the ocean. His hair that would be shining in this bright sunlight. My chest ached. He would have been with me on the beach, or he would have convinced me to go with Marie. He wouldn't have let me stay home alone in the library. Marie had tried to persuade me, but I had been stubborn. She had given up, and I hadn't blamed her. Leo, however, was more stubborn than even I was. He would have convinced me somehow.

Backing away from the water more, I found a rock where the water wouldn't reach me and perched on it. It was warm from the sun. Given the chance, I would have fallen asleep on it like I had on the windowsill.

"Is sleep your only respite, Clara?" I asked myself, shaking my head at the thought. "You spend a single summer away from the boy you love and fall apart?" Even though there was no one around to hear, I still whispered my questions.

But of course I did. If he were here, I wouldn't feel like an imposter. Like some doll that has been dressed up just to be paraded around. I closed my eyes. Marie and I had basically been left to our own devices, within reason, until this year. Until the ball. Now everything was so different. Even the friends we had known our entire lives had started treating us a little differently. They were still lovely people, we still laughed together, but under everything there was the pressure of finding good matches for everyone, of not marrying below our stations—all the things that our parents deemed important were expected to be important to us. Marie played their game well, though I knew she wanted to marry for love most of all. There were no such games with Leo.

I rolled my eyes under their lids at the idea of 'stations' for we untitled American nobility. It was a thought that prickled at me every time I heard someone say it. All these rules and ideals brought from England to the country that had kicked up such a fuss to be free from them. I was partway into writing a mental essay about the topic when I heard a shout from behind me, presumably from the house. I ignored it.

"Clara!!" That time I couldn't. At least it was someone I was glad to hear shout my name. Marie had returned, and I spun on my rock to see her on the porch, leaning against the rail with her hands cupped around her mouth. "Clara! Come in!"

I would have gotten up for only one other person, but he was hours away.

"You've been dozing off an awful lot, Clara." Marie reached over to brush a lock of hair from my face, and I blinked my eyes open. We were stretched out on the sand behind the house, parasols propped just so to keep the sun off.

"Newport is very sleep-inducing."

She giggled and shifted to lie next to me. We lay under our parasol tent, hands twined together like they always had been since we were girls. We still were girls, really.

"How much longer until we go home?" I asked, letting my eyes close again.

"A few more weeks, then we'll go straight to Brooklyn." Marie knew my soul.

"I would like a copy of that in writing."

"I'll get it to you by dinner." Her giggle made me smile and we squeezed each other's hands gently.

After an indeterminate amount of time lying there in silence, I think Marie had started to doze off, because when I spoke I felt her jump a little.

"Do you think he'll still be there, or..." I left the rest of the question unsaid on purpose. Speaking it aloud felt like we were increasing the chances of him not being there.

"Of course! Yes! It's not even his birthday yet, not for a while longer." Marie was exaggerating the time; we both knew his birthday was the next week. "They aren't even taking men his age. It isn't as if someone will show up on his doorstep at the stroke of midnight, papers in hand." She squeezed my hand again, and I did the same to hers. "We'll be home not long after his birthday, I don't think they'd change anything between then and when we get home."

She spoke so much more confidently than I felt. I'd had this dread lingering in the back of my heart ever since our nation had taken up arms, the fear of losing not just Leo but some of our other friends. The ball and all the preparation for it, as irritating as it had been, had almost been a welcome distraction. All the young men that had been at the ball, besides a few, had been too young to be taken away, and Leo would be too young for a while yet. But who knew how long this war would last.

"I don't want to lose him," I whispered, and I wasn't even sure if Marie had heard me.

"I don't either. He's too bright," she whispered back, and we both shifted to press our shoulders together and lean our heads toward each other. "He just shines so, so brightly."

"You speak every word I think." I lifted my hand not twined with hers, reaching up toward the sliver of sunlight that was peeking over our parasol tent. Marie started giggling.

"I'm sure it's not *every* word you think, Clara."

I flushed, bringing my hand down to swat at her shoulder. She started laughing, and I let myself smile. "Not every word, no. But close enough."

"Oh great Leo, our Regulus star sent down to us from the heavens, your pretty face must remain in New York City or you shall suffer Clara's wrath." Marie somehow kept her voice a whisper while putting every ounce of drama in her body into it, and I joined her in laughter.

"I don't believe he's afraid of me." I continued to chuckle, letting my eyes close again.

"I don't either, but it is quite fun to think about." Marie's head leaned back against mine, and I pressed my temple lightly to hers. "He loves you, he wouldn't abandon you. He'd leave word with someone at the station." Somehow she'd pinpointed my precise worry, my secret dread beyond simply losing him.

"I know. I love him for it. And things like it. He never lets anything go unanswered, does he?"

"Usually not!" Marie wiggled our hands between us. "Tell me, my dear Clara, what most are you looking forward to doing with our Leo when we return?" She was teasing me, I could hear the smile in her voice, but I answered honestly.

"Not feeling like I'm playing some facsimile of myself." I sighed out the confession, and Marie's fingers tightened on mine. "Being with you, just us two, has been the only time I haven't felt like that here. Every other time I feel like...my parents' doll that's already been purchased by the highest bidder, but they still want to show it off."

"Oh, Clara." Her smile had gone, replaced with warmth and a bit of pity. "Is that why you've stopped going out with us?"

"Yes. I'm sorry."

"Don't be, I only wish you'd told me sooner. I know our friends have started prioritizing different things, but maybe I should have pushed harder to not let you be alone. I'm sorry." She rolled onto her side, and I turned my head to face her. Marie's eyes, so much brighter than mine, were tinged with regret, and I shook my head.

"No, you aren't allowed to be sorry either. I was being so stubborn and childish about it all. I should have just told you." Shame was threatening to stop my tongue, but I swallowed it down. "Leo never expects anything of me besides honesty, and it's the same with you. And yet here I am, keeping things from you. I...I..." I swallowed again, squeezing my eyes shut tighter. Marie pushed herself up on her elbow.

"I know, my dear. I know. It's why we stick together, isn't it?" I nodded, and she laid back down at my side with a gentle sigh. Our hands were still intertwined. "I wish you would have told me how unhappy you were."

"I'm sorry. I didn't want to ruin our first time here." Guilt lowered my voice, and Marie tilted her head back to mine to hear me. "I was thinking the other day that perhaps I should have just stayed in New York."

"That *would* have ruined my trip, if you had." Marie's giggle was softer this time, and our temples touched again. "I feel selfish saying it, but I would rather have you here and unhappy than in New York and unhappy. At least here I can hold your hand."

It was my turn to giggle. "Marie, sometimes I wonder if people think our relationship is...*untoward.*"

"Hah! Am I a better partner than our dear Leo?" She had her hand over her mouth, laughing.

"Your manners are certainly better, but sadly, you do not make my heart race." I sighed dramatically, laying my hand over the aforementioned organ. Marie laughed harder.

"You do not make mine race either, so I believe we're even." She wiped a mirthful tear from the corner of her eye and I grinned.

"Thank you."

"For what, dear?" She turned her smile on me, and I returned it.

"For making me feel better."

"It is, in fact, what best friends are for."

Someone called for us from the house, and we waved at them over the parasols to acknowledge it before slowly getting up and gathering our things. My respite from my gilded cage had been brief, but

I no longer felt as if a light had gone out in my heart. Soon, I would return to the soul whose light matched mine, and until then, Marie would share hers.

It would be alright.

At least I believed so, until we walked into the house arm in arm and were greeted by the Warburtons. I saw Mr. Warburton first and froze in the doorway. Marie stopped when I did, looking at me curiously. When she turned and realized who was in our parlor, she squeezed my arm and tried to steer us both upstairs.

"Girls! Girls, do come here, would you?" Father called, sounding unnaturally jovial.

Marie and I sighed as one, but straightened our spines and walked into the room, still arm in arm. Father held out a hand as if presenting us, and the Warburtons made noises of approval.

"Oh, girls, you've done so well at keeping out of the sun this summer. Look how fair your complexions are!" Mrs. Warburton stood, coming over to us. She put her fingers gently under my chin, and I lifted it just slightly away. "So beautiful. Reginald has truly made a good catch, hasn't he?" She turned to her husband who nodded.

As if you hadn't planned it from the start. My bitter thought must have shown on my face, for Marie gave me the lightest pinch on my arm. I smoothed my expression.

"Thank you so much, Mrs. Warburton." I gave her my most charming smile. She flashed one at me before turning back to her husband.

"We simply must share with them the good news, my love." She practically danced across the room, Mr. Warburton's arm lifting to settle around her shoulders as she pressed her hand to his chest.

"Oh yes, dear Clara, you'll be so thrilled to know that your fiancé is officially safe from being shipped away and forced into the trenches." He chuckled, and his wife giggled. I forced a grin.

"Oh! How wonderful! One less boy to worry about!" I laid a hand on Marie's, still threaded through my arm, and turned to her. "How wonderful!" I repeated with as much fake enthusiasm that I could muster.

She picked up on the ploy easily, copying my grin and nodding. "That is amazing news! How did he get so lucky?"

"Oh, we finally found a doctor that would confirm his asthma." Mr. Warburton chuckled into the glass he raised to his lips. His wife grinned wider.

"Our son has been suffering with that terrible illness for so long now, it's so good to see someone take it seriously." She and her husband shared a secret smile, and I fought to keep from groaning aloud. I felt Marie deflate a bit beside me. Of course Reggie had absolutely had asthma all along, it absolutely had not just developed the moment the States took up arms. Marie's gentle squeeze of my forearm practically channeled her thoughts to me, and I knew they were the same as mine.

We were released to clean ourselves up and change for dinner, then forced to suffer through the Warburtons praising Reggie throughout the entire meal. It was as if he were there with us, instead of integrating himself in Princeton with everyone else starting university that year. Thankfully, he was indeed doing just that.

That night, I snuck into Marie's room after the rest of the house was quiet enough for me to assume everyone else was asleep. It wasn't difficult; our rooms were across the hall from each other. Luckily, she was still awake, reading by the light of a bedside lamp. She lifted her book as I collapsed onto her lap, then shifted it to one hand and laid the other atop my head, laughing gently.

"Can't sleep?"

I shook my head, sighing. "I sound like such a devil saying it, but I was really hoping he'd get taken away." I kept my words quiet on the slim chance someone was in the hallway.

"I was too," Marie admitted, setting the book on her little table. She leaned back against her headboard, and we stared out the window together. Her room was on the same side of the house as the library, so we could see the ocean in the distance.

"It would have been too easy, I suppose." I shifted, tucking my hand under my head.

"Far too simple. We'd have to suffer something else equally terrible if Reggie got taken away from us so easily."

"Let's not imagine it."

"Let's not."

We remained there together for a long while, Marie's fingers threading through the bit of hair that had escaped my braid. Once the moonlight shifted away from the window, I forced myself back to my own bed. It was much lonelier, but knowing Marie and I had harbored the same dark wish made me feel better about it and much less alone.

August 7th-9th, 1918

The afternoon before my eighteenth birthday, Gregory forced me to go home and spend time with my mother instead of staying at the station and pretending my birthday wasn't happening. I had been moping around for most of the summer, and it didn't help that my birthday fell on a Thursday that year, which would have normally lined up perfectly with one of Clara's visits. But no, she was up in Newport.

"You know your dear mother is home right now plotting a fantastic dinner for you and just hoping you show up, since you've spent nearly your entire summer here." Gregory crossed his arms, looking at me more sternly than he ever had. "You're to treat her right, son, you hear me?" I knew he had children, and this must have been the tone he used with them.

He was right about me spending my summer at the station. I was throwing myself into work to forget my woes. Not seeing Clara and Marie for months was one thing, but in just a little while I'd be walking around with the threat of being drafted hanging over my head. No one had mentioned it, not Clara or Mom or anyone at the station. We didn't trust the rules not to change. Every one of the firemen that was of age or about to be got sidelong, pitiful glances from the rest. We'd already lost a few.

I nodded. "Alright, Greg. I'll go."

"Good. Put your things away and get out of here. I don't want to see you until Saturday." He was waving his hand dismissively as he left the bunk room. I gaped in disbelief for a split second before following him, stopping in the doorway.

"Greg, that's three days off!" I'd already had a day off on Sunday, which I'd spent wandering aimlessly around the shops.

"Happy birthday, Leo!" His voice trailed away as he walked down the hallway. After a moment more of gaping, I turned around and gathered everything that needed to go home with me. I would get to spend so much time with Mom!

As I was leaving, bag slung over my shoulder, Timothy appeared out of nowhere as he usually did. The kid held up a hand to stop me.

"Something wrong?"

Tim shook his head. "What's your mom's address?"

Even though it was an odd and out of nowhere question, I told him. Tim was trustworthy, and

I knew he wouldn't do anything off-putting or harmful. He thanked me, asked me to keep Friday free, and disappeared off into one of his many station nests. I chuckled at him as I headed out.

Mom answered the door as if she expected it to be the landlord or a neighbor, but her expression brightened so much when she saw it was me that I couldn't help but laugh.

"What's that look for? Did you think I'd never come back?" I leaned forward to hug her, and she wrapped her arms tightly around my shoulders.

"You haven't been home in almost two weeks!" she scolded, still smiling. She led me in and sure enough, just as Gregory had suspected, Mom was doing some prep work for what was sure to be a fantastic dinner.

"Would you have eaten all of this yourself if I didn't come home?" I was inspecting a potato as I chuckled through my words, and mom grabbed it out of my hand only to shake it at me.

"I would have shared with the family across the hall. I still might, if you're a pill." She was trying to be threatening, but her smile made it hard to take seriously.

Mom made a less extravagant but just as delicious dinner that night, and we spent hours at the table just talking. She told me everything that had happened at the apartment building. The father of the family across the hall had gotten sent overseas, and the mother was overwhelmed, so Mom was trying to take as much of the burden as she could. There were other families in the building that were in similar situations, and Mom was trying to make sure everyone was as well taken care of as she could manage. She'd become a supplementary grandmother to so many children that lived in our building. I had the thought as she was talking that I should give her even more of my pay so we could help them all. I was about to bring it up but was shot down.

"I can see your thoughts all over your face, my boy, if you want to put your money anywhere there are plenty of charities around." She reached over the table to pat my hand, and I shook my head.

"But if I give it to you, I know where it's going. I know where it's being spent and who it's helping most."

It took another ten minutes of convincing and cajoling for her to finally just laugh and throw her hands up, admitting defeat.

"Fine! Alright! You've persuaded me." She was shaking her head and lowered her hands to wrap them around her long-empty teacup. "Give me your money, and I'll make sure all my new grandchildren are fed."

I grinned in triumph. "You'll be the most well-loved charity in all of Brooklyn."

I woke up Thursday morning to sunlight filtering through my curtain and the noises of Mom making something in the kitchen, humming gently as she did. I rolled onto my back, pushing my hair out of my face, and let my eyes close again. It wasn't the first Thursday Clara hadn't shown up; in truth, we hadn't had that many visits before she'd been swept away, up to Newport, but it still didn't feel good.

I hadn't quite convinced myself to get up yet when Mom bustled in, holding a mug in one hand and a steaming bowl, her apron protecting her hand, in the other.

"Good morning my birthday boy! Time to get up and eat!" She was practically singing, and set the mug and bowl down on the nightstand. I pushed myself up on my elbows, smirking in amusement. She set her hands on her hips and looked me over. "Well now, if that gal of yours ever gets to see you right when you wake up, she's in for a treat, isn't she?"

I groaned loudly and rolled back under the covers, pulling them over my head. "Ma! Why would you say that?" As embarrassed as I was, I laughed, my hands over my face. She pulled the blanket off my head and I was met with a wide grin.

"I'm not allowed to say my son is handsome?" She leaned over and kissed my temple, then dropped the blanket. I heard her move to the door, still chuckling. "Oh, what a world." I peeked from under the blanket and saw her go back to the kitchen.

The bowl was full of oatmeal, but it was sweetened with honey, which surprised me. I wasn't about to question my mother about the cost of her groceries, though. I carried the piping hot bowl (immediately regretting not holding with something like Ma had) and mug with me to the table without bothering to get dressed just yet. Mom laughed at the sight, and set about fixing her own breakfast.

After we'd finished up and I'd gotten myself presentable, we set out to the shops and I was the grateful recipient of a few new sheets of music, some laces for my shoes, and other daily necessities that I hadn't gotten around to buying more of just yet. Mom had asked what I wanted, so I told her things I needed instead. I didn't want her buying me something flashy, not this year. There were other people that we should spend money on.

We were chased home by a random spattering of rain. Mom continued where she'd left off the day before and set about finishing up the best beef stew and fresh bread I had ever eaten in my life. We did end up inviting the family across the hall over to share it with us. The mother, her two daughters, and a toddling son all piled around our little table, and between the six of us, we finished the pot.

Mom bragged that I played guitar, so I pulled it out at our neighbors' insistence and tried out the new songs we'd bought that day. I stumbled through them all a few times before giving up and playing one I knew by heart, much to the delight of the two girls who clapped and danced along. It was such a charming evening that I'd managed to forget everything that had been on my mind that morning.

The little boy fell asleep in his mother's arms as she and Mom sat at the table talking and I sat on the floor with the two girls, showing them how to play different chords. Neither of them really had long enough fingers to do it right, but they were determined to try. They both managed a few and cheered in delight over it. The apartment was filled with light and love, we were all able to forget about the plight outside the door, to pretend just for a little while that there wasn't a war on. That I wasn't of age to be drafted. And for me, I could forget that there was a chance it could happen before Clara and Marie came home.

I kept Friday free just as Tim had asked. That morning, a mother on the floor below us asked Mom to tend to her children while she was at work, so I went down with her to help feed everyone breakfast. The children ended up being a near-teenage boy with his slightly younger sister, and neither of them thought they needed a babysitter. But their mother gave them a stern look before leaving, and they both cowed. Mom wouldn't need any help with them, I was sure.

I helped the boy wash the breakfast dishes before leaving myself, kissing Mom on the cheek and promising not to stay out too late. She just waved me off, settling in to show the girl how to mend a hole in one of her dresses.

Tim hadn't told me when he wanted my attention, so I headed all the way downstairs and looked around the street for a bit to see if he was lingering. I had barely lit and taken two pulls on a cigarette before he pulled on my sleeve, and I turned to find him smirking up at me, rocking back and forth on his heels. It was so unlike him that I laughed, and his typical stone-faced expression returned.

"I'm sorry, I'm not used to you smiling." I grinned at him, and he rolled his eyes. Tim was trying to keep up his impenetrable facade, but a smile broke through anyway as he led me down the street without a word. "What's got you so excited?"

"We're going to Coney Island," he called over his shoulder, and I caught an incredibly rare sight: Tim was grinning. He lifted his hands to link them behind his head as he walked, whistling some nonsense tune. I shook my head, still grinning to myself, and hurried to keep up with him. Tim's excitement was quickening his pace.

He was just as quiet as always on the short train ride, but his knee was bouncing the whole way. The entire situation was not what I'd expected at all, but I wasn't about to refuse Tim. I did wish he'd warned me about the location at least; I would have worn a different, lighter shirt.

"Is this your first time going?" I asked him as we hopped off the train, and Tim nodded, more eagerly than I'd ever seen him. It was going to be impossible to keep a grin off my face.

"I always wanted to, but my parents wouldn't take me. So I figured you can be my adult supervision." Tim shrugged, leaving out any further detail. Now *that* was to be expected, and I didn't pry. Well, I only pried a little.

"Do they know you're here, at least?"

"Sure do. They know I'm with you too, and Gregory knows. You of all people should consider me responsible." Tim rolled his eyes and I smothered a laugh. It was probably the most I'd ever heard him talk in one sitting.

Tim had already decided on everything he'd wanted to do at Coney Island and led me straight to the entrance of Luna Park. The noise of the crowd and rides filtered out even half a block away, and I looked up at the flags snapping in the breeze. The air was a little fresher here closer to the ocean, and families and couples roamed the boardwalks and general area with smiles on their faces. It had changed a lot since I'd last been there as a child, way before I'd even met Clara. All three parks in the area were bigger, more rides and shows added, more land bought to accommodate them.

"Two please and thank you," Tim said to the lady at the ticket booth and handed over the money when asked.

"Wait a minute, why are you paying?" I asked, taking the ticket he offered me.

He stared at me as if I'd grown another head. "It's your birthday. Come on, I want to ride the Top!" Taking hold of my sleeve, Tim dragged me through the entrance and followed the signs to the ride. It was an extra charge, which I paid for before Tim could, earning me a glare that quickly dissipated as we reached the front of the line.

We were loaded onto the coaster car, and I looked up skeptically at the wooden structure. We'd been eyeing it as we walked up, watching it tilt slowly from side to side as the cars ran along the rails. It didn't look safe, but no roller coasters ever did. The operator gave everyone a final look-over, then set the ride into motion. I was gripping the rail while Tim was cheering, laughing as we were spun around and tilted. As we reached the bottom of the spiral after two minutes that felt like much more, Tim looked back at me with a grin which I returned.

Tim was bouncing, not walking, as we went around to the other shows and attractions. We didn't do everything, since most rides were an extra charge, but we did ride the Chutes toward midday when it was getting too hot to stay out of the water for much longer.

We'd mostly dried off and were walking around the park, Coca-Colas in hand, admiring everything and pointing out things we'd like to do if we came back again. I was thinking about what bits Clara and Marie would enjoy when a hand landed on my shoulder.

"What are you doing here, boy?" An older woman was glaring at me, holding my shoulder much too tightly. I shrugged her off, fighting the urge to glare back. I didn't know her, so I hoped she was just mistaking me for someone else.

"Enjoying the day. What do you mean, ma'am?" I asked as Tim shifted closer, holding onto my sleeve again. The woman glared harder.

"You're here frolicking about when all the others your age are overseas fighting and dying for our country, is what you're doing. What a disgrace."

My heart dropped. I'd been worried that something like this would happen for the entire year. Ever since the States had joined the war. They weren't taking boys my age yet, but I wouldn't have been surprised if it started soon.

"You ought to be ashamed of yourself, young man, spending the day at the amusement park instead of signing yourself up to go join your brothers." She stabbed my chest with a finger, and I covered the spot with my soda bottle.

"Ma'am, I—"

"He's only eighteen!" Tim interrupted, scowling up at the woman. "Leave him alone! They wouldn't let him join even if he asked!" He moved in front of me, and even though he was shorter than us both, he straightened to his full height and made himself a barrier between the woman and me.

To her credit, the woman briefly looked chagrined. But her glare returned quickly, and she shook her finger at me again. "You'd best get yourself signed up right when you're of age then, lest you *actually* become a disgrace." She sniffed haughtily, then turned on her heel and marched away.

I melted against a nearby railing, lifting the cool soda bottle to my forehead. Tim patted my upper arm.

"Are you alright?" he asked, and I nodded. My heart was still racing, and I reached back to grip the railing. The noise of Luna Park had been pleasantly busy and cheerful all day, but now it was overwhelming. "Do you want to leave?" He tried to hide it, but I caught the note of disappointment in his voice.

I shook my head quickly. "No, I do not." Moving the bottle, I looked Tim right in the eye. "You asked me to join you here, so we're spending the day, and if anyone else tries to tell me the same thing, I'm still only eighteen."

"That's right, you're too young." Tim nodded, and the steely determination in his eyes made me smile. He was there to back me up, he was on my side. I'd suffer every reminder of my potential drafting if it meant Tim had a fun day.

We finished our sodas, then went to see a few of the countless shows that Luna Park offered. We were down to our last few dimes and nickels when Tim suggested riding the Top again, as our last hurrah before we left the park.

So we did. Down it spiraled, back and forth it tilted, and Tim cheered the whole time. His joy was infectious and made it so easy to shake the discomfort and guilt that woman had stabbed into me.

That is, until a man cornered me with the same questions. He was old enough to be my father, and Tim and I stood up to him together.

"I'm only eighteen, sir, I'm sorry to disappoint. I'll be sure to march to the registration office first thing tomorrow and tell them to change their rules." I was glaring this time, and Tim glowered at my side like a cat ready to pounce. The man's jaw worked as he ground his teeth.

"With an attitude like that, you'll be discharged immediately," he snapped.

"It'll be the military's decision instead of mine then, won't it?" My heart was pounding again, but I wasn't going to cower this time. "If they choose to send me back, there's nothing I can do about it."

This was too logical for his anger, and the man just grimaced at me and left. Tim started laughing. It was so unusual to hear that I was startled for a moment before I joined in. We were two fools, riled up with adrenaline from the park itself and being accosted twice. I sat back on my haunches, holding my head as I panted, recovering from our hysterics. Tim slapped me on the back, still chuckling.

"Well, I guess you can tell everyone you had a very eventful birthday."

Another burst of laughter escaped me, and I covered my face. "My most eventful ever, I think."

After we took another moment to fully recover, getting all the giggles out, I lit another cigarette just to calm the lingering nerves, and we made our way out of the park and back to the subway station. Tim was quiet again on the train, both of us starting to feel the effects of being in the heat and crowds all day. About midway, Tim dozed off, and slumped against my shoulder. I snickered near silently, shifting just a bit so he wouldn't fall. I knew I'd have to keep it a secret, that he'd deny it happening, but I was glad he felt safe enough to fall asleep on the train next to me.

He woke up as we reached our stop, sitting up and rubbing his eyes and pointedly not mentioning where he'd been sleeping. We wandered back to the apartment building together, and when I asked if he wanted to come up and have dinner, he shook his head.

"I promised my mom I'd be back. It was part of the deal for letting me go without them." He was adjusting his hat, and patted his pocket, reaching into it to find the entry ticket still there. "Good." He tucked it back into the same pocket, keeping his hand around it. So Tim was a sentimental boy after all. The thought brought a smile to my face.

"I'll see you at the station, then." I nodded to him, and he nodded back. "Thanks for inviting me out. It was a good day."

"Thanks for coming!" He turned, calling over his shoulder, "We'll take your girls next time!"

Before I could respond, he was hurrying off back home.

"Yes, next time." I liked the idea of it, very much, but as I turned to head into the building, I sighed. This birthday marked a turning point. I was now officially in danger of being pulled away from everything and everyone I knew, and I didn't know if there was going to be a next time.

Despite all my attempts, it flavored the rest of the afternoon and evening, and I had to feign exhaustion to avoid worrying Mom.

But being pulled overseas before Clara got back from Newport was the last thing on my mind before I fell asleep, the woman from Coney Island's disgusted expression the last thing I saw.

November 11th, 1918

War over! L. safe! Delighted!

It was over. This long, vicious war was over. Treaties had been signed, other deals made that I didn't really understand, and everyone was happy. But all I could think about was the fact that Leo had turned eighteen over the summer, and I hadn't been able to contact him at all from Newport. I had been prepared to not hear from him all summer, had emotionally steeled myself, but the threat of the draft made it all worse.

The beginning of the season, right after the ball and the accursed meeting my family had thrust upon me—those torments were trivial compared to the thought of returning to New York and finding out Leo had been shipped overseas, with no knowledge of when or if he'd return. He was eighteen now, which wasn't a problem until we'd returned in September and the military began drafting eighteen-year-olds. Every one of our visits after had been tinged with that lingering dread. And even now, with the fighting over, some of that fear still lingered. He'd been safe for the past three months, he hadn't been called to duty, but some of his fellow firemen hadn't been so lucky. One had even been killed overseas.

The city celebrated; the air was joyous and thrilled. People were singing in the streets and even dancing, passing around newspapers sharing the grand news. But all I could think about was getting to the station, making sure some letter hadn't come between last week and now, making sure he wasn't going to have to head off to some camp only to be returned right after.

Trains were always crowded, but that day it was worse, the celebrations extending into the cars and lingering there, people forgetting their stops and all sense of decorum as they stood in front of the doors and on the stairs of the platforms, and my elbows got put to good use because of it. All thoughts of the Spanish Flu had seemingly been tossed aside, but I kept a scarf up over my nose and stayed as far from the others as I could.

The fire station wasn't far, and I stopped myself from running to it, despite the deep yearning in my soul to get to Leo's side as swiftly as possible. I reached the steps with panting breaths, having abandoned my restraint two blocks back.

"Hey Miss Clara," Tim called from where he was perched on the back of one of the trucks, the garages wide open even in the chilly air. He was smiling and tipped his hat to me. I smiled back, resting my hands on my knees to regain my breath, pulling my scarf down to get more oxygen. "I'll grab Leo." With that, the station boy was off, whistling as he went.

Leo was at the garage door only moments later, having clearly run once Tim told him I was here. He hurried to my side, and we both just started laughing before either of us said a word. As he wrapped his arms around my waist, I lifted mine to twine about his shoulders. Before I knew it, I was being spun around, our breath mingling in soft clouds in the chilly air. We twirled a few times more before Leo lowered me to the ground, squeezing me close and shivering.

"Come inside. I didn't grab my coat." He took me by the hand, and I followed him through the garage into the station kitchen, where a gaggle of other firemen and Tim were celebrating the news. Gregory looked up with a teasing grin.

"Come to see if your favorite fireman is still here?" He stood and held out his arms, and I released Leo's hand to embrace the Chief.

"Of course! My life would be so empty without you, Greg!" I exclaimed, squeezing the older man once for good measure before returning to Leo's side. The comment sent a roar of laughter through the room. Even Tim chuckled. "I'm so glad all of you are still here." My eyes grew misty as I looked around at the group of men, some I knew fairly well and some only in passing, but they were all men Leo knew deeply and had worked side by side with in some of the scariest circumstances. Losing any more of them would have hurt him, and by proxy, me.

We celebrated with the men for a while longer before Gregory shooed us off, told us that bringing a woman in here was indecent and Leo should be ashamed of himself. All of this was said with a wide, loving grin, and a repeat of nearly every other time I'd been inside the station.

So Leo and I ran off, hiding away in various shops and our diner for a few hours. He kept ahold of my hand at every opportunity, and when he couldn't hold it, I rested it on his shoulder. We were constantly touching, constantly reminding ourselves that he was safe, he was *safe.* He was home, and he wasn't going anywhere. Not this time. Leo hadn't been drafted, the war was over, and even with the looming threat of Reggie over our heads, no news could have been better.

"I need to go to my mother," he said as we were huddled in the alcove where we'd kissed the first time, his hands holding both of mine, his lips resting on my knuckles. "We haven't had a chance to celebrate together." He kissed my hands, one cold knuckle at time, and my heart fluttered in my chest. I didn't want to say goodbye, I wanted to stay at his side and celebrate more, to sit here and remind myself that Leo hadn't been taken away. But his mother deserved that jubilation and security as well. So I squeezed him close to me, kissing him until we were both breathless, and let him go with promises to come back for our normal Thursday visit.

I floated home, not even noticing the crowds and noise. I'd seen Leo in person and reassured myself again, and it all felt like a dream, a glorious dream, almost too good to be true. But the cold in my fingers and toes helped prove it was reality, the lingering tingle of Leo's kiss and the imprint of heat on my waist from his hand, all proved it was real.

The war was over, Leo was safe, and I was going to see him again every Thursday, all winter.

December 16th, 1918

Met Mrs. A. finally. Delighted. Charmed. Happy.

Sneaking away from my family in the hubbub of Central Park was nothing. I knew they were all too distracted to care anyway, so I headed toward the west side of the park, opposite of them. My grandparents had come into the city for the holiday, along with a few aunts and uncles I hadn't seen for a while. My cousins were either young enough that they were still with nannies, or too old, and celebrating with the other sides of their families. I was left adrift in that liminal space that was young adulthood, too young to truly join my parents, too old to play with the children. Although I had been playing with the children all morning. We'd played hide-and-go-seek all over the house, only a few areas deemed off-limits. They'd adored it. I had too, until Mother had pulled me aside between games and warned me that this behavior was unbecoming of a recently debuted lady. It took all my strength not to roll my eyes then, and again now as I wandered down one of the many paved paths in Central Park. As long as I was home to join them all for dinner, it would be fine.

"Hot toasted almonds! A bag for a nickel!" A street vendor was hollering, and I fought a giggle. He'd raised his prices for the tourists who had flooded the city for the holiday season. The smell was so tantalizing I nearly bought a bag but decided not to. He would make his money from unsuspecting out-of-towners, and I could come back in a few weeks when he'd lowered his prices back to normal.

Other vendors had done the same, and I started marking down the prices alongside the date in my little notebook. I was interested in just how much they'd hiked the cost up. My attention was absorbed in the small pages, and I bumped into someone while I wasn't watching where I was going.

"Well, isn't this a delight." I recognized the voice before anything else, and looked up from my notebook with a grin.

"What on Earth are you doing in Manhattan?"

Leo returned my grin with his brilliant one that always made my heart skip a beat, his eyes sparkling. He motioned to a woman at his side and tugged her a little forward. She was older than us, and immediately I realized this must be his mother. They looked so alike! He had her bright eyes.

"We're celebrating. Are you wandering about alone?" I could hear the double meaning of his question, and nodded, grinning wider.

"I am! My family expects me home for dinner, but I'm on my own now." I turned to his mother, holding out both my hands. "Mrs. Ardin! An absolute pleasure to finally meet you!" She started laughing, confused and amused all at once.

"Well, now, there's no doubt in my mind you're Clara." She chuckled, reaching forward as well. I took her hand in both of mine and clasped it, shaking it gently. "How lovely to put a face to all the stories."

"Oh dear, do I dare ask what stories?" I giggled, releasing her hand and clasping mine behind my back. We stepped to the side of the pathway to keep from blocking it, and Leo shook his head.

"Nothing terrible. There are no terrible stories about you." He had his mother on his arm but still looked at me as if I were the only girl in the world. His expression would have been considered quite indecent in the circles I was currently hiding from, but it was so pleasant coming from him that I couldn't stop myself from smiling.

"Oh, I'm sure there's a few." I giggled again. "What are you celebrating? I know it isn't Leo's birthday. Is it yours, ma'am?"

"It's the holiday season, the war is over, and Leo didn't get taken away from us." Mrs. Ardin shook her son's arm a little, smiling so very fondly up at him. Leo was bashful for all of a second.

"All good things to celebrate! I'm sure that's why so many others came to the park today as well. Where all have you been?" I was prepared to play tour guide for the rest of the afternoon and would have gladly done so.

"We've walked about and seen many of the statues, and we stopped by the menagerie, but it was..." Mrs. Ardin looked to her son as if she were trying to think of a polite word.

"Pitiful and dreary?" I offered, and she laughed.

"That's a very good way to put it, yes. I don't think any of the animals are very happy about being there." She shook her head in what seemed like disgust alongside pity, and I shook mine in solidarity. The menagerie was in fact one of the most unfortunate parts of the park. I hummed softly as I thought about where else they could go.

"Oh! If you are still going to be in Manhattan for a while, and don't mind walking across the park, the Metropolitan Museum of Art is about ten blocks down. It's a bit of a walk, but you can hail a motor cab if need be." We were about equal with ninetieth street, and the museum was across the park at eighty-second. Mrs. Ardin looked up at her son again, and Leo looked back, a private conversation passing between them. After a moment, Leo nodded, then turned to me.

"A fantastic suggestion, but I'm afraid we've stretched our purses quite a lot already." I raised an eyebrow at him. He only got explicitly formal like this when he was preparing for an argument. I wasn't going to give him one.

"Oh, Leo." I sighed, moving to dig in my purse. "Please, allow me. It will be my Christmas present to you and your mother both." I pulled out fifty cents, enough for both their museum tickets, and held it out rather impatiently to Leo. He gave me a stern look, but he took it. "I can pay for cab fare as well, ten blocks in the snow is much too far to walk." I was already counting more coins as Mrs. Ardin spoke up.

"Are you sure, my dear?" She sounded nervous, and I looked up at her, trying to force every ounce of sincerity I possessed into my voice.

"Absolutely, ma'am. Absolutely. Please, consider it my gift to you both." I stopped digging in my purse for a moment and reached out to take her hand again. "Leo has watched over me and been at my side for six years now, and I wouldn't trade that time for anything. If I could, I would spoil you both daily. I would do everything I could to make sure you're both comfortable and happy."

Mrs. Ardin's expression softened as I spoke, and she smiled. With a glance, I saw Leo still looking at me sternly. I resisted the urge to stick my tongue out at him and instead spun to take his mother's other arm, tucking her to my side.

"Leo, if you don't let me spoil your mother at least once, I shall be *so* very cross with you." I stuck up my nose in a mimicry of haughtiness, and it finally broke him. He started laughing, pushing his fingers into his hair, lifting his hat briefly.

"Fine, I admit defeat." He took his mother's hand and dropped the fifty cents into it.

Mrs. Ardin chuckled as well, hugging my arm. "Goodness, he has his hands full with you, doesn't he?"

"I have since 1912." He was trying to sound chagrined, but the grin on his face ruined it. I did stick out my tongue at him then, and Mrs. Ardin laughed, a full bodied, pleased-as-punch laugh.

"What a wonderful girl you are, Clara." She patted my arm, and I walked with them across the park to where they could easily catch a cab. If I saw my family, I'd say I was helping some out-of-towners navigate the city.

We reached Fifth Avenue, and Mrs. Ardin took both my hands in hers, leaning forward to kiss my cheek. I kissed hers back, squeezing her hands.

"I am very glad I got to finally meet you, dear girl." She was smiling fondly up at me as she said it, and I felt my heart grow warm.

"And I you, ma'am!" I kissed her cheek once more before she released me and turned to Leo. As much as I wanted to kiss him, we both knew it was too risky, so he took my hand and kissed the back of it instead. "How serendipitous to run into you here, Leo."

He chuckled and gave my hand a squeeze. "Indeed. Now you said something about cab fare as well?" His grin turned teasing, and I rolled my eyes, giving him a fond smile of my own.

"Oh yes, of course, mustn't let the fireman get his feet wet." I dug in my purse again as Mrs. Ardin snickered, then handed Leo another handful of coins. He tucked them in his pocket.

"I'll see you Thursday?"

"Of course!" I clasped my hands behind my back, swaying joyfully.

"Until then." Leo nodded at me, and my heart fluttered. My sun, my knight, staring into my eyes as if I were all he could see.

I was still giggling as I watched them walk a bit down the street, then climb into a cab.

Serendipitous indeed.

February, 1919

Devastated. An unhappy day.

The next year, I found myself alone when Mom passed. The doctors told me afterward that she'd actually been sick for a while, and the flu had just made it worse. She had always been a little weak, a little frail, but none of that felt out of the ordinary. So when she started getting more run down in the middle of winter, we both just figured it was the cold wreaking havoc on her body. I can't for the life of me remember now what chronic illness she had, only that it had been eating away at her stamina and lifeforce for longer than we realized. Catching the flu had just been the nail in her coffin.

The day I woke up to no sounds of cooking coming from the kitchen, no Mother's voice singing quietly as she worked, I immediately knew something was wrong. It had only happened a few times before, before Dad had passed, where she'd felt bad enough to just stay in bed all day. It was rare.

So, fearing the worst, I got up and hesitantly made my way to her bedroom. It looked like she was just sleeping, resting gently on her side, comfortably dozing away. The sight was a brief comfort, especially since she'd been coughing so much before, until I realized she didn't seem to be breathing. Without even thinking, my training kicked in and I went to check her pulse. Of course, there wasn't one.

I only remember the aftermath of going to find a neighbor to help me, the only one in the building that had a phone. They placed the call for me; I didn't know who to ask for or what to even say had happened. I watched from a distance as emergency responders much like myself but different wrapped my mother up entirely and carried her from our apartment.

One of them asked me for a statement, a story, just for records. There wasn't anything to tell, really. She'd caught the flu. I'd probably brought it home to her, I kept thinking to myself. She'd been frail for longer than I could remember, always suffering through her pain silently. It was a fight to get her to rest even on her worst days. That was why I was giving her practically all my money, so she could rest and not work herself all the way down to the bone. But now, it felt like my efforts for the past five years had been for nothing. I hadn't saved her. I hadn't kept her around as long as she had deserved to be. There was nothing I could have done, the doctor said, but to this day I still don't believe it. If I had stayed a paperboy a little longer instead of accepting the station boy spot, maybe she would have had enough money earlier to be able to stop working altogether. She could have stayed home and rested and read books and embroidered as much as she liked instead of spending her days washing other people's laundry and cleaning up after other people's children. I would have gotten her the kitten she had always wistfully talked about, a little companion to sit with in that little slant of sunlight that stretched into our apartment all throughout the winter. If I had given her my entire paycheck instead of keeping those few dollars to myself, maybe she could have quit her job earlier. Even just a few months earlier. If I had just stayed away during the first wave of the flu through New York, and the second, if I hadn't exposed her to everything I'd been exposed to...Everyone kept telling me over and over again that there was nothing I could have done, we didn't know she was sick before the flu, maybe resting wouldn't have helped anyway. But to this day, I still do not believe it at all.

The only comfort I could take was that she had passed in her sleep, in the comfort of her own bed and underneath her favorite quilt. That quilt was the only thing I had buried with her. It felt so wrong to let her go without it. It was irrational, but I couldn't stand the thought of her being cold underground.

Clara had come up with some lie or another to attend the funeral with me, among the rest of the small, gathered crowd. It was a budget affair to be sure. We were lucky this kind of gathering hadn't been banned because of the pandemic. But everyone still wore those gauze masks and sat a little away from each other. I'd asked my station mates to come if they could, and Marie had sent a heartfelt letter along with Clara to send her condolences and regrets she couldn't be there. Clara held my hand through all of it, and Timothy sat at my side, silent but supportive, securing himself in my mind as a younger brother for the rest of our lives. It was a short, simple little thing—Mom wouldn't have wanted a lot of fuss about "little old" her—but I made sure she had a lovely reading, and although I couldn't say anything myself, Gregory stood and spoke about the sacrifices a mother makes for her children, and how mine was one of the best mothers he'd ever had the pleasure to meet. I heard the rest of the squad agreeing, gently, quietly. They'd all had her homemade cooking at some point or another, and on the rare occasion she dropped by the station, she was always greeted warmly and affectionately. These days, she would have definitely been dubbed the station mom.

Living in the apartment without her was nigh impossible, so I moved permanently to the station for a while. Following what I figured would be Mom's wishes, I donated her clothes and most of her kitchenware to a charity that provided necessities to those who were struggling. The furniture belonged to the landlord, so that was easy enough to leave behind. In the end, the only things I kept were her and Dad's wedding rings, the family bible, and the quilt she'd made me that I had kept on my bed. We didn't have any family heirlooms that I knew of, and if we did, they definitely didn't belong to this branch of the family tree. I put the wedding rings on a chain that Gregory and the rest of the station gave me as a kind of 'I'm sorry for your loss' type gift, which I accepted graciously.

By graciously, I mean I cried in front of the entire squad. Normally that kind of behavior would garner merciless teasing for years to come, but this was the type of situation that defied normal male companionship logic. Timothy was the first to wrap his arms around my shoulders, and Gregory rested his hand on my back not long after. Everyone else stood around awkwardly in the room until Gregory released them by telling them to go clean the trucks. I called out a shaky "thank you" to them as they left and was met with murmurs and calls of acknowledgement tossed from the doorway, quickly but meaningfully.

"Do you need a few days off, Leo?" Gregory asked, jostling my shoulder just a bit and angling his head to look into my face. I shook my head.

"I don't think so, I don't know. I want to work to distract myself." I knew my words were shaking and tumbling over each other, but somehow, he still understood. He nodded. Timothy stood up, releasing my shoulders and crossing his arms. When I looked at him, the kid who had never really seemed like a kid had water threatening to spill over in his eyes.

"I think you should take a few days off," he said, his words just as shaky as mine. I smiled at him gently, grateful for his no-nonsense tone today.

"Well, if Timothy demands it, I guess we must listen to him." Gregory was chuckling as he patted my shoulder again heavily, and I felt myself shift with it. "Take some time, Leo. Your job isn't going anywhere. Timothy will tell you when you can come back." I looked up to see him grinning slightly before he nodded to our station boy and took his leave. I turned to my adoptive little brother, now even more cemented into that role than he had been before.

"How long do I take off then, Tim?"

He studied me for a long moment, eyes still glistening, and uncrossed his arms to let them hang limply at his sides. "Until I stop feeling like I have to hug you to keep you from falling apart."

My heart sank, and I lifted my arms to wrap the boy in a tight hug. I was sitting and he was standing, so his arms were closer to being around my head than my shoulders, but he wrapped me in them all the same. And I broke again, squeezing him tight as he did me, both of us falling and trying to keep the other upright.

The very next day, as soon as I woke up, Timothy was standing at the foot of my bed, waiting. I stared at him, bleary-eyed, blinking a few times to be sure of what I was seeing.

"Tim?"

"Get up, I have somewhere to take you today." That's all he said before he disappeared, leaving me confused and still half asleep. But I did as he commanded, washing my face and cleaning myself up before getting dressed and heading downstairs to find the lad. He was perched on the back of one of the trucks, kicking the leg that didn't quite reach the floor of the garage.

"Alright then, where are we headed?" I asked, slipping my hands into my pockets.

"To get breakfast first, then somewhere else." He hopped off the truck without any further explanation, heading out of the open garage door with his hands on the back of his head. I blinked after him, then followed.

He led me to a little—and I do mean little. It had exactly three tables—restaurant and ordered for the both of us. Timothy was definitely in charge today, and I wasn't about to fight him when he clearly had a plan. It ended up being a pancake breakfast, eggs and bacon on the side, with freshly squeezed orange juice to wash it all down. I marveled at the spread. Surely this cost more than Tim could afford. I thought about it, and mentally counted the money I had in my pocket. I could probably cover it if need be.

"How do you know about this place?" I asked as we ate, the first words to be spoken between us since Tim had told me not to bother looking at the a menu, he knew what to get.

"I eat here every week. They're nice to me here and don't treat me like a little kid who's supposed to be in school or at home." He shrugged loosely.

"But you don't get paid as a station boy."

"Dad gives me a little bit of money every month. I don't really have any other use for it, so I use it here."

"Oh." He had explained everything so succinctly, I couldn't even think of anything else to ask. I was also starting to realize how much about Timothy I didn't know. I had assumed he had taken the station boy position for similar reasons to me, because there wasn't much benefit to it other than free meals and a room when you needed one.

We ate the rest of our meal in silence. Timothy paid even though I tried to tell him I was happy to, but he silenced me with one of his 'I'm not accepting your help' looks, and I backed off.

"Alright, next place." He led me out of the tiny eatery and down the street, taking turns and back ways I was unfamiliar with. He was leading me toward a part of town I'd rarely been in, a mostly residential zone with a few little shops throughout, instead of the more commercial area I'd always lived in. I was lost as anything before he stopped in front of an apartment building and announced we'd reached our destination.

"This is it? I didn't know what to expect, but definitely not this," I joked, trailing after him up multiple flights of stairs. He shrugged.

"I didn't say where we were going, so of course you didn't expect it."

One more flight of stairs and then he was heading down a hallway, knocking on a door before testing the knob. When it gave, he pushed the door open and called out in a tone I'd never heard from his voice before.

"Papa? Ma? Are you home?"

The answer came from deep within the apartment, muffled by a few walls. "In here, Timmy!"

Everyone at the station was most definitely *not* allowed to call him Timmy, but the woman who had must have been an exception. I could only assume she was his mother, and was proven right as he led me to a nursery where she was sitting with a tiny baby girl who was still in diapers and cooing happily from a blanket on the floor.

"Hello darling." The woman got up and stepped carefully around the infant to kiss her son, then smiled brilliantly at me. "Who have you brought home?"

"This is Leo. He works at the station too."

I nodded, sweeping off my hat as I should have done as soon as I stepped inside. "Pleasure to meet you, ma'am."

She chuckled softly and waved her hand. "You can call me Grace. There's no formality here."

"Ma, can I help with Sally?" Timothy's demeanor had entirely shifted, and he moved to kneel down on the floor near his baby sister who grabbed onto his finger as soon as he held it out. The sight made me grin, and Grace moved to my side to watch her son.

"She's all set up right now. I just fed and changed her, so go ahead and play until she gets sleepy. Wash your hands first."

"Yes!" The single word from Tim was said with such delight, and after running to the bathroom to do as his mother bid, he very carefully slipped his hands under his sister to lift her, pulling her to his chest as he stood. The little bounce in his step was long-practiced, even for a fourteen-year-old, and I chuckled at him. That received a trademark Timothy glare.

"Ah, suddenly he's back to the Tim I'm used to." I laughed, and Grace joined me.

"He is a darling boy, but mostly to his family." She reached out to ruffle his hair fondly as he passed, taking his sister to a different part of the apartment and away from our teasing. "How different is he at the station?"

"Oh, he rules over all of us with an iron fist. Nothing gets past him, and he tells all of us what to do constantly. He actually brought me here with no explanation today, just told me we were going somewhere." I shrugged lightly, turning to follow Grace as she headed down the hallway to find her children. She laughed.

"That sounds like him. He's more gentle about it with us, always asking instead of telling, but he also rules this home with a...hm...maybe not an iron fist, something softer." She hummed in thought and led me to the parlor, gesturing to a chair for me to take while she took hers. "Perhaps a golden fist. Isn't gold very soft?"

I nodded. "As far as I know, yes."

"I do wonder why he brought you here, though. If he wanted to see Sally he could have just come. He's here as often as he can be." Her attention turned to the pair of them, sitting on the floor near the window in a sunbeam like a couple of kittens. Sally was sitting on her own, a little wobbly and definitely still learning how to hold herself up. Timothy was grinning and encouraging her, hands on either side ready to catch her the moment she toppled.

"I would wager it has something to do with my mother passing last week and Tim thinking I needed a few days off." My smile was a little sad but genuine, and Grace gasped softly.

"Oh, I'm so sorry, that's such a horrible thing to go through." A hand lifted to her heart, her face falling in sympathy. I swallowed back more intense emotions in favor of polite ones, and nodded.

"Thank you." After a breath, I was back to a slightly more jovial tone. "The chief, Gregory, asked me if I needed some time off, and when I said I wanted to work for the distraction, Timothy basically told me to be quiet and that I would be taking time off." Grace's lips curved in a smile, slowly finding the polite line between secondhand grief and amusement. "So here I am, at his command."

"Well how sweet he's decided to take care of you as well." She laughed gently. "Timmy?"

"Ma?"

"Were you planning on the two of you staying for dinner? Your father won't be home until late, so we may have to eat without him."

"If that's alright."

"Fine by me."

So it was decided that we would spend the day with his mother and sister. Sally and Tim were clearly joined at the hip, with Grace the loving guardian of them both. Being an only child, I didn't know what it was like to have siblings, but it was nonetheless heartwarming to see Tim be such a devoted older brother. Sally was delighted every time he picked her up, every time he hid behind his hands then suddenly reappeared. The parlor and my heart were full of her laughter for the entire afternoon.

After insisting on cleaning up the dishes myself, as a thank you to Grace for feeding me, I found myself alone in their kitchen for a brief moment. I still couldn't figure out why Tim had brought me here, but I couldn't deny that being around another mother had greatly eased my pain. Grace wasn't quite old enough to be my mother, but she provided a sense of comfort and safety that I hadn't even realized I'd been missing since I'd lost my own mother. I dried the last plate and set it in the stack with the rest, focusing my attention on polishing the silverware. A small smile had found its way onto my face and I caught it reflected in a fork, pausing to look at it. Whatever Timothy's family had pushed into my heart, I was grateful for.

The door of the apartment pushed open, and I heard a man who had to be Tim's father call out that he was home. Timothy responded.

"Hello Papa!"

"Well Timmy, what a lovely surprise!" His father sounded just as jovial as his mother.

"We have a visitor, dear."

"Do we now? Where are they?"

Grace chuckled. "Well he stayed for dinner and then insisted on doing the dishes himself. So I let him."

The pause of confusion that I felt more than heard made me chuckle, and I set down my towel and a spoon as I was called into the living room. Tim's father's eyebrows raised at the sight of me, and he smiled.

"Well now, you must be the Leo our Timmy has told us so much about."

I paused. Tim had told his parents about me? In my experience, Timothy was the most private person I knew, refusing to even share details of a cold so we could figure out which medicine to get him. He truly was an entirely different person around his family. I glanced at the kid to find him giving his father a withering glare. Alright, maybe not that different. I recovered from my pause with the laughter that escaped me.

"Told you about? Oh dear. It's probably all my worst moments."

"Oh no, no, he tells us all the time how much he looks up to you, how neat he thinks you are. You're practically his hero." Tim's dad laughed, grinning mischievously at his son, who was still glaring.

"Well I'm honored. He's never shared that with me." I turned my grin on Tim, who turned his glare on me.

"Your head doesn't need to be any bigger than it already is." He grumbled, setting his chin on his baby sister's head. She turned it and reached up to bap at his face.

"That's the Tim I'm used to." I chuckled, moving to sit with his parents when bid. I was introduced properly to his father, Gianmarco, and finally learned the boy's last name. Timothy Rinaldi. Now I knew what to yell when I needed him at the station.

The evening passed with light conversation. Tim set Sally on my lap when he had to run off for the bathroom, and she curled up against me, asleep after only a few minutes. Tim was very jealous when he saw but sat down at his mother's knee and kept quiet about it besides sending me a few scowls from across the room. Gianmarco was a bondsman who worked in Manhattan, taking a long commute in favor of moving his family from the home they knew and loved. Both of Tim's parents were kind, gentle people, and I came to understand where Timothy had learned his deep, secret compassion. They welcomed me to their home anytime I wanted to visit, even if Tim didn't come along as well. He took great offense to that and said that he would never tell me when he was coming again. We teased him that it wouldn't change anything, I'd still come.

As we headed home, I stopped Timothy outside the station's kitchen door, reaching out to hold his shoulder.

"Thank you. That really did help."

Tim just gave me a small smile and nodded, heading inside. "I feel much less like I have to hug you back together now, so it definitely worked."

"Your parents are very nice. I'm glad I got to meet them."

"They're good people."

His responses were coming shorter and shorter, so I took it as my cue to stop dragging the conversation out. We went our separate ways for the night, him heading off to wherever he'd secreted his little nest away and me to the bunk room. A good number of the other firefighters on call here tonight were already asleep, so I took care to climb into my own bed as quietly as possible. That night, for the first time since Mom had passed, I was able to fall asleep and stay that way. No anxieties plagued me, not a single nightmare crossed my headspace. To say I was grateful to Timothy and his family would have been the understatement of the century.

The day after Tim took me to his family home, I was due to meet with Clara. She'd had to skip our last Thursday meeting in favor of coming to the funeral, and had lied and said the painting class had moved just that one day. It worked, and as sad as I was to miss her on Thursday, it was worth it to have her hand in mine as I bid my mother farewell.

She beat me to the stairs outside the milliner's, our forever meetup spot. Her hands were clasped behind her back, and she was staring off across the street at someone doing something, I don't even remember. What I do remember is the sunlight catching her hair and casting it in a golden sheen, tipping the color closer to my own. I stopped a few steps away just to look at her, enjoying the view.

"Like what you see, fireman?" Clara asked, smirking but not even looking away from whatever she was watching. I chuckled. Of course she'd known I was there.

"Always, dearest." I held out a hand to her, reaching up to help her down the stairs she definitely didn't need help getting down. She took my hand anyway, lightly pinching the ring she'd bought me between her fingers.

"Where are you taking me today?"

"I didn't have any plans." I shrugged. The visit with Tim's family had taken all of my attention. "I do have a story for you. Timothy introduced me to his family yesterday."

Clara chuckled. "Oh? Timothy, the kid who would gladly not tell anyone his name if he didn't have to?"

"The very same."

"Well how odd. How did that go?"

"Wonderfully, honestly." I launched into the tale of the visit as we made our way to the park, a normal haunt for us for the past few years. It was a little chillier today, so instead of sitting on the grass we picked out a bench.

"Aw, I would love to see you holding a baby. That sounds adorable." Clara grinned. She was turned toward me, with her arm resting along the back of the bench, propping her head up with her hand. Her grin was infectious, and I matched it.

"She was a lovely little thing. Sally is going to grow up to be as beautiful as her mother I bet. But I have no doubt Timothy's going to teach her his attitude."

"Hah! Then there will be two of them. And they'll both adore you." She reached out to swat lightly at my shoulder.

"You're right, I have no idea how I managed to become an older brother figure, but I'm alright with it. He's a good kid, and he's learning fast at the station. I'm really proud of him."

"Aw, Leo, you sound just like an older brother now," Clara cooed, tucking her feet up on the bench beside her.

"Aw, Clara, it's almost as if I meant to or something." I wrinkled my nose at her, drawing a giggle forth, and reached out to pat her knee. "Did you decide what you want to do today?"

"Oh I was happy just listening to you talk, honestly."

"Wow."

She let out another soft titter. "I don't know. Wherever you want to go, I'm pleased."

We ended up staying at the park for a bit longer, until Clara started shivering in the late winter air and we decided to find somewhere warm to loiter in. We ended up in the music shop. It had opened not too long before thanks to the staggered work hours that were now mandatory.

"Why hello you two. It's been a bit." Mr. Weis leaned on the counter, grinning our way. We grinned back. "You two married yet?"

We both flushed, I was trying to stammer out an answer when Clara took my hand. "He won't propose until he has four hundred dollars in the bank."

Mr. Weis chuckled. "Well boy, you best get to saving."

I shook my head at Clara's smooth recovery of the situation and her lie, but my heart did a flutter thinking of proposing to her. I knew it was probably impossible, but Mr. Weis didn't, so I didn't say anything. Clara had banned all talk of her loathed engagement whenever we were together anyway. I was happy to oblige, as I didn't even like thinking about it. Even though we were supposed to be figuring out a way out of it.

Later that day, as we sat side by side at our normal dining counter, Clara's fork idled on the side of her plate longer than the normal time it took her to chew and I nudged her gently with my elbow. “What is it?”

“I wish four hundred dollars were all that were keeping us from getting married.”

I sighed, my gaze falling to my plate. "Me too, dearest. Me too."

The wistful air tainted the rest of our day. We walked back to the train station, and Clara wrapped her arms around my shoulders, leaning close. "How much money *do* you have in the bank?"

I laughed. "Nothing. I don't have a bank account." Mom had left behind some money, and the policeman that had come with the medics told me it was mine, so I'd tucked it in my trunk at the station.

Clara looked almost appalled. "You start one right now. Don't you dare just leave cash sitting around." The train pulled in and she pushed up onto her toes to kiss me, holding my face after. "Go open an account! Then you can get started on your four hundred dollars." Another kiss, and she ran off to catch her train.

I held my hand to my mouth, smiling under it. Maybe that really was all that was keeping us from getting married. That much money would be enough to run away with, to leave New York. If only I could convince her.

April, 1919

L. has own place, found such delights in it.

After a month or two of living at the station full time, Gregory not so gently told me it was time I got a place of my own. He was right; I didn't want to admit it, but he was. I couldn't just mooch off the station forever. So I went looking and found a place fairly close to work and not too far from the shopping area, just a little apartment with enough room for me and my guitar. It took up a good portion of the money Mom had left, so I started my bank account with even less money than I thought I would.

It was pretty cramped. The bedroom was little more than a closet, but by some miracle I managed to find one with a private bathroom instead of a shared one. Granted, the private bathroom was *actually* the size of a closet, but it was worth it. There was just enough room for a two-person dining table in the kitchen, and I grinned at the idea of having Clara over to eat before remembering what kind of place she was used to. I sighed, and suddenly the apartment felt like nothing more than a rat's nest.

As soon as I told her the news, though, Clara demanded to see it and wouldn't let up. I told her the pipes were loud and the wallpaper was peeling in the corners, but she absolutely insisted on seeing my new home. So I relented and led her there, dreading the whole way what she'd think of it.

Much to my surprise, the minute she walked in, she exclaimed, "I love it! It's so cozy! This is so cute!" She had her hands on her cheeks as she spun around, taking it all in. The gauze mask she'd worn on the train dangled from her fingers. "It's nowhere near what you described Leo, you liar. Yes it's small, but it's lovely! The wallpaper isn't peeling at all. You're so dramatic."

The wallpaper was peeling, but in the bedroom, not the space that served as kitchen, dining room, and parlor all in one. I opened the bedroom door and pointed. "It is, over there."

"Oh psh, *psh*. One corner. Oh no! Find some paste and it's fine." She swatted my shoulder as she moved past me into the bedroom, making her way to the bed and touching the quilt softly. I was suddenly overwhelmed with thankfulness that Clara had been able to meet my mother, even for a short time, as she touched her handiwork. Her voice was soft when she asked, "Did your mother make this?"

"She did. The one in the trunk over there too. Few Christmases ago." I allowed myself to speak a little louder than a whisper, even though it almost felt wrong to. Clara's head lifted to meet my gaze.

"She did fine work. This is beautiful." She knelt, knees hitting the floor without a sound, to lift and examine the hem of the quilt. I leaned against the doorway and crossed my arms, letting her have the moment. I knew she was trying to understand what it meant to me, why I kept it despite its age, and who the woman that had made it had been. We were quiet as she did her examination, fingers tracing the perfectly matched stitches along the hemline, toying softly along the patterned squares that had been cut out of old clothes to become what they were today. There was an entire family history in that quilt, and to this day I will forever wish I could have it back. When Clara was satisfied, she stood, coming to the doorway and lifting her arms to wrap them around my neck. I shifted to wrap my own around her waist, hugging her close. I let my eyes close, bowing my head against hers with a sigh.

"Thank you," she whispered, one hand lifting to stroke along my hair.

"What for?"

"For letting me see where you live. Letting me touch such a treasured object. I can tell it's something sacred to you and I'm just happy you trust me that much."

I smirked, just a little. Of course I trusted her. "I knew the worst you'd do is want to be wrapped in it, and that's alright with me."

"You're right." She pulled back, and when I saw her expression, she was back to grinning. "In fact, I think I'll wrap myself in it now!" She wiggled free of my arms, turning to pull the quilt off the bed. She didn't have a chance, as I trapped her back in my arms and dragged her onto the bed with me, peppering her jawline with kisses as she cackled.

"Absolutely not. I forbid it."

We faux wrestled until we were breathless and laughing, and I shifted to lean against the headboard and draw her to me, her head on my shoulder.

"Oh Leo, you horribly naughty creature, you've pulled me right into your den of debauchery and sin." She was giggling through her words, the falsely serious tone she'd tried to put on absolutely failing.

"You demanded to see it. I can't be blamed."

"You pulled me onto your bed!"

"You wanted me to." I silenced her retort with a kiss, sliding a hand down her back to tug her closer. She giggled softly against my mouth and melted into the embrace, a hand lifting to settle against my neck. Our kiss grew deeper, more breathless, and suddenly she was straddling my lap and my hands were under the hem of her dress, resting on her thighs. My senses came back to me at the touch of her garters, and I broke from her lips.

"What?" she breathed, and I looked up apologetically.

"I'm pushing my luck."

Clara regarded me for just a moment, confused and amused all at once. Then she took my face in her hands, speaking against my lips. "I'm letting you."

November 8th, 2010

"Mister Regulus!" Lorena suddenly interrupted, and I looked up to see her hands covering her face. What I could still see of it between her fingers was red, and I realized what part of the story I'd been telling.

"Oh, Miss Bisset, I'm so sorry." I lifted my hand to cover my eyes and laughed, sinking down in the chair. "Please, forgive me, I got caught up."

Lorena sighed slowly, her face still in her hands. I peeked at her through my fingers. "It's! It's fine!" She lowered her hands and looked to the ceiling, the bright red of her blush fading a bit into a strong pink.

"I really am sorry. I shouldn't have gotten carried away."

"No it's alright!" She shook her head, then picked her pen back up, making a quick note. "How about, if you want to include any more of these...memories...you write them down later and I'll just edit them in?"

I chuckled, sitting up properly. "That's better than hearing it spoken?"

"Yes!" She answered so quickly that I laughed again even harder. Lorena returned her hands to her face, and I heard her laughing behind them. "It is! Then I can just pretend I'm reading a romance novel and not being told about things that actually happened!"

I grinned. Despite embarrassing this sweet young woman, laughing with her was making me feel better than I had in over a week.

"Alright, deal. I'll write all the salacious details down for you when I get home."

"Okay! Skip it and go on then!"

Lorena's embarrassed giggle and hand wave pushed me on, and I fell back into the story.

April, 1919

Her permission unlocked the years of tightly-held desire, and my hands slid up her thighs to her hips, tracing the bone with my thumbs. Her tongue pushed its way into my mouth, meeting mine in a ferocious, needy dance that had been a long time coming.

We didn't let ourselves take it all the way that night. Both of us wanted to, but we were also far too frightened of the repercussions. Still, we were taking a risk. My fingers found the secret, soft inner folds between her thighs, and she cried out against my neck as I brought her to the first peak I'd ever led her to. She wrapped her hand around the hardened muscle beneath fabric that was far too tight, pulling a strangled moan from my throat as I joined her on that peak. Her forehead rested on my shoulder as we panted nearly in sync, coming down from the high we'd pulled each other to. My eyes were closed, so I can't say for sure, but I imagine hers were too as we both let it sink in that we'd just crossed a line we couldn't come back from, more dangerous than the one we'd crossed with that first kiss, her mother in the store next to our hiding place. Her fingers released me and mine slid away from her, but our heads remained leaned against each other.

The room was so quiet, I could hear my heartbeat pounding in my ears and could feel hers just softly against the side of my neck where her temple pressed to my skin. Neither of us knew what to do now. We'd unlocked the door already, but now it was wide open. I was trying to figure out how to break the oppressive silence, but she beat me to it.

"That was my fault. I wanted that."

Her fault. As if what we'd done was a mistake, wrong, something that needed punishment. I shook my head.

"No fault to be had, dearest," I whispered, turning to kiss the side of her head. I used the hand that hadn't been under her dress to tap under her chin and get her to lift her head, kissing her gently when she did. "Not an ounce of fault to be had."

"Are you sure? I...I feel like I pushed you, like I dragged you into it." Her voice cracked softly, and I kissed her even more gently.

"I'm sure. I wanted it too. I wanted more." I let my gaze drop to her lips, letting out a slow breath through my nose. "So much more."

"One day," she muttered, leaning in to take her own kiss. It was sweet, warm, and tinged with guilt. But I felt both of our hearts lighten.

I let her clean herself up in the bathroom first, leaning back against the headboard and staring up at the ceiling, hand in my hair. I had wanted everything she'd give me, and I would have done anything she'd asked. We'd enjoyed each other sexually for the first time, something that should have been joyous and ended with us curled around each other in bed until morning, but she'd have to leave in about three hours to be home in time. I was trying not to ruminate on it too much when she reappeared, freshened up and without the scent of our tryst on her.

"If you get cleaned up fast, I'll buy your food today." She was trying to lighten the mood, and I took it.

"I'm ordering the most expensive thing on the menu then."

Her grin was genuine. "Go right ahead."

October 16, 1919

Delightful afternoon with L.
Caught in rain also.

It was after she came back from Newport, months after that first encounter, that it happened again. The weather had turned nasty on us. We'd both gotten soaked through, and the closest shelter was my apartment. We'd been subconsciously–or rather, consciously but unsaid–avoiding it as much as we could, but now our hands were tied. I held my jacket over both of us as we ran, but it wasn't doing much to help. Clara's hair was slipping out of her pins and the rain was plastering it to her forehead and neck, and I had to keep tearing my eyes away from the sight. Something about her being slightly disheveled was lighting a spark deep within me.

By the time we made it to my apartment, my jacket was soaked through and dripping all over us, our shoes were waterlogged, and Clara's hair was almost entirely free from its pins. We dropped our shoes and jackets by the radiator, then Clara stood near the sink and started pulling the now useless pins from her hair while I closed the bedroom door between us as I dried off and changed. When I came back out, she'd gotten her hair completely loose and was wringing it out into the sink, grumbling about how tangled it was going to be. I chuckled and set my only other towel on the counter beside her, leaning forward to kiss her cheek.

"You can borrow some of my clothes while your dress dries, if you want. Everything's going to be way too big on you, but at least you'll be warm."

"Thank you," she breathed, kissing me softly before disappearing with the towel into my bedroom.

It took her but a moment to get out of her wet things and return in one of my shirts with the sash from her dress tied around her waist. I was right; the shirt absolutely dwarfed her, the hemline of it hanging down to her mid-thigh. Still, it was much, much shorter than her dress had been, and I did my best not to stare. My best wasn't great.

Clara draped her soaked dress over the rail by the radiator, sighing at the small puddle on the floor underneath our things. "I'm sorry about the mess."

I lifted my gaze from the backs of her knees, shaking my head. "No, it's fine, the radiator will dry that too." She sighed again, moving back to my bedroom. After a rustling, she returned with my mother's quilt wrapped around her like a cape, tugged tight against the chill on her legs.

"I'm borrowing this too." She declared rather than asked, and I didn't mind. It was the quilt from the trunk at the foot of my bed, and I had kept it for days like this, when it's just too cold to go and do anything else at all. Clara pulled one of the two chairs over to the radiator, re-situated the blanket around herself, and curled up as tightly as she could on the chair. Her chin rested on her knee as she watched the water droplets falling slowly off the hem of her dress.

The only noise in the room became the soft thumping of the radiator, the rain pattering against the window, and if it hadn't been in my chest, I would have sworn my heartbeat could be heard from across the room.

"I loathe getting caught in the rain," she grumbled quietly, shifting to look out the window. I smirked, softly, teasingly.

"I did warn you when the clouds started rolling in."

"Oh psh. It doesn't normally downpour like that."

I laughed, low in my chest. "Clara, you know we live right near a harbor, and therefore the ocean, right?" She turned to glare at me, and I just grinned. Getting up, I moved to sit on the floor beside her and soak up some of the heat from the radiator as well. She lifted a hand as I leaned in, stroking my hair away from my face ever so gently.

"At least your place was close."

"Mhm."

Silence fell over us again, and I closed my eyes against Clara's fingers running over my scalp. The rain didn't seem to be letting up anytime soon, but I was selfishly glad, because it meant she could stay with me for longer. I opened my eyes. Damnit.

"Your family is going to freak out."

Her sigh came from the very depths of her soul. "I'll just tell them the truth, I got caught by the rain and had to hide out until it stopped."

"But where did you hide?"

"I don't know, a shop or something. Mr. Weis will cover for me if I need him to, I'm sure." She was right, he was definitely someone we could trust.

"Do you want to go ask him before you head back?"

Another deep sigh. "Maybe. I don't know. I don't really care about anything besides being warm right now."

Her words made a horribly mischievous, slightly naughty idea come to mind. There were all sorts of ways I could think of to keep her warm, but I fought back the urge to voice them. I just adjusted my head against her leg, letting my eyes fall closed once more. Her hair-stroking paused as she tugged on a lock.

"Why are you pulling my hair?" When I looked up, her gaze was boring down on me.

"Leo, that was a hint. You're not dense." Her eyebrow raised, and I felt my blush before she saw it and smirked. So she'd had the same thoughts. Of course she had.

"Alright." I let my shocked expression melt into a grin, tilting my head to look up at her better. "How can I help?"

She slid off the chair and onto my lap, tucking herself into my arms and nestling her head under my chin. "This, for starters." Her bare leg pressed against my arm, and my heart picked up speed. Her head tilted, lips pressing to my neck, hands gently gripping my shirt. I lifted my arms, circling them around her, pulling her as close as I could. One of her hands rose to rest against the side of my neck she wasn't kissing, the other pressing against my heart. I let one of mine slide along her bare thigh, marveling at how soft she was, but was then shocked out of my thoughts at the chill she still had despite being out of the rain for so long. She really did need help warming up, innuendo or not.

"Your skin is actually ice, Clara." I shifted, interrupting her kisses to steal the quilt just briefly and wrap it around the both of us, clutching her to me underneath it. "I know what you want, but the chill is distracting me." She laughed, rolling her eyes.

"I told you to do something about it, loverboy." Her voice was so breathy, so intoxicating. So I compromised. I kept her against me, sharing my body heat, and reached down between her thighs. I was surprised to find she didn't have any underthings on, but her little gasp as I touched her was double the reward.

"Wh...where are your..." I whispered, my fingers curling against the soft curls I'd only explored one other time. She sighed happily against my shoulder.

"Hanging up in the bathroom." Her pleased little chuckle made me shake my head. She had been plotting and I hadn't seen it coming. She'd fooled me entirely, but I did not mind in the slightest. As my fingers began their work, Clara shifted to kiss my neck and jaw. I held the quilt tightly around us with one hand, keeping the other between her legs. Her idea of warming up was definitely working.

"Fine then, you win." I dipped my head, turning it to catch her lips, making her sit up a little. Her giggle betrayed just how pleased she was that she'd won our faux battle, and it dissolved into a sigh as I dragged a fingertip along the little bundle of nerves, that most sensitive area that caused all the best noises to spill from her lips. I kept my mouth against hers for the first few moments, wanting to feel every noise she made as I touched her. Then I pulled away, watching her head fall back, her eyes half closed as she stared up at me.

"Faster," she whispered, her lips staying parted on the last syllable. I turned my hand, giving myself better range of motion to do as she bid. Her hips bucked, seemingly involuntarily, against my touch as I hit the exact spot she wanted me to, and her back arched away from my arm. "Oh, oh God, yes–" she whined, eyes closing tightly as she tried not to buck again, tried to keep my touch in that same spot. A few seconds more and—"Leo! Oh!" She lost her control, her hips lifting higher, her hand reaching to grip my shirt hard. Her legs twitched, then lowered slowly as she moaned.

I smothered a pleased snicker at the sight, pulling my hand from between her legs and wrapping both arms around her to drag her against the reaction in me she'd caused. She shivered.

"Do you want another?" I whispered, turning my head to kiss the side of her neck. She groaned, nodding.

"Oh, please, yes. Please."

I gave her two more there on my lap, before shifting to sit her between my legs with her back against my chest. The quilt had fallen open, barely staying on my shoulders, and Clara's legs were spread enough I could almost see everything. If I just leaned forward a little more...I was glad she couldn't see how red my face surely was at the thought.

I kept one arm around her, a hand clasped over a breast, holding her to me tightly, using the other hand to please her at a much better angle now. My fingers slipped over her clit and downward, pressing toward the entrance to her warm core.

"Do you want–"

"Yes." She didn't even let me finish, reaching her hands up to tangle her fingers in my hair, her head falling back against her arm and my shoulder both. I took her permission, slipping just a single finger inside her, testing, probing. She was so warm, and so, so wet. I twitched against her back.

I slowly managed to find a pace and technique that she liked, listening to each little moan and whimper as if they were detailed instructions. After she clenched around me the first time, I slid a second finger in to join the first and was rewarded with the prettiest moan I'd heard so far. The grin on my face thankfully remained unseen by her closed eyes and tilted head.

"Ohhhhh God, Leo, mmm...more..." She spread her knees wider, pressing herself toward my hand, her own hands tightening in my hair.

"Like this?" I pumped both fingers slowly in and out of her. My voice was beneath her ear, lips tracing the soft skin underneath it. Her shiver was delightful.

"Mmm faster, please..."

I obeyed, picking up speed and trying to maintain it until she arched against me, her internal muscles clamping down hard around my fingers, her cry just my name, only Leo. I didn't really know what I was doing at that point, but I tightened my grip around her, lips pressed hard to the side of her neck and kept pumping into her. She cried out again, her legs twitching between mine, her hands falling to grab the arm that was around her. I kept it up, whispering low just how wonderful she sounded, how much I loved doing this to her, how *rewarding* it was to see her come undone at my touch.

All my efforts were rewarded with Clara reaching another, more desperate peak, before collapsing in my arms. She panted, head lolled to the side against me, one hand gripping my arm loosely. "L-Leo," she breathed, and I grinned while kissing her temple.

"Yes, dearest?"

"You're way too good with your hands." Her breathy response pulled a laugh from me, and we found ourselves holding each other as we laughed, pressed close, not allowing any more traces of guilt to taint the experience ever again.

We wanted each other. Loved each other, I was absolutely certain. And we weren't going to let someone we barely knew ruin that.

April 22, 1920

Reading new author – F. Scott. Enchanted.

We spent the years Reggie was at school acting as though he didn't exist. As if Clara wasn't now engaged, didn't have this unwanted, unchosen fiancé hanging over her. She told me that she saw him a few times in Newport over the summers, always chaperoned, never forced to be alone with him. It was a small blessing, but we counted it. We should have been spending all that time figuring out a plan to get rid of him, but swept up in young love and the emerging Jazz Age, we didn't. Looking back, I see how stupid it was. But I also see how happy we all were, and it makes me reluctant to trade the days for anything else.

In late March of 1920, a new author emerged and took the city–and a good portion of the rest of the world–by storm. Clara had bought his book, of course, and on one of the warmer April days, Marie and I chatted while Clara laid on the grass next to us and read.

Marie fell back onto Clara, laying across her back. "Are you going to ignore us in favor of Amory?" She giggled, and Clara groaned, trying to shake her off.

"No, I didn't mean to. Let me finish this paragraph." And so she did, Marie and I grinning at each other with a silent bet that we'd see Clara turn the page before too long. We did. Clara had gotten caught up in her novel, oblivious to the outside world even though it was literally pressing down on her in the shape of her best friend.

Another page turned, and Marie started laughing, rolling to take the book from Clara, marking her place with a finger. "You can have it back when we go home." Clara rolled over and tried to take it back, then gave up and just laid on the grass. I wanted to lean over and kiss her, but didn't want to make Marie uncomfortable.

"Who's Amory? Someone I need to worry about?" I teased. I figured it was the main character of the book. After moving to lay in the grass, I propped my head up with my hand. My ring, which I had moved to my ring finger as my hands settled into their final size, pressed into my cheekbone. Clara glared at me briefly, then shook her head.

"Not unless my type of man suddenly turns into a pigheaded, dramatic, and full-of-himself heel, you don't." She closed her eyes, relaxing into the park lawn as Marie tucked some slip of paper into the book, setting it aside.

"Well, that all sounds like Leo, so I suppose he's safe even if your type does turn." Marie covered her mouth to hide her grin, and I gasped in mock offense.

"You wound me, Marie."

She giggled. "I don't mean it." Marie shifted to lie between Clara and me, and I gently tugged on a bit of her hair. She laughed and batted me away. "Did you hear about the man who wrote that book?"

"What about him?" Clara asked, eyes still closed.

"I don't even know who he is." The novel was within reach, so I picked it up to look at the cover. "F. Scott Fitzgerald?" Marie nodded.

"He and his wife got kicked out of the Biltmore last week. Supposedly they had been causing all sorts of problems, even flooded their rooms."

"Flooded?" I hadn't heard any of this, but Marie was apparently caught right up. "How did they manage?"

She just shrugged, giggling a little. "Who knows? They do all sorts of strange things. I heard he did handstands in the lobby, and they both slide down the stair railing instead of walking properly."

"Sounds like they know how to have fun." Clara laughed from Marie's other side, and I looked over to see her eyes open, watching us. The storm gray caught me, and I only looked away when Marie spoke again.

"I heard they fight a lot too, and they're drunk all the time. Amazing he's able to write as much as he does."

The girls gossiped, and I laid there just watching them. All of this author's antics were taking place in Manhattan, not too far from where either of them lived, so it was possible they'd even happen upon the wild couple while they were out and about. But I couldn't help but think of what it would be like, to have that kind of absolute freedom. To be with the person you loved–although it seemed, by way of Marie's gossip, there were a lot of doubts about how much the Fitzgeralds loved each other–and to be able to show it in public.

I was daydreaming about staying at a large hotel like the Biltmore with Clara when Marie checked her little watch. "Oh, dear, we need to head back. I completely lost track of the time." She stood, brushing herself off and holding a hand out to Clara, who took it, then both girls held their hands out to me. The wicked thought of pulling them back down to me and trapping them on the lawn with me crossed my mind, but I shunned it in favor of letting them pull me up, then wrapping an arm around either one.

"Next Thursday?" I asked, kissing Clara on the cheek first, then Marie. They both giggled, and Marie swatted at my chest.

"Of course." Clara looked up at me, and I very nearly kissed her mouth right then and there, but Marie was still under my other arm.

"Until then, Leo!" Marie tugged away, retrieving Clara's book and their other things, linking Clara's elbow with hers.

"Til then, ladies." I watched them walk away, tucking my hands in my pockets. Thursdays never came soon enough.

July 14th, 1920

Newport party. Boring. Lonely. Want to return to city.

As if we'd thought Newport couldn't get any harder to deal with, the government had decided before the 1920 season that alcohol was an absolute sin and everyone needed to abstain from it. Of course, if you had a private supply you could finish it. And many did. Part of our wine cellar at home in New York got carted with us to Rhode Island, and to be quite honest it was one of the only decisions my parents ever made that I actually praised them for.

Marie's family had rented a house of their own that season, instead of just sending Marie along with us as they had the past few years. The forced separation made everything even worse. We still saw each other often, but not being able to just waltz into her bedroom or find her in the parlor was annoying. I liked having my best friend and confidante near.

It wasn't helping my happiness that I was continually being scolded for going out into the gardens and trying to better cultivate whatever plants the owners had decided to have their gardeners grow for them. There were so very many roses that were overgrown and having their run of the place, effectively choking out anything else trying to gain a footing in the area. After the third dress with shredded sleeves, Mother had banned me from going near the roses.

Which left me with very, very little to do other than wait for an invitation to go somewhere.

At one party, Marie and I had slumped gracefully against a wall, watching everyone else dance and chatter and generally be sociable. The owners of this house had decided to throw out all their liquor and wine and had confiscated any brought as hostess gifts. I had seen a few people with hip flasks, taking discreet swallows, but the owners had politely asked someone to leave because of just such an offense. As such, Marie and I were attempting to drown our boredom in sparkling cider and it was very much not working.

"This place is so much more rotten without a good glass of wine." I sighed into my glass, making a face at the last dregs of the cider. Marie was looking into her own glass, looking just as displeased as I felt.

"It truly is. Maybe the boys from the club have something stashed away?" She looked up and over the crowd, trying to spot one of the aforementioned boys. They were a group that we sometimes went out with, when we needed a date or an escort to specific parties or dinners. "The club" wasn't even a proper club; they didn't belong to an organization, but we met them at a dinner club, and that had become their moniker.

"I would be willing to bet my copy of *A Princess of Mars* that Johnathan does." I motioned with my glass to the man currently swinging Diane, one of our friends from New York, around the dance floor. Marie laughed.

"That's quite the wager, Clara. Of all books." She finished the last sip of her drink, setting it on a table nearby.

"That's how sure I am about it."

"Let's go find out then." She took my drink from me–I wasn't going to finish it anyway–and led me by the hand to Johnathan and Diane.

A quiet, quick conversation later, my suspicion was confirmed, and we were gathering in a parlor with some of the other boys and gals from New York. Johnathan produced two hip flasks, strapped to his calves instead of tucked near his hip, and held them up like trophies.

"Oh John, you can always be counted on." Diane was fluttering her eyelashes at him, her chin in her hand. I chose to ignore the deliberate flirting and held out a hand for one of the flasks.

"Clara, so thirsty tonight." Johnathan handed it over with a wink, and I ignored that as well, taking a long pull from the flask. I regretted it briefly as a very strong gin burned its way down my throat and I fought off a cough. The others guffawed.

"We should have warned you." One of the other boys took the flask from me, and I gave it up without a fight. The liquor was shockingly potent and quite frankly, didn't taste very good. But that wasn't the point.

Marie had claimed the edge of one of the couches and I made my way over to collapse next to her. Though I had only had a few swallows of the contraband, and I certainly wasn't a lightweight, I could already feel the muscles in my shoulders unknotting, and I closed my eyes with the sensation.

"Is that better?" Marie was teasing me, but I just nodded, folding my hands on my lap. Floating just a bit through the rest of the night would make surviving it so much easier. Marie took one of my hands and held it, keeping me from floating too far.

The rest of the people in the parlor had started singing, some song I was sure I knew but couldn't remember the words to just then. The music from the ballroom was faintly in the distance, making for a strange, dissonant mix of sounds.

"I hate this place," I whispered, and felt Marie lean closer to hear me.

"What?"

"I hate this place." I had only meant to speak it a little louder, but any control I had over my volume was gone. The others in the room paused, a few agreeing instantly, a few looking nervous and unsure. "Apologies. Continue with your frivolity." I waved my hand dismissively, and the nervous ones took the cue gladly, starting up another song. The ones who had agreed with me joined in after passing the flasks around one more time. Someone put it in my hand, but I just held onto it instead of partaking. After a bit, Marie took it from me and I peeked at her as she took a small sip.

"I hate this place too," she said, setting the flask down on the table near our sofa. "But mostly because it makes you so miserable." She squeezed my hand, and we tucked ourselves into the cushions, shoulders pressed together, hands intertwined, listening to the rest of our little club sing every song they knew and some they didn't.

May 5th, 1921

Beautiful gift from L!
Sang with M. on train.

When I met Clara and Marie at the train station, they barely noticed me on the platform. It wasn't unusual for them to be arm in arm, glued at the hip as they were, but I could only think of a few other times I'd seen them walk off the train while singing, and they'd all been around Christmas. I stamped out my cigarette before they noticed it.

"My olwd New Jousey hooommme!!" They were clear of the train now and paused on the platform to do a little synchronized kicking dance, falling into laughter after only a few seconds of it. The New Jersey accent was very overdone, very faked. I stayed in my spot to watch them. They tried doing the little dance again, but they kicked out of sync and ended up kicking each other.

"Oh no! I'm sorry!" Marie was laughing through her apology, stumbling as she tried to catch Clara who was doubling over with laughter. I stepped forward at that point, sliding my arm around Clara's waist and hoisting her up so she could drape her arm over my shoulder. Once Marie was relieved of her burden, she took my other arm.

"Leo!" they cried in unison, and I grinned.

"Our hero!" Clara reached up with her free hand to pat my face.

"Saving us from ourselves!" Marie was still giggling and squeezed my bicep with both hands.

"Don't I always?" I teased, earning a wrinkled nose from Clara and a light pinch from Marie.

After shifting her arm from my shoulders, Clara linked it through mine and we set off together to our usual haunts. If it were the park, the music store, or the diner first, I'd leave it up to the girls to decide.

It ended up being the music store, since it had started drizzling on our way from the station. Which meant my little surprise would have to be delayed just a bit. Clara and Marie both released me and pushed through the door first, calling out to Mr. Weis.

"Hello sir! We have a question!"

Mr. Weis, who had been old but spritely from the very first time we'd visited the shop, was now prone to staying behind the counter on his stool. But he never ceased to entertain us, and we him. He chuckled pleasantly as he folded his book shut and greeted us.

"Hello, my favorite trio. What can I help with?"

"Do you have any of the music from the new show at the Ambassador?" Clara asked, leaning on the counter in front of him.

"It's called *The Rose Girl*. Just opened!" Marie added, leaning on Clara's back and peeking over her shoulder.

"Oh, well, can't say that I do unless they're using old songs. If it's just opened, they'll still be guarding their music like treasure for a while yet." Mr. Weis pushed himself up off his stool, making his way to the rack that held all of the sheet music. "Just got this in, though. You might know it."

The girls followed after him like a pair of baby ducks, Marie's arm sliding through Clara's as they went.

"Can Leo play it?" Clara asked, and I laughed.

"Is that the basis of every sheet of music you buy?"

"Of course! If it's not playable on your guitar, I'm not buying it." She shot me a grin over her shoulder and I shook my head. I shouldn't have thought any different. Mr. Weis was chuckling at us again.

"Yes, he can play it. Here you are." He pulled the sheet and handed it to Clara, who gasped in delight at it.

"'Ain't We Got Fun'!! You ordered this just for me, didn't you?!" She giggled, and Mr. Weis smiled.

"Not only for you, but I did think of you three when I ordered it."

"How lovely!" Marie clapped, and the girls followed him back to the counter to buy it.

I tucked my hands in my pockets, curling my fingers around the little box in the right one. I couldn't wait to show the girls what was inside it.

"Leo! We bought it! You have to play it for us now!" Clara was holding the sheet of music up in front of my face, and I lowered her hands gently with a laugh.

"Of course I will. Let me learn it first."

We chatted with Mr. Weis a little longer. The girls made him promise to find the music from *The Rose Girl* as soon as he could, and he cheerfully agreed. He really had become a surrogate grandfather to us all and tended to indulge us like one. We took our leave and I took charge of the direction, looping a girl on each arm and heading toward the diner for a late lunch.

"I am absolutely withering away. I cannot wait to eat." Clara pushed open the door of the diner and led the way in, so I caught the door and held it for Marie. She did a little curtsy, holding one side of her dress out and bowing her head.

"Dear sweet Leo, such a better and more polite friend than Clara could ever be." She started out the sentence seriously but was giggling by the end of it.

"I heard that!" Clara called from a nearby table; our normal booth was occupied. She pulled out one of the chairs and gestured at it. "My darling Marie, if you'd accept this seat, I'd be most delighted."

Glenn, who had been our regular waiter for the past couple months and was therefore used to our shenanigans, was already setting down a pitcher of iced tea and some lunch menus, looking amused. Marie strode over to the seat and sat down as dramatically as she could, swishing her skirt over her knees as she did. Clara pushed in Marie's chair for her, dropping a napkin on her lap as well.

"Oh, I must retract my earlier statement." Marie covered her mouth as she giggled and Clara took the chair next to her. I curled my fingers around the box in my pocket once more before I joined them at the table. "You might be equal now."

"This is acceptable." Clara and I both grinned, then looked up as Glenn came back.

"What'll it be today, friends?" His smile was always so charming, but I caught his gaze lingering on me just a bit longer than was proper that day. We wore about the same hairstyle—it was popular at the time—but his was a dark red, with brilliant green eyes to complement. He was exceptionally handsome, with a face truly wasted as a waiter. He should have been a model or film star, at the very least. I turned a little toward him, draping my arm across the back of the empty chair beside me.

"I'd like to hear your best guess. How well do you know our orders?" I said it with the most sincere grin I could manage because I didn't want him to think we were taunting or picking on him. Luckily, he caught my intent and grinned back.

"Well, Clara will most likely have the turkey sandwich. It's warm today, so Marie will want something cold..." Glenn shifted his pen and notepad into one hand so he could hold his chin in thought. "Probably the sliced chicken and potato salad. And for Leo, hm." He looked at me, pretending to be serious but I could see the glint of mischief in his eye. It was undeniably attractive.

Clara and Marie had been watching the proceedings with their chins in their hands, giggling in agreement with everything he'd said so far. We hadn't known him all that long, nine weeks at most, but the waiter had our habits figured out. I was waiting for him to choose for me, but he seemed to be taking the excuse of thinking it over as a chance to look at me for longer. I had to admit I didn't mind in the slightest. He was handsome. It was nice to look at him as well.

Glenn snapped his fingers, then pointed at me. "Toasted ham and cheese." He nodded, absolutely sure of his choice.

"You've got every single one of us pinned." Clara laughed. "That's exactly what I was thinking of ordering."

"Me too. I would love some potato salad right now." Marie leaned back in her chair, her hands falling to the table. "Go ahead and ring that right up, Glenn!"

He chuckled, pleased with himself. "I'll do just that. Leo? Was I right?" He had already scribbled the girls' orders down on his notepad, and added mine as I nodded.

"You've got us pinned for sure, Glenn." I gave him another grin, which he returned before scurrying off to the kitchen. Clara and Marie giggled very hard at that, and I turned to face them.

"What?"

"Glenn only has eyes for you, it seems. He barely glances at me or Marie whenever we're here." Clara reached across the table to pour herself some tea, and I caught her hand to kiss it. She blushed.

"Are you worried I'll follow him to Hollywood when he finally goes?"

"N-no." Clara shook her hand free and laid her hands on her cheeks, giggling. Marie poured the tea for all of us with a wide grin.

"Every time you kiss her hand it's as if it's the first time you've ever done it."

"Stop, stop. Cease!" Clara was waving her hand at Marie, who only laughed. I settled back in my chair, arm still draped comfortably over the back of the empty one. If Clara reacted like that to my kisses every time for the rest of our lives, I would live a happy life.

It didn't take too long for Glenn to bring our food out, and he set it all down with a flourish as if we were at the Plaza instead of just a little diner in Brooklyn. We all applauded him for it and he took a bow with the same amount of flourish.

"Please go to Hollywood already, Glenn. We would miss you so much, but you are wasted here." Clara had her sandwich in one hand and her other on her heart, pleading. Glenn only smiled.

"Ah Miss Clara, I cannot afford it." He held up a hand before she could speak. "You wouldn't be the first person I've refused money from for it, either." His smile grew into a true, brilliant grin. "But I'm flattered you think so highly of me."

"We all do! Maybe you could try Broadway?" Marie was mixing her potato salad to her satisfaction but glanced up at him. "Have you already done that?"

"I haven't, but I do always hear of auditions opening up."

"Please go to one! We'll come see whatever show you're in." Marie looked up at him with puppy-dog eyes. Glenn put a hand over his face to laugh.

"You're going to break me with that expression." He lowered his hand but looked to the ceiling. "I will go to the next one that strikes my interest, I promise." He looked back at her, and Marie grinned.

"I hope you know we will all be holding you to that," she said, then dug into her meal.

"Will you come as well? To my show?" Glenn turned to me, and I nodded.

"Of course. Glenn on stage would be a spectacle to behold."

He was floating on air the rest of the time he served us. He did go to Broadway once and ended up in Hollywood not long after. We found this out by going to a movie and seeing him in the background as an extra. It was a non-speaking role, but he was still there, and it was the only time we'd ever applauded and cheered at the cinema.

The day we'd begged him though, his shift ended before we left the diner and we were still sitting at the table chatting when his replacement came over to clear dishes away. When he was finished, I reached into my pocket and set the box on the table.

"What is that?" both girls asked, Clara closing the novel she'd just opened.

Marie leaned closer. "Leo, this has a jewelry store logo on it. What have you done?"

"Open it and find out." I motioned to it, and Clara picked it up. They both gasped in delight once she removed the lid.

"Leo! What have you done?!" Marie asked again, but this time as she reached over to take the box from Clara, who was still looking into it with her mouth open. "Is that a real ruby?"

I nodded. "A ruby and a moonstone, for your birth months." Moonstone was a common replacement for the much more expensive diamond at the time.

"Oh, Leon," Clara whispered, plucking the moonstone ring gently from the box. "This had to be so expensive."

I shook my head. "Not at all. You girls only cost me about four dollars this time."

"That's still unnecessary!" Marie had already slid the little ruby and gold ring onto her middle finger and was holding it up to the light to watch it sparkle.

"It wasn't. I had to do this." I shifted to rest my arms on the table, taking Clara's hand gently to slide the moonstone onto her middle finger. My gold band that she'd bought me all those years ago tucked right next to it when I interlaced our fingers. She looked up at me and I saw her eyes watering, but she was smiling.

"Why?" Marie asked, laying her hand on top of ours, the little ruby topping it all off like a cherry on a sundae.

"Clara's birthday was just a bit ago, and yours is soon, but you'll be in Newport for it. I wanted to give you both something for them." I squeezed Clara's fingers gently, then lifted my other hand to lay on top of Marie's. "I wanted you both to have a set that matched, so you could tell everyone who asked that you bought them for each other as a pair, but the gold is the same as the ring Clara got me, so it's a trio. Like we are."

Both girls stared at me, obviously touched, eyes watering, and I laughed. "Goodness, I didn't realize you both would get so upset over it, maybe I should take them back..." I moved to grab both rings and they both jerked their hands away, Clara pressing hers to her heart and Marie holding hers high out of reach.

"Don't you DARE!" they both said, and I laughed harder.

I never saw either of them without the rings from then on.

March 9th, 1922

New F. Scott not as good.
Teased at lunch.

It was just a couple years later that Fitzgerald put out another novel, and the Thursday after it released, Clara was once again absorbed in the book instead of talking to Marie and me. This time, we were in the diner instead of at the park because the snow was refusing to give up its hold.

"Leo, do you think Clara reads to avoid talking to us?" Marie asked from across the table, and I laughed.

"Oh, probably. She doesn't like to discuss her stories with us. Have you seen how possessive she is over John?" Clara's Barsoom series had been published as more novels, and she'd collected every one. There was a new one finishing up in the

All-Story at the time as well. Clara told us it was about John and Dejah's daughter.

"I'd be worried about John if I were you. I'm sure she'd drop you for him in a heartbeat, Dejah or no Dejah." Marie propped her head up in her hands, elbows on the table. We'd both been looking at Clara as she read, and she was steadfastly ignoring us. Or so we thought.

"I'd never drop Leo for anyone," she said, turning the page. "It's not my fault neither of you appreciate a good story."

"I've read every single book you've lent me," Marie pouted, reaching over to lay her hand across the pages. Clara glared up at her, but it was soft and unserious. "All of them. Just not at the table with friends." Marie grinned, and Clara relented, tucking the book away.

"Ah, she returns to us." Her glare turned on me as I spoke, and I could tell she was trying not to stick out her tongue. I just grinned.

"It's not my fault you don't know how to read either, Leo." She picked up the mug of coffee she'd ordered, shuddering at it as she discovered it was cold.

"I do too know how to read. I read over your shoulder all the time." I leaned back against our booth seat, crossing my arms in mock offense. Marie giggled, copying me. Clara rolled her eyes.

"You two are insufferable. But so is that book." She put it back on the table. "I liked *This Side of*

Paradise much more, and I'm not even halfway into this."

Marie picked it up, opening to the first page. "Is Anthony an even bigger popinjay than Amory?"

"Worse, he's a popinjay who pretends he isn't one." Clara chuckled. "I haven't even gotten to the main point, I don't think."

"Which one's Amory again?" I asked, reaching for the book. Marie handed it to me.

"The lead of *This Side of Paradise*. A rotter, really, but watching him grow up was amusing." Clara had turned a little in the booth, leaning back against the wall to better face Marie and I.

"'In 1913, when Anthony Patch was twenty-five, two years were already gone since irony, the Holy Ghost of this later day, had, theoretically at least, descended upon him.'" I read from the book, then laughed. "Clara, how do you read this? That sentence alone is so hard to follow." The girls laughed with me, Clara nodding.

"Fitzgerald likes to take the path least traveled when he writes a sentence."

I read aloud a little more from the book, dramatically, but softly. We were still in public. I did hear a chuckle from the booth behind us, and the girls were both smothering laughter. After the first little section, I snapped the book shut and handed it back to Clara.

"I told you that I could read."

She grinned, leaning forward. "I knew you could." I didn't normally kiss her while around Marie, but she was close and smiling and open to it, so I did. Marie made a fake noise of disgust, and after we pulled apart I saw she had her hand over her eyes. She was still giggling.

"Behave yourselves. Everyone around us will think I'm a terrible chaperone." She lowered her hand to her mouth, but her grin was still obvious behind it.

"You *are* a terrible chaperone. Look what's happening on your watch," Clara said, and grabbed my tie just to kiss me again, making Marie laugh even harder.

June 19th and 20th, 1922

Bought time. Displeased still.
R. is vexing.

In Newport, I was stationed next to Reggie at the dinner table while his father and mine discussed some business or another and Reggie tried to engage me in a discussion of his own business. It was the first time Reggie was joining us for the entire season. He had gotten a job at a lending firm in Connecticut right after he had finished his schooling, and it was apparently going well for him. The more he spoke about it the more I saw my future laid out before me, just like the food laid before me on my dinner plate. The roast chicken representative of the meat of the relationship—our unwanted (at least on my side), unchosen betrothal, and my loathing of him—the side of potatoes smothered in gravy playing the part of our families supporting the union and smothering us in their expectations. I hadn't quite decided what the vegetables would be when my father spoke, in a voice clearly directed to our side of the table.

"Now then, how are things in Connecticut, my boy?" Father leaned back in his chair, hands folding over his stomach as our footmen started clearing the plates. I managed to steal the last carrot from mine before it was taken away.

Reggie beamed, shifting to rest his arm along the back of his chair, his fingertips lightly grazing the back of mine. I could feel it like a bolt of electricity, as if he'd touched my shoulder instead. "Oh perfectly well sir. I've been told that I should make partner in just a few years if I keep on as I am. And I plan to." The glasses hadn't been cleared yet, so he lifted his toward my father and drained the last of his wine.

I saw my opportunity and swallowed a gasp. Father hadn't responded yet, so I did, grinning at Reggie for good measure. A little show couldn't hurt. "Oh, Reginald! How wonderful! You should absolutely keep on as you are then and make partner without a home life to distract you."

Reggie's grin sharpened, and his black eyes turned to me. I knew he could tell I was up to something, and he did not appreciate it. I refused to recoil under his oppressive gaze. "Whatever do you mean, love?" His hand took hold of the back of my chair properly, and I leaned away from it as surreptitiously as I could. It was raining buckets outside, but I was tempted to run right into it and away from him. I forced myself to stay put.

"I just mean that you're doing so well, and learning to live with another person, take care of them, and having their schedule interrupting yours...it would make it so unnecessarily difficult on you." I tilted my head, telling myself that laying a hand on his arm was probably too obvious of a show. "I so very much do not wish to make your life difficult."

"What are you talking about, girl?" Father called from the end of the table, and I spun to find both pairs of parents looking at me quizzically. I just smiled, fluttering a hand to my heart.

"I am a person who demands so much attention; my mother can attest to this." I looked at her, and she laughed and nodded, as if on cue. "I desperately do not wish for that to be a problem for our Reginald as he's working so hard to climb the ladder in his office."

Reggie's mother smiled in what seemed to be approval, and his father laughed. "You're a very smart girl, Clara!" he said, and I smiled bashfully.

"That she is," Reggie said from beside me as he set his wine glass down sharply, catching the edge of a remaining spoon as he did. "That she is."

It took great efforts to suppress the shudder that traveled down my spine at the tone of his voice.

The next day, we were meant to go to the Newport Casino to watch the tennis championships since the rain had stopped and the matches weren't canceled. Mother and Father had decided to stay home, which left Reggie and me going on our own. I wanted so badly to refuse, but I knew after my line-toeing the previous night, that would have been a terrible idea. So, dressed in one of my favorite summer dresses, with a reminder that Marie would be there in my heart, I held tight to the seat of Reggie's car as he sped down the road. I liked the car very much. He'd said it was a Rolls-Royce Silver Ghost, and it would be the crown jewel of our estate once we built it. That part I didn't like nearly as much. Or at all.

The casino was hosting the championships on the lawn, surrounded by two layers of viewing porches where people of society mingled and talked during the games. I found Marie and linked her arm with mine as she introduced me to the man with whom she was speaking. His name left my mind immediately, and I felt no remorse, for she abandoned him quickly to be at my side instead. I asked her if she would be in trouble for being rude to him, and she laughed and said she'd only met him a few minutes before I'd found her.

We were pressed against a railing on the second level, leaning out and watching the tennis players bat the tiny ball back and forth across the field, when Reggie found us.

"Clara, Marie, finally. I can't let either of you out of my sight for a moment, can I?" His smile was not happy.

"Oh, Reginald, nice to see you. It's been—" Marie started.

"Since last summer, of course." Reggie finished for her. Marie's and my hands found each other on the railing, silently agreeing to stay by the other's side until we were forced apart. I could feel her little ruby ring pressed against my finger, and I pressed my thumb into my own moonstone one on my other hand. Reggie pushed past me to the railing. "Your lovely friend has delayed our nuptials once more, my dear Marie. Whatever am I to do with her?" He looked over, and Marie shrugged, pretending to be casual.

"I'm sure dear Clara has her reasons. What are her conditions?"

"She wants to help me make partner at the firm by not distracting me." He grinned, and I looked away from the black holes of his eyes before they could swallow me.

"That seems reasonable." Marie squeezed my hand, as Reggie's eyes landed back on the field.

"Hmm, I suppose," he mused, and I straightened.

"Oh, Marie, I see Diane. Let's go say hello." Thankfully, I *had* seen one of our other friends from New York across the way, and tugged Marie behind me. "I'll find you again, Reginald!"

He glared after us.

Diane absorbed us into her party, and we were able to spend the rest of the day with them. It was far preferable to being at Reggie's side, although the few glimpses I caught of him as we moved about the casino provided me with enough information as to his mood that I never did more than glance.

Even though he was silent the entire way home, the grip on his steering wheel and the aggression in his driving were enough to betray his thoughts. Before I got out of the car, he caught my wrist, tugging me to him.

"I will make partner before we wed, Clara, but only because our parents have agreed to it. Then, you will be mine. Do you understand me?"

All I could do was nod. My heart was pounding too fast and his eyes were too black, too deep, already trying to consume me.

"Good." With the final word snapped, he released me and I scurried out of the car, up the stairs, and all the way to my room. It was an hour before I even told my parents I'd returned, and I excused myself from dinner that night, hiding behind the lie of badly cooked fish at the championship.

I'd bought myself a little more time, but who knew how much?

Halloween, 1922

Séance! Utter nonsense. Spooky.

"Would you gals," I started, sliding into our normal booth at the diner, "like to go to a séance with me?"

They both started laughing as they settled in their seats. Clara alternated between sitting next to me and sitting next to Marie, and this time she was at Marie's side.

"A séance? Those are all fake. Don't you know that?" Marie giggled, and Clara leaned her chin on her hand with a grin.

"Gosh, Leo, have you been swindled by a great madame promising you can speak to your loved ones?" Clara's grin softened just a little, and she gave me a specific look, one that I decoded as, 'I don't mean to disrespect your mother's memory.'

I winked at her and clasped my hands on the table, leaning toward the girls as if delivering a secret.

"I have not. But I have been told that the great and powerful Madame Prudence Ethel will be in Brooklyn for Hallow's Eve, and I already bought three tickets to her Halloween show."

"You bought them before you asked us?" Marie shook her head, but she was still smiling. "Were you going to drag Timothy along if we said no?"

"Of course I was. He could use a little whimsy and magic in his life, don't you think?" I nodded along with my comments, as if it were the best life advice I had ever given. Clara laughed, and Marie just shook her head again.

"Well then, I suppose we'll have to attend." Clara picked up her menu and started flicking through the pages we all knew so well. Marie copied her. "When is it? Right on Halloween?"

"Yes, and it's rather late at night, so I suppose you'll have to find some excuse." I lifted my hand to hold my jaw as the girls looked at each other, communicating silently in that way women can.

"I'm sure we can think of something. There's no shortage of parties on Halloween." Clara shrugged lightly, and the matter was settled. I gave them the rest of the details over lunch and Clara penciled them onto the endpaper of the novel she had in her bag.

"You'll regret that, defacing your books," Marie twittered as Clara tucked the book back away.

"I'll erase it later. I would more regret forgetting the details of our soirée with Leo." Lifting her head, she returned my wink from earlier, and I found myself wishing we were alone and not in public. But I got myself together quickly, and we spent the rest of our lunchtime speculating on what might happen at the séance.

We found out half a week later. Marie and Clara had discovered one of their other friends was hosting a dinner party they could attend for a while and then head to Brooklyn after, all while pretending they'd been at the party the whole time. It meant we couldn't have dinner together, as we'd talked about at the diner, but it was a small price to pay.

With a girl on each of my arms, we made our way to the auditorium where Madame Prudence Ethel was giving her performance. It seemed like overkill for a séance, but I was sure we were in for a fake Halloween show instead of an actual meeting with the dead. The auditorium was normally used for Vaudeville and had been ever so slightly converted for the night into a spooky, dimly lit space with more curtains than normal.

We settled around our table, a single candle in the middle of it and a drink menu next to that. I chuckled; we were definitely in for a show.

"Mother would have a fit if she knew where I was," Marie said through laughter, and Clara agreed, hers would as well. "How indecent of us to associate with such *charlatans!*" I could only assume she was mimicking her mother's voice, but Clara's reaction confirmed it.

We were still snickering softly when the house lights dimmed further, and the stage curtains parted enough for a woman to step through. She wore long, flowing robes, and had a jeweled turban perched on her head. With long necklaces around her throat and draping over her chest, stacks of bracelets on her arms, and at least one ring on every finger, she absolutely looked the part of mysterious fortune teller and bridge to the spirit world.

"Welcome, my dear friends, welcome." Her overdone accent which might have been trying to be Russian or something similar was ultimately impossible to place. Marie and Clara both smothered laughter behind their hands. "We gather here on this night when the veil is at its thinnest, this sacred day of Samhain, All Hallow's Eve, to speak with those who would speak with us."

I coughed, masking a laugh. *To speak with those who would speak with us.* The woman ignored similar reactions from others in the crowd, lifting her hands to the sky. The curtains parted the rest of the way behind her. A table with a crystal ball and candles stood alongside a large ornate chair, which the woman spun around to sit in.

"Spirits, spirits be with us now! We call upon you who have words to share! We summon ye, we summon ye!" Her calls and cries continued for at least a full minute, accompanied by mysterious music played from somewhere out of sight. The music got louder until there was a loud crash of thunder, and the great Madame's head and hands hit the table in sync.

All was silent. I felt Clara and Marie reach for either one of my hands. Even thinking she was a fraud didn't erase the discomfort of watching her just lie there after her head had smacked the hard wood.

After a few uncomfortable moments, the entire audience seeming to hold their breath, she lifted her head and hands with a drawn-out groan. The lighting shifted to just a spotlight on her, and she reached toward it.

"Ohhhh spirit, tell me your name, tell me who you wish to speak with, spirit!" she called, her arms trembling with how far she stretched them. "Henry! Henry speak with us!" At the name, there was a small gasp at the back of the room. Someone must have known a Henry.

"He says...Henry says! He wishes to tell..." Her words were stammered, her head tilted as if she was listening. "Henry says he is sorry! He is so sorry! He is in tears! Sobbing!" It was just vague enough that whoever had known a Henry would take it to heart, and I shook my head. Clara lifted her other hand to rest her chin in it, and Marie released my hand to lean back in her chair.

Four more spirits visited Madame Prudence Ethel that night, each with similar vague things to say. A woman asked her to contact her late husband about a matter involving their safety deposit box at the bank, and Madame could not get him to speak. The woman would have to try again in a private setting; her husband did not wish the entire audience to know the secret. Clara had to smother a cackle behind her hand, pressing her palm hard to her lips, eyes twinkling with amusement. I squeezed her other hand and smirked. Marie was rolling her eyes to the ceiling, slumped enough in her chair that her head nearly rested on the back of it.

Madame was halfway through the next requested connection—this time a departed son, lost to the war. Madame said he was lost in France and the mother said he'd never left England during his tour—when Clara suddenly froze, her eyes fixed to a point on the left side of the stage. I followed her gaze and just saw curtains.

As the great Madame finished her act, rising from her table and bowing so low her turban nearly touched the floor, we all applauded politely even though we knew she'd been faking it all along. It was entertaining, at least. The girls slid their arms through mine on either side as we made our way down the sidewalk, mimicking her accent.

"Oh great spirits of Halloween, please bring us an actual medium! One who can speak with spirits for real!" Marie's accent fell apart on her last few words, and we all laughed. Clara's faded first, and her gaze dropped. Marie and I both looked at her.

"What is it, dearest?" I asked, tugging her closer to my side.

"Oh, I just..." She bit her lower lip, shaking her head once. "I thought I saw something in the auditorium. It was probably just part of the show, but it looked like a man standing on the left side of the stage."

So that's what had gotten her attention. "I didn't see anything."

"I didn't either. What did it look like?" Marie leaned around me to look at Clara, who shrugged.

"Just a man, maybe a little transparent? I'm sure it was just a Pepper's Ghost effect or something like that, to add to the atmosphere. Maybe it was best seen from where I was sitting?"

"Maybe so." Marie nodded, but her brow furrowed. I squished Clara's arm into my ribs, giving her an encouraging grin.

"You got the best seat in the house then," I offered, hoping to ease her tension.

Clara grinned, but it wasn't quite in her eyes. "I guess I did."

April 12, 1923

Safety Last! with L. and M. Very funny. Long talk with L. after.

The sunlight was absolutely blinding as we stepped out of the cinema. I lifted a hand to block it from my eyes, Clara taking my other one as we stepped onto the sidewalk.

"Gosh! That was so fun!" The girls were going on about the film we'd just seen. "I thought he was going to fall off the building at least four times."

"Me too!" Marie exclaimed. "Those pigeons really gave him a run for his money!"

I was navigating the sidewalk now, the girls too distracted to do anything but follow. Honestly, the film *had* been very funny, and I'd had a great time. But Marie and Clara whispering to each other about how handsome Harold was through the entire thing had been very grating.

"I wonder if he looks just as charming off screen as well," Clara mused.

"Oh I'm sure, the camera is an exact image, isn't it?"

I rolled my eyes, shaking my head. They didn't even notice, and I decided to tune them out unless I heard my name. I was a little annoyed at myself. I wasn't normally the jealous type at all. Something about Clara praising a man who wasn't fictional was clenching my jaw.

You can listen to her sigh about and moon over John Carter for years, but the moment she praises an actor you lose your composure? I was in the middle of admonishing myself when I finally heard my name.

"Leo?" Clara tugged on my arm, and I looked back at her. She and Marie were both peering at me curiously.

"What is it?" We'd stopped at a corner, waiting for the street to clear so we could cross.

"Where are you taking us?" Marie giggled a little nervously, pointing up at the street signs. I'd led them four blocks farther than I'd meant to.

"Damn." I sighed, pushing my hair back. "Sorry." I pulled Clara's arm through mine and did the same with Marie with the other. Both girls laughed as they settled on either side of me.

"What on Earth are you thinking about, dearest?" Clara took hold of my sleeve, and she grinned teasingly up at me. I frowned. My actual thoughts were too damning.

"Were we annoying you at the cinema?" Marie's voice, sweet as sugar, carried a note of worry, and I shook my head immediately.

"No, no, you weren't talking any more than anyone else there."

The girls glanced at each other and took a firm hold of my arms, and I found myself being marched back a few blocks to the diner we usually went to. The girls pushed me into a booth and sat across from me, Clara with her arms crossed.

"What is it that's bothering you?" she said a little more sternly than normal, Marie looking at me pityingly from her side.

I sighed and pushed my hands into my hair. "Nothing. It's silly."

"It isn't silly if it's bothering you." The girls said this almost in unison, and I couldn't help but laugh at it. There was no getting out of this.

"I got a bit jealous, is all," I mumbled my words, keeping my head in my hands. I saw Clara's hands rest on the table as she leaned closer.

"What was that?"

Another sigh before I spoke. "I got a bit jealous."

"Over Harold?" Marie was trying not to giggle, and I heard it in her words. I folded my arms and rested my head on them. "Aww, Leo." She did giggle then, just a little.

Clara patted my head with her hand. She was giggling too now. "Aww, Leo indeed. We just think he's handsome. For all we know he's a terrible jerk."

"You know we would rather spend our time with you." Marie reached out to pat my head as well, which did not help the embarrassment that was turning my face red and keeping my head down.

They didn't tease me further but did stop talking about Harold. They turned their discussion to the plot itself, all the stunts, how they could have been filmed, everything but the lead actor's looks. I kept my head down until I felt the blush fade. Clara grinned at me as I lifted my head. They'd ordered some lemonade and a couple of pastries while I recovered, and she pushed a glass to me.

"Feeling better, my dear possessive boy?" I must have looked much better if she was back to teasing me. I sipped the lemonade and glared at her over it, but it only made her laugh.

"He just wants us all for his own." Marie set her chin in her hand, grinning.

"Is that so bad?" I asked, mimicking her pose. "How dare I not want to share the two best girls in the city."

It was their turn to blush, even though I'd said similar things in the past. But I grinned all the same, even as they jokingly swatted at me. My revenge was as sweet as my company.

Marie had to leave before Clara did—some dinner or another she was expected at. We walked her to the station, Clara kissed her cheek, then as Marie's train left, Clara wrapped her arms around my waist with a grin.

"Were you really that jealous over Harold? That's not like you, dearest."

I blushed again, groaning as my head sank to her shoulder. "I'd nearly forgotten, why did you have to remind me?"

Clara was laughing, patting my back sympathetically. "Aww, I'm sorry. I only wanted to know." I sighed, standing straight and pulling her arm through mine.

"Yes, a little, like I said at the diner." With my free hand, I pushed my hair back again. There was no use lying when I'd already admitted it once. We left the station, weaving our way into the foot traffic on the sidewalk.

"You've never seemed to get jealous of anyone before." She clutched at my sleeve, and I glanced over to see her concerned expression turned up to me. I rubbed the back of my neck.

"I suppose it's different when I'm looking at him at the same time? I'm actually not sure." I shrugged, and Clara tucked closer to me.

She stayed quiet for a bit, seemingly thinking things over, and I returned to berating myself. It was so ridiculous, both girls had cooed over plenty of handsome men before, and it had never bothered me. I reached my hand into my jacket pocket for my cigarettes, but Clara laid a hand on my arm and forced me to lower it.

"Leo, is it perhaps the plot of the movie you're jealous about, and not the actor?" Her question was quiet, and we paused at a new corner. Her look of concern had remained, the furrow between her brows deepened just a bit.

I looked back at her, into that storm gray of her eyes, then closed my own. She was right, by the stars, she was right. Her arm threaded a little tighter through mine, and she pulled my bicep to her chest.

"Let's go to your apartment, hm?" I opened my eyes to her soft smile, and she reached up to kiss me just as softly.

"Gladly," I whispered, stealing another soft peck of her lips before crossing the street.

We had barely gotten through my door when she pushed me back against it, turning the lock and shutting out the world as her lips met mine again. I settled my hands on her hips, bowing my head to deepen the kiss.

"I want to be successful for you," I was whispering against her mouth, keeping our lips close. "I want to climb buildings for you. I want to be able to buy you beautiful things and have you come to live with me so we can get married."

Clara didn't respond right away, only kissed me harder. After a few long moments she leaned back, taking my face in both her hands. "I don't need beautiful things from you, I don't need you to climb buildings. I just need you, here, waiting for me. You are the best part of my life. You know that, don't you?"

My hands tightened on her hips, and I bowed my head to press my forehead to hers. "You're the best part of mine."

I just want you here forever, instead of once a week.

Clara leaned in to kiss me again, pushing her hands up into my hair. Sliding my hands from her hips, I wrapped my arms solidly around her waist as I pulled her close to me. I spun to press her against the door, lifting her a bit. She gasped, draping her arms over my shoulders.

Desperation clouded my thoughts. I wanted her, in so many ways. I *needed* her. Our hips pressed together, and Clara hummed pleasantly against my mouth. My body was reacting as expected, but my heart was taking a while to catch up. Clara noticed.

She pushed me back ever so gently. "Leo," she breathed, leaning in for a single, soft peck.

"I'm sorry." My forehead met hers again, my eyes shut against her searching gaze.

"What is it?"

I shifted to hold her hips again, and felt her fingers trace up my neck to my cheekbones.

"I just want to figure this out. I want you to be with me all the time. I want to be at your side." I was whispering. It was all I could manage. Clara sighed, slowly, gently.

"We really have just been ignoring it, haven't we?" She'd bought time with her excuses in Newport. She'd dodged the actual proceedings for at least a couple more years, but we hadn't settled on an actual plan.

"Neither of us ever want to think about it."

"And that will be our ruin." She slid her hands off my face, leaning back against the door.

"I don't blame you for the delays."

"I do. I blame myself." She had her eyes closed when I opened mine, and I moved to intertwine our hands, pulling her over to the table. She collapsed into one of the chairs and I took the other, holding her hand across the tabletop.

"We've both been avoiding the subject like the plague, Clara."

"I do everything I can to pretend he doesn't exist."

"I do too."

She heaved a much heavier sigh, slumping in her seat. I squeezed her hand. There were other, more dangerous thoughts trying to take control of my emotions, and I set my jaw to keep them from spilling out.

You can't give her the life she's used to. She's probably hesitant because of that. Why would she give up all her beautiful things and high-class friends to live with you in a rotting apartment in Brooklyn? Why would she want anything more from you when you can't give it?

Clara squeezed my hand again, turning to take it in both of hers. "I'm sorry. I should be putting more effort into this. I should talk to my parents. It's been long enough now that maybe I can show them just how badly suited we are."

"You haven't spoken with them?" I was shocked, sure, but it gave me no right to snap. Clara instantly pulled her hand from mine.

"I asked you years ago not to do that." Her voice was as level and as calm as it could be, but I saw the hurt in her eyes. My head sank into my hands.

"I'm sorry. God damn it, I'm so sorry."

I heard her breathe slowly, and when I peeked she had her eyes closed and hands folded in her lap. I decided not to speak until after she had. I didn't have to wait long.

"I have *tried*, Leon. They don't want to listen to me. They think I'm just coming up with complaints, because he sits at our table and acts completely differently around everyone else. You haven't seen him in Newport. He charms literally everyone to the point I wonder if he has an evil twin at times."

I could believe it. I'd known similar people before; they'd come and gone from the fire station. Duncan had been an excellent judge of character and had always gotten rid of them quickly, if not immediately, but Gregory took a while to see it.

"I will go and speak with my mother again tonight. *That* I can promise you. But I don't need to remind you that not only my entire family, but *his* entire family is going to work against me if I try to break off this engagement. This is a business transaction for them, nothing more. I can't promise anything more than talking to her." Clara's voice softened as she spoke, quieting to a whisper on her last sentence. I looked up again and saw her fiddling with her lace gloves, picking at a stray thread on the seam.

I pushed myself up and went to kneel before her, taking her hands in mine once more. "I'm sorry. I know you're just as upset and frustrated about this as I am." She nodded, squeezing my hands. "I would love it if you spoke with your mother again, and I understand that's all you can do right now." I lifted both her hands and pressed them to my forehead. The rings we'd given each other tapped together lightly as I did. "I want you so desperately, Clara. I love you."

"I love you, Leo. I'm sorry I haven't tried harder." She was still whispering.

"I can't even begin to imagine the kind of relationship you have with your parents. I can't believe anyone would treat their child the way your parents treat you. I'm the one who's sorry." I kept her hands to my head until she gently pulled away.

"You don't need to grovel, dearest." She reached forward to tap under my chin, mimicking what I did to her whenever she had her head bowed. "All I ask of you is patience, but I know yours must be running out. We wasted the four years he was in school doing nothing and look where it's gotten us."

We had, but we were both loathe to admit it. I stood, holding out my hands. She took them to pull herself up, then stepped into my arms. I held her tightly, tucking my face into the side of her neck. I'd already apologized but I could feel it bubbling to the surface once again. Clara was usually the impulsive one, I was the one who caught the back of her dress and tugged her back. This time our positions felt swapped.

"Should I just show up at your house and demand your parents turn over my love to me?" I managed a joking tone, somehow, and was rewarded with a quiet laugh.

"Please don't. I fear my father would beat you over the head with his cane." She was giggling so softly, and shifted to rest her forehead on my shoulder. "It is fun to daydream about, though."

"I do it frequently."

When she left that afternoon, it was after we'd kissed and made up, enough that she'd had to freshen up in my bathroom before heading out. She'd gotten my belt undone and taken care of me *very* well with her hands, and I returned that specific favor. I saw her out the door with my tie askew, hair mussed, and some of her lipstick on the side of my mouth. But the dreamy, hazy, afterglow of having her in my arms had chased all the gloom from my walls, and suddenly my rotting apartment felt like a palace.

February 14th, 1924

Met L. for celebration, told him about the music. It was delightful.

The only time Clara and I got to spend Valentine's Day together was in 1924. She bustled off the train and I met her at the station, all normal, all usual. It had snowed, just a little, while I was waiting for her. She was humming something softly to herself and as we settled down at the diner I finally asked her about it.

"Dearest, what is this you're humming under your breath? Are you composing a song for me this time?" I was grinning and slid my arm along the back of the booth behind her. We'd sat on the same side despite it being just us that day because it was more romantic. She giggled.

"Marie and I attended a concert a couple days ago. It started off just horribly, just terribly. The air at the venue got messed up somehow. It was so stuffy and uncomfortable." Clara shook her head, pulling off her gloves and tucking them into her bag. Her little moonstone ring caught the light and I lifted her hand to kiss the finger it was on.

"Why did you stay?"

"Well, we were about to leave, but the next song started and it was just...enthralling. I can't think of a better way to describe it. This clarinet started playing and all the other instruments came in as if the song itself was waking up somehow. It was marvelous." She was talking with her hands, trying to shape the song in the air. I was fully turned toward her, with my cheek rested against my hand, elbow on the table. The waiter that had come over took the hint and decided to come back in a few minutes.

Clara continued, describing the piece as sounding like the city itself. "It just felt like it was New York speaking. I can't explain it better than that. Every bit of the city was in there. Gershwin did absolutely amazing work with composing it. I would like to find a recording of it, if I could. I doubt Mr. Weis has anything yet." She laughed, covering her mouth.

"It sounds wonderful. I'd like to hear it as well."

"We'll find out how! I'll keep an ear out and see if anyone around here will be playing it. It's going to get so popular, I'm completely certain." Clara nodded, entirely sure of it.

"What was it called?" I turned so that we wouldn't be completely ignoring the waiter when he came back, and she picked up the menu in front of her.

"Oh! 'Rhapsody in Blue'! George Gershwin. I'm sure everyone will be all a-buzz about it in no time."

I never doubted her, but Clara was right. "Rhapsody in Blue" did, in fact, become incredibly popular.

May, 1924

Spoke to L. about idea, he was receptive. Hopeful.

"I've figured something out that I think will help our case, but I'm not sure if you'll agree to it." Clara was sitting next to me on my bed. I had been home sick for two days already and Tim sent her my way when she showed up at the station looking for me. It had been particularly rainy and gloomy that May, and I could hear the raindrops hitting the window as we lay together.

"Whaisit," I mumbled, rolling over to lay my head in her lap. She lifted a hand to run her fingers through my hair. It felt like heaven against my headache.

"If you converted to my church, it'd be a mark in your favor to my parents."

It was definitely not what I had expected. I had never even thought of Clara's family's religion beyond her and Marie telling me about Christmas masses and some of the old ladies at church. It wasn't an important topic to either of them.

I hadn't responded, so Clara kept talking. "*His* family is protestant, and I know that's been the only issue about the betrothal. My parents don't want me to convert, they want him to instead, but I don't know if he'll agree. So I had the thought: maybe if I present you as a Catholic boy whom I wouldn't have to change anything for, it could be a point for your side."

I kept my eyes closed as I thought it over, her fingers still combing through my hair. Mom and I had never been to church seriously. We'd gone with our neighbors on Christmas and Easter sometimes but not regularly.

"Not gonna have to go every week will I?" I whispered, and Clara bent over me to hear, then started giggling.

"I don't know, you'll have to talk to the priest who presides over your parish. Marie and I don't go every week. Mostly just Easter, Christmas, other random Sundays when we're forced."

"Hmmm." I nuzzled into her lap, curling up tighter. It was definitely a step toward what we wanted. And asking me while I'd been at her mercy, in her lap, was probably meant to persuade me further. Sneaky, clever girl.

"I understand if you don't want to." She leaned down, kissing the side of my jaw. "It was just an idea."

I shook my head, then regretted it as the motion made the pain in my sinuses flare. "Mmm no, it's fine. I'll do it." She giggled with a touch of nervousness.

"Really?"

"Anything for you, to have you, my Clara."

She kissed my jaw again, a few times, and resumed combing through my hair, humming some song I didn't know.

"What is that? 'S pretty," I mumbled, and Clara chuckled softly.

"It's the 'Polovtsian Dances' from *Prince Igor*. It's an opera. Next time it's performed in New York, I'll take you. But get well first."

"I will."

Clara sat with me, still humming, well after I had fallen asleep. She woke me up and made me eat before she left. The next morning, I woke up almost completely recovered.

"I think I just witnessed a miracle," I chuckled to myself in the mirror, wiping shaving cream off the spot she'd kissed. "Been healed by a saint."

A few days later, I traveled to the nearest Catholic church. It was south of the station, past the park, so I got to walk past our normal haunt on the way.

I still had a bit of pressure in my head, but it was nothing compared to the day before. I did get winded about halfway to the church though and had to lean against a building to rest. Clara had asked this of me, so I'd push through. It didn't matter to me what church I belonged to, anyway.

I picked Sunday to go to the church on purpose, since it would obviously be open, with the priest going about his duties and hopefully easy to spot. And so he was, and I waited in the back of the room until the service was over and approached him as he was stacking some papers up on his pulpit.

"Father? Could I speak with you?" I held my hat in my hands, trying to look patient and polite. The man looked up at me over his little spectacles, his balding head catching the overhead light briefly. I bit back a joke about heavenly light, but filed it away to tell Gregory later.

"How can I help you, my son?" The priest came around his pulpit, reaching a hand toward me. I took it and we shook hands.

"I'd like to join your church, sir."

The process didn't take long back then, not like it does now. A few weekly meetings with the priest and a bit of learning, and I was in. The priest scheduled my baptism and confirmation once he felt I was ready, and I told Clara the dates next I saw her.

"Ah! Leo! You're doing it, really doing it!" Clara clapped, Marie laughing softly beside her and catching the tea mug Clara had nearly toppled over.

"I said I would." I spoke around a bite of my sandwich, and Clara tapped her foot against mine under the table.

"Do you want us both to come and witness everything? We could be your audience." Marie took a bite of her own sandwich, and I smiled.

"Sure, I'd like that. If you can both get away for it."

"We'll figure something out." Clara was still grinning and hooked her foot around my ankle. It was a normal thing for her to do, but something told me this time she was doing it out of pure hope and joy. Maybe this one little change could be the step forward we'd been trying to find. "Have you given any thought as to your confirmation saint?"

"None at all. Who're yours?" I asked, turning back to my sandwich.

"Saint Brigid of Kildare." Marie set her chin in her hands, smiling at some fond memory she must have been recalling. "It was a bit of a fight with our priest, since she's mainly an Irish saint, but I won in the end."

Clara grinned. "It was very fun to witness. I picked Saint Michael."

"The archangel?" That had been a bit of the teachings the priest had drilled into me the past few weeks. Clara nodded.

"I just felt very drawn to him at that time, it felt like the right choice. I wish I could have picked Joan of Arc, but she wasn't canonized yet." She sighed and shrugged.

"Maybe I'll pick him as well. He's a guardian, isn't he? That would suit me."

"Oh! He would!" Marie was nodding, and she and Clara shared a glance. "You two *would* match, of course." We both chuckled. Of course we would.

"Maybe someday, I'll be up in heaven as his right-hand man." I lifted my right arm and flexed it, and both girls bursting out laughing.

"Oh, but of course! You absolutely will!" Marie was shaking her head, and Clara was holding hers up in both hands. Marie turned to Clara. "You could pick Joan now, you know." Clara brightened.

"You're right! I could just say I picked her then, who would know." She started giggling, taking Marie's hand. "On this day, Clara chooses Joan of Arc as her official confirmation saint, and no one is allowed to argue with me about it."

I grinned, leaning back in my seat. The weekly meetings with the priest had been worth it for the plan, but extra worth it for this. "We wouldn't dare."

Both girls somehow managed to make it to both events, which meant I got to hold Clara's hand as we sat through mass together. I knew she wouldn't expect me to go to church every Sunday with her, but the thought that we could had me distracted all through the service. I gave up trying to fight away thoughts of Clara and I getting married in that very church, with the same priest that had overseen my conversion confirming us as man and wife.

I'd joked about reaching heaven before, but Clara and I sitting together on a church pew, hands intertwined, with only Marie in our little bubble, sure felt heavenly enough to me.

July 14th, 1924

R. early. Displeased. Want to go back to city.

I hated Newport. It was a contempt I'd felt nearly from the beginning that only got worse with every summer I was forced to travel there. At least this season I'd remembered to bring along all my Barsoom novels, and some others, including *Tarzan*. The libraries of the rented homes simply could not be trusted. It was extremely tempting to cart all of my back issues of the *All-Story* with me as well, but I refrained.

I had been lying on one of the house's library sofas around midday, re-reading *Thuvia, Maid of Mars* for probably the fourth time when the door opened. I thought nothing of it; my mother had been in and out of the library all morning to check on me, and Marie was supposed to be joining us for dinner. So I remained on Barsoom, one arm dangling off the edge of the couch in what was absolutely a most unbecoming pose for a young lady of status.

"You make yourself so easy to find, love."

My arm flew back up, taking hold of my book with both hands as I pressed it to my chest. Reggie wasn't supposed to be here today! I was meant to be free of him until next week! He chuckled, coming to sit on the arm of my sofa.

"You look so surprised to see me! How charming." He reached down to pat my hair, and I did all I could to keep from squirming away. "I decided to come earlier so we can spend more time together."

"Ah, I see. What a surprise." I had recovered enough from the shock to speak, at least, and pushed myself upright into a more poised position. I folded my book around my finger to mark my place and crossed my ankles, looking every part the perfect debutante that was very much not a debutante anymore.

Reggie slid off the arm of the sofa to sit at my side, and I forced myself not to lean away or just stand up. He took my hand and then my book, losing my place. "You spend far too much time reading, love. Your brain is going to be filled with such nonsense." He was rubbing the palm of my hand with his thumb, and I urged my fingers to stay still, forced them not to curl and dig my nails into the offending digit.

"I like the nonsense. It's delighting and entertaining." *And John is a far better man than you could hope to ever be*, I thought.

Reggie chortled, and it wasn't pleasant. It never was. "I have news, my darling Clara." I tried not to shudder at the adjective. "Work is going exceptionally well. I hope to make partner within the year."

Damn it. The time I'd bought myself last season was running out, and all I'd managed to do was get Leo to convert. Father would never listen to me, and Mother only did until I said I wanted out of the engagement, then she pretended not to hear me. I wanted so desperately to convince them of more than just a delay.

"No words for your successful fiancé?" Reggie was nearly pouting when I looked to him, and I gave him a thin smile.

"You've done excellent work, Reggie." The snap of his expression from teasingly pouty to furious made my eyes widen as I realized what I'd said.

"Reginald, love. As you will do well to remember." His grip on my hand tightened, and I nodded.

"I'm sorry, it won't happen again." It would, just not in his earshot. He released my hand and I pulled it to my lap, pressing my fingers into the now slightly aching tendons of the others. He didn't notice. Thankfully he hadn't squeezed the fingers of my right hand, or my ring would have made it all the worse.

"I'll see you at dinner." The library door slammed, and I slumped against the sofa, closing my eyes. I didn't want to see him at dinner. Could I fake something? I had hours between now and then. Maybe it would be easy to make myself sick for the rest of the week, if I found something terrible in the kitchen. My nose wrinkled at the idea of it, but I couldn't deny it was tempting.

With my book stashed safely back in the trunk in my room, I went out into the garden. I'd already been scolded a few times for plucking dead leaves and flower heads off the various plants out there, but if no one saw me, I could get away with continuing my work. The hollyhocks in the farthest corner were in some desperate need of pruning, and the gardener had left his shears out in the open. I felt bad about hiding them, but hopefully he had another pair.

I had already set about snipping away the dead flower heads when someone cleared their throat behind me, and I turned to see the one person who wouldn't scold or question me about doing a gardener's work. Marie had her hands clasped behind her back, her face shaded by a very pretty straw hat. I had one of my own upstairs, and should have been wearing it, but had been distracted.

"Did you know Reggie's here?" she asked, and I sighed so heavily my head dropped back.

"Yes, unfortunately early." I turned back and rather savagely snipped off a bit of withering stem, then dropped the shears to the grass. "He already cornered me in the library."

Marie came closer, leaning forward to breathe in the hollyhocks' scent. "I'm sorry, I should have come sooner. Then you wouldn't have had to be alone with him."

I waved her comment away. "You and I both thought he was going to be here next week, not today. You carry no blame."

Marie sat on the little stone bench beside me as I worked out my frustrations on the hollyhocks, innocent as they were, and told me about the picnic she'd gone to with Diane and the others. It sounded pleasant enough.

After a while, the gardener showed up. "Ah. I seem to have found the thief who nicked my shears." He had his arms crossed but was chuckling good-naturedly. He reminded me so much of the gardener we'd had in New York before I had made the mistake of helping him as a child.

"My apologies, sir. I have a deep love for the garden and only wanted to help." I closed the shears and held them out to him, and he took them with a grin. Thank goodness he wasn't offended.

"Not a problem, miss, not a problem at all."

"Clara, love? Are you out here?" Marie and I both froze at the sound of Reggie's voice, and glanced at each other, quickly sharing the cover story without words.

"We're both here, Reginald," Marie called, and I quickly sat on the bench with her. Reggie came around a hedge not long after, trailed by my parents. How fabulous.

"Gracious dear girl, out in the garden again? We'll have to chain you to your bedframe at this point." Reggie was grinning, shaking his head as if his threat wasn't at all serious. Unfortunately, I knew him better than that.

"Might be the only thing to work, at this rate." The tip of Father's cigar was glowing with the same intensity of annoyance and disproval of his gaze, and I slid my hand into Marie's.

"I was only sitting out here, I hadn't done anything."

Marie nodded, motioning with her head to the gardener who had been silently picking up everything I'd pruned. "We were conversing with the gardener as he pruned. He told us about the hollyhocks."

The gardener caught on blessedly swiftly, nodding to my father. "It's true, sir. I was tending to these myself." I shot him a look of pure thankfulness.

Father harumphed. "Mhm. As you say, then." He took a long drag on his cigar, then turned to Mother. "Tell the girls about tonight, would you? Come, Reginald, show me this plan you've brought." He dismissed the womenfolk with a turn, gesturing for Reggie to follow.

He didn't, not at first. Instead, he stepped forward to take my right hand, then bent low to kiss the back of it. The gesture could have been tolerable, even slightly charming, if he hadn't gripped my fingers tightly enough to turn them red. My ring was pinched painfully in between. He'd done it on purpose, I was sure.

"Listen to your father, love," he whispered, masking it as a kiss to my cheek before turning away and following my father inside. Marie took my hand into her lap and pressed her own fingers into mine soothingly.

Mother had seen it all but somehow remained oblivious to everything. "If we could be alone, sir." She sounded pleasant enough giving the order, but if the gardener's quick collecting of his shears and the small basket he'd been gathering the cuttings into was any indication, he was not displeased to remove himself from the situation.

"Reginald's parents will be joining us tonight, as will yours Marie, as a surprise. Obviously they need to think we've taken very good care of you here, so please look your best." Mother smiled, but it was half-hearted. Marie's parents had sent her with us to Newport more times than they'd come up themselves—of course we took very good care of her.

"I will, ma'am, thank you for letting me know." Marie's fingers had relaxed my own, and our hands now curled together on her lap. "Shall Clara and I wear matching dresses?" She giggled, and Mother's smile became a little more real.

"If you wish. I will see you at dinner then, girls." She gave us a little wave over her shoulder as she turned, and I collapsed into Marie's lap.

"I am so, so deeply glad you were here for all of that." I sighed, and Marie laughed. But it was just a single note of breath through her nose.

"Ah, the great Princess of Barsoom has been struck down once more." She poked a finger to my forehead, and I batted her hand away. Out of everyone's teasing and taunting, hers was the most welcome.

For dinner, Marie and I had decided to wear our matching dresses. On a whim over the spring, we'd tried to find a shade that was somewhere between her favorite lavender and my navy blue and partially succeeded. We'd found out what they created when mixed instead. The result was a deep, dusty purple, and we'd gotten two dinner dresses made in the color. We walked into the dining room arm in arm, skirts brushing each other and blending together, as was our desired effect.

All three sets of parents were delighted by us, and we both smiled and posed to their approval and light applause. Mrs. Warburton was giggling into her pre-dinner cocktail as she spoke.

"Oh, if only we had *two* sons, who could just snatch you both up."

"Don't worry, Mother, I'll take them both." Reggie was lounging ridiculously casually on the sofa farthest from us and gave Marie and me the most devilish grin I had ever seen.

"Rake," Marie chided, covering her mouth to laugh. Reggie's eyes darkened but everyone else in the room laughed loudly, as if she'd told the funniest anecdote. Reggie had never paid her much mind before, and now I was afraid he would.

Dinner continued without incident. Reggie never stabbed Marie with some terrible retort, and she escaped unscathed. I tried drowning in my wine but Marie stole my glass from across the table when she noticed. Everyone else had fortunately been too distracted by whatever story Father was telling.

Before we left the dining room, Reggie caught me by the arm. I was so startled by how gentle he was about it that I jumped, and then his grip tightened.

"Clara, love, did I frighten you?" he asked, voice all soothing and charming, eyes boring twin holes into my own.

"A little, yes." I laid a hand over my heart to keep up the charade, as all the parents and Marie were still gathered nearby.

"Like a rabbit being caught by a fox, this one." He chuckled, sliding his hand down my arm to take my hand. He tugged me close with it. I saw him leaning toward me, felt him pulling my hand to his chest, my arm closer, me closer. I tried not to yank my arm away, but it twitched. He lifted his other hand to hold the back of my neck, pulling my entire body to his. Everything about this was improper. It was wrong. But his lips touched mine anyway. Mine refused to soften under his, no matter how hard he pressed. I could feel his teeth outlined under his lip.

Father cleared his throat, and Reggie hurriedly pulled back, a mock sheepish grin on his face. It took everything inside me to keep my hands at my sides, to not raise them and wipe all traces of his 'kiss' from my mouth. Marie looked horrified, the parents a mixture of amused and disapproving.

"Reginald, such a rulebreaker." Mrs. Warburton was laughing, her husband chuckling beside her. Of course they'd see nothing wrong with their son's behavior. Their shark-eyed golden boy.

"Apologies, all, my deepest apologies." He lifted my hand to kiss it, and despite the gentle touch, my stomach flipped. Golden boy or not, *Leo* was the one with the heart of gold. Reggie's was more like tar. "I cannot keep myself away from my darling fiancée."

"Restrain yourself, boy," Father harumphed at him, but he was smirking under his mustache. Marie and her parents were standing awkwardly, her father looking into his drink as if there were something much more interesting happening in the liquid.

The moment successfully swept under the rug, Mother clapped her hands together and declared we ladies should leave the men to their cigars and retire to the drawing room. I was the first one out of the door, Marie close at my heels. She took hold of my arm as quickly as she could.

"I hate him," I whispered, wiping at the tears forming at the corners of my eyes.

"I know," she whispered back. We tucked ourselves into the sofa farthest from the mothers and shared a book until they decided to retire. Marie's mother retrieved her from my shoulder when they were leaving. Marie leaned down to kiss my cheek.

"I love you, my dear, stay strong," she murmured before squeezing both my hands and turning to follow her mother.

"I'll try." I said softly, closing my eyes as she left the room. Mother left as well, and I was alone in the parlor long enough to allow myself to crumple onto the sofa, pressing the book to my forehead sharply just to make sure I was still alive and not in hell. But Marie couldn't be in hell, I reasoned with myself. And Reggie couldn't be in heaven. So clearly, this was still Earth, and I was still alive.

"Go to bed, Clara," Father called as he passed the doorway, stopping only long enough to make sure I heard him.

"Yes father." Book still in hand, I made my way upstairs and passed Reggie as I did.

"Another John Carter?" he asked, nodding to the book in my hand.

"*The Marvelous Land of Oz*." I held the book up so he could see it. His interest in my reading was suspect.

"Always off in other worlds, aren't you? We'll have to do something about that when we're living together." He was pulling a cigarette out of his little case, patting his jacket pocket for matches.

"Indeed," I said, my hand tightening on the novel. "Goodnight, Reginald." I started to make my way up the rest of the stairs, but he caught my wrist.

"You'll eventually learn I have nothing but your best interests at heart, Clara." His tone sounded so sincere but was betrayed by the glint of anger in his eyes. I pulled my arm away as gently as I could.

"I'm sure you do. Thank you." I was staying as polite as possible on the chance that someone was able to hear us, all while praying Reggie would do the same.

"Goodnight, Clara," he finally said after a few long seconds of staring at me with those black holes of his. Reggie turned and all but stomped down the stairs, and I caught myself against the railing for a brief moment to regroup and breathe. I pressed the edge of the book to my forehead again, not caring about whatever marks it might leave there.

Unfortunately, my peace after Reggie parted didn't last long, as Mother came into my room not long after I'd changed into my nightgown.

"What was that, after dinner?" she asked, closing my door behind her. I lifted my hands in a helpless shrug.

"He's never done anything like that before; I could not tell you a thing about his thought processes." I returned to brushing my hair for a few strokes before mother came over and took the brush from my hand, doing it herself.

"Marie was right, he is indeed a rake sometimes." She sighed as she pulled the brush through the strands, her free hand holding the bulk of my hair at the base of my neck.

"I have tried to say similar things in the past. I've told you how I feel about him." I was keeping my voice level despite the urge to shout. This was a well-worn path of conversation. I would tell my mother that Reggie was a terrible person, she would wave it away. Someone else would say something I already had, she would get upset about it for a moment or two and then wave it away once again when I agreed with them.

"It doesn't matter, darling. Everything is settled." She set the brush down on the vanity and set about separating my hair into three parts for a braid.

"I wish it would matter." I was near whispering, but Mother heard me anyway.

"Clara." She was warning me not to start the cyclical conversation again.

"I hate him."

She dropped her hands, the half-formed braid unraveling. "Clara, I do not want to have this discussion again."

"Why do you always back away from it? Why won't you help me when I've said I don't want him, I don't want this, over and over?" I turned to face her, still sitting, but my hands were trembling with the urge to reach out and shake her by the shoulders.

"This was all planned long ago. There is a lot of money and business maneuvers involved, and your father has everything laid out." She folded her hands in front of her, pointedly not looking me in the eye.

"So you'll happily see me sold off?"

"I do so wish you wouldn't think of it like that." She almost sounded sad, and the idea of it made me laugh. But there was no humor in it.

"How else am I meant to think of it? My father made a deal with a man: a daughter for a large sum of money and access to whatever business he runs. That is a transaction, Mother! A sale!" I stood then, my fingers curling into fists at my sides. It was a struggle not to raise my voice.

"You are simply doing your duty as the only child of the household. You are keeping the business alive and the money flowing and providing children to enjoy that wealth later on. You're providing for your parents and your future children all in one action, Clara, doesn't that please you?" She reached out to touch my cheek and I pulled away, nearly tripping backward over my little vanity stool as I did.

"I HATE him, Mother." I spat the words at her, gripping the edge of my vanity that I'd caught when I stumbled. I was sure my nails were leaving marks on the wood. Mother's face fell, her gaze dropping to the floor as she sighed pitifully.

"It doesn't matter, Clara." Her voice was soft, her hands twisting together.

I only had one final card to play, one I had held closely to my chest all these years, tucked away and never shown to anyone but Marie and Juliana. But I played it.

"I'm in love with someone else."

Mother froze, her wedding ring pinched between the thumb and forefinger of her other hand. Her eyes closed. I watched her waver. Would I catch her if she fainted? I was no longer sure.

"Every time you've wanted to delay the wedding makes sense now." She was still whispering as she lifted a hand to pinch the bridge of her nose, then rub her eyes. "Don't tell me a single word more. I do not want to hear it. Whoever he is, let me be ignorant completely. Let me know nothing. If you continue seeing him after the wedding, never let me know where you're going. I do not want to have any knowledge that could condemn me if you were caught."

I was aghast. My heart had fallen to the floor alongside my jaw. My final play, my last chance, shattered. My grip on the vanity faltered, and I collapsed back onto the little stool.

"You wouldn't help your own daughter marry for love instead of money?" I felt tears fall from my cheeks to the backs of my hands before I realized I was crying. Mother refused to look at me.

"Not if it would bring about the ruin of our family, Clara." She started toward the door, pausing with her hand on the knob. "If what you say is true, put it aside and never speak of it again." The door opened, and I felt my hopes leave the room. "Goodnight." Mother left before I had a chance to respond, the door closing behind her.

It took me so very long to work up the strength to move from my vanity to my bed that night. The moonlight was shining through the window, rudely beautiful, and I stared at it as my pillow grew damp.

If I wanted to live in the sun, I'd have to leave everything else behind. Mother had just told me, in no uncertain terms, that marrying Leo would be the ruin of our family. All the wealth, our house, our belongings, I didn't know what all would be lost without the money from Reggie's family. My thoughts began to spiral.

Had Father been hiding the fact we were in a dire position this entire time? Did Reggie's family pay for the debutante ball? Were they paying my allowance? Was I already beholden to Reggie because of it? Did every penny I ever spent on Leo actually belong to him?

I was tying myself into knots trying to figure it out. How deep did this deal run? Why hadn't I been told anything? Why was everyone so insistent on it? The sun peeked through my window before I finally dozed off out of sheer exhaustion, my face itching from dried tears.

April 16th, 1925

Spoke to L. about new F. Scott, new ideas about book now.

Seeing Reggie only in the summers was somewhat of a blessing despite the fact that it had been made crystal clear to me that I would receive no support from my own household. Every time we spoke, Reggie told me how wonderful he was doing at work and how much his bosses were praising him, how much they trusted him to handle everything and anything without being asked. With how often he went on about it, I began to wonder if he was making it up. Surely a new graduate couldn't have taken things over that quickly? I didn't know enough about the business to question it, and I refused to ask lest he take it as genuine interest in his life. My summers were spent in a haze every moment I wasn't with Marie or our other friends, lying on sofas and window seats, reading whatever books I had brought with me to Newport and doing my absolute best to avoid seeing Reggie.

Fitzgerald had released a new one in April, and as soon as I finished it I handed it over to Marie. In my opinion, it was his worst, and I proclaimed as much to Leo on one of our final visits before I was shipped back to Newport to waste away without him.

"It's just so hard to believe." I shook my head, holding his arm as we strolled around the park. Marie hadn't joined us, so even though we delighted in her company, we were enjoying being alone together. "I don't believe that Daisy would claim she loved Gatsby and then just abandon him. I can't believe someone would do that." Leo chuckled.

"I'm sure she had her reasons," he said, patting my hand. "But I'm glad you don't approve of her actions." He leaned over to kiss my cheek softly, and I swatted at him, laughing.

"Of course I won't abandon you, my heart." I tugged his arm, pulling him closer to kiss his cheek in return. It was a gift to see his cheeks color pink, the grin break out across his face.

"I'm glad." He had lowered his voice, moving to twine our fingers together and then lift my hand to kiss it, all while looking me in the eye. I was sure my knees would give out. "Tell me more about the book."

I gave him a basic overview, touching on all the major plot points I could remember, and bemoaning the entire character of Tom. I didn't like him at all and was still reeling that Daisy had chosen him over Gatsby. Leo hummed in thought, squeezing my hand as we found the bench we normally rested on. I sat, and he stayed standing, holding his chin in a dramatic thinking posture.

"Oh, what?" I laughed. "Are you going to give me some long ramble about all the reasons you could leave someone you love behind?" He smiled and shook his head.

"No, I'm only thinking. Based on what you've told me, I think Daisy knew she couldn't be herself around Gatsby. He wanted the ideal version of her that he'd made up in his mind over all those years. He made up all those lies and façades just to catch her attention. Even his name was a fake, as you say." I nodded, fascinated by his words, and he continued. "Tom sounds like a rotter, I agree with you, but at least she knew what to expect from him. They were themselves with each other, right down to knowing each other's affairs without saying anything."

"You haven't even read the book and already I think you understand it better than I do." I smiled up at him, and he finally sat down next to me. As was customary, we turned toward one another,

Leo's arm resting against the back of the bench for me to lean my head on. I pushed up my little cloche hat a bit as it sank over my eyes. "I'll get my copy back from Marie, then we can have a proper intellectual conversation about it all." Leo chuckled, shaking his head.

"I just might know a thing or two about a woman who's free to be herself with someone she loves, and has to hide behind a façade with someone else." He reached up to tap my chin, smiling tenderly.

I stared at him, lips parting just a little. I hadn't even made the connection. I'd been so caught up in the tragedy of lovers being forced apart, of Nick Carraway being left alone, that I hadn't fully considered Daisy as a reflection of myself.

"I hope I'm not as much of a bastard as Tom is, though. I know I am one, but he sounds so much worse." Leo's joke broke me from my thoughts, and I swatted at him, making him laugh.

"How dare you! You are not!" He just laughed harder, holding up a hand in defense as I went to swat him again. "You really aren't!"

Leo lowered his arm from the bench, reaching to take both of my hands in his own. His smile hadn't faltered, and he kissed the backs of both hands. "I know, I just wanted to see your reaction." He kissed my hands again, and I squeezed them as hard as I could. It wasn't very hard and only served to amuse him more.

Leaving him after that realization made the 1925 season all the harder. I had always known I was more comfortable with Leo, felt more like myself around him and Marie, but no one had held up a mirror to it before. I'd been exposed, lovingly and gently, and it was making playing my part in Newport that much more difficult. Marie noticed, of course, and asked me about it at a party early in the season, so I pulled her aside and explained. From that night on, she promised to help me rebuild the façade, just long enough to figure out how to rid myself of it forever.

September 10th, 1925

L. has dedicated a song to me.
I am all aglow.

I hadn't seen her all summer. This was sadly normal now, had been for years, but it didn't make it any easier. Especially since Reggie now spent every summer up in Rhode Island with her. The idea he could see her as often as he liked, take her to all the parties and dinners and outings they got invited to, and I had to just sit and wait for her to come home to me? Maddening, absolutely maddening. I was pure green, all the way to my bone marrow, every single summer.

But it made my falls, winters, and springs all the sweeter. In the fall of 1925, Clara met me at our normal spot alone, instead of with Marie like she usually did. That was the first odd thing.

The second was that she kept rubbing her wrist, pressing her thumb into the tendons as if they were sore. The third was her telling me that Marie had a new suitor and was likely to be engaged as soon as her parents and the man discussed her dowry.

"Her dowry?" I was confused. I knew what a dowry was, but I didn't know they were still an actual thing. My mom, Gregory's wife, Tim's mom—as far as I knew, none of them had dealt with one. "I thought that was a Victorian thing."

Clara shook her head, rolling her eyes at the same time. "They might not call it by the same name anymore, but high society is still stuck in its ways. There's always some financial compensation included with the bride."

We walked in silence to the park, Clara still idly rubbing her wrist, strangely silent, oddly absent. Once we'd settled on one of our normal benches, she leaned back against it and closed her eyes with a sigh.

"What's wrong? Did something else happen in Newport?" I laid my arm across the back of the bench behind her, and she tilted her head to rest it on my bicep. Her face turned toward mine, and she opened her eyes. The stormy gray in them was darkened, and she sighed again, nodding. I felt the worry stutter my heart.

"Reggie was there, and now that he's met my condition of "establishing himself" and becoming an executive at the office, he's demanding we finally set the date."

Now, almost everything made sense. Her silence, her distance, but not her wrist. I reached out to take it, rubbing my thumb along the tendons beneath her palm. My molars clicked together briefly as I composed myself, forcing my hatred toward him down in favor of my love for her. "Did he hurt you?"

She shook her head. "No, thank goodness. He might have bruised it a little had he been more rough, but Mother came into the parlor and he let me go. I think she saw how uncomfortable I was because she took me with her right away." Her eyes were on our hands, and I shifted to use both of mine to massage her wrist. There was anger sparking in my chest, but I pushed it down and focused on comforting Clara. Each time Reggie did something, anything, to make her uncomfortable or threaten her, it became harder and harder for me to contain my blistering rage toward him. And now he'd actually laid his hands on her.

"What happened? Besides this, I mean."

Clara told me the full story. She'd been cornered by Reggie at a dinner last week in Newport while they were all preparing to leave, and he'd demanded to know why she was still delaying the wedding. Clara had tried to joke with him and laugh it off, tried to say it was much luckier to get married in a year ending with an even number, shouldn't they wait just one more year? But Reggie hadn't appreciated the joke and had grabbed her wrist, threatening her instead.

"He said I'd regret it, and he'd make my parents regret it too if we weren't married by the end of 1926. I have one more year to figure all of this out. One year to get out of it." Clara's eyes had closed again, and I'd stopped my massaging to hold her hand. We sat like that for a while, my thumb tracing patterns into her palm and Clara's fingers flexing ever so slightly with the movement.

"We'll run off, like you said," I whispered, not realizing I was speaking aloud. Clara's two note laugh of disbelief made me turn my head as she shook her own and lifted her free hand to her eyes.

"Oh, Leo, he'd find us somehow, I'm sure." She curled into my side, face pressed to my shoulder, laughing painfully into my shirt. I tilted my head to rest it against the top of hers. Her hairpins jabbed at my cheekbone, but it was nothing compared to the pain from being kept apart. "Unless we went all the way to California, I suppose. Somewhere out west, so far that we'd be away from anyone at all who knows us."

"We could go that far. Easy. Few stops along the way, lots of trains." I shrugged, just with one shoulder so I didn't jostle her.

"Stop making it sound like an option." Her voice had softened, the laughter dying. It had been mirthless anyhow.

"It *is* an option, Clara." I pushed back the annoyance at the brick wall she always threw up around this conversation, knowing her hesitance was out of fear, knowing she desperately didn't want to leave Marie on her own.

"Stop, Leo. Please," she whispered, her fingers tightening around my thumb that was still on her palm. I sighed out my irritation.

"Of course, dearest."

A moment or four of regrouping later, we decided to go to the music shop. On our way there, I asked about Marie's new suitor.

"Oh, Lucas." Clara rolled her eyes again. "He's an old friend of my family. My father and his did some business together when I was very small, so he's been at all our parties and such for years. He's been away at school and working, too, so this was the first time he and Marie had met as adults."

"Is he nice?" Marie deserved someone that would protect and appreciate her tender nature.

Clara shrugged. "Polite enough, I suppose. He's good in public, but I've never been around him in private, not since we were small."

"Do you think Marie likes him?"

"Enough? He made her laugh quite a few times and she was comfortable enough to stay with him at a party when I went to talk to someone else."

"Maybe she'll be set up then." I shrugged, and Clara squeezed my arm in warning. She'd seen right through my single comment. If Marie were happily married and living safely with her husband, Clara could feel less guilty about leaving. I was quiet the rest of the way to the store.

Once there, we greeted Mr. Weis, and he excitedly brought me a new song to learn. "Here, your lady will love this." He handed me the pamphlet and I flipped through it, nodding appreciatively. It was called "A Cup of Coffee, a Sandwich, and You." I was grinning at the lyrics; it sounded similar to so many of Clara's and my conversations. Mr. Weis knew us so well.

"This is top notch, thank you sir." I counted out the price printed on the cover from my wallet, but he held his hand up.

"It's a gift. I know you don't have that four hundred in the bank yet." He winked at me, and Clara, who'd been browsing nearby, laughed. "Does he yet, my girl?"

"He doesn't!" Her shoulders shook, and despite the fact that they were having fun at my expense, I grinned.

We headed out of the shop not long after, Clara thumbing through the pages as we made our way back to my apartment. "I know how to play these on the piano, but guitar still makes no sense to me."

"And I have no idea how to play the piano," I responded with a smile. "So, get us a couple of instruments, we'll have a full song." She laughed and hummed out the notes the rest of the way to my home.

I played the song there for her, peering at the pages propped up by a mug on my little kitchen table. She sat in the other chair, chin in her hands, looking at me with the dreamiest and softest expression. This was definitely *our* song now. Her eyes were half closed, and she hummed along softly with my playing. It was, quite honestly, distracting. I was struggling to keep my fingers on the right strings with my attention not-so-firmly above the table. The guitar, as much as I loved it, was absolutely not what I wanted to have in my arms just then. But I finished the song and played it once more for good measure and Clara's amusement.

"You really do have a wonderful talent with that thing. I hope you play it always." She was leaning her head softly in her hand, her palm and fingers resting on her cheek as she grinned across the table at me, and I looked back with my own grin.

"I'll play as long as you draw breath, then once you're gone, I'll be too heartbroken to do so anymore." I hadn't said it to be sad, or even serious, but I realized my mistake when her grin fell.

"No! Oh, no, Leo! You have to play after I'm gone too. How else will my spirit know where to find you?" She seemed to genuinely mean it, and I had to take a moment to regroup at the idea of her passing before I did.

"Alright, I promise I'll never stop playing guitar. They'll hear music from my grave and find my skeleton moving, playing every song I know over and over."

That got her to laugh, and my slip up was amended. Nothing more happened that afternoon. She left my apartment and kissed me tenderly goodbye, but I was left alone with the memory of the first time she'd been there, years ago. Just like every other time she left my apartment. Everything about our relationship was a risk, and every time I was left on my own to remember that, I spiraled.

It tormented me. I wanted her, desired her, needed her. But she couldn't be mine, shouldn't be mine. Acting like a couple in public was risky enough, even if it was clear across town from her family and anyone who knew them. I lay on my back staring at the ceiling that night, an arm thrown up across my forehead, the quilt and sheet suddenly too much heat even in the chilly fall weather. I was *burning*. For her, because of her, and all my training as a fireman wouldn't be enough to save me.

September 24th, 1925

In bed. Miserable. Sleeping mostly.

"Leo! Hey! Get up!" Tim's voice sounded somewhere beyond my dream, and I rolled over to face him. He had his arms crossed and kicked the side of my bed for good measure. "Someone's here to see you."

"What time is it?" I grumbled, rubbing a hand over my eyes. There had been a late-night blaze, and I'd collapsed on my bunk at the station instead of going home.

"Two-something. Come on, don't leave her waiting." Tim yanked the covers off me and I shivered, glaring after him.

Leave *her* waiting? Clara usually didn't show up until after three. I sat up and finished rubbing sleep from my eyes before forcing myself out of bed and into yesterday's clothes. I was running my fingers through my hair in an attempt to get it presentable as I walked downstairs.

In the kitchen, a young lady sat with Gregory, laughing politely at some joke he'd told. It sure looked like Clara from behind, but as Gregory lifted his gaze to me and she followed, I saw Marie instead. She smiled at me over her shoulder.

"Good morning, Leo. Sleep well?" she teased, and I shook my head.

"Yes miss, I did." I moved to stand next to her, leaning down to kiss her cheek in greeting. She returned it, giggling at her own joke. "What brings you to the station?"

"Oh, my painting class got out early, and I've come with a message. Clara's sick, so she won't be coming today." Marie must have caught the brief flash of worry and panic cross my face because she lifted her hands and laughed. "No, don't worry! It's nothing serious! She'll be fine in a few days! She'll be back next week."

I felt my shoulders fall away from my ears. "Well thank goodness for that. Thank you for telling me." I put every ounce of sincerity I felt into my words.

"Well of course I must! Couldn't leave you wondering." Marie stood, pushing the chair back under the table. "I'll get out of everyone's way now. Thank you for welcoming me, Gregory." Her smile turned on him, and he nodded.

"You and Clara are both welcome, as long as you stay out of trouble." He stood as well, taking his coffee with him, presumably into his office.

"Are you heading home?" I asked, and Marie nodded.

"I have no other appointments today."

"Well, I have the day off, so we could have a late lunch if you'd like." She knew that Thursday was my guaranteed day off every week. I tucked my hands in my pockets, realized my suspenders were still dangling off my waistband, and hurriedly pulled them up. Marie giggled.

"I don't know if I should be seen with you in such a state of dishevelment, Leo."

I gave her a look of false offense, my hand going to my chest. "I get back from fighting a terrible fire in the middle of the night, and still get tossed aside just because I'm not wearing suit and tie? What a world."

Marie laughed, her hand covering her mouth. "I don't mean it."

"I know you don't." I grinned, and she agreed to walk with me to my apartment and wait while I changed and got myself together. I let her in and she took one of the chairs at my table, chuckling over the stack of books Clara had left.

In just a few minutes I was looking presentable again, and stepped out of the bedroom, adjusting my hat. "Alright, I think you can be seen in public with me now." Marie laughed at that, and we took the few-block stroll to the diner we frequented. She slid her arm in mine and told me about the painting class as we walked.

"We're on still life at the moment, fruits and flowers, vases and such. According to the teacher, it helps to learn values and shadows." Marie lifted her fingers, wiggling them as if painting a shadow in the air in front of us.

"Do you have any of your sketches with you?"

She shook her head. "Oh, no, I realized I'd left my entire portfolio at the school once I was on the train here. I can bring them with me next week."

"I'd like that. I'd love to see some of your art." I meant it, and Marie blushed a little, but she smiled.

"Clara isn't here for you to charm, so you turn it on me?" She swatted my shoulder, and I opened the diner door for her as we reached it.

"Have to charm someone, or else I'll lose my skills." My wink was returned with a smirk and an eyeroll, and we settled into a booth.

We ordered and our food was brought out rather quickly. Marie and I fell into a companionable silence as we ate. It was a much quieter meal than it would have been with Clara, but that wasn't a problem. Marie was a much quieter girl in general, and it suited her. She was sipping at her tea when I spoke next.

"Clara told me you found yourself a new beau up in Newport?" I leaned back in the booth, lifting one arm to rest along the top of it. Marie blushed, hiding her smile behind her teacup.

"Nothing is safe from you, is it?" She chuckled. I grinned encouragingly.

"She didn't give any details. Just said his name is Lucas, he was an old friend of her family, and he made you laugh."

"He did." Her blush deepened a little, and her gaze slid past me, out the window. A little smile crossed her face, and I assumed she was turning Newport memories over in her mind.

"Do you like him?" I lifted my hand to rest my head on it, and Marie glanced back at me before looking down into her tea. Her face was mostly hidden but I saw the smile.

"I do, I really do. He's very charming, very polite, he absolutely enthralled my mother." She chuckled softly, picking up a spoon and stirring her tea absentmindedly. "I think my father wants to demand a proposal from him immediately but I would like to actually get to know him first. We only met a few months ago."

"That sounds very responsible. I wouldn't want you to marry someone you barely know." Clara had seemed very lukewarm on the matter of Lucas, but she'd also been distracted by her own suitor, unwelcome as he was. Maybe she hadn't been able to see the things Marie had.

"Aww, Leo, you do care." Marie had gone from shy to teasing in an instant, and at my second expression of mock offense that day, she laughed loudly enough a couple of people at the counter turned to look. She didn't notice and giggled into her hand. "I know you do, I'm only teasing. I'm very thankful to have an older brother to come to if I need to."

"Aww, Marie." I leaned my head more into my hand, smiling broadly. "You do care."

She threw a balled-up napkin at me, and we both collapsed into laughter. We left a good tip as an apology for our disruptions, and I walked Marie to the station. Her arm was in mine again and everything seemed so pleasant, as if we *were* brother and sister, out for a stroll and a meal. Marie had been in my life as long as Clara had, and I was grateful for it. I tried to show it as I kissed her cheek again at the station.

"I'll bring Clara with me next time, I know how much you like her." Marie giggled, and the whistle blew.

"Please bring her *and* your art. I'd like to see them both."

"Ha! Of course! See you next week!" She turned and hurried to catch her train, and I stayed to make sure she got on before heading out myself. I hadn't gotten to see my love that week, but Marie had made my day off enjoyable all the same.

I stopped in front of the station, out of the flow of traffic, and took in a deep breath of air that was getting colder the closer we crept to winter. If we could just find out a way to push Reggie out of the picture, everything would be perfect.

Christmas, 1925

Convinced L. to join us!
Will be the best fun.

"Oh Leo! It will be so much fun! Come with us! No one else from the houses are going, none of our other friends either. It will be completely safe, I promise." Marie was shaking my arm, Clara giggling on my other side. "We can't go without a chaperone!"

I scoffed, shaking my head with a grin. "A chaperone? You two?" I laughed, shaking Marie gently off my arm. The idea of going to a New Year's Eve party at a dance hall did sound like a good time. The only thing that gave me pause was that it was in Manhattan, where many people knew Clara and Marie, where word could spread much more easily about Clara dancing with someone who wasn't her fiancé.

"No one we know will be there, we've already confirmed it." Clara was smiling rather triumphantly, hands behind her back as she swayed a little, her skirt swishing across her knees. Oh, I enjoyed flapper fashion far too much. "Everyone is going to other parties."

"Exactly! It'll be a hoot, Leo. A real party with your favorite gals!" Marie spun away from me, taking Clara's hands instead. They were laughing, and I heard Mr. Weis chuckling behind his counter.

"You'd better say yes to them, lad. They're not going to stop." Amusement was glittering in his eyes, and I finally just gave in.

"Alright, but the first sign of trouble, we're out of there. And you'll have to find me something to wear."

Both girls cheered, throwing their hands up in the air, then clapping, spinning about in the middle of the store. Mr. Weis and I laughed, and I shook my head again. I'd have to go talk to Gregory, but I was sure asking for one night off wouldn't be an issue.

"Let's go to that shop two blocks down right away. I saw the most dashing suit in the window earlier." Clara and Marie had stopped their spinning, and Clara's arm was sliding through mine. "Come on, it can be your Christmas gift! We'll split the cost so you feel less bad about it." Clara was making fun of me, and I lightly pinched her arm between mine and my ribs for it. She just laughed, unphased.

"Let's go! Leo's first fancy party! It's to be celebrated!" Marie was practically dancing a jig, her excitement palpable and infectious.

"Mind the ice, youngins," Mr. Weis cautioned, and we called our assurances and goodbyes over our shoulders as we headed out into the cold. Clara and Marie both had hats and gloves and thick coats, but I'd lost my hat and hadn't been able to find my gloves that morning. I tucked my hands deep into my pockets instead, and Clara slipped her hand into one with a grin.

"Poor Leo, first he has no suit, now he has no gloves."

"We'll have to spoil him for Christmas, Clara!" Marie giggled, and Clara took Marie's arm, hooking their elbows together.

"We'll buy him a whole new wardrobe. He'll have to look his best at all our parties, after all." Her eyes were twinkling, rivaling the cheery decor in all the shop windows. The gals' good mood had infected me, and we all sang carols as we made our way to the shop where Clara had seen the suit. Most passersby grinned at us, the holiday spirit shared between souls.

Before too long, I had been stripped of my coat and jacket and tie, positioned on a little platform, and was being measured by an attendant at the shop. Clara and Marie were seated nearby, drinking tea that a shop employee had brought over, and giggling over something or other together. I watched them in the mirror with a smile until the attendant told me to turn. The whole thing took the better of an hour, Clara and Marie shooing me away from the fabric samples and picking which colors and material would be best. I wasn't allowed to decide any of it, but I did veto a bright green tie when it was held up to me with laughter. The girls didn't let the shop employees say the cost aloud, just counted bills between them, and Clara hurriedly tucked the receipt deep into her bag, where I'd have to really dig and make a nuisance of myself if I wanted to see it. But I'd learned to not worry as much about the cost of things over the years, to just trust the girls when they said it was alright. I did draw the line at them paying any of my bills, though. And I made sure they let me buy them lunch a few times a month. We'd settled into the arrangement fairly nicely.

"They said they'd have it ready by next week!" Clara took Marie's arm and slid her hand into my pocket again as we left the shop, and both girls were still all smiles and song. "How thrilling. We get to show you a little bit of our world that you haven't seen before."

"A good part, even!" Marie giggled, and Clara laughed with her. My heart felt like it was glowing, and I squeezed Clara's hand in my pocket.

"All parts of you two are good parts."

Both girls flushed at that, jokingly admonishing me for being fresh. I walked them back to the train station, kissed Marie's cheek and Clara's mouth, lingering with her as I always did, and saw them off until the next week.

They made me try on the suit when we went to pick it up, and it only needed the pants shortened slightly. Other than that it was a perfect fit. I turned in front of the mirror and inspected myself, Marie giggling and Clara sitting with her hand over her mouth, eyes wide. I smirked at her in the mirror.

"What is it?" I knew what it was, but I wanted to hear her say it.

"You just..." She paused to look me up and down, all but fanning her face. "You look so, so handsome. Amazing. Spiffy. Bee's knees. I should have bought you a suit ages ago." Her cheeks reddened, and my smirk spread into a grin, holding back a rather inappropriate retort I'd have to share with her later.

"Well he has one now at least!" Marie was grinning. She very likely knew what was going through both our minds, and she leaned over to whisper something to Clara, whose blush deepened as she hid her face in her hands, laughing.

"You're right but stop it," she hissed back, just barely loud enough for me to hear. I grinned wider.

With the suit packaged and safely tucked away in a box under my arm, we went to drop it off at my apartment and then had a late lunch together at the diner. It was a shorter visit than normal, as the holiday season meant a lot of parties and dinners both girls were expected to go to, but I didn't mind. I'd get to spend nearly a whole night with them soon, and dance with Clara in public. The short visit was more than an equal payment.

The days between picking up the suit and the dance seemed to fly by, besides Christmas itself. I spent it with Tim and his family, an invitation graciously extended to me every year since losing Mom. Sally was no longer a baby, and she had started to take over Tim's job of ruling the household. I'd known all those years ago that she'd get her brother's personality, and was pleased to see I was right. The six-year-old girl bossed everyone around, even me, and for some reason we let her.

"Leo you sit here," she commanded as we gathered around the table, pointing to the chair next to hers. "You sit by me." I grinned and took my seat as ordered. Tim frowned at her across the table; he probably wanted to be next to his sister. He was a man of twenty now and had started his training at the station just a little later than I had.

Gianmarco led us in grace, a short blessing and thanks for the feast prepared lovingly by his wife. We ate heartily, talking about anything and everything. I told them all about the party at the dance hall, and Grace jokingly scolded me for not wearing my new suit to dinner.

"Ah it's too good for our little apartment, is it Leo?" She laughed, covering her mouth with her napkin. I shook my head, laughing as well.

"No, no, I just don't want to get it dirty before the party. I don't know how to take care of it. I would definitely ruin it trying to get mud or some other stain off of it, I'm sure."

She just laughed again. "Bring it to me after your fancy party and I'll show you."

After dinner, we exchanged a few gifts. I'd brought a few books for Tim—Clara had helped pick them out—and some clothes for Sally's favorite doll, a new pen set for Gianmarco and a brooch for Grace. They were all well received, and my still-glowing heart was made brighter by it.

They had one gift for me, and how I wish it were still in my possession. A few years back, I'd entrusted the chain with my parents' wedding bands to Grace's keeping, fearful I'd lose it in some blaze or it would get stolen out of my apartment. Tim's family had a small safe, and she'd kept them in there, tucked in an empty cigarette box.

Until that year, that Christmas. They presented me with a small wooden box, gleaming and polished to a nearly mirror-like finish, inlaid with a thin band of a blue stone I didn't recognize.

"What is this?" I chuckled, holding it up to the light. The box fit in my palm and weighed basically nothing.

"Open it, obviously." Tim rolled his eyes from where he sat with his chin on Sally's head, and she laughed, clapping.

"Open it!"

I did as my little siblings instructed and flipped back the lid of the box. My eyes were full of tears nearly instantly, as soon as I realized what was inside. My parents' wedding bands were tucked into a velvet cushion, the chain I'd worn them on wound around the inner edge of the box. I lifted my hand to my mouth as the one holding the box shook slightly. Grace stood up to steady it, smiling tenderly.

"Now, now, don't drop it." She laughed softly, closing the lid and my fingers around it.

"We thought your memories deserved a better place to rest," Gianmarco said, grinning from his chair. "A cigarette box isn't very sturdy, son."

I laughed, breathlessly, gripping the box. "It's not. Thank you." Looking down at the box again, I squeezed it gently. "Thank you so much." It was a custom box, and it had to have cost a small fortune. This family that had already shown me so much kindness and warmth was spoiling me, almost more than Clara and Marie ever had. The girls had money to burn, but the Rinaldis had to be more careful with their funds. This gift would have required careful planning, careful rearranging of the budget. I silently hoped they hadn't forgone anything just to get me this.

"Could I keep it here still? Just until I find a better place," I asked, looking between them all.

"Of course, we'll happily keep it safe for you." Grace was the one that had responded, but everyone was nodding their agreement, even little Sally. She shook Tim off, stood and held her hands out, motioning for the box.

"I'll go put it away!"

I laughed, kneeling down to her level. "Thank you, but I think I'll have you do that before I leave. I want to hold it a bit longer." I reached out to smooth her hair, and she grinned, holding my face.

"You can cry if you want. Only Tim will make fun of you." She giggled, and Tim scoffed behind her.

"I won't make fun of him this time. It is Christmas after all."

That brought a laugh from everyone, and the rest of the night was filled with that grateful mirth. Sally did put the box away for me, even though she wasn't strong enough to open the door on her own. She set the box on the shelf almost reverently, and I knew it would be safe even in the clumsy hands of a six year old.

How blessed was I to be adopted into such a family.

New Year's Day, 1926

Party at dance hall! Absolutely wonderful. Brilliant.

A quick week later, New Year's Eve was upon us. It was odd being the one getting met at a train station, rather than doing the meeting. But as promised, Marie and Clara were at the platform as I got off, both girls grinning hard and waving harder. I couldn't help but laugh.

The new suit was at odds with my old coat, but I was sure I'd be forgiven for it. It was too cold for anyone but the snobbiest to argue about it anyway.

"Hooray!! He's here!" Marie was practically jumping up and down and clapped her hands excitedly. Clara laughed, reaching out to take both of mine in her own.

"He's here!" She looked up into my eyes, and I felt my heart stutter. "So strange seeing you anywhere but Brooklyn. It's almost as if you're rooted to the place." Her grin widened, and I leaned down to kiss her cheek.

"I will uproot myself anytime if it's for you." Another peck to her cheek and we arranged ourselves so I had a girl on each arm, and they directed me to the dance hall a few blocks away. They'd told me it was a good blind pig—there'd be enough giggle water to go around all night. The weather was cold but forgiving, and the snow that fell was light and melted on our shoulders almost instantly. It felt like being in a snow globe that was starting to settle.

Manhattan was full of light, just like it is now. Light and noise and people. So, so many people. Brooklyn wasn't a ghost town by any means, but here, in the heart of the city, the center of commerce and tourism and right near Broadway, it was as if the whole world had gathered to just this peninsula. The girls kept tight hold, refusing to let us get separated, and we made our way to the dance hall quickly.

Somehow it was as if the light, noise, and people had all followed us there. Inside the hall, everything was glittering, jewels wrapped around wrists and throats and tied in hair, sparkling on dresses. Even some of the men had glinting pins on their lapels.

"I see why I needed a new suit," I said with a bashful smirk. It was probably obvious I felt out of place, but I was trying to pretend, to play the part. I was doing my best to act like Clara's proper suitor, and Marie was our always-welcome plus one. The girls laughed my comment off, and I was pulled to the dance floor with them, lavender and blue lace skirts trailing after them. Both girls had pinned their hair up in fake bobs, trying to match the current fashion while being forbidden to actually cut their hair. They were both glittering just as much as the rest of the room, but there was some sort of air, some bubbly, shining aura about them that set them apart. I felt lucky just to be surrounded by it.

We danced, and I switched off between the girls as other men held out their hands and they accepted, just happy to be twirled around, knowing none of these men would care about them beyond that night. At one point, Clara was in my arms and Marie was across the room at the buffet table taking a rest. Clara looked at her, then started giggling.

"Oh Leo, look, she's flirting with the waiter." She was well on her way to being drunk and so was I, and we both started laughing. Still spinning around the room, we swung close to Marie and the table, Clara laughing, me blowing my hair out of my face. It had started to fall in the warmth and movement; dancing would ruin all my work entirely by the end of the night. Not that it mattered, everyone else's hair looked about the same at that point.

A dance hall party in Manhattan with this crowd was the fanciest thing I'd ever been to, even though Clara and Marie had insisted it was a purely casual affair. Things were just too shimmery and dazzling to be considered casual. Later in the evening, I pointed that out to Clara as we rested against the wall, Marie off dancing with someone new. She snickered at me, shaking her head, curls swinging about her face.

"Oh Leo. Sometimes I swear you're from Barsoom."

I smirked at the mention of her favorite books and finished off the drink I was holding. Taking her arm, I pulled her closer and leaned down to whisper in her ear. "Show your favorite Martian some earthly delights then, hm?" I kissed the spot below her ear, lifting a hand to settle on her waist. She laughed again, breathily, leaning into my touch. Her hand rose to trail through my hair, her hips leaning toward mine.

"Here?" The single word was full of her laughter, and before I answered, her mouth was on mine. The groan that came from my chest was drowned out by the music, and my hand moved from her arm to the back of her head. She pulled back first, grinning, mischief gleaming in her eyes. "Come with me then, I'll give you the grand tour."

Taking me by the hand, she led me down a hallway near the coat closet and we found ourselves in a storage room occupied by mops, brooms, and various other cleaning supplies. She perched herself on top of a crate, beckoning me over. I locked the door before I obeyed.

"What an interesting place to first show me, Earth girl." I leaned over her, a hand on each side of the crate, and she lifted her hands to take my face between them. She bit her lip, leaning in to kiss me, and all further thoughts of interplanetary communication were silenced.

Her hands dragged down my chest, unbuttoning the jacket and vest, pushing them aside. Her lips trailed away from my mouth, over my cheek, my jaw, all the way to my collarbone. I closed my eyes, keeping my hands still for now as she did as she pleased. She had just started undoing my belt when the door rattled. We sprung away from each other, laughing as the handle shook and someone banged on the other side.

"Unlock this immediately or get thrown out! You hear me!"

Clara and I looked at each other and burst out laughing. I managed to stumble to the door and unlock it, opening it wide as Clara finished adjusting her dress and I hurried to button at least my vest.

"This is an employee-only area!" said employee shouted, glaring at us from the doorway then stepping aside and pointing back out to the public areas. "Out! Or I'll have security throw you out of the entire building!"

Clara hopped off the crate and took my hand, and we both ran out the door, trying not to laugh. She called an apology over her shoulder as we scurried down the hall, back toward Marie. We caught up with her near the buffet table again, but there was a new waiter instead of the one she'd been flirting with before. One of her eyebrows rose as she looked us over, then she pointed to her jaw.

"Leo, you have something just here." Her lips curled into a smirk, a bit smug, a lot amused. Clara looked up and I looked down at her, confused, then Clara started chuckling, fished into her little purse for her handkerchief, and wiped at my face.

Marie sipped her drink with a smile as Clara cleaned her lipstick off my jaw and neck. "Looks like you two had a good time, wherever it was you disappeared to."

"We got interrupted." Clara's giggles quieted but her grin didn't waver, and the girls both started giggling, falling into each other. Had it been any other night, if everyone else around us hadn't also been absolutely plastered, their loud, bright peals of laughter would have drawn everyone's attention. But I could hear others doing the same all around the room. No one was paying any mind, and in my blotto state I didn't care. My girls were laughing and having a great time, and so was I.

We stayed through the countdown, confetti falling over the crowd at the stroke of midnight. Clara and Marie were laughing again, holding onto each other and me, and I leaned forward to kiss them both on their cheeks. Clara turned and caught my mouth at the last second.

"How—" She hiccupped, laughing more. "How dare you! Kiss me properly." The girls were much drunker than I was.

"No! Not here!" Marie cried, although she was laughing too. She swatted at us both with fake disdain, only to fall into our arms, both girls stumbling and me only barely managing to hold them up.

"That's it, you're both done." I maneuvered, looping an arm around each of their waists. They gratefully but not gracefully settled their arms over my shoulders, Clara trying to dance as she did.

"Ah! Leo! No! It's a good song!"

"Then listen to it as we sit down." I chuckled, pulling them away from the dance floor, all of us slipping on confetti and spilled alcohol. But we made it to a trio of chairs set against the wall, collapsing into them. They both leaned against me and I shook my head, lifting my arms to wrap around their shoulders. Somehow, they both got ahold of another glass each, and sipped their drinks while using me as a prop.

"I'm so glad you came with us, Leo," Marie said, her head falling on my shoulder.

"Why's that?"

"Because you're holding us up!" Clara answered for her, and both of them started drunkenly laughing yet again.

"Oh you two are zozzled. No more." I was trying to be stern but the lingering alcohol in my system kept me laughing with them.

We sat for three songs, danced to two more, then decided to call it a night. I had a girl on either arm again as we made our way to the station, Clara loudly singing one of the songs we'd danced to and swinging her little purse around. Marie was humming along, much softer, and ended up taking Clara's purse from her.

I just basked in their presence.

Marie pulled Clara away from me at the station. She'd started kissing me goodbye and I hadn't told her to stop, even when the train showed up.

"If you get him fired for being late, you'll be soooo guilty, you'll feel so bad!" Marie couldn't come up with a proper threat, and I was in no danger of being fired, but it worked. Clara pulled away from me after one more peck of a kiss, and they both shooed me onto the train. I waved through the window, and they both waved handkerchiefs at me and pretended to cry, chasing the train down the platform just a little way before stopping and doubling over laughing. I carried the image of them in my heart all the way back home.

It was a glorious holiday season that year, Christmas and New Year's both. 1925 faded happily into 1926, and even though in the earliest hours of the year we'd been happy and celebrating, we were not prepared in the slightest for what would come next.

June 23rd, 1926

Charity dinner. Forced to choose. Unhappy.

A charity luncheon was a common enough event, so I agreed to sit through one for my mother's sake. Marie and her mother were hosting it at their home, and they had chosen a buffet style for the food. That was always more fun, in my opinion, because you got to sit and watch people sneakily try to add more to their plates. The only issue was that Reggie was there. He was one of the few men that had joined this legion of ladies in their altruism, but I was sure he hadn't actually donated anything to the cause but was rather using it as an opportunity to have a public appearance with me. We hadn't gone to Newport that year since my parents were expecting a wedding announcement from us. They had to keep every date open for it, of course. I'd been flat- out avoiding Reggie at every opportunity, feigning weakness or illness for any event that I could, finding someone else to speak with at every party I was forced to attend at his side. I made it a point to never be alone with him. This was the first time I'd failed in that endeavor.

"Clara, love, could you come with me for a moment?" he asked, after all the most important speeches had been made and the event speakers had joined the line for the buffet. I squinted, and I saw the same waiter that Marie had been flirting with on New Year's. What a coincidence. "Clara. Love." Reggie's voice came through his teeth, and I quickly took his outstretched hand before he caused a scene. He led me out of the main hall where the festivities were taking place, and into a small, attached parlor, small enough it felt awkward being in it without the owner of the home present. The rain that had been lightly falling all day was louder there. "It's the lucky year you requested, Clara, and now we're halfway through it. Make your choice." In private, his façade dropped, all of his faux charm evaporating in an instant. His smile melted away, and he pressed his lips together in a thin line as he stared at me.

My choice. Because I'd come up with a lie on the spot about even-numbered years, not knowing what else to do. I'd been running away from this instead of solving it for eight years, taking solace in the fact that for half of those I'd only had to see him for three months out of the year, and the other half, not at all. I was running out of places to run and hide, and Reggie knew it. He had backed me into a corner. Literally, at that moment.

"Clara, pick a day or I will pick for you. And you will not enjoy how soon it will be."

"Fine, August eighth." I hated myself immediately for picking Leo's birthday without a second thought. Now I had a little over a month to figure out how to break this. Why hadn't I chosen a date in December? Why not New Year's Eve? Whatever was wrong with me, I needed to tear it out of myself.

Reggie grinned, pulling something from his pocket and taking my hand. "Now that it's official..." A ring appeared, and he shoved it roughly onto my finger. "I've been carrying that around for far too long. I'm so glad you're finally coming to your senses. Now come with me."

He wrapped his fingers around my wrist, tugging me out of the parlor, back into the hall where everyone was gathered. I was too stunned to protest, and he was much too strong for me to resist without my wrist breaking. Once in the hall, he swiped a glass and a knife that hadn't been cleared and tapped them together, gathering the attention of everyone in the room. As he did, he nudged me to the little platform in the corner where a small band would usually be set up, but today had held the speakers for the charity.

"Hello everyone!" Reggie called to the room. Curious and confused faces turning toward us, as he handed me the glass. "I have an amazing announcement to make!" He took my hand—it was so aggressively that I was shocked the people closest to us didn't say something—and lifted it, letting the handcuff of an engagement ring he'd forced onto my finger catch the light. "Clara has finally agreed to become my wife!"

I smiled, tightly, hiding it behind a sip from the glass, not caring whose it used to be. The room cheered and applauded politely, even though this was such a breach of decorum that no one knew what to do with themselves. A few people came over to admire the ring and offer their congratulations, so I humored them until Reggie had absorbed himself with telling stories of all he'd done at the firm lately, and I found my chance to slip away and cross the room to Marie. She was speaking with the waiter again, and I wrapped my hand around her arm.

"Marie, Marie. We have to disappear. Please." I pleaded with her, my eyes wide. The only thing keeping me from running outside and into the rain was her concerned expression. Marie immediately tended to me, apologizing to the waiter and asking him to pretend he didn't know we'd agreed to go to her mother's parlor, where Reggie wouldn't be welcome. I cried to her for the remaining hour of the luncheon.

June 24th, 1926

Had to tell L. He cheered me up a bit.

Clara turned up on Thursday looking run down and defeated. I gathered her in my arms immediately, and she slumped against me, her hands gripping the back of my shirt.

"Oh, Leo. It's all a mess." She sighed, rubbing her forehead against my chest. I lifted a hand to rub her back.

"What's happened?"

"He made me pick a day." She was speaking so quietly I had to tilt my head to hear her.

"Oh."

"Yes."

We stood in silence for a moment, then I squeezed her tight as I pulled in a breath, then released it as I moved back to look at her, taking her hands. "What day did you pick?"

For some reason, this made her start laughing. But I could hear the bitterness and pain in it. "Your birthday. It was the first one that came to mind." She hadn't looked me in the eye yet and made it even harder to catch her gaze by dropping it to the ground. "I'm so sorry."

"Of all days." I shook my head and squeezed her hands. "Alright, I suppose we better decide on something then."

"Can we do it later? I am too exhausted today." She leaned her head against my shoulder, and despite my desperate need to solve this issue once and for all, I agreed.

We took our normal stroll around the park, and I found myself thankful that her family hadn't gone to Newport this year. She'd told me it was because of the wedding, because she'd chosen this year and now all long-term plans were on hold until she had picked a date. I wondered if her parents were trying to find a house to rent in Rhode Island for after the wedding. Knowing what I did of them, it wouldn't be shocking.

We ended up on our bench, Clara leaning her head back and me just looking at her. She had tugged down her little hat a bit to keep the sun out of her eyes and had her hands clasped in her lap. I reached over to take one.

"That other option *is* still an option, Clara," I said softly, tracing the lines in her palm with a finger. She laughed, but not nearly as bitterly as before.

"I'm starting to consider it."

Don't give me hope if you don't mean it, I thought, closing my eyes briefly to steel myself. "Just give the word."

"I will."

We made a brief visit to the music shop and bought a new song from Mr. Weis. This time it was "Tea for Two" by Vincent Youmans. Clara took her leave early. She was genuinely exhausted and I couldn't fault her for wanting to rest, even if it meant less time for us. So I kissed her tenderly, lovingly, before she got on the train and I waved her off.

I wasn't paying much attention to where I was headed as I left the station, busying myself with my matchbook, and my shoulder slammed into a man with black hair as we went in opposite directions.

"Watch where you're going!" he hissed, brushing his jacket off furiously. I held up my hands in surrender.

"I'm so sorry."

"Yes, you should be," he spat at me, and then left.

I made my way back to my apartment and started figuring out what all it would take to leave, just in case.

June 30th, 1926

Horrific day. No words. None.

Since Reggie had gone ahead and broken high society rules by announcing our engagement at a dinner that was not meant for us, he had also forgone any sense of remaining decorum and started treating me as a full-fledged fiancée. Most of the people in our social circle already knew about the betrothal, but it had been taken for granted all these years and hardly mentioned besides a few, "Well, Clara won't have to worry about that sort of thing," comments in regard to dealing with suitors at balls and other events during the season. They were always laughed and waved off, mostly ignored, and I wanted to ignore the situation just as I'd done with the comments. But it was out now. People were congratulating us. Gifts were being delivered to my house already, and it had only been a week! He'd been coming over to have dinner with my family nearly every night as well. My Thursday meeting with Leo had been my only respite, and even then it had been far too short. I'd only kissed him the one time and found myself craving so much more. I missed him desperately. I wistfully searched for the star that Marie had pointed out to me all those years ago each night, my eyes wanting to see the heart of the lion every moment I wasn't able to hold it.

"Clara, my dear? Are you in here?" As soon as I heard his voice, I wanted to shrink myself and hide amongst the pages of my book. My father was hosting yet another small party for the men of his office and their wives and children, and I'd sneaked off to the library between dinner and cocktails. It was far too big of a gathering for my liking, despite it being perhaps fifteen people total. I just wanted to be on my own, to read and pretend that none of this was happening. But Reggie had to come in and ruin that all for me. I sighed, dropping my book to my chest.

"Yes, I'm here," I replied, closing my eyes to build up the emotional and mental energy I'd need to speak with him for more than a few moments. I wanted to pick up my book again and hide behind it, pretend I was too engrossed with the story to answer him, but I knew he would just rip it from my hands.

"Why are you hidden away? We should be showing everyone how happy we are together." The smile on his face was far from pleasant, and I hid a wince as he sharply tugged the door shut. "You keep running away like this, people are going to think you don't want to marry me." He laughed, but it was clearly a threat. I stayed quiet and just looked up at him as he made his way across the room, planting a hand on either side of my chair and staring down at me. I lifted my hand to my book, pressing it lightly to my chest like a shield. He may have won my hand, but he would never have my heart.

"We can't have people wondering, can we?" I replied cordially, keeping the book pressed to me as I made to sit up and get out of the chair. But Reggie didn't move. "Let's go out there and show everyone what a fine couple we are, then." I tried a small smile, but Reggie remained still, jailing me in my chair and pinning me with his gaze. My heart stuttered, and I pressed the book more firmly against it. "Let me up, and I'll go with you."

His lip curled in a mean smirk, and one hand lifted to toy with a curl that had escaped my style and landed against my cheek. "We will. First, I have something to share with you, pet." He tugged on the curl and I kept my expression stony.

"What is it?" I managed to keep my voice level despite working valiantly to suppress the urge to shove him and run as fast as I could.

"I know why you don't want to marry me, Clara." He said it without looking up at me, his eyes on the curl around his finger. "I found out why two days ago."

My heart stopped. "Oh?" Was all I could manage.

"You'd rather marry that fireman in Brooklyn. What was his name?" He paused in a mockery of thought. "Ah, right, Leon Ardin."

Despite the sentence being irrevocably true, the absolute truth of my soul, Reggie was not supposed to be the one to voice it. He wasn't supposed to know Leo's full name. He wasn't supposed to know *anything.* I remained still, watching his face as he continued playing with the bit of hair between his fingers.

"I saw you with him, two days ago. I followed you. You don't normally leave the house while I'm in town. But you were so very adamant about getting to your painting class that I just had to see it for myself. This great teacher that Clara thinks so highly of and doesn't want to disappoint." He twirled the curl around his finger, tighter, causing it to pull against my scalp. I winced.

Reggie had followed me. We were ruined. As easily as that, after all these careful years. All we'd done and how many lies we and people we loved had told, the entire thing was about to come crashing down. My future had never looked so fragile. Leo was in danger. It was possible Reggie had already hired someone to deal with him. I swallowed the tears.

"Please tell me you didn't hurt him," I whispered, and Reggie laughed, releasing my hair.

"She doesn't even deny it! Hah!" He was laughing, spinning away, reaching for the mantle. I thanked the stars there was no fire lit; I didn't want to think about the pain that could be caused with fire and a murderously angry fiancé. Reggie looked back at me, his sharp, dark grin widening. "He remains unharmed. For now. But now I see why it's taken so long to convince you. Where all your lies and delays were seated." He laughed again, and my core turned cold. Tears that I'd tried to swallow pricked at the corners of my eyes. His own eyes had always been fathomless depths, always black holes which absorbed every bit of light in the room. But now they were lit from within, a glowing ember of hatred burning in both pupils as the rage and jealousy devoured him on the inside.

"For now?" I breathed, my hand gripping the arm of my chair. "What are you planning? To blackmail me with his safety and well-being?"

He laughed again, nodding. "Oh Clara, you are too smart for a woman. That head of yours would be so much better placed on a man. You almost got away with it. Almost." He pushed away from the mantel, each heavy step filling me with another ounce of dread. I pressed back into the chair. "Yes, that is the solution. Your lover will remain safe and whole for as long as you do as I say. Hell, I'll even let you keep meeting with the bastard as long as it's on my terms." He had reached my chair and taken ahold of my chin, keeping my eyes on his. "You just can't sleep with him, you see, because if our child has blond hair, we'll be caught out immediately. So bear me a little brat first at least." He chuckled, and my grip on my book faltered. It landed in my lap.

"Let go of me." My weak request was laughed away, and Reggie gripped tighter.

"Never again, Clara." His false jovial tone was gone, engulfed by the light of anger in his eyes. The black holes returned and threatened to swallow me once more. I felt my rebellious tears sliding down my face and prayed they weren't taking any of my mascara with them. The last thing I needed was more evidence. "If you think I'm letting you out of my sight ever again after discovering what I have, you're more dense than I thought."

I pulled away from him but his hold on me only tightened, and he grabbed my wrist. I tried to twist away but he gripped harder, lifting my arm higher. I whimpered.

"Reginald, please." It was a pathetic attempt and did as much as I figured it would. He hauled me up by my wrist, nearly dangling me from it since he was so much taller. I stood on my toes and scrabbled with my other hand to try and pry his fingers back, but he caught me around the waist with his other arm, laughing maliciously again.

"Clara, please," he mocked, pressing my body against his. "Clara, let me kiss you like Leo does. You'll like it more I'm sure. You'll drop him in a second." He was still laughing as he pressed a cruel kiss to my mouth, hard and bereft of any emotion other than possessiveness. I yanked myself away as hard as I could, which only served to wrench my wrist. Reggie's laugh continued as he shoved me onto the couch, quickly climbing on top of me and pressing his hips down against mine. His teeth were all showing in his smile.

"Reginald, please! Stop!" I tried pushing him away with my other arm, but he was so much heavier, stronger than me. I sobbed. "Please, stop."

"No." The word was growled, and he reached down to yank at my skirts. I tried to twist away but he pressed my arm upward, against the arm of the couch. It was bent backward, much too far and much too roughly. My moonstone ring, my treasured gift, was cutting into my finger. Another sob escaped me. "I will have what I'm sure that bastard has already had, what was meant to be mine. You've already given it to him, haven't you? You're ruined now, and I'm left to have his scraps."

My skirts were already up around my hips and Reggie was clawing at my undergarments as I twisted my hips and tried to shove him away. "I'll scream! I will scream and everyone will come see what you've done!" It was my last-ditch effort. He probably could have had his way with me and murdered me in that room with no one noticing. But my wrist was burning, I needed to get him to let go before it snapped. It felt like it was on the edge. His fingers tightened around it, but his other hand shot to my throat and gripped it instead of my clothes. His eyes were on fire again. I tried to gasp.

"For the sake of my reputation, fine. Fine!" He threw himself off me, wrenching my wrist the other direction in the process, and I cried out as something popped. "You dirty little whore, if you go back on this deal we've finally made whole, after all these fucking years of making me sit around and wait and jump through hoop after fucking hoop like some sort of goddamn circus animal, you mark me, Clara. I will murder him myself. If you back out of this marriage, I will throw him in the fucking Hudson and you will never see him again."

Reggie slammed out of the room, and just a minute later I heard him speaking politely and calmly to someone else in the hallway. He'd left me a mess, my clothes astray, my hair falling out of its pins, mascara probably smeared. I knew I would be a sight to the rest of the party.

Seeing how recovery was far from an option at this point, I gave myself a moment to regroup, then listened at the door and waited until I heard the voices of the partygoers regress down the hall. When they seemed a safe distance away, I ran to the powder room at the end of the hallway, locking the door behind me. Thanks to all the stars in the heavens, my mascara somehow hadn't run. My hair was easy enough to fix and my clothes hadn't torn, so I adjusted everything as well as I could, willed my red eyes to clear, and went to find my mother.

I told her I'd fallen asleep reading, and wanted to go to bed properly, and since I'd already done my duty as daughter-of-the-hostess, I was let go. I managed to do this while keeping my right arm to my side without raising suspicion, but that may have had more to do with the champagne flowing like water rather than any budding acting skills I was putting to use. I stayed in my room long enough to change out of my dinner clothes and take my jewelry off, and wiggled into a much plainer dress. I was favoring my wrist, and doing everything with one hand was so much harder. What a brute, what an absolute horrid brute. And I was meant to be marrying him? I had the brief thought that I'd rather die, but it wasn't true, I just wanted a different choice. I needed to talk to Leo. Reggie would be caught up with the party for a while longer, and wouldn't expect to see me back. Hiding my hair under a hat and grabbing my darkest, plainest coat, I hurried silently down the back staircase and out the kitchen door. It should have been nothing to slip through the gate and scurry to the nearest subway station, which was close enough on a normal day. But it was a full test of endurance with an injured wrist and shaking legs. One quiet train ride holding my wrist close to my chest and avoiding glances later, I was in Brooklyn.

Most everything was closed, but I knew my way to the fire station and who would still be awake at this hour. The city was so quiet away from Manhattan, away from all the glitz and glamour and nonsense. And all the families just wanting 'what was best' for their daughters. When I knocked, it was Timothy who answered, glaring sleepily at me from the kitchen doorway until he recognized me. I would have taken anyone, I knew all their names, but my heart overflowed with thankfulness that it was the one person at the station who loved Leo as well as I did. Timothy, the little brother. Timothy, the secret keeper. Our little guardian.

"Clara?" He'd never been one for formalities and I appreciated him for it. "It's so late, why are you here?" All of Tim's harshness softened. He was too perceptive for me to hide anything. He knew something was wrong. His eyes went right to my arm, my hand covering my hurt wrist. He frowned but didn't say anything. Another thing to be thankful for.

"I really need to talk to Leo." My voice was more desperate than I'd wanted it to be, more strained, and it cracked on his name. I felt my eyes start to water. Timothy nodded, then rubbed his hand over his face.

"He's not at the station tonight. I can take you to his apartment though. Come in here." He moved to usher me into the station kitchen, sat me at the table, and scampered away to wherever it was he slept at the firehouse. I was so grateful to be somewhere quiet and safe, as far away from my family home as I could be just then. Only a few minutes later, he returned with his hat in hand and boots on his feet. "Come on, Clara."

I pushed myself back up with my uninjured hand—quite a feat—and followed Tim out the door. I knew how to get to Leo's apartment but having Tim with me meant I could get lost in my own misery a bit and look down at the sidewalk instead of where I was going. Timothy noticed and reached back for my hand, looking again to the injured one. I positioned it across my chest to protect it and keep it steady.

"You don't have to tell me what happened, Miss Clara, but know I'm on your side."

Something about the tender note in his voice cracked my heart back open, and I lifted my injured hand gingerly to my face to muffle the sob. I didn't see it, but I felt Tim's pitying glance back at me, and the reassuring squeeze to my hand. The boy was so much younger than I was but already taking charge of so much, from duties at the firehouse to his friend's secret lover showing up in the middle of the night. What a heavy burden we'd placed on his shoulders. I hoped he held no resentment about it.

As we walked up the stairs to Leo's apartment, Tim dropped my hand and hurried a bit ahead of me, perhaps to check if any of Leo's neighbors were about. It was the middle of the night, but I appreciated his caution. I waited on the landing until he peeked back around and motioned for me to follow. Tim knocked on the door as I stood with my hand wrapped lightly around my wrist and we waited for Leo to wake up and answer.

It didn't take long, and had I been in a different mindset I would have taken the time to appreciate his unbuttoned shirt and rumpled hair. But as it were, I could hardly look up.

"Clara said she needed to talk to you." Thankfully Tim still had his voice and was able to answer Leo's question before he even asked. I'd lost mine somewhere between the station and the apartment building. I looked up to see Leo pushing his hands through his hair, worry and rage building in his eyes, no doubt immediately and accurately placing the blame on Reggie.

"Thanks, Tim." Leo's voice was thick with sleep, and he reached around Tim for me. I slowly let go of my injured wrist, keeping it tucked against my chest. "Come in, then." He motioned for Tim to follow as well but the boy shook his head.

"I'm going back to the station. Do you want me to tell the chief you'll be in late?" Tim was already readjusting his hat, backing away from the door. I took Leo's hand, and he tugged me closer to wrap an arm around my waist.

"Yes, thank you Tim." Leo glanced at me before turning back to the boy. "I'll make sure Clara gets back safe before coming in. Just tell him it was an emergency."

"Planned on it. Let me know if you need anything." His last words were for me, and I met his gaze and nodded. *Please don't resent the load we've made you carry, dear Timothy.*

"Thank you, Tim." For answering the door, for leading me here, for speaking the first words when I couldn't. I didn't say it but I knew he felt it. I'd repay him properly as soon as possible.

Tim gave us a cheery grin, clearly false but charming all the same, tipped his hat, and headed off. As soon as he was down the stairs, Leo pulled me into his apartment and locked the door.

"What happened?" I could hear the barely contained concern, the bubbling anger as he ran through scenarios of what could have driven me to his door at this hour.

I slumped against him, keeping my hurt wrist tucked against me and holding onto his shirt. Leo wrapped his arms around me with a sigh, his head tucked against my hair. "Reggie threatened me."

"Again?" Leo started to pull back to look at my face, but I hid it against his chest. "What did he do?"

"I think he broke my wrist." My voice was small with the admission, and I timidly leaned back to lift my arm to him. Leo's face was contorted with rage, and his chest lifted with a steadying breath.

"Let me see." He lifted my arm, holding my hand and forearm, and gently bent it back and forth. I winced, but noted the pain was already easing. He shook his head. "I don't think it's broken." He closed his eyes and pulled me back into his arms. I leaned back against him, closing my eyes as well. We were both silent for a moment before I coughed, and Leo moved to get me water. After I drained the glass, I told him the whole story, and Reggie's threat against him if I backed out of the marriage. I even told him the twisted condition of me being allowed to continue seeing Leo as long as I gave Reggie a child. Leo stood in silence for a long while, anger radiating off him in waves. I stared at my empty glass, and we shared the quiet until he spoke again.

"We should leave. I know we keep joking about it, but this just proves it." He was right; he knew it, I knew it, lord knows every ghost and spirit listening in knew it. The truth reached from his small apartment all the way to Barsoom.

"Where would we go?" My voice was hardly a whisper. I couldn't gather enough strength to have any sort of volume.

"Anywhere. Out of New York."

"But you love it here." It was a weak argument, but I couldn't help myself. Leo belonged to New York the same way a fish belonged to water. Imagining him elsewhere seemed like a crime, like treason, like *blasphemy.* I would have happily just stayed in the city with him, in a different neighborhood. There were enough people that it would be easy to hide. We could change our names.

"I love you more." His gentle determination broke me, and I collapsed against his chest as sobs freed themselves from my throat.

He lifted his arms to wrap back around me, hands at my back and fisted together. "You can't marry him, you don't want to, and you shouldn't. God knows what he'll make you do, what you'll become, if you're forced into his house."

Once more, he was right. But I couldn't stop crying long enough to say so.

Leo guided me to sit on the edge of his bed, kneeling in front of it with the first aid kit next to him. He'd gently pulled my ring off my swollen finger with the help of some soapy water and now he took a hold of my hurt wrist, gently prodding it and examining it. "He's lucky nothing's broken. Just badly bruised." The bite at the edge of his voice was revealing his lingering anger, and I wiped at my tears with the back of my uninjured hand. I was still sniffling, trying to get my breathing back under control, trying to ignore the fact I was an absolute wreck and looked like one.

"It hurts a lot," I managed to whisper, and Leo nodded, the set of his jaw telling me far more about his mood than anything else could. He was livid. Furious. Every other synonym that could be found in a thesaurus. But he was controlling all of it just to be able to tend to me properly. In silence, I watched him wrap my wrist and part of my hand with a long bandage, stabilizing it so I couldn't bend it and injure myself further. His gold ring, still on his finger after all these years, glinted here and there in the light. His silent and steadfast promise to me, the one I'd never actually asked him to give, but he'd offered it all the same. He was mine. He had been long before we'd confessed our feelings to each other. And all I wanted was to be able to make that same promise in return.

"Do you want a sling? So you can keep it close to your body?" Leo was already digging in the kit for one, so I just let him put it on me, tying the cloth at my shoulder. As he finished, he lifted his hands to my face and held it softly between his palms. "All of your eye paint is on your cheeks, my dearest." He brushed at what was surely a dark streak along my cheekbone, then leaned forward to kiss my forehead. "Let's get you cleaned up." I hadn't bothered to wash any of it off before I'd left my family's house.

Ten minutes and a washrag later, my face was bare and free of the mascara that had bled over my cheeks as I cried, and I was sitting at Leo's kitchen table as he worked the tangle of knots out of my hair with his fingers and the singular comb he owned. It was slow going because he was intent on not hurting my scalp or pulling any hair out. So far, he'd managed. I stayed quiet and examined the bandage, doing my best not to pick at the tied edge and unravel it.

"Do you want to leave?" Leo's voice was quiet, and he paused his work with the comb. The entire apartment felt like it had frozen, and I closed my eyes against the sensation. Of course I wanted to leave. I'd wanted to run away the moment I'd been engaged to Reggie, the first time he'd cursed at me and tried to hurt me. I'd wanted to run away for years. But Mother being on my side and guarding me, at least at first, had kept me here, and Marie, she'd kept me here. Leo had kept me here. There was so much to love in New York and one thing to hate. But the thing to hate was beginning to eclipse all the things I loved. I must have been silent for too long because Leo moved to crouch at the side of my chair, lifting a hand to touch my chin gently and turn my face toward his. I looked down at him through bleary eyes that were slowly refilling with tears.

"Clara, dearest?" he whispered, and his expression looked as stricken as I felt. "Answer me, please."

I bit my lip, turning away from him, my throat tightening around my answer. I wanted to just take off right then, go hide somewhere deep in the parts of the city where my family would never look, even if Leo didn't come with me. I wanted to be as far away from Reggie as I could be. Leo sighed, letting his hand drop. I knew I was adding to his frustration, I knew he wanted to just toss me over his shoulder and carry me away. But he was letting me make the choice.

He returned to untangling my hair, silently, but I could almost feel the clench of his jaw, hear the soft grinding of his teeth as he worked his thoughts through his head instead of voicing them.

After a while, I lost track of the time, Leo set the comb down with a click of finality on the table and stood next to me, looking down expectantly.

"I can get you out of here. I can make us both disappear, but you need to be willing to come with me." This was a conversation we'd had before, only half-seriously, but this time he was deathly serious. He motioned to my bandaged wrist. "He's only going to do worse from here on out. Especially after you marry him and are forced to move in with him."

I nodded, holding my injured wrist tenderly and keeping my eyes on it. I could so happily abandon

Reggie, but everyone else would be so much harder to let go of. Leo crouched down again to be on eye level with me. I finally turned my gaze to his, trying not to be intimidated by the spark of anger in his eyes. I knew full well it wasn't directed at me, but I had never seen it in my love's gaze before, and the same gleam in Reggie's dark pupils was freshly haunting me.

"At your word, I'll organize everything. All you'll need to do is go back and grab whatever you want to keep, tell your mother if you wish, leave notes, whatever you want to do, and we'll be gone as soon as Thursday." His eyes bore into mine, digging for answers, for permission to put his plan into action. I closed my eyes, sucking in a giant, steadying breath and holding it for just a moment before nodding.

"Let's go. Let's leave," I whispered, leaning toward my fireman, my protector, my guardian. He enveloped me in his arms, and I let my head fall to his shoulder, let my eyes close, let him take my weight.

"I'll arrange it all tomorrow. You need to sleep, and you're not going anywhere tonight." His tone was final enough that I didn't even dream of arguing, and I let him pick me up and carry me back to his bed. Then he disappeared into the hall, and I heard him talking to a neighbor. Upon his return, I looked quizzically at the ladies' nightgown and robe he was carrying.

"My neighbor is letting you borrow these. I said my sister had run away from a terrible man and I was keeping her safe for the night, but she hadn't brought anything." He laid the clothes on the bed next to me, then pulled a proper hairbrush out of his back pocket. "She said to return it all tomorrow when you're dressed again."

I lifted the brush from his hand, pulling my hair over my shoulder to finish the job Leo had started. Luckily, my left hand, the one I normally used for this, was the uninjured one. "She's a darling." My voice was cracked but sincere, and Leo smirked.

"You can thank her properly in the morning."

Leo shooed me away into the bathroom to change, and I hung my clothes on the hook on the back of the door. The nightgown was just a little big, the robe the same, but it would do for one night. Plus, it was a lovely pink, and so soft, so I wasn't about to complain about the size.

After allowing myself a few minutes alone in the bathroom to regain my composure fully, I pulled open the door and slipped back into the bedroom to find Leo lying back on his bed with his hands behind his head. He was also stripped down and, thanks to the blanket across his lap, I couldn't even tell if he was wearing his underthings. My face burned, my heart thumped loudly, and I quickly slipped back behind the bathroom door to *once more* regain my composure. It didn't work. So instead I closed my eyes, took in another large breath, and decided to charge in headfirst. It wasn't as if this hadn't been coming for years, anyway. And what better way to commit ourselves to each other, and to our plan?

He opened his eyes when I stepped on a creaky floorboard and smiled at me, his eyes darkening as his pupils expanded.

"You took your time," I said, and she took my words as permission to come closer. As if she needed permission.

Clara shifted onto the bed, still holding the robe closed against her chest. I was lying as I had been for ten minutes, on my back with my hands behind my head and eyes slipping closed.

"Were you primping and preening in the mirror?" I joked, lowering an arm to smooth my hand along her hip. She shifted closer, leaning down to kiss me instead of answering, her injured wrist tucked back up against her heart. I lifted my hand to her cheek, holding her gently to me so I could let the kiss last longer.

"I'm nervous," she admitted, whispering softly against my lips before claiming them again. I let her hide the nerves in our kiss, moving to wrap my arms around her as she moved to lie on top of me, her legs to the side of my hip instead of straddled like I so desperately wanted her to be. We'd always avoided going this far, to keep other complications from arising, but what did it matter now? We were getting out of here. There was only one precaution that I needed to take now.

She lowered her head to my chest, a hand spread across my heart as she listened to it. I bowed my head to kiss the top of hers, taking in the soft floral scent of her perfume that still hadn't faded from the day.

"I'm still a little shaky, and I can't do anything with this hand," she whispered, trailing her fingers into my chest hair and then up my neck, her nails dragging so gently along my jaw. I took a breath to suppress a shiver.

"It's alright, just come here." I kissed the top of her head again, and she lifted to take my lips with hers, sliding a leg over my hips, settling on them, pulling a low moan from my throat. My hands found her hips, sliding along the gentle silk of the nightgown she'd left on. I could feel there was nothing on underneath, and felt my body react to that knowledge. I squeezed her hipbones to keep myself from bucking up against her.

She pulled back, her hand gliding along my chest, her eyes downcast, her bottom lip gently held between her teeth.

"You...you might have to tell me what to do." Her whisper was hardly more than a breath, I took a moment to smile at her. To call it innocence would have been a lie; we'd gotten nearly this far before, hidden away in closets and tucked into this very bedroom more than once. But she was nervous, still reeling from earlier, and wanted me to take control of the situation. Lucky for her, I didn't mind.

"Lean back a bit, you know this part," I murmured, pushing myself up, adjusting so that I could sit up a bit more against the headboard. I slid my hand—the left one, the one I held my guitar strings with—under the hem of her nightgown and trailed up her leg. I made it a point to hold her gaze once I had it, but it was broken the moment my fingers slipped into the soft pile of her curls and farther against her inner folds. She closed her eyes, whimpering. Her hand tightened on my chest, nails digging in just softly. I played chords against her skin, sliding my fingers along her as she wept for me from her core. It was slow, and tender, and I kept it as such until a single whimpered word drove me to sit up and hold her tight, pushing my fingers inside her.

"Faster."

She didn't speak again until she'd hit her limit, an arm wrapped around my shoulders, her head pressed hard against my neck as she whimpered and moaned into my skin. She clenched around my fingers, three of them slid inside her, the others fondling what they could reach.

"Leo!" she cried, shuddering against my chest and squeezing me close. I smirked, knowing she couldn't see, allowing myself a moment of pride that it was my name she called, my hand that drove her to cry it out.

"Did you like that?" I whispered to her, trailing my free hand down her back to make her shiver, kissing her shoulder and the curve of her neck.

"You...you know I did..." She may have stammered, but the gentle exasperation and contentment shone through, and I chuckled.

"Can I have you, Clara? Fully?" This time, it was my whisper that was naught but a breath, spoken directly into her ear. Only the sheet separated us, and I could feel myself trying to break past it.

Clara leaned back, a little hazy from the pleasure, and laid her free hand on my cheek. The sight of her just slightly above me, lips parted, looking at me through lidded eyes, sent an entirely new, stronger wave of desire through me. The moonlight and glow from the streetlamp outside was hitting her eyes just perfectly, highlighting her cheekbone like no face paint ever could, and I couldn't stand it.

"I'm yours, Leo."

It was all the permission I needed. I pulled the sheet away and rolled her underneath me, minding her injury, and she raised her hand to brush my hair from my face. The light from the window was directly on her now, the gentle curve of her breasts and the small glimpse of her nipples standing out amongst the shimmer of the silk keeping me from it.

"Fuck me, I'm a lucky bastard," She definitely heard me, but I didn't care. I dove toward her to kiss her, work my tongue between her lips, hear her muffled whimper as I reached back down between her legs.

She came for me three times more before I entered her. I needed to hear her noises, feel her call my name against my shoulder. I was absolutely mad with desire by the time I centered myself against her, easing in slowly, our gazes locked once more. Clara's eyes widened and she bit down on her lip, sucking in a slow breath. It was a feat of strength to keep myself from just diving in and taking what she was offering, but there was never going to be a world in which I hurt her. We'd move as slowly as she wanted. Keeping my eyes on her, I pulled back just a bit, pushing forward, repeating the pattern as her eyes fluttered with pleasure. Then she spoke.

"Harder," she panted it, her hand gripping my shoulder, her hips lifting to meet mine.

I obeyed. How could I not? Every command she moaned to me I obeyed. If she needed me to slow down, I did. If she wanted me to use my hand, I used my hand. Every single request, whimpered or shyly nudged for, was obliged. It didn't matter how long it took me to reach my own peak, she would have every bit of pleasure she wanted from me before I finished.

She whimpered and nearly fought me as I tried to pull out, but I managed to lock eyes with her for just a split second, just long enough to remind her of the consequences. The one bit of safety to ensure, just for a little while longer. The noise she made as I pulled away from her to replace her warmth with my own hand is forever branded into my mind as one of the most musical, most spine tingling and incredible sounds I have ever heard.

With a strangled moan I hit the peak, emptying myself against her thigh. I was shivering and barely managed to hold myself up long enough to grab the blankets before collapsing against her with a groan. Her arms slid around me, her injured wrist resting on my back and the other hand trailing up into my hair, her lips pressing against my temple.

It was silent in the room besides our soft panting, and we both broke into a tired laugh at the sound of shouting outside. Someone was arguing with his neighbor about where to park his car, and the neighbor told him where to stick his own.

"Please never stop playing guitar." I had dozed off slightly and her words brought me back, processing them for a moment before laughing.

"As you wish, dearest."

One of my favorite discoveries I made in bed that night was that Clara fell asleep best curled up on her side. And I fell asleep tucked behind her, my forehead pressed between her shoulder blades. We breathed nearly in sync. I could feel it as her ribs rose and fell under the arm I had secured around her.

It was the best sleep I'd had in years.

Clara had gotten up before me. I heard water running in the bathroom and then the door open and shut as she presumably took the nightgown and brush back to my neighbor. I rolled over and pulled my pillow to my face, breathing deeply and relishing the scent of her still on it. We'd spent the night together for the first time, and even though it had been tainted by that foul demon, the end result was wonderful.

I still had my face in the pillow when Clara returned, and I heard her rustling through my cabinets. There wasn't much, but she could have what she liked. I dozed off to the sounds of her cooking something and woke up to quiet besides the clink of a spoon against a bowl. I decided to roll over and get up, pulling on my drawers and going to see what she was doing.

In the kitchen, Clara was curled onto one of my chairs, a bowl of oatmeal in front of her, her eyes on a familiar book. The spoon I'd heard clinking was hovering between the bowl and her mouth, and I chuckled, bringing her out of the trance.

"Oh, good morning." She smiled, then flushed as she realized I was mostly undressed. That made me grin.

"Good morning yourself. I see you've found the tome you left here." She'd brought one of the Barsoom novels on her last visit, one I hadn't read yet, and left it for me.

Her grin matched mine. "I can stay away from John no more than I can stay away from you."

Before she could continue reading, I went to the table and leaned over to kiss her, cupping her cheek in my hand. I rested my forehead to hers, closing my eyes and savoring this precious little domestic moment. "I hope I wake up to you reading about him every day after we're out of here."

Clara giggled, reaching up to touch my jaw. "Me too."

July 3, 1926

M. Birthday. Mostly delightful. Very distracted.

Before I left his apartment that morning, I'd told Leo I didn't want to leave until after Marie's birthday party. I wanted to have that lovely time with her before abandoning her, possibly forever. He understood.

So just days after I'd run to Leo's apartment in the middle of the night—Marie helped me cover things by saying I'd gone to her family's home—she and I were spinning around a ballroom together, laughing as if nothing was wrong, as if my wrist wasn't purple and tender, didn't still twinge when I worked it too hard or tried to lift something too heavy. As if I could get my ring back on my finger and it wasn't tucked under my dress on a chain. Marie knew what had happened and was gentle with me. She was horrified, of course, and at first she insisted I go to my parents once more, maybe even Reggie's parents. I'd reminded her through tears whose very life was at stake and how quickly my father would shove me into Reggie's arms anyway. She relented, but not before making it clear she didn't like the idea of me trading my life for Leo's. Still, every time we were near each other at her party she stood on my injured side, taking my hand gently in hers so it wouldn't be bumped or jostled. I loved her all the more for it. My darling girl. I couldn't believe that I hadn't told her we were leaving yet.

We spun again to the music, panting, ignoring everything else in the world besides ourselves. Then as the song ended, she slowed, shaking her head in amusement. We came to rest against the wall and she took my hand again, protecting it in the simplest and least suspicious way. We'd held hands since we were small, and everyone who knew us knew we were joined at the hip. Claraand-Marie, instead of two distinct people. And we enjoyed that. People always introduced us together, and often the person who'd gotten the introduction didn't know whom was Clara and whom was Marie. We loved it.

"I'm famished." Marie was giggling as she said it, but I followed her eyes and found her favorite waiter in her gaze instead of food. I laughed and shook her hand off mine.

"Go and eat then, dearest." I winked at her, nudging her forward. "I'm going to rest a bit and then we can dance again." I shouldn't have encouraged it, tentatively promised as she was to Lucas, but her sparkling smile and the bubbly air about her when she got to speak with the waiter from New Year's Eve was so difficult to say no to.

"You have yourself a deal!" She leaned over to kiss my cheek, squeezing my upper arm gently before striding away. I tucked my hands between myself and the wall, sinking against it. My eyes unfocused as I looked around the room, all the people Marie and I had grown up with, along with some new faces, piled into the ballroom I'd spent nearly as much time in as my parents'. What would it be like to no longer attend parties like this? To have no reason to be trussed up, dressed to the nines, just to have dinner with my father's business partner. To not have to make an *impression* every single time I was put on display.

To not have to obey every order given to me.

My thoughts consumed me. Somewhere in the back of my consciousness I knew my expression had fallen and I likely appeared as if some tragic thing were happening on the outside of this party, as if it weren't a day of mirth and laughter and celebration of one of the most darling souls ever to grace this earth.

That very soul shook me out of my reverie, scampering back to my side with a wide grin and holding out her hands. I returned her grin and caught her by the arm, taking her back to the dance floor to resume our spinning, dizzying step. Marie was the light of the ballroom and everyone knew it, especially the waiter who kept smiling fondly at her whenever he thought no one was looking.

Marie told me when we were resting again, in chairs this time, that his name was Jackson and she was going to go talk to him again. I waved her off, telling her to bring me back a drink, and she practically skipped away. As I gently massaged my injured wrist, I watched her, laughing and flirting with Jackson. I swore I could hear her bright, happy giggle across the room.

A shadow moved past me, and I looked up to see Lucas making his way to Marie's side. Oh, curses. That would make her laughter quiet very quickly. Lucas had been charming and friendly all last summer, then returned to work in the fall and we'd seen less of him. Of course, as Marie's official suitor, he'd been to all our parties and the more important dinners, but it was rare to see him without a schedule. Marie had confessed to me just recently that he'd been telling her that he couldn't wait to be living together and he could show her how a real married couple behaves, and she wasn't sure she'd liked the gleam in his eye when he'd said it. She'd also told me a story about him yelling at a waiter at the Plaza. I'd told her that they were far from official and she could break it off, but she wanted to give him a bit more of a chance. I told her she was too nice for her own good, and it had nearly brought us to an argument, so I'd agreed to keep my thoughts to myself unless he got worse.

Unfortunately, it seemed to be getting worse over at the buffet table. Lucas had settled his hand on Marie with blatant possessiveness, and even across the room I could see her shrinking into herself.

My heart sank with another ton weight of guilt.

July 8th, 1926

M. wanted to go to bakery. Feeling apprehensive.

It was because of my guilt that, when Marie asked me after the party if I would go with her to the bakery where Jackson worked, I agreed. I worked it out to where we'd go on Thursday, so I could try to talk to Leo as well. I told Marie I'd meet her at the station we usually met at and left an hour before the time we'd agreed on to go to Brooklyn and find Leo.

He was waiting for me on the steps of the milliner's, arms crossed, elbows resting on his knees, and his face holding displeasure. I sighed, knowing its source. Moving closer to him, I held out a hand and tried to smile. He looked up, and the smile he gave me in return didn't light his eyes.

I think he was trying to do it secretly, but I saw him look pointedly at my lack of luggage.

"Hello, dearest." He stood, taking my hand and kissing it. "I take it we're not heading out today?" I could very nearly taste the disappointment on his lips when he leaned forward to kiss me. As he pulled away, I shook my head, looking down to hide the tears gathering in my eyes.

"No, I'm sorry."

He pulled a deep, steadying breath into his lungs, letting it out slowly. "Alright." He took my hand again, threading my arm through his. "Where *are* we going today then?"

"Marie asked us to go with her to meet with that waiter from New Year's Eve. She's found out he works in a bakery as well and wants to see him."

"Is that safe?" I'd told Leo about Lucas and how I didn't trust him, that his eyes were the same as Reggie's, but I didn't want to ruin Marie's relationship when she seemed happy. Was she still happy? Maybe not, after her birthday party.

I sighed, resting my head on his shoulder briefly. "I hope so."

We made our way to the train station, catching the train back to the one I'd just left. Since we were in a part of town where seeing people who knew me was much more likely, we sat a seat apart and didn't touch, waiting for Marie to show. It was almost a relief, to be forced to not talk about why we hadn't left yet, why I was delaying our plan. I knew I had to explain, and I would, but it would be in private.

I was planning out my explanation in my head when Marie showed up, seeing Leo first and going to greet him before pivoting to me with a wide smile. I treasured her ability to immediately read a situation. She and I hooked our arms together, moving to stand on the platform, and I glanced back at Leo who nodded nearly imperceptibly. He sat two seats behind us on the train, close enough to see when we were getting off and far enough it didn't look as if we were traveling together. Marie told me all about her and Jackson's conversation at her party, and I hate to admit I only half-listened to her. I was trying not to notice the sensation of Leo's gaze on the back of my head, or at least, that's what I imagined. When I glanced back to check, he had his cheek in his hand and was staring out the window as if we weren't two seats in front of him. His gaze was so, so distant. Almost like it had been after losing his mother. And I'd thought my heart couldn't get any heavier.

Before long, Marie was readying to get off at the next stop, and Leo looked up in time to see us standing. He exited the train with a few people between us, just in case, but we were far enough away from the heart of Manhattan that we'd be safe. I slid my hand into his as soon as he came close enough, and my heart tensed as he squeezed my fingers. He'd fought us when we asked him to join us at the New Year's Eve party, he didn't think it would be safe. It had been, but had it been worth this tension? Was it worth making him this deeply uncomfortable? Was any of his pain worth the love I had?

We walked in silence all the way to the bakery, and Marie was on a high enough cloud at the thought of seeing her waiter again that she didn't even notice. We reached the door of the bakery—I only knew because Marie stopped and turned to set her hands on my shoulders—and she grinned.

"If you see anyone, you can drag me out, and I'll know it's a sign." She was grinning so brightly, at odds with the gloom in my heart. I knew by anyone she really meant Lucas, and I quickly sorted through the possibilities of him being nearby. Luckily, they were low.

"Are you sure about this? Lucas was so angry last time. I thought he was going to punch a hole in the door." The last time had been right after her birthday party, when I'd had the unfortunate pleasure of witnessing Lucas admonishing Marie for spending all her time with me and the waiter instead of the rest of the guests and most importantly, him. Marie just nodded encouragingly, and I bit down on my lower lip before finally sighing. "Fine, alright. But Leon and I are going in too."

Leo followed us silently into the shop, and he and I took up a post where we could watch out the window. Not that he'd recognize anyone troublesome, but it was nice to have someone else on the lookout. We peered at the pastries, chocolates, and a whole display of different types of breads, all while listening to Marie and Jackson flirt over a box of chocolates. At one point, another bakery employee entered the room, and I glanced at his red hair as he praised his own creations, then Marie stammered out that she needed to leave. I nudged Leo gently with my elbow, and he nodded.

As soon as we hit the street, I caught Marie by the arm and didn't let her go as we made our way back to the station. "Why were you flirting so much?" I hissed, my heart pounding behind my ribs. I shouldn't have encouraged this, I shouldn't have agreed to come with her. I should have pushed her harder to break things off with Lucas.

Marie flushed, shaking her head a little. "He was too." Her words were just a breath, and she squeezed the little box to her chest. I closed my eyes, just briefly, to regroup. *Oh, dear.*

Leo and I parted ways with Marie at the train station, her heading back toward the Financial District as we made our way back to Brooklyn. He sat next to me on the train, not holding my hand or even inviting me to rest my head on his shoulder, and it felt like a dagger in my heart. I finally worked up the courage to talk when we were in front of his apartment building, which we'd walked to without thinking.

"I'm sorry." My voice was smaller than I'd wanted it to be as I anxiously twisted my gloves between my hands. Leo turned to me, one eyebrow raised quizzically, waiting for me to continue. "I'm sorry it keeps getting delayed. I'm sorry we haven't left yet. It was supposed to be days ago. We should be so far away by now." I pressed my gloves to my mouth, feeling a single teardrop escape the prison I'd tried to lock them in. Leo sighed slowly and ran his hand through his hair.

"Come on, let's go inside."

I nodded and he took my hand, and we walked up the stairs to his apartment in silence, just like the walk to the bakery. He only let go of me to unlock his door, then guided me to sit down on one of his chairs. He took the other.

"You told me you want to leave, and I understand why you wanted to wait until after the party. That was fine, I'm not bothered. But what happened with this?" I'd expected anger, a blowup, Leo shouting at me and telling me that it was all off unless I was going to be serious and take off with him right that moment.

I twisted my gloves between my fingers some more, searching for answers, wishing I were on Barsoom instead. I'd almost rather take my chances with the white apes and Tharks or set myself up in Helium and live out my days as a scribe. Leo's elbows settled heavily on the table, his hands catching his head between them. His loud sigh brought me back down to earth.

"Everything's ready to go but you, Clara."

Somehow his soft, tender whisper was worse than a shout.

"I'm sorry. I just...it's..." I held my gloves to my face again, smothering a little sob. "Marie, she..."

"If you told her, she would understand." His patience was undeserved.

"I'm so afraid for her. Lucas reminds me too much of Reggie and it frightens me. I'm so scared she's going to end up like me." The words flooded out, muffled slightly by my dampening gloves.

"In love, ready to leave with the man she loves? I'm sure if she found the will, she'd break things off in a heartbeat. She's just as strong as you are, Clara." I couldn't bear that he was complimenting me at that moment.

"I don't want Jackson threatened! I don't want his life to be in danger!" In that moment, I realized that I'd never told Leo about Reggie's threat against his life. The room went quiet, still, and I hid behind my gloves.

"Clara..." Leo began, and I peeked to see his hands in his hair, his eyes closed. "Did Reggie threaten me?" He kept his voice steady, but I'd known him long enough to hear the thread of rage lacing it. I didn't want to tell him, but he took my silence as confirmation. "God damn it, Clara." He pushed away from the table, standing and pacing the room. As his anger grew, I shrunk.

"I'm sorry," I whispered, and Leo stopped his pacing, lowered his hands, and came to kneel in front of me, taking both my hands in his. When I didn't meet his eyes he sighed.

"I'm not angry with you, I just..." He huffed in irritation, shaking his head. "Why didn't you tell me? Why didn't you let me know my own life was in danger from that bastard?"

"I don't know." My voice was just a squeak, and Leo gently released my hands to start pacing again. He linked his fingers behind his head, standing at the far side of the room, clearly working to control his breathing.

"I understand you don't want Jackson threatened. I understand. But you can't stay here and try and guard Marie instead of protecting yourself."

I started stammering, words flooding from me once more. "She is just too obsessed with that waiter. Lucas is going to find out, and he's going to just chain her to the hous—"

"Just like Reggie found out about me, Clara?" Leo was forcing himself not to snap, just like he'd promised me years ago. But he was moving closer and closer to the edge.

"I don't want her to be in this situation!" I shouted, collapsing, my head touching my knees as I sobbed. "I don't want her to be in this spot, torn between her heart and society and danger and love and everything else. I couldn't bear it if she had to make the choices I'm having to make."

Leo made his way back across the room as I sobbed, kneeling in front of my chair once more and reaching out to hold my shoulders. When he finally spoke after some long moments, it was gentle, hardly any of the lingering anger audible. "You can't sacrifice your own happiness, Clara." Just like Marie had said about going to my parents about Reggie. I couldn't trade my life for someone else's, no matter how desperately I wanted to. All I could do in the moment was sob harder. Leo pulled me gently off the chair and gathered me to his lap, his arms around me, hands fisted at my back and his head against mine. "You love her, I know. I know you love me. I'm not asking you to choose between us. I'm asking you to choose yourself." He was whispering, and he tilted his head to kiss my temple, just a graze of his lips. "Just choose what will give you the happiest life. And if it means staying here, instead of going away with me, I'll stay here too. I'll deal with Reggie's threats and conditions and whatever else the son of a bitch wants to try and force us into, because without you, my life will never be happy. If I only get you on another man's terms, I will accept it. It will hurt, it will be hell, but I would rather burn in hell with you than be anywhere else without you."

I couldn't take it. His sincerity felt absolutely undeserved, There was no way I had gained this deep of a love from a man that I had already hurt so much. It was unbelievable. And all I could do about it was cry. Hard, loudly, holding onto Leo as if he were the only thing keeping me together. He just held me, arms like steel bands around me, his head resting on mine as he rocked us both on his kitchen floor. It took a while, he wouldn't tell me how long, before I calmed down enough that he felt it was alright to let me go, and he helped me back into the chair before making some tea. The water was heating as he leaned back against the counter, arms crossed, looking me over. I was futilely trying to straighten out the hem of my glove, which I'd gripped too tightly and now was creased. It was also wet, but that was easier to fix. Leo's kettle whistled, and he turned around at its call. He dragged his empty chair closer to mine, our knees touching, and set the mug in front of me.

"How about tomorrow? You can go home, get everything that you want to keep packed up, leave a note for Marie, and we will leave in the morning." His eyes were searching my face, and I glanced up at him briefly before wrapping my hands around my mug and staring into it. "Clara?"

I just nodded, taking a sip. I still didn't want to abandon Marie, but if I wrote her a really good letter, I wouldn't feel as guilty. I had already planned on leaving her a note, but maybe I'd just talk to her in person? No, no. If she cried in front of me

I'd never be able to leave. I'd never, ever be able to leave her side, even if she told me to go.

"We could take her with us, Clara. It wouldn't be difficult." Leo's voice had gotten softer, all the anger dissipated, only quiet exasperation remaining.

"I know."

He lifted a hand to rub his eyes and pinch the bridge of his nose. "I know I gave you no time to think, I'm sorry. I'm sorry I'm being pushy, I'm sorry I'm trying to force you into this." His hand laid on the table between us, his fingers stretching toward mine. "I want you to choose, like I said. But please, don't make me wait a long time." I finally looked up, matching his gaze, and his earnest, begging expression almost sent a new wave of tears to my eyes. "Please."

"I won't. I promise." Somewhere, while staring into his eyes, I'd found my strength again and used it to stand up and kiss him. He let go of his mug to cup my face between his hands, and I slid onto his lap. "I'm sorry. I'm so sorry," I whispered between kisses, threading my fingers through his hair. "I'm sorry I didn't tell you everything, I'm sorry I've made you wa—"

"You already apologized, dearest." Leo quieted me with a gentle kiss, his thumb running along my cheekbone. I moved to wrap my arms around his shoulders and we gradually became more intertwined, Leo's lips slipping down my neck and trailing along my collarbone before he paused, panting softly as he looked up at me. "Is this alright? Right now?" I nodded, catching his mouth with my own again, starting the process over.

Distract me from all this right now, please, I thought, tilting my head to the side to allow Leo more room. His lips trailed along the tendon in my neck, his hand pressed between my shoulder blades as he leaned me back ever so gently. I closed my eyes, shifting when needed to give him room, gasping near-silently as Leo laid me on the table and buried his face between my breasts, tugging the collar of my dress down just a bit, enough to let his lips brush the skin of my sternum, trailing over the chain that held my ring. I lifted my hands to his hair.

"I love you, Clara." His voice was muffled in my dress, and I felt the rumble of it in my ribs. I tightened my grip on his hair, not enough to hurt.

"I love you, Leo," I whispered, and his head sank lower, lower, disappearing under my dress. He spent the next little while reminding me just how *ardently* he adored me.

I returned home later that day a little lightheaded, most of my makeup scrubbed away, and with a flush to my cheeks. I'd had the foresight to clean myself up in Leo's bathroom before leaving his apartment, and my gloves had dried, so I didn't think any evidence of my day's activities would be noticeable.

"Gone to dally in Brooklyn again, Clara?" Reggie's unnerving voice called from the library as I passed it, and I froze, then spun around to see him sitting in the chair that faced the door. I quickly made my way into the room, relieved upon noticing there was no one in there with him. He laughed. "Your parents aren't here at the moment. Don't worry, your secret is with me. Not safe, by any means, but with me." His grin lit rage deep in my chest. I wanted to swing my purse across his face.

"Why are you here?" I demanded, forcing myself not to cross my arms and pout like some little girl not getting her way. I squared my shoulders, looking down at him. He just grinned wider.

"I'm sure your mother will tell you when she gets home. Why don't you go wash the fireman off of you and we can find out together?" He already knew, I was absolutely sure, but I stormed out of the library anyway.

I did take a bath, behind a locked door with one of the maids positioned in front of it as a chaperone since Reggie and I were the only ones in the house. Society rules were in my favor for this, at least. I could use them to keep Reggie and me from being alone together as long as my parents were out of the house. If only it had worked a few weeks ago, but that party had consisted of a few too many guests for my parents to worry about any one person in particular, even their own daughter.

Mother came directly to my room with a jubilant air, knocking a bright tune on my door before poking her head in. I looked up from one of my Barsoom novels, and she smiled. "Come downstairs, darling, there's great news!" I did as she bid, sighing all the way. I met them in the library, where Reggie was still perched in the same chair, and I realized with absolute horror he was holding the copy of *A Princess of Mars* that Leo had bought me. It took every single shred of willpower and decorum to clasp my hands behind my back instead of smack my precious keepsake out of his.

"What's this grand news?" I asked, trying to keep my tone light and unbothered, as if Reggie hadn't already harassed me earlier. Father straightened, his hand resting on the back of the chair Reggie was sitting in. As if he were already a son, as if Father had already claimed him as one of his own.

"Since you two have finally made it official, after all these years of waiting"—here he paused to give me a stern look, and I knew that he blamed me for every delay, possibly even Reggie's schooling—"we're holding your engagement party this weekend." He was grinning, and I returned it, but I could hear my heart drop to the floor. This weekend? How terrible would it be if I didn't attend, how quickly would Reggie figure it out? Would he go to the station? Would he threaten Tim and the others too? Could I get away with it if I ran to Leo tonight?

Reggie snapped my book shut, his vile grin still splitting his face. "We'll have so much fun it'll *slay* you, Clara. Enough to light a fire in your soul."

The coded message turned my soul to ice instead.

July 10th, 1926

Dreaded party. Horrible.

In the end, against everything in my heart screaming at me to run to Brooklyn, take Leo's hand, and run farther, I forced myself to stay. At least for the engagement party. Reggie had threatened Leo again, and I'd caught the spark in his eye, the sharpness of his grin that my parents hadn't seen. But now I wanted it to be over. I was praying for it all to be over. He'd already made his big announcement, and I'd raised my hand dutifully to show off the giant new rock on my finger, letting it sparkle in the light.

I found Marie's eyes across the room; she was standing next to the refreshments table. Those same two caterers from her birthday party were behind her, and I felt the deepest wave of sympathy from all three. Marie looked as if she were about to cry, and I had to look away from her to keep my own eyes from welling up with tears. I tightened my grip on the champagne glass in my hand, willing myself not to break it. It was thin enough I likely could have. Probably very expensive as well. The temptation to do it and use it as an excuse to leave the party swelled dangerously within my heart, but right as I'd worked up most of the nerve, Reggie led me off the little platform for the band and dropped my hand.

Relief flooded me, and I found enough of a smile to placate all the well-wishers in the crowd as I made my way to Marie. It was the least suspicious and most relieving thing I could do, and it would keep me from fleeing the room.

She lifted her hands to my arms as soon as I was close enough, and I stepped into my best friend's embrace, suppressing my shudder.

There were others nearby so I tried to keep a jovial, light tone, remarking upon all the gifts my fiancé had heaped upon me. Jewels, furs, more than I could ever possibly wear. What was I to do with them all? It was only a small exaggeration.

Marie took her part in this farce easily and without complaint, giggling and saying perhaps I should share some with her. We kept up the charade until the crowd shifted away, out of earshot. We lowered our voices.

"Honestly though, what does he think I need all this for? It's not as if I'm some costumeless girl from the streets, and he knows that." I sighed, our hands finding each other's and holding tight. She sighed with me.

If I had been a woman of a different station, Reggie showering me with gifts and clothes befitting who I'd become after marriage would have made more sense. But my family was in a better station than his! Weren't we? We'd been part of society for far longer! I was still unsure thanks to Mother's words from Newport. Before, I would have thought it would have been more accurate for me or my father to be buying him new suits and shoes so that he'd look better at our table, and not embarrass us in public, but now I had no idea. I shivered at the idea of being forced to be with him in public, more than I already had. Marie lifted her free hand to my other arm.

"I don't want to keep any of it, but he's already chastised me for not wearing any of it tonight." I felt pinpricks at the corners of my eyes, recalling the whispered admonishment as we waited to make our entrance into the party. "As if he didn't dump it all on me this morning, I barely had time to even see if anything fit." My voice was trembling, and Marie squeezed my hand as it started shaking too.

When she spoke, I knew she'd somehow read my thoughts. "I know, the more you let him put on you, the more it feels he owns you."

I nodded, my shoulders rounding forward, lifting my hand so I could mimic a yawn to anyone watching. Someone came over to the table to pick at the spread, so Marie and I quickly picked back up our banter about the clothes I seemingly had no idea what to do with. It wasn't said, but I could tell we were both thinking about burning them.

As the crowd ebbed away once more, I allowed my head to droop, my eyes to close. "Leo's going to be so upset," I whispered, pulling my hand from Marie's grasp to spin the heavy engagement ring around my finger, again and again, letting the too-large jewels catch my skin. Marie reached up, taking my hands in hers, making me stop.

"He can't do anything," she said, and although it would have sounded cruel to anyone else, I knew she was just as distraught about that fact as I was. Leo, my love, my darling, had no power here. No standing, no money, not even a name among these glittering fools.

Just for a moment, not even sure I was safe to do so, I let my façade shatter. The devastation and heartbreak, the fear for my love's life, I allowed it all to show for one brief moment. Marie matched it with her own pained look, understanding entirely.

She glanced to the caterer she'd been speaking with before, and I looked as well. I'd suggested their company for this event solely for Marie's benefit, but finding another pair of sympathetic eyes was an unexpected balm on my heart. This man barely knew me, but he felt sorrow for my situation. I wanted to laugh almost—even near strangers could see how badly I didn't want this if I let it show.

It was that glance that made me decide I needed to leave New York.

July 11th, 1926

Followed Mother on her errand, distracted, unhappy.

Manhattan

I'd have left that night, if it weren't for Mother insisting that I needed to go with her to New Jersey for a couple days, at the engagement party, no less! There was a charity luncheon there, one of her many groups, and she'd promised to bring me along. Without telling me until the day before, of course. I'd thought all of my obligations had been taken care of. I'd quietly spoken to the leading ladies of each organization to which I belonged, and, under the guise of a leave of absence due to wedding planning, withdrawn my membership with a promise, of course, that I would return after I was happily wed and settled after the honeymoon. It was an easy enough lie to concoct and eased much of the guilt surrounding Leo's and my flight from New York. But Mother's charities were not the same as mine, and so I hadn't needed to speak to them. I didn't belong to any of them, but for this one in New Jersey, benefiting orphans or veterans of the war or someone else, I couldn't remember, Mother and her friends had been doing their absolute best to bring me into their ranks. I'd been toying with the idea until Leo and I had decided it was time to leave, at which point I told my mother I simply had too much on my plate with my own organizations.

But still, she insisted I accompany her to this damned event. And so, bound by familial duty, societal obligation, and that ever-present, ever-pressing shadow of guilt, I failed to get a message to Leo and went to New Jersey with my mother early Saturday morning. I had even been tempted to ring the station, but the thought of one or more of our neighbors overhearing me on the party line was simply too terrifying. It's what had kept us from using it all this time, and without Juliana acting as buffer as she had before, it would be too easy for anyone to figure us out.

The trip was meant to take two days, and it was easily the most agonizingly long two days of my life. It wasn't as if New Jersey was far from the city, much closer than Newport of course, but it was miles away from Leo and our plan and my freedom, his survival. I tried vehemently to behave as if nothing were bothering me, as if I were simply tired from wedding planning and nervous to be a new bride. All lies easily told and accepted.

Everything passed in a haze, a swirl of conversation, tittering laughter, teacups clinking against saucers, passionate speeches delivered by the most well-read women in each room, more speeches from the wealthiest women in the group. Deciding where best to send the funds, what the theme of the next month's fundraiser would be, should we do a bazaar? Should we host a formal and charge a price at the door? What food should we serve, what decor, what color this, what shade of that. I lost track of every bit of it. My heart and mind were back in Brooklyn, waiting with the fireman who was going to rescue me from this blaze.

Brooklyn

I hadn't seen her for three whole days. It would have been normal, it would have been fine, if we hadn't been trying to leave. I'd made the mistake of expecting her to come back to Brooklyn the day after the bakery, packed and ready to go. But she hadn't, and doubt was making its vile way into my heart. It was Monday and I hadn't seen her, hadn't gotten word through Marie like I had before, since

Thursday. We'd first agreed to leave on the night of the thirtieth, and it was already the eleventh of the next month. I knew about Marie's party, but she'd made me wait nearly two entire weeks. I was going mad with impatience. Why did we keep getting delayed? Where was she?

As I paced around the station kitchen, out of things to clean and sort and put away, Tim stepped right in my path. "Will you stop that?" he snapped, and I glared at him. He glared right back. "What the hell is going on?"

"I'm waiting for something important." I turned away from him to pace in the opposite direction.

"What, Clara to show up finally so you can leave?"

I stopped. "Yes."

Tim sighed, moved to sit in one of the chairs at the table, and patted the one beside him. I took it, catching my head in my hands.

"Listen, Leo." Tim suddenly sounded like his father, like Gregory, like my father. "She loves you. It's obvious. You'd have to be a total sap to not realize. She'll show. I'm sure there's something going on that she can't get away from."

"Or she's just decided that living with that bastard is easier than running away with me." I mumbled, and Tim slapped me on the shoulder. I jumped and turned to find him staring down at me furiously.

"Knock it off! Damn it, Leo." He sighed again, harder this time, and stood. "She bought you that ring didn't she? She's come to see you as often as she damn can. She. Loves. You." With each of the last three words he stabbed his finger into my shoulder, then whipped around and left the kitchen, his irritation trailing after him.

He was right, I knew Clara loved me. My eyes landed on the gold band, my thumb shifting to press it into my finger. It was still early morning, so there was the rest of the day to wait.

But she didn't show on Sunday.

July 12th, 1926

Home again. Thank goodness.

Brooklyn

Or Monday.

That night, one of my chairs hit the wall of my kitchen and a leg broke off. I stared in horror at it until I realized I had been the one to throw it, then my horror was turned to my own hands.

I'd broken something in anger for the first time in my life. My knees hit the floor, hands covering my face. Clara wasn't coming. Either something horrible had happened and I'd never get to know what, or she'd chosen Marie. She'd chosen life in a cage, gilded as it was, over freedom with me. It was the only thing that made sense. These past two weeks she'd just been trying to figure out how to tell me.

She was never going to leave with me. I had convinced myself of it and I had no way of finding out if it were true short of going to her family home and demanding answers, but I realized with embarrassment that I didn't even know where it was. If I'd known her address, I could have asked the phone operator to connect the station phone to her, but I didn't. Of course, it was better that way, but it meant I truly did not know how to find her, talk to her, convince her that we needed to leave. She couldn't marry him. She'd become a husk of herself, and even with his twisted proposition of allowing her to come to me after they were married, I wouldn't be able to stand watching it happen.

I cleaned up the broken chair silently, carrying it down to the dumpster in the alley. I'd have to pay the landlord for it, no matter if we left or not. But we weren't leaving, so maybe I'd just buy a new one. It didn't matter. It wasn't like anyone was going to be coming over anymore, anyway. I stood outside and smoked two cigarettes in a row just to get myself back under control. This habit was becoming a crutch, I realized.

I went to bed that night curled around the hollow in my chest, Clara in every heartbeat, in every dream. I knew I'd sleep like this for the rest of my life.

New Jersey to Manhattan

It was a relief to be on the train back, Mother across from me in the lady's section of the first class area, the little table between us shivering with the car's movement. I sighed in relief, but I was too obvious. Mother chuckled.

"Was the meeting truly that exhausting, my love?" She smiled into her teacup, still looking down at the paper in her lap. I looked up at her, startled, then forcefully relaxed my posture.

"It is simply a lot of travel and discussion for two days, is all. I'm glad that there's nothing planned for the coming week." I casually rested my chin on my hand, elbow on the arm of my seat. It was a probing statement, to make sure my plans would not be thrown askew once more.

Mother chuckled softly again. "Yes, darling, you can hide yourself in the library and read all your books for the hundredth time." Her attention was firmly on her paper once more, and I took the quiet dismissal of conversation gratefully.

Leo had said he was ready to go; everything was in place. He'd spoken to the chief of the fire station, to Timothy, and gathered everything we'd need. His landlord knew, his things were packed, and he'd managed to buy a car from someone in the neighborhood for a fair price. It was sitting behind the station now, waiting for us. I had begun sorting through my things at night when everyone else was to bed. I'd only been asked once by a maid what had happened to one of my dresses, but I'd shrugged it off, saying I must have left it at Marie's and would check next I was there. She'd accepted the explanation, but I made a mental note to not actually pack anything else until the night I left, and instead secretly started moving it all to easy-to-find places in my bedroom. No one had questioned me thus far.

The only thing I had left to do was write a letter to Marie. I'd been avoiding it for so long. I'd even considered waiting until after we'd left to send it to her from somewhere along the road, but that could be dangerous, and, more than that, I knew it would shatter her. So I couldn't. I wouldn't.

I also couldn't tell her to her face and watch her shatter. Every bit of resolve that I'd managed to build, all of the courage I had screwed to its sticking place, would wash away with Marie's tears. I was cursing myself for being such a coward, for not just taking her with me. But Lucas's family had more connections, more money, than Reggie's. He would find her—find *us*—far too easily. So as much as I hated it, I had to leave my darling girl behind. It would be a miracle if those resources sat untouched after our flight, anyway.

I was halfway into planning her rescue, coming back a while after Leo and I escaped to take her away, when we pulled back into New York. Thoughts for another time, I supposed. There was always a chance we could come back, sneak into her home quietly, and carry her off. It was an option. I contented myself with that as Mother and I made our way back home.

I spent the rest of the day curled up in the library as mother had said I could, hidden away from everyone. Thankfully, not a single person called on me.

Monday night, it was time to start packing in earnest. I'd go to Leo in the morning and tell him it was time, that I was sorry I'd made him wait. I'd take hold of his hand and not let it go. I'd explain everything, why it had taken so long, why I'd made the choice to wait when we could have left right after Marie's birthday. I hoped he'd understand; he usually did, but I knew his patience was thin after Reggie had hurt me.

I sorted through my books. Obviously I had to take the novel Leo had bought me and the rest of the series. I'd given all my Fitzgeralds to Marie, and the others I frequented weren't really mine. So in the end, it was to be just John Carter and me braving the world together. I laid the books on my dressing table. I'd left them there enough times that no one would think it odd.

I slipped some jewelry into pouches, things I liked, things from Reggie that I hated but could sell. Leo said he'd gotten enough money, but I wanted to be useful. I didn't want the burden to fall entirely on him. I left Reggie's engagement ring in the middle of my jewelry box, safe but hidden. I didn't want to sell that. It would be too easy to trace. But taking it with me was not even remotely in the cards.

Clothes were harder. I had shunned all of my most gaudy and extravagant costumes, choosing only the plainest and simplest things to take. But it still felt like too much. Too many of them would make it obvious that I was from a well-to-do family, a rich girl running away. I knew well enough how big of a target that would paint on our backs. In the end, I picked three dresses and two pairs of shoes. Somehow even that seemed a bit much, but at least it all fit in my bag alongside undergarments and two nightgowns. I tried not to consider finding my winter things, tucked away by maids and packed for the season.

I spent far too much time packing and repacking my bag, the biggest one I could find without digging too deeply into the closet all our luggage was stored in. I thought about taking one of the trunks, just to take more with me, but I couldn't pull it off the shelf, let alone carry it to Brooklyn.

So, the bag would have to do. It was the subject of all my attention, adjusting everything in it just so, turning the shoes this way and that to see if they'd fit better. But it was a ruse. I was still avoiding writing the letter to Marie.

After the fifth time of taking everything out of the bag and replacing it, I finally relented and pulled stationery from my drawer. I couldn't leave my darling girl without an explanation. I wouldn't.

Marie, my dearest...

The letter finally written, teardrops dried as best they could be from the page, I sealed it in an envelope and signed her name on the outside. It would be nothing to hand it to one of our maids or footmen and have it delivered to her house, have her maid slip it under her pillow like it was a little game. Easy enough to present it as such, easy enough to believe that two grown childhood friends still acted as if they were both in the nursery. If only it were a game.

July 13th, 1926

Going. If Mother or Father reads, I'm not very sorry.

Manhattan

Sleep evaded me the entire night. I was still up, caught between reading idly and looking out the window, when my maid came in.

"Oh! Miss! You're already up!" She was surprised, but smiled and came over to me, gesturing for me to sit at my vanity. "Here, let me help you with your hair. Did you forget to take it down when you came up last night?"

I had, and so I allowed her to brush it all out and put it back up in a lovely style, all my curls restrained and artfully arranged. With a genuine grin I told her as such, and she giggled, flushing.

"Thank you miss. Please let me know if you need anything else!" She was already heading out the door as she called, carrying the linens from my bed down the hall. I peeked, and no one else was about, so I quickly changed into the dress I planned to wear for the journey, handed Marie's note off with instructions, gathered my things, and slipped out the back gate just like I had the night Reggie had nearly broken my wrist. I almost felt sad that no one had caught me, that it had been so easy to simply disappear. I wondered how long it would take them to notice me missing as I waited at the train station, tying a scarf around my hair. The more of my features I could hide, the better.

The train pulled in, and I stepped on. It was time.

Brooklyn

It was barely past dawn when I heard the knock at my door. I didn't even fully register it, until it came again. Shoving myself up, I made my way across the kitchen and pulled it open.

Clara fell against my chest, and immediately I lifted my arms to wrap around her. "Oh, dear god." I breathed, feeling my legs shake and knees start to buckle. "You came." It was a silent whisper, and I squeezed her to me tightly, feeling the hollow place in my chest twist painfully. Had I been wrong? Or had she come to tell me that this was our final meeting?

"I'm so sorry! Leo, please, please forgive me, I'm so sorry!" She was already in tears, and I managed to gather enough strength to pull her inside the apartment and close the door. She had a scarf tied around her hair, damp from the drizzling rain and falling off a little, and she tugged it away as she set her bag on the floor. "Leo, I swear I didn't want to make you wait this long, everything got thrown at me, there was so much going on."

I pushed my hair back from my face, ready to soothe her if need be. When I reached my out hand to her, she immediately took hold of it. "What happened?"

She laid out the events of the past few days to me, the engagement party, Reggie's latest threat, the trip with her mother. All since we'd gone to the bakery together. I stared at her, stunned.

"All of that?"

"All of it." She nodded, wiping under her eye with the back of her hand. "I didn't know what to do. Reggie threatened you again, and I couldn't take the chance he'd just march down here and stab you. I'm sure he knows where you live by now."

I pulled her back into my arms, bowing my head so my face was in her hair. We were silent for a long while, just standing in the middle of the kitchen holding each other. I still couldn't quite believe she was here. She tried apologizing again but I shushed her gently, shaking my head.

"Clara, the only thing you have to apologize for is making yourself miserable. When I said choose the path that makes you happiest, I didn't mean try to tie up every loose end you possibly could before you did so."

"I just didn't want to leave things unfinished," she whispered, and I squeezed her tight again. Of course she didn't. Anything she could have done to make her disappearance easier on other people, she would have done. She was that kind of woman.

"Well, it seems you haven't." I pulled back, holding onto her shoulders. "Does the bag mean you're ready to go?" I asked it hesitantly. My hopes were trying to soar but my doubt was tearing them back down.

She nodded, and the gloom from yesterday that had slowly been ebbing since I answered the door finally faded away. Hope won out. The hollow in my chest had started to refill. I'd never been so glad to be wrong.

Clara settled on the remaining chair, looking quizzically at the empty space where its match used to be, and I went to pack up the last few things and get dressed. My trunk with the majority of my belongings—Mom's quilts, my guitar, and my parents' wedding rings included—was already in the car parked behind the station. Clara's grin was impossibly wide as I stepped out of my bedroom wearing the suit she and Marie had bought for me. It was probably too warm for it, but I didn't care.

So, with a bag that nearly matched Clara's, her hand in mine and an umbrella over our heads, we walked to the station for the last time.

Tim was already up and opening the garages, airing them out and dragging a length of hose when we saw him, and he grinned. He dropped the hose and he came running over, going for Clara immediately. She was as shocked as I was when he wrapped his arms around her and spun, settling her back on her feet just to kiss her forehead. I lowered the umbrella; it wouldn't fit all of us under it and I didn't think any of us cared.

"What was that for?" She laughed, patting his face softly. He pulled back, still grinning, and leaned forward to kiss her cheek.

"For finally showing up. Now get outta here, would ya?" Tim was laughing through his words, and he looked so unlike the iron fist we all knew that I wondered if it was all a dream. His hair was starting to gather little droplets of moisture, making it look like it was holding stars or pure light, which only added to the surreal scene.

Clara's lip quivered, and she bowed her head. "Oh, Tim, I'm so sorry."

"For what? Loving this sap and making him happy? Being nice to everyone here?" Tim lifted his hands to hold her shoulders. He was so much taller than her now. "Then I'm sorry too, for keeping your secrets and helping you out. What a terrible thing for me to do." He grinned again, and I felt my eyes start to water. Clara laughed, shakily, and wrapped him in another tight hug. Our little brother, the boy we'd both unofficially adopted.

"Thank you, Timothy. We both love you so much." They both tightened the hug then released each other, and I moved to wrap Tim in my own arms, holding him as firmly has he had me when my mother had died. He returned it, hands twisting in the back of my jacket. Getting this suit wet couldn't have been good for it, but oh well.

"Thank you, Tim," I whispered, closing my eyes against tears. "When we get settled I'll write you, call you. Something. We won't lose you."

"No, you won't. You won't get away with it." I recognized the emotion hidden underneath the bossy, stubborn tone, felt him grip tighter. "I'm going to miss you, Leo." The last part was a whisper, and I tightened my hold.

"I'll miss you too, my brother."

I felt him shudder, take in a shaky breath, then he squeezed me hard, just once before pulling away. "I'll tell everyone you've finally left, and we don't have to deal with you anymore." His normal stoic stare was clouded with tears. Clara and I both chuckled lightly.

"Please do." I paused, then looked toward the firehouse. It didn't seem as if anyone was up yet. "Is Gregory awake?"

Tim shook his head. "Not yet." I sighed. I'd been hoping to see him again before we left, but I didn't want to linger and have Reggie show up at the station. As much as I hated it, it was safer to leave without a proper goodbye to everyone.

A few more words of parting later and Clara and I were pulling the cover off the car, packing our bags inside, and finally heading out of the city and into the Catskill Mountains.

Clara whooped with joy as we sped away from the city limits and the rain, her scarf waving above her head as our new car carried us along to the little hotel that we'd talked about a couple weeks prior. She took a moment more of triumphant scarf waving before collapsing into her seat and resting her head back against the top of it.

"Oh, we did it. We're out, we're free, we don't have to go back." Her sigh released every bit of tension she'd been holding for the past several years and she closed her eyes. I reached over to lay a hand gently on her thigh, my other gripping the steering wheel.

"We're free."

After about an hour and a half, we were checked in miraculously early, bags already tossed to the floor, and tangled together on the bed. She had undone my tie and was working on the buttons of my vest, giggling against my lips while I worked the pins out of her hair.

"You've got to stop laughing, you're making this so difficult." I grinned at her, tapping a pin against her jaw. She only giggled more, mischief in her eyes as she popped the last vest button.

"It would be easier if you just left it."

"Oh, fine then." And so I did, instead focusing my attention on her garters and stockings, gently unclasping the delicate chain around her neck and setting it aside. Her moonstone ring clicked lightly against the nightstand as I did.

Before long we were both bare, thankful for the distance between us and everyone else, for the locked door, for the knowledge that only Marie knew we'd left and no one else. My face was against her thigh, lips trailing down the inner side of it, her hands in my hair as I knelt at the side of the bed before her.

I looked up at the sound of her soft sigh, seeing her looking down almost sadly. Shifting, I reached up to cup her cheek, pulling her close for a kiss. Her hands slid up my chest, curling into fists near my collarbones. The kiss didn't last long, and she broke it with a hard swallow.

"What is it? What's wrong?" *What could possibly be wrong?* I wanted to ask, but it felt too forceful, too demanding.

"I just...can't believe it took literally running away to be together. I can't believe we had to go to such lengths." Her voice was so quiet, whispering as if we weren't hidden away miles from the city. I didn't have a response. I agreed, wholeheartedly, but there wasn't anything to add. So I kissed her forehead, her cheek, her jaw, letting her sort out her grief and anxiety.

"Come here, dearest," I whispered back at her. I scooped her up and tugged her into the bed with me, settling the covers around us and resting her head on my chest. "Let's postpone that for a little while." She nodded, and I felt the soft brush of her eyelashes as her eyes closed.

We sat together in silence, listening to the far-off sounds of a bustling hotel in the middle of summer and letting the knowledge that we'd gotten away soak in and sink deep into our bones. As we sat together, I worked the remaining pins out of her hair and combed it with my fingers, separating her corkscrew curls into softer waves.

Without meaning to, we both drifted off, my head slipping and tilting to the side to rest on hers. The soft tickle of her hair against my nose is what woke me, and I blinked awake, gritting teeth against the tight muscle in my neck. The sun slanting through the window had shifted position, the only marker that time had passed.

"Mm, Leo?" Clara mumbled, her fingers reaching up for my jaw, her head lifting to look at me with bleary half-awake eyes. The expression was heart melting.

"I'm here." I took her hand, kissing her fingertips one at a time as she smiled and settled her head against my collarbone.

"I guess we passed out." She was whispering still, but not from the habit of not wanting to be found, just the voice you have when you first wake up and haven't rediscovered your normal volume yet.

"We did." I nuzzled into her hair with a soft sigh, squeezing her to me gently. I let my eyes close again as we lay there for a moment together, enjoying the music from the lobby as it drifted up and under the door of our room.

I was quite honestly content to stay like that with her, just resting in silence and savoring the fact we could be together openly. But she had other plans.

Her hand slid up my thigh, fingers soft and teasing, lingering on the tendon in my inner hip before circling around the muscle that hadn't quite lost all its firmness during our nap. I sucked in a sharp breath through my nose, tilting my head back against the headboard. She took it as a chance to lift her lips to my throat, breathing soft, warm breath across my skin and leaving a tingle. My eyes fluttered closed as her hand moved under the covers, bringing me back to full mast. An involuntary moan escaped me, and I bit down on my lip to muffle it. We may have been away from the people trying to keep us apart, but that didn't mean we got to annoy everyone in the hotel. Clara chuckled softly under my jaw.

"Too bad you couldn't get us a bungalow instead of a hotel room," she teased, gripping harder for just a moment then resuming her stroking.

"Th-that's...what happens when you run—fuck. Run away on a moment's notice...god damn it Clara, oh fuck me." I couldn't keep my words straight. It was taking so much of my self-control not to just thrust up into her hand. She knew it, too, and laughed gently against my neck once more. My hands were tight against each other at her back, the back of my head pressed sharply against the headboard.

"I think you're the one who's supposed to do the fucking, Leo..." her tone was still teasing, taunting me into action. I could feel her grin against the side of my neck.

If I had been an actual lion, I would have roared as I swept her underneath me, tugging her hips down the mattress so her head didn't hit the headboard. I parted her legs, tucking my knees under her thighs and holding them open as I looked down at her. She was pretending to be demure now, head tilted to the side, hands above her head, a badly hidden smirk threatening to break out any minute. The light blue sheets were a contrast against her nutmeg brown curls, her fingers lightly tangled in them as they fanned out over the pillowcases. I momentarily forgot what I was supposed to be doing and just stared at her, cream and spice and storm in her eyes.

"You're so beautiful." I leaned down to kiss her, sliding my hands farther up her thighs, all the way to the tendons that hid in her innermost curves. She parted her lips against mine, pressing her hips toward my hands with a soft whimper. My thumbs brushed against her outer folds, gently parting them and slipping between. She was already wet for me, and so I parted our lips and kissed along her jaw, down her neck, to her breasts. Her hands slid into my hair as I tended to each nipple in turn, biting them gently and teasing my tongue around the stiff nubs I had only seen once before now. Her gasps and soft groans were the only payment needed for my work, and with that job complete I slid farther, kissing a trail down her stomach and toward my own hands that had been idly fingering her as I worked.

"Ohh, Leo, Leo yes, please..." she breathed, her back arching as she pushed her hips toward me. I smirked, replaying the last time I'd done this for her, the day we'd gone to the bakery with Marie. The memory of her laid out on my table, her skirt over my head, one leg over my shoulder as she muffled her every noise—it made me harder, and I had to bite down on my lip hard to keep myself from just taking her then and there. She'd asked me to finish what I started, and by God I would. So I set to work, finding the most sensitive bundle of nerves with my tongue and lips, teasing it and sucking on it, licking with the tip of my tongue while holding it flat. I hadn't even slid a single finger back into her before I felt her thigh muscles trembling and her breath catching in a tell-tale fashion. Knowing she was close, I kept up what I was doing, my lips closed around her as I ran my tongue back and forth across that most sensitive area as quickly as it would move. Her hand fisted in my hair sharply and I heard the slap of her hand over her mouth as she muffled her cry. I allowed myself a brief smirk before opening my mouth, sweeping my tongue from her entrance to the tip of her clit, tasting her pleasure and humming against her in my own. She whimpered, still muffled into her palm, but her grip relaxed and her hand fell to the mattress. After one more slow, drawn out lick, I lifted my head to find her gaze. She was staring down at me, biting down on her first knuckle with pupils so dilated they threatened to overtake the silver in her eyes.

I shifted, planting an elbow on the mattress and setting my cheek in my palm, managing to trap her thigh in the crook of my elbow.

"Good?" I grinned, and she flexed her legs to trap me briefly between her thighs. I laughed and pressed a few kisses to her lower stomach, and she released me.

"Did that really need confirmation?" she hissed quietly, reaching down to urge me forward, pulling me up to her. Clara captured my lips and gave me no choice on the matter, but it's not like I would have refused. I deepened the kiss, shifting my legs to find balance on my knees as she spread her legs for me once more, welcoming me inside.

Our moans were muted against each other's mouths, breathed across each other's lips. It didn't take long to find the rhythm, gasping as our hips rocked back and forth in sync, pushing against each other to drive me ever deeper inside her. She bent her knees and flexed her hips until her legs were pressed against my ribs instead of my hips, giving me the angle I needed for the depth she wanted. Her gasps dissolved into moans and whimpers as I thrust into her, one hand on the mattress for balance and the other gripping one of her hips. My head bowed, forehead nearly touching her shoulder as we both absolutely lost ourselves in the pleasure, heightened by the fact we didn't have to part right after, we didn't have to scurry away from each other as soon as the act was over. She was whimpering my name repeatedly, fingers trying to find purchase on my back without digging her nails in, her thighs flexed against my sides to hold me inside her.

"C-Clara, Clara, I'm...fuuuck...Clara I'm going to—"

"Do it...do it Leo," she gasped, and I lifted my head to meet her gaze. She was nodding, gripping my shoulders and staring at me, the want clear in her eyes. "It doesn't matter anymore, do it."

She was right. We didn't have to be careful. We didn't have to deny ourselves anything anymore.

I leaned over her, pressing our bodies together as closely as I could and taking her lips in a deep kiss. My range of motion was shortened but we were both so close it didn't matter. A few more thrusts and her legs became a vice grip around me, her internal muscles doing the same as I broke our kiss to muffle my cry of pleasure in her neck. My fingers dug into the sheets, hips driving down against her as I shouted against her skin. She was trembling beneath me, moaning and panting as she clenched in pulses around me, pulling every drop from me. The pulses slowed, we caught our breath, and my muscles gradually began to relax and give up. I was on my elbows above her, shaking with the effort to keep myself up, but goddammit she was kissing me and her tongue was in my mouth and her trembling fingers were in my hair and I was still deep inside her and I would not move until she told me to. It didn't matter if my arms wanted to give out, I would stay right there.

I let her break the kiss, groaning slowly as she did and taking it as my cue to gently, slowly, so fucking slowly, pull out of her. She slapped a hand over her mouth to muffle the shaky whimper it drew from her, and once we disconnected, I collapsed to my side and pulled her to me. She settled against me, her head tucked under my chin, hands on my chest.

"I suppose this means you have to marry me tomorrow." She giggled, her voice soft from the exertion. My eyes had been closed but they flew open, staring at the door across the room. *Oh.*

I must have been silent for longer than I realized because she tilted her head back, trying to look at my face. "Leo? I didn't...really mean—"

I quieted her with a kiss, cupping her cheek in my palm and grinning at her as we pulled back. "Clara, my dearest, my love." I kissed her quick once more before pulling back, stumbling on shaky legs and holding onto the wall as I made my way to the trunk on the other side of the room. Hidden inside was a velvet box I'd been saving until we got farther away, but well, she'd started it.

I knelt at the edge of the bed again, opening the box to reveal the bright white gold ring with the tiny white stone set in the middle. Her eyes watered, and she sat up, bracing herself against the mattress with one hand.

"Oh, Leo, do you really mean it?"

I laughed, taking her other hand down from her mouth, kissing it. "Oh, Clara, I really do mean it. I will marry you. I will be yours, if you'll be mine."

Her tears broke then, and she started laughing, diving forward to wrap her arms around my neck. I held her, nestled my face in her shoulder, letting my eyes close to savor the peace and joy that had flooded into our room.

"Tomorrow then. Before we leave here." Clara's voice was muffled in my hair but they were still the sweetest words I have ever heard. I squeezed her tighter, breathing deeply and trying to brand this moment onto my soul, deep in my heart.

She pulled back and I slipped the ring onto her finger, glad I had guessed the right size. She held it up to the light, turning it this way and that to watch it sparkle. I got back into bed with her and we cuddled and dozed for a little longer, kissing softly when the moment hit us and allowing ourselves to bask in the reality that we were free, and tomorrow we'd be wed.

At one point, near sunset, Clara wrapped herself into one of the bedsheets and went to sit by the window, combing out her hair with her fingers. The golden light filtering through the thin privacy curtain lit her up and made her glow. She giggled at people down on the street, telling me a couple was arguing but she couldn't tell over what. I leaned back against the headboard, just staring at her. Even though I knew I was going to see this so many more times, Clara bare, glowing, happy, I wanted to just freeze us in that moment. Everything had finally worked out. We had made it out, we were safe behind our fake names at the desk and the single note left behind purposely not betraying our location.

We cleaned up in time to head to dinner, whispering our toasts to each other and tapping our glasses together so softly we couldn't even hear the clink. Everything still felt secret, something meant for only us. So we kept it that way, knowing we'd allow ourselves to be louder the farther away we got.

We didn't enjoy each other again that night, as we had the rest of our lives to do so and we were both a little drunk and just exhausted from the drive. So we allowed ourselves to sink into a deep, peaceful sleep, tucked together behind a locked door with the chain set on it and windows shut tight against the rest of the world. I fell asleep against her as I had in my apartment, forehead pressed between her shoulders, but this time my hand was laid over hers with the ring I'd given her under my palm.

Unfortunately, the towel we'd rolled up and tucked against the crack beneath the door to muffle the noise of the rest of the hotel meant we didn't smell the smoke until it was far, far too late.

November 8th, 2010

My office was deathly silent besides Leon's slow breathing, the gentle creak of the arms of the chair as he gripped them. I stayed quiet as well, pen stilled, just watching him. His eyes were distant, still in 1926. Still with Clara. After a few more moments, I spoke.

"What happened after the fire?" Leon had said he'd lost Clara to a fire, so it didn't take a genius to know he meant the one he had just described. But it didn't explain how he was sitting here, nearly a hundred years later, on my chair, almost crying in my office.

It took him awhile to respond, fingers again trying to spin a ring that wasn't there, and I almost repeated the question.

"I got out, she didn't." He was whispering, and his eyes closed. "She didn't." Then he laughed, bitterly, lifting a hand to push into his hair as he slumped down in the chair. "My love, swallowed by a blaze. Some fireman I am." His hand dropped to cover his face. I put my pen down.

"I'm so sorry, Leon." What did someone even say in this kind of situation?

He slowed his breathing intentionally, laying his arm back along the arm of the chair. I moved to rest my elbows on my desk, looking down at the notebook between my arms. Clara's life, their love, all inked onto these pages. Even if Leon forgot—and it didn't seem as if he would—they'd be here forever. I'd made the decision to have the archival team give my notebook a once-over when I was finished with it when I had another thought.

"How did you get out?" I asked, and Leon's bitter laugh filled the space. Clearly it was something still deeply uncomfortable for him.

"That, my dear archivist, will have to be a story for another time."

He stayed in my office until he'd regained most of his composure. We discussed the logistics of things and I gave him a ballpark date on when he could expect the full write up of everything, then he left.

At the time of publishing, it's been sixteen years since that day. And now, Clara and Leo's romance can never be forgotten. Not as long as it lives within these pages.

www.ingramcontent.com/pod-product-compliance
Lightning Source LLC
La Vergne TN
LVHW041138150826
845673LV00001B/27

* 9 7 9 8 9 9 1 1 0 6 9 8 6 *